James H. Graff, Catherine Grace Frances Gore

Cecil

The Adventures of a Coxcomb

James H. Graff, Catherine Grace Frances Gore

Cecil
The Adventures of a Coxcomb

ISBN/EAN: 9783337341541

Printed in Europe, USA, Canada, Australia, Japan

Cover: Foto ©Andreas Hilbeck / pixelio.de

More available books at **www.hansebooks.com**

CECIL.

CECIL;

OR,

THE ADVENTURES OF A COXCOMB.

BY MRS. GORE,

AUTHOR OF "PIN MONEY," "THE DOWAGER," ETC.

"He was such a delight,—such a coxcomb,—such a jewel of a man!"
BYRON'S JOURNAL.

A New Edition.

LONDON:
ROUTLEDGE, WARNE, & ROUTLEDGE,
FARRINGDON STREET;
NEW YORK: 56, WALKER STREET.
1860.

CECIL;

OR,

THE ADVENTURES OF A COXCOMB.

———◆◆◆———

CHAPTER I.

Vanitas,—vanitatis !

BIOGRAPHERS are fond of attributing the tendencies of their heroes to heroic sources. Since it is my fate to tell my own story, I choose to tell it in my own way, and confess that the leading trait of my character had its origin in the first glimpse I caught of myself, at six months old, in the swing-glass of my mother's dressing-room. I looked, and became a coxcomb for life !

My Self consisted, at that epoch, of a splendid satin cockade, with a puny infant face thereunto attached ; while a flowing robe of embroidered cambric, four feet by ten, disguised my nonentityism. The spectacle, enhanced by a showy sash of gorgeous ribbon, was the very thing to captivate a baby's eye ; and it was soon discovered that Master Cecil was always screaming, unless danced up and down by the head nurse within view of the reflection of his own fascinating little person.

"Take him to the glass, nurse !" was my mother's invariable mode of pacifying my shrieks, when my fractiousness interrupted the process of her toilet, rendering it inconvenient to contemplate her beauties in her own.

B

"Take him to the glass, poor little fellow ! He loves to look at his ribbons fluttering in the light."

I suspect that, even then, what I loved to look at was the same personal reflection that delighted the eyes of her ladyship. But no matter.

When my little self, or rather my great nurse, grew tired of the dancing system, there were other glittering objects in my mother's sanctum which I found almost equally attractive—jewels, feathers, flowers, and frippery of all descriptions. I usually visited her at dressing-time. The baby was less in her ladyship's way while adoring,

> With head uncover'd, the cosmetic powers,

than when adored, in her turn, by the men of wit and pleasure about town ; colonels in the Guards and memberlings of parliament, who had the honour of being inscribed in the visiting-list of the young and fashionable Lady Ormington.

As soon as I grew old enough to roll about the Axminster carpet, the rich garlands interwoven in whose soft tissue delighted my eyes by their gay colours, the nurse was desired to leave me ; and while the lady-mother and the lady's-maid were engrossed in their mysteries, paying no more attention to *me* than *I* to my neglected rattle, I watched unnoticed the play of the waving satin train they were adjusting, the glitter of the diamond tiara, and the turn of the snowy feather. Gewgaws were my earliest playthings ; and my primer consisted of the flourishing capitals at the head of a milliner's bill.

I have described my face as puny ; but I know not why I pay it so poor a compliment, since there is no one to gainsay me and do it right ; for it was unquestionably to my personal charms I was indebted for my *entrée* into Lady Ormington's *sanctum*. I was the first of her children admitted to be danced before her glass, or roll upon her soft carpet. Yet I had a brother and a sister ; a brother destined to inherit the honours of the family, and a sister born to share its affections. But the Honourable John squinted, and the Honourable Julia had red hair ; and our lady-mother was as heartily ashamed of them both, as if they had been palmed upon her from the workhouse.

From the day of my birth, on the contrary, nurses and toadies were unanimous in protesting that *I* was the living image of my sweet mamma ; and as my sweet mamma was the daughter of a country squire, whose face had been her fortune, and whose fortune it was to win the heart and hand, or rather the hand and coronet, of the Right Honourable Lord Ormington, she might be reasonably excused for some maternal partiality for her miniature, adorned with a satin cockade and twelve yards of superfine French cambric.

My mother's vocation was for the toilet. Beauty had been her stepping-stone to distinction ; and she seemed to think too much care could not be bestowed on its adornment, as devotees erect a shrine to a favourite divinity. It was true, the worship was gratuitous. There was nothing further to gain ; no more hands, at least, and no more coronets. As for hearts, it is to be hoped that Lady Ormington neither brandished the powder-puff, nor spread the rustling hoop, with any mal-intentions towards those fragile superfluities of the human frame divine.

But if fashionable notoriety constituted the object of her desires, the ambition was gratified. There was an Ormington *pouf*, and an Ormington *vis-à-vis ;* an Ormington satin and an Ormington minuet. In those unlettered times, Annuals were not. But a languishing portrait, limned by Cosway, was charmingly engraved by Bartolozzi ; and the Right Hon. Lady Ormington, leaning on a demi-column, with " Sacred to Friendship " engraven on the plinth, a stormy sunset in the background, and a bantam-legged silken spaniel staring its eyes out in the foreground, figured in all the print-sellers' windows ; immortalized by certain stanzas, silken as the spaniel and flat as the landscape, from what

Dr. Johnson and courtesy used to call "the charming pen of Mrs. Greville."

I recollect contriving to convert the favourite scarf of her ladyship into a bridle for my rocking-horse, on the day when the said engraving, richly framed, was first placed in her boudoir ; and so delighted was she with the print (which, I concluded, was intended as a *cadeau*, for I never saw it again), that she magnanimously overlooked my misdemeanor.

There was something else, by the way, which we all seemed inclined to overlook ; *i.e.* the Right Honourable Lord Ormington. I hardly recollect hearing his name mentioned, either in the dressing-room, drawing-room, or nursery. The scholarship derived from the important great letters heading the Christmas bill of Madame Lebrun had not assisted me a sufficient number of steps up the ladder of learning to enable me to decipher the newspapers, even if my "sweet mamma" had not been too fine a lady to admit them into her boudoir ; or I might have found it written down there, in malice, that his lordship was one of the heaviest prosers, supporting, in the Upper House, the country-gentleman interest of Great Britain. As it was, I knew nothing about him, except that there was a cross, gaunt, pig-tailed old fellow, much scouted by the livery of the house, who went by the name of "my lord's own man ;" and that every evening, as the under-nurse was hushing us off to sleep, the rumble of wheels from the door of our house in Hanover Square used to be hailed with a remark of, "There he goes to the 'ouse ; much good may it do 'em !"

Upon *whom* his lordship's departure for the House was likely to confer a benefit, I was not of an age to trouble my head. Let us hope that the nurses pluralized the nation, referring the collective interests of the three kingdoms to the collective wisdom of Parliament.

Time progressed. I had fallen in the world four feet and a cockade ; *i.e.* from my nurse's arms to a go-cart.

To contemplate myself in the glass, I was now forced to climb into a chair. But I was rewarded for my pains. The puny face had expanded into a fine open countenance surrounded by hyacinthine curls. Impossible to see a more charming little fellow! Lady Ormington seemed to fancy that everybody was as pleased to look at me, as *I* was to look at myself; for I now superseded the spaniel in the Ormington *vis-à-vis*, and was as constantly seen lounging out of *one* window as Sir Lionel Dashwood lounging *in* at the other. Many people fancied they could discern a resemblance between us. For my part, I think Sir Lionel bore a much stronger affinity to the spaniel, my predecessor, both in point of fawning and foolishness. Yet I don't know why I abuse him; for, while he never alluded to John and Julia otherwise than as "those unfortunate creatures," he invariably qualified myself as "Cecil, my boy!" or, "There's a darling!"

I can scarcely say whether Lord Ormington's predilections, or my mother's, kept us resident in town eight months of the year. The only point on which they seemed to feel in common, was a detestation of Ormington Hall; perhaps because, at the family place, there was no pretext of parliament or parties to keep them asunder. My sweet mamma, however, usually spent her summers at Spa, occasionally visiting Paris; and the breaking out of the war was a serious evil to a family which it reduced to the necessity of domestic peace. I remember feeling as strongly inclined to join the outcry against Pitt and Cobourg as the Convention; for while John and Julia were left safe at the Hall, I had always been promoted to the honours of La Sauvenière; and the rooks, the avenue, and Dr. Droneby were antipathetic to my nature I was in despair at the closing of the Continent! *Bonbons, maréchale* powder, *chocolat de santé, pommade à la vanille*—how were we to exist without these necessaries of life? What was to become of England and her stupid martello-towers—the Pitt-posts, as they were called, for which the country was to supply railing.

A worse evil than war, however, impended over me. John had long disappeared from the nursery. On returning from our last expedition to Flanders, we found that, during our absence, the young gentleman had been made over to roast mutton, Latin grammar, and Dr. Droneby ; while Miss Julia was transferred to a school-room as cold as a church, and a governess as stately as the steeple.

The head-nurse, who had presided over my cockade, seemed to think it a good riddance. A similar opinion was expressed by Lord Ormington and his own man, when, six months afterwards, that lady herself was postchaised off from the Hall in one direction, while I was postchaised off in another to a preparatory purgatory at Chiswick ; where they began with me as in a lunatic asylum, by cutting off my curls, choosing my head to be as unfurnished without as within. I remember weeping bitterly for the loss of my nurse and my locks. I was ashamed to look myself in the face after being shorn thus vilely. But the only looking-glass within reach was a thing as large as a half-crown, in the lid of an enamel *bonbonnière*, given me at parting by my mother. Moreover, I dared not cry too loud over my disfigurement ; for the horrible Dalilah by whom my clustering curls had been curtailed talked of corduroys, highlows, and a leathern cap, in case I was refractory. The dread of seeing myself transformed into an errand-boy suppressed my tears.

Let me pass lightly over my school-days, though Heaven knows they passed heavily enough over me ! Biographers, whether of themselves or others, seem to luxuriate in pictures of academic innocence. For my part, I have a horror of birch and bread-and-milk, even in reminiscence. There is something excruciating to a well-born young gentleman in being reduced to the toilet of a Newfoundland dog ; viz., a rousing shake, a plunge into cold water, and the eternal rusty coat of the day before.

Even at Eton I was a miserable dog. In the first place, because I was called Danby Secundus (the Honourable John having the advantage of me); and in the second, because the duncehood, which had been passed over as a minor evil at the preparatory, seemed likely to be flogged out of me among the antique towers where "grateful Science still adores her Henry's holy shade," and where humbugging tutors still adore the flagellation of innocent defaulters in classic lore. John was a regular sap. Droneby and roast mutton had made a scholar of him. Ugly little brute! what was *he* good for but Virgil and corduroys?

At college he obtained still further advantages over me. He was beginning, indeed, to have the best of it everywhere. From the date of the abrogation of my curls, I was out of favour, even in the boudoir. Sir Lionel Dashwood had been unable to repress an ejaculation of "little monster!" on seeing me again; and by the time John was entered at college, something of a paralytic attack seemed to remind my sweet mamma that the Right Honourable Lord Ormington was to survive in her elder son, when her noble spouse took up his rest in the family vault, instead of on the benches of St. Stephen's.

Neither he, nor I, nor Dashwood, nor even Dash, were now admitted into the dressing-room. Matters were growing too serious there. With sons of eighteen, ladies who have stood godmother to a minuet or a taffeta, are not fond of exposing to investigation the mystery of their washes and pommades. The *flacons* which formerly contained *bouquet de Florence* or *verveine,* now held the lights and shades of her ladyship's complexion. Blue veins were sealed in one packet, and a rising blush was corked up in a crystal phial. Eyebrows—eyelashes—lips—cheeks—chin—an ivory forehead, and a pearly row of teeth,—all were indebted

for their irresistibilities to a certain Pandora's box of
a dressing-case, furnished by Thévenot, which sent
forth Lady Ormington, full-armed for conquest, like
the goddess that emerged from the brain of the father
of the gods.

But her ladyship was no longer the same woman as in
the days of the spaniel and the cockade. It was not alone
because Dashwood was in the Bench and I out of
favour, that I discovered a change. But she was
growing almost domestic, almost reasonable. She had
given up balls,—would not hear of an opera box,—and
for a year and a half scarcely stirred out of her own
boudoir. In place of Sir Lionel there was a pet
apothecary, who came every day with his little budget
of scandal, just as Madame Lebrun had formerly made
her appearance with her little box of laces ; and
though certain persons, to wit, two old-maidenly
sisters of Lord Ormington, two card-playing, blue,
Honourable Misses Danby, with brown-holland complexions and tongues of a still deeper dye, protested
that the only disorder afflicting their noble sister-in-law
was an ugly daughter, of an age to be presented at
court, her ladyship resigned herself to the sacrifices
exacted by an elegant valetudinarianism.

In winter, she seldom rose till candle-light ; in
summer, the muslin curtains of her chamber were
never undrawn. A perpetual twilight surrounded her.
Though blessing her stars for not being hereditarily
exposed to the cruel revelations of the peerage, so as
to be hopelessly branded with the shame of having
attained her eight-and-thirtieth year, *she* could not
blind herself to the fact, as betrayed in the very
looking-glass which had exercised so singular an
influence over my nature. Eight-and-thirty was
written *there*, in words as terrible as those of Bel-
shazzar's warning,—even in characters of crow's-
feet !

Eight-and-thirty is a frightful epoch in the life of a
woman of fashion. Hot rooms and cosmetics place it

on a level with fifty, in the lady of a country squire.
The struggle between departing youth and coming age
is never more awful. A little older, and the case
becomes too clear for dispute. At forty, she gives up
the field, allowing that time has the best of it. But
for the five preceding years, those years during which,
though no longer pretty, a woman may be still handsome, the tug of war is terrific. A woman never
prizes her beauty half so much as when it is for-
saking her; never comprehends the value of raven
locks till revealed by the contrast of the first grey
hair; never finds out that her waist was slim and
her form graceful, till she has been accused of
corpulence.

Brother coxcombs! if you would have a proper
value set upon your homage, pay your court to a
woman of eight-and-thirty. The flutter of a little
miss of sixteen is nothing to the agitation with which
the poor grateful soul uplifts her head above the waters
of oblivion, in which she was succumbing. At that
crisis, a dreadful revolution occurs in the female heart.
The finer sensibilities have lost their edge; self-
veneration is impaired by the slights of society; the
injustice of the world, in scandalizing virtue and
exalting vice, has produced a peevish misappreciation
of the value of reputation. After all, *was* it worth
while to break so many hearts? Others, less cruel,
are more respected. She puzzles herself in wondering
whether they are more happy. It is a dangerous
thing to wonder on such subjects. It is like a
hypochondriac feeling the edge of a razor.

At forty, she wonders no longer. She has resumed
her trust in excellence, her reverence for the spotlessness of virtue; thanks Heaven for her escape; and
renouncing for ever the influence of the puppies,
betakes herself for consolation to the tabbies. Cards,—
universal panacea!—cards, that knit up the ravelled
sleeve of care, boon Nature's kind restorer, balmy
cards,—inspire her with a new insight into the

purposes of existence.   Lovelace himself might do his
worst.   The votary of the odd trick

passes on,
In matron meditation, fancy free !

Foreseeing no improvement to Lady Ormington's
delicacy of health, my father at length decided that
Julia should be introduced into society by his sisters.
So much the better for *her*.   The poor girl, who was
really plain, looked twenty times as well in contrast
with *their* frightful faces, as when approximated with
her sweet mamma's still lovely features.   Julia was
not altogether amiss, when seen between Miss Mary
and Miss Agatha Danby.

Lord Ormington generously provided them with a
family coach and an opera-box ; and the daughter, of
whom his right honourable lady had seen so little
during her school-day martyrdom, took up her quarters
with her maiden aunts in Queen Anne Street, almost
without her absence being perceived ; leaving the
woman of eight-and-thirty to hope that the fashionable
world would not trouble itself to trace the connection
between the beautiful Lady Ormington and a Miss
Danby in the enjoyment of red hair and eighteen
years of age.

Of Julia, beyond this, I knew nothing.   Having
seen her banished by my mother, and sharing to the
utmost her ladyship's abhorrence of the Judas complexion, I looked upon her as a species of Paria.   Of all
physical defects, red hair is one of the least remediable.
The blackest of wigs only renders the disfigurement
more glaring.   Apply what pigment you will to the
eyebrows, the lashes remain a burning accusation.
Nay, were even the eyelashes put in mourning, there is
a peculiarity of complexion induced by the coating of
the epidermis, as ineffaceable as the blackness of the
Ethiopian or the spots of the leopard.   I scarcely
wondered that Lady Ormington should give up Julia
as hopeless.   Who would marry her ?—Who perpetuate

in his race a stigma so repellent?   Unless Miss Mary and Miss Agatha were kind enough to die, leaving her their heiress, she must inevitably succeed to their honours of single blessedness.

I have survived to see wondrous reforms in Great Britain, even leaving out of the question that of parliament.   In the days of my cockadehood, it was cited as an exemplary thing on the part of the charming Lady Ormington, to have even one of her three children sprawling in her dressing-room.   The elegiac poets wrote verses about it; and every other ugly little anecdote affecting her renown, was hushed at the clubs by the rejoinder of—"but then she is *such* a mother!"

The cockade generation of succeeding times is far better off.   The cockade generation of to-day is at a premium.   One might fancy all the little boys one meets were heirs-apparent, and all the little girls, countesses in embryo.   For them, the Tyrian murrey swimmeth.   They are not only clothed in purple and fine linen, Flanders lace and Oriental cashmeres, but we hear of nursery-governesses, nursery-footmen, the children's carriage, the children's pair of horses; and, Turkey being civilized, the only despotism extant in Europe is the nursery-archy of Great Britain, with its viziers and janizaries,—head nurses and apothecaries,— ladies' doctors and Lilliputian warehouses.—I thank Heaven I was born a coxcomb, for coxcombs are bachelors by prescriptive right: and it would have stung me to the soul to find myself tied down like Gulliver, in my middle age, by the authority of pigmies.

To return to my mother.   No sooner had Julia grappled herself so fast to the fond bosom of her maiden aunts that they proposed to her parents retaining her as a permanent inmate, than Lady Ormington was pleased to accomplish the recovery of her health.   Luckily for her, the Revolution had occurred during her seclusion: and revolutions in politics have the singular faculty of accomplishing revolutions in dress,—as the moment-hand and hour-hand of a dial are actuated by the same movement. The Reign of Terror had frightened people out of their wits, and out of their hair-powder. Buckles had given place to shoe-ties ; and love-locks and *chignons* to crops *à la victime*, and *à la guillotine*. London, it is true, had not advanced further in revolutionary terrors than by making a bonfire of Lord Mansfield's wig and MSS. But being accustomed to accept its fashions from Paris, neat as imported, their powder went off, and their locks were polled, as though the clubs and coteries of St. James's Street and Hanover Square had prepared themselves for the cart and scaffold.

The transformation thus effected was peculiarly favourable to Lady Ormington. The hair, so long snowed over by the powder-puff, came out a rich auburn ; and in her Roman crop and tunic *à l'Agrippine*, she was still a bewitching creature. Several of her adorers underwent a relapse ; and we all know that a relapse is the most fatal period of a disorder.

All I *now* knew of her ladyship's triumphs, however, was derived from the newspapers. I was banished from her presence, from the moment of my degradation into a schoolboy. Even when matriculated at Christchurch, I remained an exile from her good graces. On taking leave of her on my way to the University, she complained bitterly that my father should send me to Oxford. "What was the use of college ?—I should only become a brute of a fox-hunter. It was quite enough for John to acquire a taste for buckskins and High Toryism, without infecting *me* with Oxonian propensities. *She* wished me to go straight into the Guards. I knew quite enough for the Guards. The humiliation of maternity would be less galling if she had a son in the Guards. In the Guards, I should be on the spot to swear at her chairmen when drunk, or her coachman if disorderly. John was unpresentable ; but, if properly drilled and tutored, dressed and *re*-dressed, she should not be so much ashamed of Cecil."

An involuntary smile overspread my features while hinting my suspicions that I was intended by my father for the Church ; and a faint shriek burst from Lady Ormington's lips at the announcement. The horror of being mother to a parson,—a licensed dealer in sermons,—a privileged preacher of prose,—a fellow in a black coat, holding a patent to exhort her to repentance ! After all, I believe some feeling of maternal affection lingered in her heart ; for as I held the salts-bottle to her nose, she faintly ejaculated, " Cecil, were I to see you in a shovel-hat, I would not survive it ! " The idea of the cockade of my infancy,—the Antinous curls of my boyhood,—giving place to a shovel, was too much for her.

It would have been *far* too much for *me*. I, Cecil Danby, whose name was already whispered in St. James's Street, as having taxed my bill at the Christopher, on account of a semitone too much in the complexion of the pink Champagne,—*I*, to be swamped in a country parsonage. It is true, my father's church patronage was such as a bishop might have envied. It is true, his lordship's parliamentary interest was such as might in time have made me a bishop. But then the wig !—" Angels and ministers of Grace " (and of the Church of England) " defend us,"—the episcopal wig ! I could almost as soon have borne to defy the derision of puppy-life as a Lord Chancellor.

It did not much signify. Alma Mater proved as little in conceit with me as Lady Ormington. In less than a year, I was rusticated. Why, it is not my province or pleasure to communicate to the reader. If my contemporary, he may happen to know ; if my junior, let him read, mark, and learn in the archives of my college. I love a little mystery. So did the public, till Mrs. Radcliffe gave them a surfeit of it. The only mysteries in fashion nowadays are Speeches from the Throne and " Tracts for the Times."

I commenced this chronicle of my adventures with a predetermination against " University Intelligence." College life,—a low, vulgar, stupid thing in itself,— has been written down still lower by smart periodicals and fashionable novelists. Instead, therefore, of sketches of Christchurch in the year of (dis)grace 180–, suffer me to favour you, gentle public, with the " Portrait of a Young Gentleman," as I figured that season in the eyes of the fair sex and the foul, in the city of high-churchmen and sausages.

Standing five feet seven in my pumps, and five feet ten in my boots, with a trifling hint of the Piping Faun softening the severity of my Roman nose and finely-chiselled mouth, I should, perhaps, have passed for effeminate, but that the sentimental school was just then in the ascendant. People went to the play to cry at the " Stranger " or " Penruddock ;" and subscribed to a circulating-library to weep over " The Father and Daughter." The severest poetry tolerated by Mayfair was that of Hayley, William Spencer, and Samuel Rogers. In short, people had supped full of horrors during the Revolution, and were now devoted to elegiac measures. My languid smile and hazel eyes were the very thing to settle the business of the devoted beings left for execution.

Self-reliance was one of the strong points of my character. I had always a predisposition to womanslaughter, with extenuating circumstances ; as well as a stirring consciousness of the exterminating power. But, as the most tremendous-looking piece of ordnance is non-existent for her Majesty's service, till after progressing through the department of the proving-house at Woolwich Warren, I almost blushed for my own beauties, till they had been labelled with " deadly poison " by the experience of the sex.

I attained my majority without a catastrophe : the cause of much heart-burning, but not a single heart-break ! The plebeian conquests of the University, or the sighs of the lady's-maid and vicar's daughter at

Ormington Hall, are unworthy of record ; their sensibility being quite as much at the service of my elder brother, with his frightful phiz and ill-built coat. My pen lends itself only to adventures proper and specific to the Honourable Cecil Danby, the arch-coxcomb of his day.

Not that I was without rivals near the throne. At Oxford, where my acquaintance lay more among the moderns than the ancients, I picked up, or, truth to say, was picked up, by a man—ay, a man !—though I, but six months his junior, remained a boy,—destined to play a distinguished part on the stage of puppyism. In the course of my first lounge down the High Street, I was rash enough to show my rawness by inquiring the name of a figure much resembling one of the models serving as signs to a Parisian clothes-shop ; and, "Not know Jack Harris ?" was the lofty reproof of my ignorance concerning one never, of course, heard of beyond the bounds of the University.

I did *not* know Jack Harris ; and I suspect no one knew him less than my rebuker, who was no other than my whipper-snapper cousin, Lord Squeamy. But I was willing to extend my knowledge ; and Squeamy accordingly chirruped in my ear that Harris was a nobody, who had made himself somebody, and gave the law to everybody. This was accomplished per force of some talent and much impudence. Squeamy did not call it impudence. The word was too substantive for his puny lips. *He* called it coolness. "Jack Harris was the coolest fellow in the world !"

"A man of family ?"

"Nobody knows."

"A man of fortune ?"

"Nobody has an idea."

"He must indeed be cool and clever, then," was my secret reflection, "to have kept his secret among people so distinguished by ill-manners as the academic youth of Britain."

I soon discovered, in my proper person, that Jack Harris was something more than impudent.   He was impertinent.   Impudence is the quality of a footman ; impertinence, of his master.   Impudence is a thing to be rebutted with brute force ; impertinence requires wit for the putting down.   Had Jack Harris been simply impudent, he would have been repaid with a kick ; he was impertinent, and his obnoxiousness was recognized by a low bow.

His talents, however, received higher recognition. Some time previous to my rustication, Jack Harris took an honour.   He had probably tact to perceive that he was not sufficiently well-born to aspire to the honours of duncehood.   It sat well upon such fellows as Squeamy and myself to defy all pretence to scholarship ; for in college life there is no middle course for a nobleman.   A lord must be cited either for the highest acquirements, or the boldest contempt of them ; whereas your Jack Harris, or your John Thompson, Esquire, is *bound* to afford evidence of possessing the use of his faculties.   Harris quitted college, accordingly, with the reputation of being an excellent scholar, wanting only application to be the first man of his year.   No one had ever seen him with a book or pen in his hand ; and my subsequent knowledge of him has often led me to conjecture how hard must have been the course of secret study, which enabled him to reconcile the pursuits of a man of pleasure with the acquirements of a sap.

The first thing that startled me in Jack, was his refusing to make my acquaintance.   I could detect the negative air with which he received a proposal to that effect, whispered by that ninny of ninnies, Squeamy. Involuntarily, his eyebrow became elevated, and his lip depressed ; saying as plain as lip and eyebrow could speak,—" Thank you—I know quite enough of the family."   At that moment I should have had much pleasure in knocking him down ; but, as I said before, it is impudence and not impertinence that challenges physical correction. I accordingly prepared myself for inflicting moral castigation.

Ten days afterwards, at the close of a supper party in which I distinguished myself by the display of certain saucinesses studied in my boyhood under Sir Lionel, Jack carelessly requested the favour of an introduction.

Squeamy's lack-lustre eye was upon me. I saw a smile of triumph irradiate his unmeaning face, evidently anticipating an act of retribution. Had he been at my elbow, he would doubtless have suggested a dead cut.

" With the greatest pleasure ! " cried I, rising and offering my hand to the offender. " The acquaintance cannot fail to be a mutual benefit. I shall be proud to place my rawness under the tutorage of Mr. Harris, as regards the habits and customs of that part of his Majesty's dominions called Oxford ; and equally pleased to afford *him* some hints concerning those of a less circumscript region, denominated the world."

The blow was felt, and resented as it deserved ; that is, by a pressure of the hand denoting sympathy and bad-fellowship. As Saladin and Cœur de Lion rushed into each other's embrace after the mutual trial of skill described by Scott in " The Talisman," the two coxcombs recognized each other's merits by a secret sign, mystic as the tokens of freemasonry.— We became allies for life.

Jack Harris was an amusing fellow,—that is, amusing for the University. I should never have got rusticated, but from the *ennui* consequent upon his quitting Oxford. In my own defence, I was forced to descend to the vulgar exploits of gownsmen to keep myself awake.

On arriving in town after undergoing the extreme penalty of the law (of the University), I underwent, of course, a further sentence of parental condemnation. Lord Ormington favoured me with a longer sentence than I had ever heard from his lips. " I expected no

better of you," said he ; "you have disgraced yourself,
and done justice to my prognostications." Lady
Ormington merely observed, " Rusticated ?—What *is*
rusticated ?" and on learning that the verb had no
reference to rusticity, was satisfied that it meant
something very incomprehensible and very uninteresting ; like the capitals M.A. or D.D., which she had
never been able to interpret otherwise, than a Double
Dose of Divinity, and More Anon of promised preferment.

But Jack Harris was better versed in the obliqui-
ties of the case, as well as more inclined to dissert
thereon, than either my genitor or genitrix.

" A sad affair ! " said he gravely, at the conclusion
of my narrative. "I fear, my dear Cis, you stand
convicted of heinous vulgarisms. How would your
prospects in life be injured by the rumour that you
have condescended to break lamps, and carry your
poodle to chapel, like any other blackguard of fashion.
Expulsion, to a man in your position in life, is rather
a feather in your cap. Next to a high honour, it was
your only mode of obtaining college eminence. You
had no professional prospects to injure ; and people of
the world attach little importance to the pranks of a
gentleman commoner, a sillier sort of schoolboy."

Instead of being affronted, I congratulated him in
my turn upon the exquisiteness of the little snuggery
in which he had installed himself.

" I don't complain ! " replied Jack, looking round,
with an air of ineffable coxcombry, upon furniture
composed of the richest foreign woods and marbles.
" I am an easy fellow in these particulars. Provided
things are clean and comfortable, I make no pretence
to ostentation."

" I suspect you have a pretension to non-ostenta-
tion," said I,—" the less vulgar affectation, perhaps, of
the two."

" Not so bad for a beginner," retorted Jack Harris
coolly. " You are, however, safe in venting your

sarcasms on my establishment; for it will be long enough before you incur retaliation by a household of your own. Yours, my dear Cis, will be the poet's and the younger brother's portion,—an airy attic, containing three cane-bottomed chairs and a chest of drawers."

" Had you heard the admonishment with which Lord Ormington received me this morning, you might have judged it problematical whether he would afford me either lodging or board!" said I laughing.

" You would be bored enough, I fancy, by any lodging he could afford," cried Jack. " His lordship's lodging would prove harder than board."

" I should be somewhat soft to accept it," replied I. " If I can persuade him to continue my Oxford allowance, I will look out a bachelor den, within distance of the clubs and the opera, and——"

" Get through the probation of your whelphood as best you may," interrupted Jack. " Cis, my boy,—take my advice on the matter. So long as you can, live at free quarters. If I had Lord Ormington's house in Hanover Square to fall back upon, his man-cook, and choice cellar of wines (as the auctioneers have it), would I mulct myself, think you, of rent and taxes at the rate of ten guineas per inch, for a snail-shell in Dean Street, Park Lane?—*I* have my way to make in town; yours is made for you. Between ourselves, Cis, it was my intention, on quitting Oxford, not to consort with any fellow less than ten years my senior. At your age and mine, one must live for improvement. No man has a right to study his pleasure or convenience, till thirty. It takes till then to make up his mind and character. Once established, let him follow the bent of his inclinations."

" You intend, then," cried I, interrupting him, " to improve yourself by the society of fogeys?"

" I intend*ed*,—but I recant. *You*, my old chum, shall march hand in hand with me in the path of perfectionment. We have been boys together; we will

cease to be boys together ; or rather, together we will
learn to be men——"

" Of fashion," added I ; " for such I conceive to be
the object of what you call making up a character.
But for my part, I frankly tell you that, having as you
say Lord Ormington's house, cook, and cellar,—such
as they are,—to fall back upon, I shall give myself
no great trouble about the matter. You observed just
now that I was able to dispense with scholarship. I
consider myself as well able to dispense with ambition."

" Ambition ?" reiterated Jack Harris.

" What signifies the object to be attained ? The
art of rising in the world is still the same, whether
it be

Th' applause of listening Senates to command,

or to conquer the plaudits of White's. For my part,
I despise both. Provided I secure the roses of life,
confound its laurels. By the way, Harris, where
did you get that love of a waistcoat ?" said I, perceiving that Jack was nettled at finding his affectation
outdone, and his air of patronage discountenanced.

" It was got *for* me," he replied, with a peculiar
smile. " These rumours of wars make one shudder to
think how soon the Continent may close again, to the
utter discouragement of our attempts at humanization.
There is only Paris for a waistcoat. London produces
buckskins and boots. Germany has its coats. But
nothing like Paris for a waistcoat !"

I saw he was determined I should inquire into the
origin of *his*, and disappointed him. But I could
scarcely support the self-sufficient air with which he
first glanced at the pattern, and then at me, as with
a tacit assertion of superiority. That the waistcoat
was neither French nor a gift, I was persuaded. Jack
would not, however, have troubled himself to assume
the smile of a lady's man but for a foregone conclusion.

" By the way, Cis," said he, when, after taking leave of him, I was about to retread the miniature staircase carpeted to the brink, so that neither the blind mole nor Jack Harris could hear a foot fall,—" one little piece of advice,—the advice of a man who has six months the start of you on the *pavé*. Drop Oxford. Be not a hint of the 'damned spot' perceptible in the garnish of your discourse or of your garments. A man fresh from the university is infected with slang or pedantry. Avoid both. Cut the college-cut,—or prepare to be cut in your turn."

I could have killed him for the air with which he uttered this warning. I was Lord Ormington's son,— that is, I was Lady Ormington's. *Who* was Jack Harris, that he should be a plummet over me ? Alas ! it was less *who* he was, than *what* he was, that endowed him with the right. He was a monstrous clever fellow ; or, with a problematical fortune and doubtful origin, he would not have come to be called Jack Harris by the best men of his time.

Next to the mortification of Harris's nonchalance, was the dryness of my father. Lord Ormington, indignant at losing in me the family incumbent of a family living of two thousand a year, referred me, in the fewest possible words, in the fewest possible days after my arrival in town, to his men of business, Messrs. Hanmer and Snatch, of Southampton Buildings, for intimation of his paternal projects for my advancement in life.

There is something offensive in being despatched, even by one's father, to Southampton Buildings. When a gentleman intends to shoot you, he refers you to his friend ; when to persecute you according to the law, to his man of business. I felt the menace as it was intended. But I went. Old Hanmer was my father's man. In such firms, there is usually a thinking partner and a talking partner. Hanmer was the talker ; the partner who received orders from the clients, while Snatch gave orders to the clerks. I

had seen him once or twice in my boyhood at Ormington Hall, when he brought down a post-chaise full of
deeds to be executed, and carried up a post-chaise full
of venison or pheasants on which execution was to be
done. Hanmer had a good-humoured jocular face, of
most unlawyer-like promise; and was especially odious
to me as a man who made merry with a solemn subject. I never liked Shakspeare's grave-diggers. Above
all things, I hate a comical physician or punning lawyer, whose good-humour is as nauseous as the lump of
sugar infused into a black dose prepared for the use of
schools.

I was compelled to swallow him, however, or, at
least, consult him as the way-post of my future career.
Having borrowed a horse of Jack Harris, I sauntered,
at an hour when least likely to find Christians in the
streets, and most likely to find a lawyer at his office,
towards what have since been facetiously denominated
the wilds of Bloomsbury.

The irritation of my mind probably rendered me
inarticulate in my inquiries of a pepper-and-salt non-
descript that opened the door ; or, perhaps, my appearance announced a person somewhat different from
the usual clients of Messrs. Hanmer and Snatch. For,
instead of conveying me into the chambers of the old
lawyer, Pepper-and-Salt ushered me to a barn on the
first floor, which, I suppose, called itself by courtesy
a drawing-room.

Having desired me to "please to step in," which I
did please, a certain confusion at a table in one corner
of the room made it apparent that some one else was
pleased to step out. There was a lady seated at
the table, writing, drawing, sketching—no matter
what—who had her back towards me. But as
there were petticoats in the case, I took Jack Harris's
advice, forgot Oxford, and was civil; begging I
might not disturb her, and feeling, with perfect
sincerity, that whether old Hanmer's drawing-room
contained or not a piece of quizzical human furniture

in addition to its quizzical chairs and tables, mattered not a jot.

Advancing towards the fireplace, though it was April and the weather balmy, I took up that national position on the hearth-rug, from which John Bull, like

> Andes, giant of the western star,
> Looks from his throne of clouds o'er half the world;

and in the present instance overlooked something, which was something worth looking at.

The fireplace commanded the table where old Hanmer's better half or quarter,—his wife, or daughter, or niece,—was fussing together her rattletraps preparatory to escape. I suppose it was the recollection of Jack Harris's waistcoat that determined me to stare her out of countenance. For, to own the truth, my practice was to include in one vast horde (good to sew on buttons, get up fine linen, and compound cheese-cakes) all that portion of the sex not entitled to walk at a coronation or kiss hands on a birthday.

A single glance at the beautiful creature who was shutting up her writing-box in the corner of old Hanmer's humdrummery, brought a flush of surprise to my cheek and a stammering apology to my lips.

Never had I seen so sweet a face, so graceful a figure! Falling shoulders, trimly waist, a profusion of chesnut curls, falling from the smallest head I had ever seen, on either side a throat as white as it was slender,—all were exquisite! There was an air of elegance, more distinguished than even an air of fashion, in the girl; and though her mourning dress was simple to homeliness, she seemed far from oppressed by a sense of my affability, when I once more " begged that I might not disturb her, as I was merely waiting the arrival of Mr. Hanmer." She requested me to take a seat, much as Lady Ormington might have offered the same courtesy to her apothecary, and left the room.

My first impulse, on her departure, was to turn round and look in the glass ; no uncommon movement with me, certainly ; but, on the present occasion, it was accompanied by a note of interrogation, rather than admiration. I wanted to ascertain *why* this girl of Hanmer's had been able to confront me without confusion. Had I, in anticipation of my fusty visit to my father's man of business, neglected to arm myself with my usual implements of destruction ? No ! my tie was sublime, my shirt frill of " lawn as white as driven snow ;" my buckskins and tops unimpeachable ! (Shudder not, gentle reader, and more especially reader fair ! for I write of a year whose decimal is zero, 180- !) There was every reason the young lady's civilities should be incoherent, and her curtsey tremulous. I felt, therefore, inexpressibly injured by her self-possession.

My meditations were interrupted by the entrance of old Hanmer, rubbing his hands and drawing in his breath with a hissing inspiration ; while good humour shone upon his cushioned cheeks, and sparkled in the cold blue eyes, which looked as if they had frozen into icicles the shaggy white eyebrows by which, like stalactites, they were overhung. I abhor people who enter a room rubbing their hands, and drawing in their breath. It is the favourite *début* of dentists, attorneys, and other excruciators of the public mind and body. My bow to the man of business was indicative of suitable repugnance.

" Glad to see ye, Mr. Danby — glad to see ye ! Take a chair !" cried he, not a whit abashed by the non-extension of my hand to meet the one he offered. I saw, at once, that my father had invested him with some sort of authority over me.

" My lord, pretty well this morning ?" continued he. " I had the honour of seeing his lordship yesterday forenoon." And he spoke in a tone proprietary of my lord, as if in daily attendance upon his moral nature as the apothecary upon his gout.

"Lord Ormington sent me hither, sir," said I, as grandly as twenty-and-a-half, with its modicum of beard and whiskers, is able to look at a barbose old monster of sixty-five, "to learn his pleasure on the subject of my future career." And I tried to insinuate into my tone an implication that my father's pleasure and my own were not necessarily concorporate.

Old Hanmer regarded me with the complacent smile of pity with which the Ogre may have examined the condition of Hop-o'-my-Thumb, ere he put him by in a child-coop to be killed when wanted for table. The man of business had no mind, perhaps, to grind my bones to make his bread, because at present my bones were marrowless as those of Banquo's ghost. He saw that I should make prettier pickings hereafter.

"My dear young gentleman," said he, with the most nauseous cordiality, "it grieves me to be under the necessity of explaining, in the name of my noble client Lord Ormington, his heartfelt disappointment at the recent——"

I spare my readers the preamble. Most of them must be capable of supposing the sermon of a rich lord's man of business, commissioned to inflict an exhortation upon a younger son. The pith of the argument was—"You can't go into the Church, Mr. Cecil Danby—you shan't go into the army. If you choose to embrace a diplomatic career, there is an opening in the Foreign Office. But I will neither accept the obliging offers of my friend Lord Votefilch to advance you in diplomatic life, nor continue your present allowance of four hundred per annum, unless you pledge yourself to punctual habits, and submission to the powers that be."

I seemed to have acquired one of the indispensables to my advancement in diplomatic life; for instead of closing with the offer, I replied, with a countenance and voice most mysteriously inconclusive, that, "I would reflect upon the proposal, and have the honour of delivering my ultimatum in the course of a day or two."

I had, of course, already made up my mind,—that is, as much mind as I had to make up,—to accept the offer. Nothing could have suited me better. I had anticipated a hundred horrors ; a residence on my father's Irish estates (where the agency was worth two thousand a year and the rent-roll three), or extinction in a parsonage with a private tutor, during the half-year still to elapse previous to my coming of age ; and to a minor, half a year is half a century. In that said month of April, with the London season before me, I would not have bartered the ensuing six months against an eventual mitre or Mastership of the Rolls.

The career of diplomacy flattered my dearest ambitions. Diplomacy is almost the only profession where a man gains nothing by appearing a beast. Slovenliness is esteemed an evidence of scholarship in almost every calling save that which renders one the mouthpiece of kings, redeeming their gracious majesties from the trouble of communicating per speaking-trumpet from one end of Europe to the other. Downing Street exchanged only for some foreign mission enchanted me. The diplomatist's is a metropolitan existence. The diplomatist is fated to progress, like a child learning its alphabet, from capital to capital. His post lies in some focus, concentrating the rays of civilization. His place is the bull's-eye of the target. The diplomatist can never subside into the commonplace of life.

Instead, however, of making these cogent reflections manifest to the man of business, I observed, rising at the same time to take leave, that I regretted to have been the means of driving Mrs. Hanmer from the room. I never knew an old fellow of sixty-five who was not pleased at having a pretty wife of eighteen ascribed to him, however inveterate his bachelorhood. A glance towards the table and the writing-box served, of course, as note explanatory to my text.

"Mrs. Hanmer ? " repeated he, exactly in the tone

I had anticipated. " Oh ! ay,—you mean Emily. It was no interruption, my dear sir. I was expecting you this morning. I had desired you should be shown in here. It was her own fault if she did not remain in her room."

To me the fault appeared a venial transgression. The case was clear. " Emily," whether Miss Hanmer or Miss anything else, had evidently heard of Cecil Danby, and wished to ascertain whether fame had been a flatterer. But then, since aware that the daughter of Lord Ormington's man of business had the honour of standing in the presence of Lord Ormington's son, why was not her deportment more demonstrative of her consciousness of the distinction ?

Determined to vouchsafe no interest in her favour, and looking unutterable solemnities at old Hanmer in rebuke to his familiarity, I made my parting bow.

On entering the house, I had taken little heed of the meanness of the staircase, or the unworthiness of the thing in pepper-and-salt, considering it all highly becoming in the abode of my father's attorney. If attorneys *had* houses with staircases and serving-men, such was probably *hoc genus omne.* But as I went out, it struck me with disgust that a being so inexpressibly lovely as " Emily," nay, so thoroughly on a par, in manners and appearance, with any *Lady* Emily I had ever seen, should be condemned to so mediocre an existence.

The creaking stair,—the yellow paint, omitted in a central stripe intended for a carpet, though carpet there was none,—the dirty hall, with its worn-out floor-cloth,—the very street-door, with its unsightly bolts and chains,—were such as should never have met those soft eyes, overshaded by such lashes, and gracing a countenance worthy of a diamond coronet or garland of roses.

Southampton Buildings, however, was not the place for soliloquy. So, throwing a shilling to the boy holding Jack Harris's horse at old Hanmer's door, and

trusting that Emily might be peeping from the window
of her room, I leaped into my saddle with the air of a
Bayard, and made the best of my way towards the
haunts of civilization.

———•◦•———

CHAPTER II.

Immortalia mortali sermone notantes.—LUCRET. 1. v.

Comme les gens dont la taille est bien prise, il s'habillait avec
esprit, et se portait une espèce de culte.—MICHEL RAYMOND.

I HAD seen little of my brother during my college
days.   John was a Cambridge man.   John, as became
his ugliness, had taken honours ; and John, as also
became his ugliness, was not only devoted to study,
but pursuing it at Ormington Hall.   He usually remained there long after the rest of the family were
settled in Hanover Square ; and even when in town
seemed to take delight in maintaining the same distance between himself and my mother, now he was a
man, that *she* had maintained betwixt herself and *him*
when he was a boy.   With my father's sanction he
occupied sober lodgings of his own, not very far from
the residence of his maiden aunts ; and, except when
Lord Ormington gave a political dinner, seldom dined
at home.

This suited me perfectly.   John was still the same
lump of clay banished by its mamma to the nursery in
its infancy, and self-banished to the study in its
maturity ; and I felt that, to be seen walking down
St. James's Street, hooked to the arm of such an
elder brother, would be to stand for my picture to
Deighton.   I accordingly established myself with him
on the footing of, " How are you, John ?"—" How are
you, Cecil ?" and as such intimations of fraternal coolness are by no means uncommon in that model country

of the domestic affections, Great Britain, no one was surprised to see us nod to each other in the street, aware that we must have nodded in each other's company in all other times and places.

Jack Harris noted with a smile, that "'twas no wonder we should dislike each other, without a feature or idea in common;" and as Lord Ormington and his elder son's ideas and features were not only in common, but uncommonly common, I was by no means jealous of their sympathies.

My father was a man such as one rarely sees out of England; reserved, without being contemplative; convivial, without being social; not mistrustful, yet having confidence in nobody; cold, unexpansive, undemonstrative; fulfilling his petty duties so gravely, as to impress people with a notion they were of some consequence; and by his gravity of air and paucity of words, imparting a tone of mystery to his insignificance.

He seemed afraid of letting himself know what he was about. Yet he had nothing to fear. God knows he never did anything worth speaking of. He was a moral man. His business with Hanmer, with his banker, or with Lord Votefilch, might have been transacted at Charing Cross without discredit to his public virtue, or private virtues. Yet he seemed to dread that even his own man should be aware on Tuesday, that on Wednesday he had an appointment with either of the three; and as to his wife—but for *that* reserve there was, perhaps, sufficient motive.

When, at the close of two days' cogitation, I approached him with the intention of signifying my acceptance of his terms, it did not surprise me to find myself a second time referred to Southampton Buildings. "On everything relating to business," he said, "it was his wish to communicate with me through a third person."

But that I anticipated some such regulation, I should not have volunteered my "ultimatum" to his

lordship. It was my full intention to make my way
a second time up the creaking staircase, lacking a
carpet. And lest the *sang-froid* evinced by Emily at
our last interview should prove the means of disappointing me, I rode straight to Hanner's door, without
warning or appointment.

"Mr. Hanmer was not at home, and Mr. Snatch
had quitted London on business, by the Leeds mail
the preceding night."

The murmured ejaculation, not intended to reach
beyond my lips, unluckily caught the ear of Pepper-
and-Salt.

"I could speak to the head-clerk if I liked. The
head-clerk would be disengaged in the course of a
quarter of an hour."

Satan, or some other of the invisible esquires of the
body to Adam's grandsons, at that moment seemed to
flourish before my eyes the waistcoat of Jack Harris,
which I had seen dazzling the eyes of Fop's Alley the
preceding night.

"Be so good as to inform Miss Emily," said I,
"that I have a message to leave with her, from Lord
Ormington."

The latter name had an instantaneous effect upon
Pepper-and-Salt. It was that of the presiding divinity of the house of business of Hanmer and Snatch.
The deed-boxes most reverentially lodged of their
whole cliency, were those inscribed with the designation of "the Right Honourable Lord Ormington,"—
their solitary link with the peerage. It was from the
park and preserves of Ormington Hall, that corn,
wine, and oil,—haunches of venison and leashes of
pheasants,—reached the meagre kitchen of the firm.
To Pepper-and-Salt, accordingly, his lordship appeared
to be the fountain of all goodness,—the king of
Cockaigne,—a man to be venerated even in the person
of his messenger.

Without further hesitation, he conducted me once
more into the drawing-room; then hurried off, ob-

serving, that he would see whether Miss Emily could be spoken to. For there was no Miss Emily in the chilly chamber, no fire in the grate, no writing-box on the little table. Her intrusion on the last occasion had perhaps excited the displeasure of her father, and brought down upon her a sentence of perpetual banishment. In that case, she would not now venture to obey my summons.

In so short a time, however, as to afford no hope that she had added a single touch to her toilet on the announcement of my name, the graceful creature who had produced so startling an effect upon me at our first interview, glided into the room. Still, no embarrassment,—still, no emotion. Nay, she did not even request me to be seated ; and I stood, looking like an oaf, with my hat and riding-cane in my hand, like a subject receiving orders from his sovereign.

" You wished to speak to me ?" said the sweetest voice I ever heard, as if in compassion to my awkwardness.

" Understanding that Messrs. Hanmer and Snatch were absent from town——" said I, wholly incapable of assuming the tone of superiority I had premeditated.

" The clerks of the establishment, sir, are in the office," observed Emily, almost haughtily.

" I was anxious," I stammered, as if not noticing her interruption, "to request the favour that you would charge yourself with a confidential message to to your father."

In a moment, every part of Emily's person, that was visible to eyes profane, became flushed by the deepest crimson ; and her eyes seemed to dilate with inexplicable emotion, — surprise or indignation, or both. I saw that I was somehow or other confoundedly in the wrong. She made no answer. But I neither dared reiterate my question, nor hazard another. I was conscious of looking like a pickpocket.

" What do you wish me to communicate to Mr.
Hanmer on his return ?" said she, after a minute's
silence, and in so subdued a tone, that indignation,
at all events, was not the passion I had excited.

" Simply that I accept the terms proposed to me
through his mediation," said I, not daring to excite
her surprise, by the preposterous fact that herself and
Mr. Hanmer, of Southampton Buildings, were the
chain of communication between a peer of the realm
and his son, residing under the same roof.

" I have the honour of speaking to Mr. Danby ?"
she inquired coldly.

I bowed my affirmative.

" I will not fail to deliver your message," she continued, advancing her hand towards the bell, by way
of an intimation, and not a very gracious one, that my
audience was at an end.   There was no remedy.
Away I went, like a beaten dog ; having effected
nothing by my impertinent intrusion, except a still
deeper descent in Emily's opinion, and my own.

" Southampton Buildings ?   An attorney's daughter ?" muttered I, as if to revenge myself by the contemptuous inflection with which I pronounced the
words, as I galloped off in the direction of the west-
end.   And again, the waistcoat of Jack Harris seemed
to flutter before my eyes, as a memento of my insignificance in the field whose laurels are myrtles.

On the strength of my " ultimatum," I was now
mounted on a horse of my own ; as I had good reason
to discover, on encountering the smile of Jack Harris
in Rotten Row.   Harris was one of those who never
break out into condemnation.   A withering glance
or smile was sufficient.   Towards myself, he affected
indulgence.   At *me*, he looked leniently, as much as
to say, " Poor fellow ! it is not *his* fault if taken in by
a dealer to purchase a screw."   At my elder brother,
he would have sneered outright ; at such a fellow as
old Hanmer, gazed with horror.   But his clemency
was far more galling than his utmost rigour of the

law. A boy can never stand being treated as a boy ;
more especially by another boy assuming the importance of a man.

" Who was that with whom you were riding to-day
in the park ?" observed my mother (the Ormington
vis-à-vis, now that Julia was rusticating with my
aunts in the country, permitting itself to be seen once
more in the ring).

" A college chum."

" A *what ?*" reiterated my mother, opening her
eyes as wide as Emily had done that morning, but
without the accompanying blush.

" Jack Harris, a Christchurch man," said I, not
deigning to notice the shrug with which she listened
to the announcement.

" Yet he had nothing of the horrible Oxford cut ?"
observed my mother, as if muttering to the spaniel
nestling under her white hand on the sofa. At that
moment, Harris's warning about dropping the University recurred to my mind.

" It will give you pleasure, perhaps, to learn," said
I, perceiving that she was about to coax herself as
well as her lapdog into a doze, " that Lord Ormington has procured me a clerkship in one of the public
offices."

" A WHAT ?" again reiterated my mother, twenty
times more shocked than at my Oxonianism.

" A clerkship. As soon as I can compass a legible
hand and the rule of three, I am to be provided for
by Government, at the rate of £75 per annum."

" You have not surely accepted ? " exclaimed my
mother, shoving away poor Bibiche with more vivacity
than I had ever seen her exhibit. "He has no right
to expose you to such a degradation. *That* were a
breach of all our compacts."

In compassion to her emotion, I condescended to
expound, that the £75 per annum, at twenty, was a
necessary preliminary to the ambassadorial £12,000
per annum crowning a diplomatic career ; and that of

D

my brother-clerks in the office, three were sons of earls and four of members of Parliament.

"So that, some day or other, you will be an ambassador ? " said she, resuming her languor and her spaniel.

" *Deo,* or rather, *diabolo volente !* " I replied.

"In that case, I am glad you are going to stay in town," said she. "I will give you one of my Opera tickets, and introduce you to the duchess of Money-musk. I dare say you will get on very well. When Lord Ormington said something about the necessity for your living at home, to redeem your character after disgracing yourself at Oxford, I thought it would be a bore. But if you manage properly, you need not be in any one's way. You have only two things to avoid,—play and politics. Play and politics are for elder sons. It would be the making of John to go into Parliament, or upon the turf. But John is such a stupid young man, that there is no doing anything with him. John does nothing but read. John was never intended to play a gentleman's part in the world."

"And how do you recommend me to fill up my time ? " said I, by way of humouring her absurdity.

"Not in exhibiting yourself as the companion of a Mr. Harris, whom no one ever heard of," she replied. "Ah ! my dear Lady Harriet, how are you ? " cried she, interrupting herself, on perceiving that a pretty little woman had entered the room, unnoticed by either of us. " You are come to take me to the duchess's loo, and I have not even begun to dress ! "

"Make haste, then," replied her friend, dragging a chair to the fire, and seating herself as if at home. " You forgot your appointment, I suppose, in the pleasure of lecturing your son. Pray are *you* the young gentleman who has got himself expelled from Oxford ? " she continued, addressing me over her shoulder, and extending her hand towards a fire-screen, as if to command me to reach it for her. The movement discovered to me the pretty, but somewhat *passé* face of a woman half a dozen years younger than my mother, whom I had no difficulty in recognizing as one of the intimates of her coterie.

"And who cannot regret, still less repent, a step that procures him the honour of presenting himself to Lady Harriet Vandeleur," said I, offering the screen with an air of gallantry, which I flattered myself was irresistible.

Her reply was a burst of laughter.

"Is the Grandison style of compliment still in vogue at our seats of learning?" cried she, turning and contemplating me from head to foot. "My dear Lady Ormington, off to your dressing-room, I beseech you, for we are late already : and *I* will continue your jobation to this junior incumbrance of yours. He is not so ill-looking! I was afraid we should find him much more of a cub. Leave him in my hands, and I will see what is to be made of him."

I was again on the point of being betrayed into a compliment, expressing my delight at falling to the share of such a preceptress. But something in the arch eyes of Lady Harriet warned me to desist. She was an Irishwoman, whose *naïveté* bordered on effrontery. It *would* have been effrontery in an ugly woman. But in the pretty, pouting, piquante Lady Harriet, it was enchanting.

"Is the cub to sit or stand, or will you permit him to kneel?" said I, falling into her vein, the moment my mother quitted the room.

"Your height and figure warrant my refusing you a chair," she replied. "But I have a mind to ascertain the colour of your eyes, which flashed so furiously just now, at my condescending to laugh at you. So draw a chair, and let me proceed in my investigation."

I replied, of course, to the summons, by falling at her feet.

"Not ill done, as regards the attitude," said she,

examining me without embarrassment. "But a blunder as regards intention. By hazarding a burlesque declaration, you admit your conviction that you shall never be tempted into a serious one. In your ignorance whether I am maid, wife, or widow, you are right. Any, but the last, might take you at your word, and you would stand committed! So now, rise;—gently,—or you will throw down the Chelsea *déjeûner*. Take your seat with the modesty becoming the junior member of the house; and contrive, if you can, not to look hampered in your own cravat."

The levity of Lady Harriet struck me dumb. I was tamed, as brutes are, by the coolness of their keepers. I had not even courage to inform her that I was perfectly aware of her being a rich widow.

"It is not a horrible vulgarism," said she (again adverting to the china, that I might recover the breath of which her *sang-froid* had deprived me), "to cram a habitable room with trumpery, of which one risks the fracture of a hundred pounds' worth, at every turn? One might as well lay out, for show, one's stomacher and diamond necklace. Look at my friend Lady Ormington's confusion of cabinets and tables, rivalling an old curiosity-shop, or Weeks's museum. Twenty years hence, perhaps, even the little mousetraps of Marylebone will have their knick-knackery, and Birmingham *virtù*."

In my boyish susceptibility, I fancied she was talking at *me;* my rooms at Oxford having been renowned for their foppery. I stood accountant for as great a sin as Lady Ormington, and consequently broke out bravely.

"As you say, an odious weakness," cried I; "dilettantcism viewed at the wrong end of the telescope! If people *must* affect the fine arts, be it nobly. A fine Dominichino, a Giovanni di Bologna, affords a diploma of taste to the possessor. Whereas these less than nothings of Sèvres or enamel, require a microscopic eye. Were Nollekens's Venus smiling upon her pedestal in yonder corner, I should adore her in the distance, without losing sight of Lady Harriet Vande-- leur ; and enable myself to decide at a glance whether the smallest foot in Europe, slippered by Taylor, be not a prettier sight than the same charming feature in its primeval symmetry."

"Not so bad," cried Lady Harriet. "But another time don't call a foot a feature. It is William Spencerish. The school is obsolete. Try reality. We are all pretending to be natural with all our might, till the affectation of nature has become as natural as any other affectation. And now pray what is Mr. Cecil Danby going to do with his younger sonship, after proving too wicked for the Church? Not a man of wit and fashion about town, I trust. The ranks are overflowing : an inundation of the *nihil !* The army, too, is out of date."

"I am about to devote myself to the cause of my country in a more modest capacity," said I, "by sketching dogs and horses on his Majesty's blotting-paper in Downing Street."

"Official?" cried Lady Harriet, withdrawing her feet from the fender, and throwing the lustre of her dark eyes full upon my face, as a watchman turns the light of his lantern. "You are becoming natural indeed. You are flinging away the poetry of life with a vengeance. Official? Have you reflected on what it will be to extend your finger-tips to ours, black with the inky business of the state ?"

"You authorize me then to decline a diplomatic career?" cried I, starting up as if about to rush out of the room. "I have not heard Lord Ormington's carriage drive off. I shall perhaps be in time to catch him on his way to the House of Lords."

"Let me recommend you not to jest with Lord Ormington," said she gravely, motioning me to be re-seated. "It is playing with edged tools. If you are to be pushed by *his* interest in public life, accept and be thankful. Do you go with us to the duchess's to-night ?"

"Am I to have that honour? I wait your ladyship's
orders," said I, again mistaking myself and *her* so far
as to play the gallant.

"Then I order you to stay at home. Nay, I order
you to stay at home till qualified for society. At
present, you do not approach within millions of miles
of even the very small thing indispensable to obtain
endurance among us. You would easily make a sensation,—but a sensation is a vulgar triumph. To keep
up the excitement of a sensation, you must always be
standing on your head ; and the attitude, like everything overstrained, would become fatiguing to yourself
and tedious to others. Whereas, to obtain permanent
favour, as an agreeable well-bred man, requires simply
an exercise of the understanding. To ascertain whether
you possess one, get rid of your conceit."

"I will learn anything you deign to teach me," said
I. "But how could *you* teach me to be humble, when
your interest would a thousandfold increase the self-
conceit you reprobate?"

"From Oxford, yet a logician ! I thought young
men went to the University to get rid of their learning? However, for my own sake, I *shall* take you in
hand. For as it must be my fate to see a great deal
of the pet son of my bosom friend, it would be a
serious evil were I always to find him presuming,
abrupt, and coxcombical, as to-night. Don't bristle
up so furiously. You will gain nothing but being
laughed at. I tell you again, that to succeed among
us, you must reduce your laugh to a smile, your voice
to a whisper, your assertions to surmises. For some
years to come, you have no right to have an opinion
of your own. You will be coughed down by the 'most
potent, grave, and reverend signors,' who are ten years
older than yourself. For it is of *them* the jury is
composed. The men of thirty carry all before them in
London ;—men old enough to pretend to tact, but not
to wisdom. As soon as we grow really wise, we become indulgent ;—witness myself, who am three-and-

thirty. And now, good night! I hear the rustling of Lady Ormington's sarsnet; for which I am grateful, as I perceive that you are about to explode."

I had, in fact, been making sundry efforts to interrupt her, but without success. There was no putting down her audacity.

"Good night!" said she, kissing her hand in the Italian fashion. "You are not yet sufficiently in my good graces to admit of accepting your arm to the carriage. Prove your docility by staying at home, while we proceed to throw away our time, money, and temper at the card-table."

When, in spite of her prohibition, I had conducted her to the carriage, and taken remarkably fast hold of the hand which she placed on mine as she stepped in, I found myself almost out of breath with pique and wonder.

I was a Christchurch man. Yet here was a pretty woman, who had both looked and talked me down. There was only one word of her rambling discourse which operated as a saving grace in Lady Harriet's favour. I should have called her bold,—I should have called her flighty,—I should have called her flippant,— nay, I would have repeated, after her own authority, that she was three-and-thirty, and after my own, that she looked her age; but for the monosyllable "*yet!*" That "yet" was a peacemaker! She did not "yet" like me sufficiently to put up with my boorishness.

This was throwing down the gauntlet. The ambitions of the Foreign Office were too prolix for the hot blood of twenty and six months. I might be an ambassador at forty,—an ambassador with a bald head and chinchilli whiskers. The prospect was too remote. But a pretty woman who told me so frankly, that she did not "yet" like me, was an immediate incentive. I swore,—as my uncle Toby swore, that Lefevre should not die,—that she should NOT like me; that, by Heavens! she should *love* me,—to desperation,—to madness.

Next day, I contemplated Jack Harris's waistcoat
with calmness. I felt myself on the road to preferment.   I was convinced that there were waistcoats in
the loom for me, and consequently discovered that
his was frightful : a waistcoat calculated, according to
Lady Harriet's system, to produce a sensation,—to
induce questions.   I had already ordered myself half
a dozen of the plainest pattern, and simplest fashion ;
such as would enable no one to swear, half an hour
after parting from me, whether I had a waistcoat on
or not.

I took care not to utter a syllable to him, either of
my haughty attorney's daughter, or my familiar
fashionable widow. Time enough to talk about them
when I had something to boast of. To quote them
prematurely, and to a Jack Harris, might prevent my
ever having cause for boasting. I told him, therefore,
that I had not accompanied Lady Ormington to the
duchess of Moneymusk's, " because it was a bore."

It was the fashion in those days to call one's
mother a bore. Mothers have rather risen in the
market since, and fathers gone down. Fathers soon
afterwards came to be called " the governor ; " but
this was by the generation that grew up in the nursery,
before the nursery became council-chamber to the
house. The creatures who are cockading it nowadays, have every reason to call their parents your
Majesties, and address them on their knees,—I mean
the children on their own knees, not upon the knees
of their parents.

Jack Harris sank a fathom in my esteem, by the
frankness with which he allowed me to discern his
surprise that any one should think it a bore to go to
the loo-party of a duchess. *I* was unaffectedly surprised that any one should think a duchess worth
thinking of; not only because my head and heart
were running upon pretty widows and attorneys'
daughters, but because the habits of my youth
familiarized me with social distinctions. It would

have been as difficult for a mere duchess to impose upon the sprawling pet of Lady Ormington's *boudoir*, as for a man to be a hero to his *valet-de-chambre*.

Jack was no longer to me the Infallible. His *à plomb* delighted me no longer. It was the *à plomb* of the adroit mountebank, not of the graceful opera-dancer. His vivacity had lost its charm. There was a brazen twang in its note. The sallies of Lady Harriet, on the contrary, if they had not a silver sound, were at least Corinthian metal. I saw that though Jack might launch me on the waves of the great world, it was Lady Harriet who must officiate as my pilot. Of the three modes in which society may be contemplated, from above, below, or level ground, I preferred the last. Since I was to live with those of my own class, it was better to examine them on a fair footing, and not from the point of view appropriate to a *parvenu* like Jack Harris.

> Quod petiit, spernit ; repetit quod nuper omisit :
> Æstuat, et vitæ disconvenit ordine toto.

In the order of things which condemned *him* to an Ishmael's portion in the land, there was everything to provoke his animosities or rouse his envy. But for *me*, the son of the free woman, an aristocrat, one of the privileged, the malediction that became *his* lips, or the petty arts indispensable to *his* progress in life, would have been out of place. Our principles of action could never be the same. He might be honest,—*I* must be honourable. Generosity might become *him ;* from me, nothing short of magnanimity would suffice. All this, at least, I whispered to myself, as a plea for paying a long visit on the morrow to Lady Harriet Vandeleur, and for nodding to Jack Harris, as we crossed each other at a brisk trot on Constitution Hill.

That night I received a professional letter from Messrs. Hanmer and Snatch. If there be an object in this world from which every particle of the poetry of life is excluded, the very *caput mortuum* of the

crucible of common-place, it is a lawyer's letter. There
is a savour of pounce about it—a dryness—a senten-
tiousness, as if a pen plucked from the wing of that
dullest of birds, the owl, had ministered to its indite-
ment.   Yet, strange to say, I tore open old Hanmer's
long, narrow, wire-wove wafered epistle, his thirteen-
and-two-pennyworth of epistolary civilities, with an
impatience savouring of the lover.

Messrs. Hanmer and Snatch (for old Hanmer addressed me as Wolsey addressed the pope, in the first
person, though hooking in *rex meus* into a parenthesis,
"for partner and self"), Messrs. Hanmer and Snatch
informed me that Messrs. Drummond and Co. had
orders to pay one hundred pounds a quarter to self or
order ; and that I was to present self, without further
orders, on the Monday next ensuing, at the office
of his Majesty's Secretary for Foreign Affairs, in
Downing Street, where Lord Votefilch would have
the honour of explaining to me the nature of my
duties.

I did not pause to exult in the petty triumph of being
handed into office by one of his Majesty's ministers,
while Jack Harris would probably have been thrust
forward by some junior clerk.   I was examining the
date of the letter, as if there were magic in the words
"13, Southampton Buildings !"—The sight of the
Lesbian promontory would scarcely have excited more
emotion in the heart of a young gentleman well
grounded in his Ovid !   I certainly had no reason to
expect that old Hanmer, in writing to me profession-
ally, would hazard mention of "Emily ;" yet, strange
to say, I did not reach the signature of the letter without a sensation of disappointment.   Some emanation,
some hint, some reference, some something, of *her*, ought
to have intermingled itself with that soulless epistle !

Such was my mode of characterizing (at twenty and
a half) a letter conveying a permanent income of four
hundred per annum, and an appointment leading in a
direct line to an embassy.

I know better now. *Now*, I can discern more
poetry in such a despatch than in the collected works
of Wordsworth and Byron !

CHAPTER III.

" Ca ! quelle figure allons nous prendre, Don Juan ou Lovelace ?—Don Juan est usé comme la soutane d'un séminariste.
Lovelace est un peu plus inédit.   Dans sa perruque poudrée, il
a bien meilleur air que Don Juan, ce mauvais râcleur de
guitare."

Nam quodcunque suis mutatum finibus exit,
Continuò hoc mors est illius quod fuit ante.
LUCRET.

SHAKSPEARE'S commentators have disputed much in
disserting on Othello's tender rhapsody, whether the
bronzed generalissimo originally complained that his
" *way* of life," or his " *May* of life," had "fallen into
the sere and yellow leaf." The quarto edition says one
thing, the folio edition says another thing, and the
various buz-wigs, who have overlaid the great poet
with their leaden weight, say a hundred other contra-
dictory things.

I, Cecil Danby, decide for the " MAY of life."   For
what so charateristic of youth and hope as MAY,—the
summer month of the soul, whatever the calendar may
say to the contrary.

It was MAY when I took possesion of my liberty,
and the town.   And what a month it was to me !—
Though, in point of fact, I became, for the first time, a
slave, the slave of the nation, on the trifling acknowledgment of seventy-five pounds per annum, paid
quarterly, I fancied myself, for the first time, my own
master. I had youth, health, spirits ; and the world—
that ugly, old, brown, leathery football of Fate—seemed
to me *then*, young, healthy, happy, hopeful as myself.

I looked upon it as a fresh flower, bursting from its calyx, and exhaling a thousand perfumes. Pah! I could hold my nose now at the mere thought of its exhalations.

Yet the world, errors and steam excepted, remains pretty much as I found it. The eye of twenty-and-a-half discerned only its passions and its picturesque ; while the eye of ——ty-and-a-half descries its muddy roads and arch hypocrisy.

Pass a sloe-leaf, plucked from the nearest hedge, through the hands of half a dozen different men, and each shall see it in a various point of view. The first, if a botanist, will note its specific character ; the second, if a chemist, will opine upon its juices; the third, an artist, will descant upon its colouring ; and the fourth, a tea-man, will examine its eligibility to become Souchong or Bohea. Even so differently do men decide upon the phases of society. At that time, I regarded London as the garden of the Hesperides, where demi-goddesses and the golden apples of preferment awaited the all-subduing club of that great Alcides, Cecil Danby. To Jack Harris, it was a game of skill, where the cleverest player wins the greatest number of court-cards,—*Anglice*, where a low-born man consorts with the greatest number of lords and ladies. My brother looked upon it as an unmeaning hubbub, interrupting the great business of life ; *i.e.* the study of dusty, fusty, musty tomes, in a musty, fusty, dusty library ; and my father, as a place where a man was compelled every Christmas to the unprofitable waste of certain moneys, carefully screwed out of his tenants four times a year.

Let posterity decide which was the greater blockhead.

On second thoughts, I am not so sure that London *is* altogether now as then. When I said, " steam excepted," I should have added " smoke." Every year the atmosphere, as well as the plot, thickens. Every year manufactories arise in Southwark, to suffocate the denizens of London and Westminster. We no longer send to Birmingham for our buttons, or Dorchester for our ale. Like some bumpkin squire, we

take pride in brewing at home. " London's column,"
though still "a tall bully," has rivals in a forest of
steam-chimneys t'other side the water ; and, like
other old foxes, we may end in being smoked out.

The suburbs, too, like a lady's hoop, have extended
so widely as to treble the dimensions of the body they
enclose.   The lungs of London are compressed by the
enlargement of the circumjacent membranes ; and the
atmosphere assigned her is not only less clear and
salubrious, but her breathing-pores are stopped up, and
air-vessels abridged.   Her gardens are built over.
Paddington-fields smoke, like a cigar-divan, from
thousands of ignominious tissues ; and Willan's farm,
instead of feeding hundreds of cows, affords lawn to
five villas, dens to twenty lions, and areas and dust-
holes to five hundred genteel residences, " for the
reception of small families of respectability."   For, lo !
the builders have passed like a swarm of locusts over
the land, and left all barren.

I enlarge on this, lest the dandies of to-day may
find it difficult to account for my boasted enjoyment
of good health and spirits.   As regards the former,
there was less quackery in the world ; as regards the
latter, less smother in the air.   People in general
were more agreeable.   Knowledge did not pretend
to be useful.   There were almost as many courteous
readers as there are now writers ; and authors were
a sort of people who dined with a great man on a
Sunday, in their best clothes, when, indeed, they had
a coat to boast of.   Like mothers, they have since risen
amazingly in the market.   They owe *that* to Scott and
Byron. Sir Walter was the first who wrote up author-
ship ; and, to quote the words of his lordly contemporary, " it was not the least conquest of his fertilizing
and mighty genius."

But if there was little good writing in London
during the first half-dozen years of the nineteenth
century, there was no end of good talking.   In war
time, the dinners, from the hands of native cooks,

were so bad, that people were forced to have recourse
to colloquial entertainment. In the best days of
Conversation S—— and Lord ——, and ——, ——,
(fill up the blanks for yourself, good sir, as you do your
assessed tax-papers, but more honestly; for in *them* you
write down your pointer a cur, and yourself an ass, by
protesting that the demi-lions on your tea-spoons are
not armorial bearings), in the days, I say, when these
blanks were prizes at a dinner-party,

> Roast was the saddle, and the pudding boil'd;

and *entrées*, or, as female cooks denominate them,
" made-dishes," implied anomalous compounds emitting
savours of something between a perfumer's and apothecary's shop,—black, spicy, opaque, and mysterious as
one of Radcliffe's romances. Now that these peppery
forgeries have given place to *épigrammes d'agneau à
pointes d'asperges*, the epigrams of the table-talkers
have become less pointed.

Having asserted (by way of taper burnt to the
memory of the dead) that those in possession of the
ear of the town were better worth hearing, I would
fain prove that those in possession of its eyes were
better worth looking at. Who will deny the beauty
of the Howards and Villierses; two Lady Williams
whom I could name, and two or three Lady Others,
whom I can *not;* to say nothing of my friend Lady
——, next to Fountains Abbey, the finest ruin extant.
They were loveliness itself. Witness the miniatures of
Mrs. Mee, the journals of Sir Lumley, or the ghost of
Harry Mellish. It is true they enabled one to judge
somewhat too accurately of their symmetry. In the
scanty gowns into which they were squeezed, like pillows into their cases, little was left for the imagination;
whereas, in the present day, beauty in her five-and-
twenty breadths of petticoat lies concealed, like the
mummy of Cheops within the labyrinths of the Great
Pyramid.

Lady Harriet Vandeleur was just the fairy on whom

these tight-fitting habiliments sat to admiration. With her snow-white skin, fair ringlets, and luminous dark eyes, she reminded me of one of those French lap-dogs which look so earnest about nothing, perched on a silken cushion in a lady's chamber, or lying among the folds of her lawn apron. Nothing angular or un-sightly was revealed by the winding-sheet in which she was swathed. A single row of pearls or brilliants adorned her white neck in the ball-room; an almost invisible Venetian chain on minor occasions. How preferable to the harness-like ponderosity of modern carcanets; allowing as little of a pretty woman to remain perceptible as one sees of the table-cloth at a country christening.

Coquette,—jilt,—flirt,—angel,—Lady Harriet ex-celled in refinement of taste. Her house was charm-ing; neither overloaded like my mother's with porcelain and gauds; nor affectedly simple, like the matter-of-factory of Jack Harris. Fancy had some scope, but her wings were clipped. She was allowed a flutter, not a flight. Intuition seemed to have dictated my code of *virtù* on our first acquaintance; for the little widow's rooms were adorned with a few *chefs-d'œuvre* by the first masters; a few cabinets, in their places, not thrusting themselves importunately forward, like a young member in the House, or a young miss in a ball-room; and a sufficiency of rich furniture, as studiously assorted as that of my poor mother was mismatched and fanciful.

Poor Lady Ormington had, in fact, never recovered her first glimpse of the boudoirs of Paris and Trianon, in Marie Antoinette's time; when my father, under the domination of her bright eyes, was weak enough to pass his honeymoon on the banks of the Seine. Snatched from the simplicity of a country parsonage into a paradise of buhl and ormoulu, her ladyship's ideas received an ineffaceable impression, which pro-duced and reproduced itself in her tawdry domain in Hanover Square. Apple-green and turquoise-blue,

lacquer and Japan, Chelsea and Sèvres, ebony in-
crusted with ivory or mother-of-pearl, dainty comfit-
boxes of Dutch enamel, curious snuff-boxes, which,
on the lid, displayed the lady wife, and, by a secret
spring, the lady fair of the Lauzuns and Richelieus of
their day, abounded in her brittle domain.   Her existence was all Watteau, all Pompadour, all powderpuff,
all musk, all ambergris ! Time need have had gold-sand
in his glass, and an agate handle to his scythe, to deal
with such a life of trifling !

There was more character in the frivolity of her
friend. It was Greuze, rather than Watteau ; it was
Voltaire, not Voiture. I am speaking of Lady Harriet as I saw her, face to face ; not as I recollect her,
reminiscence to reminiscence. To the Cecil Danby of
twenty-and-a-half she was irresistible ; an epitome of
all that was pleasant (but wrong) in woman.

I was never sure of her. Compared with *her*, a
weathercock was a fixture and a chameleon permanent.
A bevy of those

> gay creatures of the elements
> That in the colours of the rainbow live,

a swarm of humming-birds, a French brocade, a
Neapolitan brigand, an edition of Horace Walpole,
do not combine a greater variety of hues and fantasticalities. After uttering a series of brilliant repartees
and biting truths, that would have made the fortune
of Conversation Sharpe or of a witty parody like Canning's Pocket-book, she was indignant if one presumed
to consider her anything but a fool. Yet, after behaving
like one for four-and-twenty hours (by angling for
gudgeons, such as my cousin Lord Squeamy or Sir
Moulton Drewe, and flinging them back, when caught,
into the waters), she would not suffer *me* to presume
one quarter of an inch upon her folly. On the slightest
act of forwardness, Lady Harriet made me draw in
my horns and sulk back into my shell ; like any other

wretched snail who, presuming to trail itself upon a rose, gets a thorn in its side for its pains.

It was like poetry after prose, it was like grace after meat, it was like a ballet with Angiolini after an opera without Catalani, when, at the close of my official day, I was admitted into the charming drawing-room in Grosvenor Place, confronting the elms of Buckingham Gardens, and opening into a gay conservatory fresh with a profusion of the sweetest flowers.

Pimlico was then a remote suburb of London, losing itself in gravel-pits and fields covered with scrubby herbage that vainly endeavoured to look green. Lady Harriet preferred the situation, as the thing in town that most resembled the country; a place where the houses affected rurality, with laburnum-bushes, and other odd conceits, trained over their frontage. I remember that, in my short cut across the park, along the Birdcage Walk to Buckingham Gate, I always felt as though I were living in the reign of Queen Anne, and as if Lady Harriet were living at the antipodes. On the days I paid my court to her, there was no getting near St. James's Street; for Downing Street, Grosvenor Place, and the clubs, formed the extremities of a triangle.

The lovely tyrant was never visible till four o'clock; but rising at noon, how did she employ the interim? In the circle I usually found assembled round her, consisting of about a dozen of the chosen of the day, there was no one to excite my jealousy: the men were chiefly men of forty; who, in the eyes of twenty and a half, possessed about the attraction that a venerable classic, though printed by Aldus and bound by Du Seuil, possesses in those of a schoolboy, compared with some new romance by M. G. Lewis, in gaudy accoutrements of modern calf. Lady Harriet might as well have selected, as an object of jealousy, one of the wrinkled and painted cats abounding in her loo-playing coterie, as *I* one of the contemporaries

E

of Sir Lionel Dashwood, who were the Celadons of
the flock in Grosvenor Place.

But how, then, *did* she fill up the hours when I was
idling through the business of the state in Downing
Street? How was it with her from noon till four
o'clock? I had seen in my cockadehood Lady
Ormington devote half a dozen hours to the toilet,
painting, patching, frizzing, fastidious in the turn of a
feather, irresolute in the disposal of a curl. But
those were the days of elaboracy, when the mere act
of lacing was the affair of an hour ; whereas Lady
Harriet was one of the least dressy of the present
school of dishabille. Morning, noon, or night,—I lie,
afternoon or night being the only epochs at which I
saw her,—she was attired in a muslin dress of exquisite whiteness and fineness ; having her hair
dressed in the simplest fashion, without trinkets or
ribbons to set off her face or figure. Her simplicity
amounted almost to the puritanical.

It was clearly, therefore, not her "toilet's fragrant
task" which caused her door to be denied ; though,
at the happy hour appointed for her manifestation to
eyes profane, she had just the bright look of a person
who has been spending her time to her heart's content ;—eyes beaming with intelligence,—lips vivid
with quickened circulation,—cheeks brightened by
the consciousness of beauty. Dull or cunning indeed
must be the woman's countenance, that does not
betray to a jealous man whether she has been too well
amused during his absence.

I had no opportunity of resolving my doubts.
Chance had favoured me with a *tête-à-tête* at our first
interview ; but from that period I never saw her
alone. We met in the throng of the world, or at her
own house. But I could never manage to arrive
there till between four and five, when her rooms were
crowded. Nay, once, when by dint of shirking my
officialities I managed to arrive in Grosvenor Place as
the clock was striking four, I found myself distanced

by a certain Colonel Morley, a fellow in the Guards, ugly as the devil, and, like that great potentate, extremely well-mannered and prepossessing.

I do not mean that Morley was prepossessing to *me*. There was something in his shrewd glance that cut me to the soul. The superiority affected by Jack Harris roused my indignation; but the unaffected contempt of the guardsman depressed me to the earth. So sure as I entered Lady Harriet's presence with something witty or agreeable on my lips, the calm investigating eye of Morley threw a damp over my spirits. My squibs were damaged, and would not go off; my fireworks exploded in my own face; and, when floundering in the midst of an entertaining anecdote which his malice marred in the telling, he used quietly to ask me, what next? Had I not forgotten something? Was that all?—How could I do otherwise than detest such a man. He was my evil genius; and an evil genius I was sure to meet at Philippi.

One morning, when several of the accustomed visitors had taken leave of Lady Harriet on the threshold of her little conservatory, at the ringing of the postman's bell, the usual signal for her airing, I managed to linger a moment behind the rest; and was rewarded for the quiet way in which I accomplished my little manœuvre, by the gift of a branch of heliotrope.

"A token of approbation and encouragement, Mr. Cecil Danby," said she, still continuing to examine her flowers and occupy herself with their arrangement. "You have made fair progress. You have almost mastered the most difficult of London lessons; to subside into a fraction of the multitude, and satisfy yourself with being a link in the chain of society. Those who pretend to more, will never become even *that.* You have no right, at present, to individualize. You must live and move, and have your being, in the life, movement, and sensibility of the mass."

" In one respect, I certainly feel with the mass,"
cried I, with warmth ; " in my adoration of——"

" My carriage is at the door," interrupted Lady
Harriet ; " and if you have no better acknowledgment to offer for my graciousness than such platitudes——"

" Your graciousness ?" I ejaculated, with an appropriate sigh of reproach.

" Don't treat it too lightly," she replied ; " for it is
the result of my indulgence rather than of your merits.
You are doing pretty well. You have learned to
dress simply, to ride a quiet hack, and place yourself
in the background of the picture. But you have still
worlds of wisdom to acquire. You talk too much ;
you laugh too much. Your teeth are good, and your
spirits high. But this does not suffice as an excuse
for being heard in company, when others, with greater
minds and smaller voices, are compelled to silence by
your chattering. Look at Colonel Morley——"

" Thank you, I had rather *not*. He is better to
listen to than look at."

" A case directly contrary to your own," was her
provoking retort. " You would do well, however, to
take pattern by the good breeding with which he contents himself to remain unnoticed, in order that a
cleverish lad, who has his way to make in the world,
may have a fair field."

Was this sufficiently insulting ? But for the dim-
ples softening the sarcastic smile accompanying her
attack, and for the exquisite whiteness of the little
hand that withdrew itself out of a verbena-bush to
emphasize her harangue, I think, I should,—I scarcely
know what !

" Where is the flower I gave you ?" said Lady
Harriet,—discerning, perhaps, something of the irritation of my feelings in the expression of my face.

I replied by laying my hand, with an expressive
gesture, upon my heart.

" Be so good as to put it in your button-hole," said

she coolly. " Do you suppose I like you well enough to
give you a flower, which I do not intend you to make
a show of ? I gave it as the French Emperor bestowed
an order. The Legion of Honour would cease to
create heroes, if worn secretly."

On my arrival in town, an injunction from Lady
Harriet Vandeleur to make an exhibition of her gift
would have flattered my vanity. I knew better now.
I saw that she had no fear of being compromised by
me ; and scarcely was I in the street, before I flung
down the sprig of heliotrope on the pavement ; trusting Lady Harriet would note it lying there on her
way to the carriage.

Nam cupidè conculcatur nimis antè metutum.

Young gentlemen of tender years, when in love,
are almost as susceptible about being laughed at, as
very elderly gentlemen labouring under the same
distemper. I was angry. I assured myself that I
was not going to be made a plaything by a coquette :
that I would not remain the butt of Colonel Morley.
For a week, for a fortnight (ten days I believe in
reality, but the profound *ennui* to which I was a
victim, made me fancy it a fortnight), I abstained from
the house ; secretly flattering myself with the hope of
receiving one of those little three-cornered notes which
I had seen superscribed with other names, on her
ladyship's table.

But I waited in vain. No note, not even a message !
I contrived to make myself apparent twice a week to
the inmates of Lady Harriet's opera-box ; and posted
myself resolutely at the opposite side of the room,
whenever we met at assemblies. But this was not
often. She belonged to a set which rarely forfeited
caste in the indiscriminate mobs of large parties ; and
to the small ones, I was not yet sufficiently in fashion
to obtain an invitation.

I could bear it no longer. Lady Harriet's piquant
society was as essential to me as a pinch of macauba

to a snuff-taker. I found myself growing lethargic ;
yawned in the face of Lord Votefilch, while he was
pointing out to me, that I neglected to dot my *i*'s, in
a *précis ;* and in that of my mother, while informing
me that Dr. Blane had insinuated that Bibiche was
suffering from a liver complaint. Still smarting
under these double reprimands, I rushed to Grosvenor
Place.

"When did you come to town, Mr. Danby ?"
inquired Lady Harriet, in a patronizing tone, breaking off her conversation with the young Marchioness of Devcreux, the prettiest of the brides of
the season.

"I have not left London," said I, provoked at being
compelled to proclaim a fact of which I knew her to
be perfectly aware.

"I mistook, then, what Lady Ormington told me
about you. I am sure she said something about
absence. I dare say she spoke of your being absent
and out of spirits, and I mistook it for absent and
out of town."

"I must still plead not guilty," said I ; "having
enjoyed excellent health and spirits ; and not the less
for having ascertained by ocular demonstration, at the
opera and elsewhere, that your ladyship was enjoying
the same advantages."

"How bad the opera is getting. Unless they do
something better for us before the close of the season,
I shall give up my box next year," said Lady Harriet,
suddenly addressing her visitor.

"People always say so ; nothing better is done; yet
they renew their engagement," replied the Marchioness, smiling. "However bad the opera may be,
we can better spare a better thing."

"At the beginning and end of the season, when
there is nothing going on," observed Lady Harriet.
"But just now, one has as little time as patience."

I had no patience with her hypocrisy ; for never was
she known to miss an opera ! I went that night, and

planted myself, as usual, opposite her box, with the view of bringing her, if not to shame, to remorse. As I expected, she was there. As I did *not* expect, the pretty marchioness was her companion.

"I thought you were hand and glove with the pretty widow?" observed Jack Harris, accosting me familiarly, as I directed my moody looks towards the box of Lady Harriet; which, being on the pit tier, allowed the curious in fashionable movements to obtain a surmise of Colonel Morley and Sir Moulton Drewe, occupying the background. "How come you to be standing here, with your eyes fixed on her like those of Romeo on Juliet's balcony, while others, armed 'with love's light wings,' have overtopped the barrier?"

"Because I am fonder of the warbling of Catalani, than of the gabbling of even the prettiest woman in the world."

"Not badly parried," cried Jack Harris. And as he spoke, I saw him glance at a new waistcoat, in nature and origin evidently an improvement on the last.

I would have given worlds, at that moment, to have been in possession of a sprig of heliotrope, even in my button-hole.

Lady Harriet was right. Such a trophy was not without its value. Still more would I have given for the privilege of intruding into her box, which I had forfeited by my foolish irascibility. Three weeks before, I might have laid Jack Harris low with envy, and shrivelled up his gay waistcoat at a glance, by my familiar attitude in that envied spot. But now, I dared no more confront the scrutinizing eye of Morley, or the reprehensions of Lady Harriet, than leap on the stage and take a part in the ballet. I was inexpressibly vexed. For boys such as we then were, half the agonies of life arise from petty rubs of vanity. Self-consequence is our idol; an idol that imposes on its votaries a perpetual hair-shirt, and never-ending flagellation.

I saw that Lady Harriet was contemptuously regarding us ; and not to afford her the triumph of
fancying she imposed upon me, affected to talk and
laugh familiarly with the companion she had pointed
out to my avoidance ; passing in review the beauties
present, with all the impertinence of a novice ; when
lo ! while affecting to run my eye along the several
tiers, it rested suddenly upon a face, half hidden by
the curtain of one of the upper boxes, which put a
period to my mirth. " Aut Erasmus, aut diabolus."
It was either Emily's or an angel's ; beautiful as ever ;
so beautiful, that the surprise of seeing her there, was
quickly followed by still greater surprise, when I reflected that I had allowed nearly a month to elapse
without recalling her to my recollection.

Freely as we had been discussing the women present
(and Jack Harris belonged to the class of men super-
abounding in London, who, without access to good
society, familiarize themselves at public places with
the names and persons of those between whom and
them there is a great gulf fixed, but concerning
whom they assume the privilege of uttering the
grossest scandals), I recoiled from exposing Emily to
the freedoms of his sacrilegious tongue. Nay, when
following the direction of my eye, and noticing my
sudden flush, he exclaimed, —— But I will not record
what he exclaimed, further than that it contained a
fitting tribute to the loveliness of the fair unknown.

I forbore to hazard a syllable implying knowledge of
her name or person. But I was now more eager than
ever to shake him off. Nay, my eagerness was dictated by a feeling so much more genuine than the
dread of exposing myself to the quizzing of a Lady
Harriet Vandeleur, that I succeeded. I was intent
upon a nearer survey of Emily's box ; for, if there
with her father alone, Lord Ormington's son had
every pretext for intruding upon Lord Ormington's
man of business.

Having hurried up one staircase, accordingly, and

down another, in order to give the slip to Jack
Harris, who, in spite of his assumption of superiority,
neglected no opportunity of clinging in public to
my arm, I made my way to the upper tier of boxes ;
pigeon-holes, to which I had occasionally glanced
upward from Fop's Alley, as a boy looks upon a kite
traversing the fields of air, and with about as much
idea of ever finding myself elevated to the same
altitude.

No sooner had the box-keeper complied with my
request, and opened an empty box for me, than I
ascertained that old Hanmer was not on guard.
Emily's chaperon was an elderly woman, arrayed like
herself in mourning of the simplest fashion, and
stationed behind her as if in studious concealment ;
perhaps to command a better view of the stage,
perhaps because too homely to warrant a display at
the opera. I had little leisure, however, for conjec-
tures. My attention was engrossed by the beauty of
her companion. I had thought her handsome as she
stood, cold and contemptuous, in the dull drawing-
room in Southampton Buildings. But now, with the
brilliant light of the chandelier irradiating her fair
face and tinging with gold her chestnut ringlets, I was
startled by her surpassing loveliness.

For a month past, my eyes had rested upon nothing
but those withered complexions and hardened countenances of fashionable life, which, when viewed in a
mass, with their paint and varnish fresh upon the
surface, excite neither surprise nor disgust. But the
aspect of this young, bright, innocent-looking creature,
so impressed me with admiration of its freshness and
purity, that there needed no severer criticism upon
the deficiencies of Lady Harriet and her companions.

Unconscious that she was the object of peculiar
attention, Emily's eyes were fixed upon the stage ;
and her smiling face seemed to reflect back all the
brightness and interest of the ballet of " Anacréon,
ou l'Amour fugitif," in which Deshayes and his wife

were displaying their matchless graces. She was a study for an artist; with her white, gracile, swan-like throat, stretched forward, so that the auburn ringlets hung tendril-like over the hand supporting her cheek!

Without so much excuse for the liberty of a visit to her box as to that of Lady Harriet, I found it impossible to resist the temptation; no reminiscence of Jack Harris's waistcoat, however, among my motives. My feelings were for once genuine.

I could have found it in my heart to reward with a kick the insolent smile of the box-keeper, when, pointing out the box, I desired him to open the door. I saw, as plainly as though he had spoken, the vile surmises passing in his mind concerning its inmates.

But that his key was already in the door, methinks I should have rescinded my order. Another moment, however, and I had passed the Rubicon; and was blending with my incoherent excuses the most courteous inquiries after the health of Mr. Hanmer, whom had I met in the street I should have found some difficulty in recognizing.

Emily's answers were as cold as succinct. There is a favourite phrase of "putting people in their place." If it was in *my* place she put me, it was a very humble one. After encountering her chilling glances, I could have crept into a nut-shell.

I attempted the remarks that were probably made in every other box that night, to every other woman present, concerning the voice of Catalani, and the victorious rashness of her genius. But Emily would not be beguiled into more than monosyllables. She evidently considered me as much out of place in her aërial den at the opera, as in her horrible drawing-room in Southampton Buildings; and after flinging a word or two at my head, as if throwing a stone, turned suddenly towards her venerable companion, to whom she had made no movement to present me, and began to converse cheerfully with her in some unknown tongue. Ignorant as most young men who have received a first-rate education, I knew not exactly what. It might be Spanish,—it might be Portuguese, —it might be Polish, Hungarian, or Russ. All I knew was, that it was neither French nor English, German nor Italian; and further, neither Eton nor Oxford enabled me to determine.

In the mouth of the elder lady, it was a grave, sonorous language; in that of Emily, rich and flowing. Her countenance brightened as she talked, till it became almost as intelligent as before my arrival in the box. Even though she deigned not to notice my presence, it was a sufficient enjoyment to listen to her melodious intonation, and watch the "liquid lustre melting in her eyes."

Rather from awkwardness than audacity, rather because I knew not how to retreat than because resolved to stay in her despite, I stood my ground; and on a sudden exclamation of delight which directed the attention of her chaperon to what was passing on the stage, I deliberately took possession of the unoccupied chair immediately opposite Emily, on pretext of interest in the performance. Perhaps I wished to draw a little nearer to her. Perhaps I wanted to exhibit myself to the *roué* world in the pit, in company with the most beautiful woman in the house. Perhaps I was anxious to attract the attention of Lady Harriet Vandeleur to my superior good fortune. At all events, the movement afforded me an excuse for expressing to Emily my regret that she should occupy so vile a box, where seeing or hearing was out of the question.

" Would you permit me," I added, in my most insinuating tone, " to send you, some night, my mother's box, which is on the ground tier, and commands an excellent *coup d'œil* of the ballet ?"

She gazed at me with a calmly inquiring eye; but uttered not a syllable.

" Had Lord Ormington been aware," said I, by way

of recalling to her mind the exact nature of the
link connecting us with each other, "that you
were fond of the opera, I am convinced he would
long ago have had the honour of offering it to
Mr. Hanmer."

I was convinced of no such thing. For Lord
Ormington would just as soon have thought of in-
terfering with my mother's opera-box as *she* of dis-
posing of his service of plate. But I chose Hanmer's
daughter to bear in mind the courtesy due to the son
of her father's favourite client.

Again, after a slight bend of the head by way of
acknowledgment, did she turn towards the grave old
matron in black, with a thousand lively comments
upon what was going on, either in her own box or
in the ballet. With the vulgar susceptibility of
ignorance, I was convinced, at every fresh smile and
ejaculation, that they were talking of *me*. At length,
I felt so uncomfortable, that I hazarded no further
attempt at softening her rigour beyond a deferential
bow, and hastily departed.

"You were scarcely fair with me, Cis, in allowing
me to run on unchecked, while passing my opinion
just now on your lovely friend," cried Jack Harris,
whom I encountered in the lobby of the fifth tier ;
and who, I saw plainly, had ascended so much above
his usual altitude only that he might interrogate
the box-keeper touching the two mysterious ladies.
"Another time, my dear fellow, spare my feelings and
your own, by saying, 'I can't be explicit, but I won't
be unfriendly. Don't persist in your inquiries.'"

"I should have been sorry to excite your curiosity
by any prohibition half so mysterious," replied I, assuming the tone of coolness with which he so often
martyrized *me*. "Nor was I aware that it was
essential you should be warned, to a day and a
minute, whenever I had occasion to form an agreeable acquaintance."

Having uttered these oracular words, I left him,

looking vexed and malicious; and, in the rccklcss-
ness caused by the triumph of the moment, made my
way straight to the box of Lady Harriet; having
noticed, from the opposite post, that Drewe and
Morley had quitted her, as even the most devoted
men are apt to quit the most charming of women,
when the back of their box does not command a view
of the dancing.

Why was it that both the marchioness and her
friend received me so affably? Why was it that,
throughout the remainder of the night, their conversation with me was so unintermittingly kept up,
that it would have been difficult to find a moment
for leaving them? Had my recent emotion imparted
unusual expression to features not altogether deficient
in merit? Had the ambition of conquering in the
fifth tier, endowed me with the power of conquest in
the first? Had they noticed me leaning familiarly
over the box of that lovely creature? Or were
they, after all, simply intent upon avenging the base
desertion of their recreant knights by a manifest
flirtation?

The latter supposition presented itself in time to
prevent my making a fool of myself. The dread of
being accepted as a *pis aller*, saved me. The torch
might burn and sparkle as brightly as it listed, but
they should see that Cecil Danby was not the silly
moth to singe his wings. I made myself irresistible.
The jargon of London life, which at first appeared
so difficult of acquirement, is as easy as lying, when
studied by an enlightened mind. Early education
had taught me the rudiments. I had stood in the
stocks of fashion in my infancy; and my toes being
properly turned out, dancing came by intuition. I
was already a tolerable trifler; could recite a piquant
anecdote without losing the point, embroider upon
a slender hint of scandal, and twist a *bon-mot* so art-
fully, that my fair auditresses had a right to suppose it
their own.

To the marchioness, I chattered ; with Lady Harriet,
I listened ; and consequently, was successful with both.
It has been told of a late nobleman, equally distinguished by his abilities and absence of mind, that,
having talked to himself in his travelling-carriage from
Brighton to London, he ended at Hyde Park Corner,
by inviting himself to dinner, as the pleasantest companion he had ever travelled with. Lady Harriet
evidently thought as much of *me;* because what passed
for dialogue between us, was a soliloquy of her own.

Never had I seen her so gracious. Not a sarcasm,
not a reproof. Kind, encouraging, it needed all the
beauty of the expressive face on which for an hour
past I had been gazing, to convince me that the
charming little widow from whose mouth dropped
pearls and diamonds, and in whose large eyes sparkled
shrewdness and wit, was three-and-thirty years of age,
a hardened fraction of that adamantine temple called
the world.

After wincing under the haughtiness of Emily, such
brilliancy *ought* to have dazzled, such affability ought
to have overwhelmed me. Far from it. The chaste
moonlight imparts no charm to the glaring sunshine ;
though glaring sunshine disposes us for the refreshing
softness of the moon. For the first time, I discerned
effort in Lady Harriet's wit, and restlessness in her
vanity. But as my admiration declined, my embarrassment vanished. My tongue was loosed. I
became natural in her presence ; that is, natural as
the clipped hedges and formal flower-plots of a Dutch
garden. My fair friends were content, however, with
the gaudy blossoms tendered by my gallantry. Both
smiled on me " delightfully with all their might ; "
and, accordingly, at the most earnest moment of the
conversation, I started up, as if recollecting an engagement, made a profound bow, and—

—————— nec ultra
    Errorem foveo—

vanished.

Nothing in the world provokes a woman of the world more than that the man who has found refuge in her comfortable opera-box, and amused himself with her lively chat, should take his departure five minutes before the conclusion of the ballet ; a deliberate avowal that he disdains the honour (that is, that he chooses to shirk the bore) of escorting her to her carriage. But to leave her alone in her glory, to leave her when the kindnesses lavished upon you have been the means of keeping more assiduous beaux from the field, is an " ungrateful injury," past forgiveness.

Morley, I knew, was off to White's. Morley was the strongest whist-man of his day ; one of those whom one knows as well where to find, at a certain hour of the night throughout the season, as the Speaker during the session. Squeamy and Drewe were lounging in the pit, directly under Lady Harriet's box, where I made it my business to pin them firmly by the button. No mistaking our united intentions to convoy nothing but ourselves and our canes out of the opera-house that night. Indeed, I had already engaged my companions to sup with me at Watier's ; a new club, the head quarters of the *roués*, of which our three insignificances were component parts.

My plan was to remain ostensible, till the last moment ; then, just as the curtain was falling, rush up to the skyey regions of the fifth tier, to ascertain by what fortunate cavalier Emily and her chaperon were escorted. I did not foresee that the stairs would be crowded with people hurrying down ; and that, as usual, where a single person attempts to combat the mass, the mass would have the best of it. The upper part of the house was half empty before I reached the spot.

Everybody in the unlucky habit of frequenting the London theatres, either in those days or these, must have found their choler excited, on some occasion or other, by the coarseness of the Rule-Britannia class of

the community frequenting the galleries ; and just as
often, by the indecorum of a class of men, who, if
better born and bred, are scarcely better-mannered ;
dandies of a secondary order, whose gallantry consists
in staring women out of countenance, and whose
heroism in knocking a man down.

On reaching the door of the box which so strongly
excited my interest, I found it besieged by a group of
Lovelaces of this description ; and, unless I am much
mistaken, my eye caught a glimpse of Jack Harris
himself, hurrying off on my approach, as if ashamed of
such company. But the lights were all but extin-
guished, and I was unable positively to determine.
Even the box-keepers were gone ; and but that the
doors of the adjoining boxes stood open, while that
of Miss Haumer's remained closed, I should have concluded that I was too late, and that Emily had taken
her departure.

Something in the triumphant air of the scamps
stationed in the vicinity, convinced me they were
lying in ambush for her exit, to molest her with
insult. But how to obtain admittance in the box-
keeper's absence, with a tender of my services? I
knocked at the door of the box ;—no answer. At
length, it occurred to me to enter the one adjoining,
and to lean over for a parley. Anxiety on her
account imparted courage for so bold an intrusion.
I was boiling with rage. I felt convinced that
she was held prisoner by those ruffians. It was
in perfect good faith, it was with the truest and best
intentions that I pushed my way into the next box,
drew aside the intervening curtain, and addressed
her.

For a moment, I suspect, Emily mistook me for an
auxiliary of her persecutors ; for her first movement,
on hearing herself spoken to, was to retreat into a
corner behind her companion. I raised my voice, however, to re-assure her.

" I fear you have no one to see you to your carriage ?"

said I. "Will you do me the favour to accept my arm?"

A few hurried words addressed to her companion, in which I could detect, though altered by a foreign accent, the names of Lord Ormington and Mr. Hanmer, seemed intended to explain the connection between us. But the agitated tone in which they were uttered served to convince me that I had not mistaken their situation; that they were alone, unprotected, terrified. Emily advanced to the front of the box to explain that they accepted my offer with gratitude; and the sight of her blanched cheeks and tremulous lips excited so much emotion in my breast, that I forgot to congratulate myself on having vanquished her scruples.

"I fear, I greatly fear," cried I, "that you have experienced some annoyance? If you would only point out to me, as we go down, the individual by whom ——"

She stopped me. "If I profit by your kindness," said she, "it is only on condition that you take no notice of anything that has occurred, or may occur, concerning us. Nothing would annoy me more than to become the object of a dispute."

"Do me the favour then to admit me into your box till you are sufficiently composed for a sortie," said I, "in order that it may be seen you have an authorized protector."

No need of the precaution. On making my way round, the coast was clear. I had consequently no difficulty in persuading Miss Hanmer to hasten from the spot, where only a glimmering light remained to render our situation more embarrassing.

"The gentleman who accompanied us hither, the husband of Madame d'Acunha," said Emily, in a low voice (as we hurried down stairs together, closely followed by the old lady, whom she seemed to introduce by the latter name), "must have met with some accident, which prevented his rejoining us. He

F

usually leaves us during the ballet, to obtain a better place in the pit ; but has never before failed to be in time for escorting us out."

"And you have consequently been exposed to annoyance. I am convinced of it, it is useless to deny it ! " cried I, with swelling bosom, when, on reaching the lobbies adjoining the crush-room, now nearly empty, I perceived the four vulgar brutes already noticed, leaning against. the wall, as if to wait our passing. They were indulging in noisy mirth. It was the epoch of "coaching," and with the abuse of propriety distinguishing the genuine Bond Street lounger, these individuals were dressed in the bang-up style, which the Barouche Club had brought into fashion ; their dialect being the newly-discovered European tongue, called slang. I saw at a glance that I, Cecil Danby, should irremediably soil my fingers by contact with such gentry ; and with the most valiant intentions, was grateful to Emily's moderation, when she persisted in assuring me I was mistaken. Instead of casting a triumphant glance upon the baffled enemy, she quietly, but firmly, impelled me in a contrary direction toward the chair-door.

I inquired if it was *there* her carriage was waiting?

"I have no carriage," she replied, without the slightest embarrassment. "Perhaps you will have the goodness to call a hackney-coach for us, as Monsieur d'Acunha is not here."

I was horrified. *Not* at the idea of calling a hackney coach ; not even at the degradation awaiting the beautiful and queenly creature leaning on my arm ; but at the prospect of leaving her alone, while I proceeded along those horrible avenues of Shepherd's Market, which the awkward issues of the Opera House at that period rendered inevitable. Candour was my only alternative. "I *dare* not leave you," said I. "Accompany me out, and a link-boy will procure us a coach."

At the chair-door stood Jack Harris, in company

with two other Christchurch men ; their hands in their pockets, and insolence in their eyes.

" Please to want a coach, sir ?" cried half a dozen link-boys, surrounding us, as we emerged into the dirty passage.

" Please to want a coach, sir ? " mimicked the voices of half a dozen other frequenters of the detestable spot, on perceiving that we were not attended by a servant, and that my companions were not in what is termed full-dress.

Heaven knows, I cared nothing about "pleasing to want a coach." I flatter myself my worldly position justifies my being seen in such a vehicle, whenever or wherever it suits my convenience ; and, saving for their noise, the chorus of link-boys would have little moved my spleen. But that Emily should be exposed under such circumstances to the sneers of Jack Harris and his companions wounded me to the quick. The whole gang was now united, and followed us leisurely to the spot where, after the departure of the sedan chairs, a few miserable king's coaches, looking as if they wanted only a touch to tumble to pieces, were permitted to jolt their way to the pavement.

One of these, summoned by the link-man's twang, was already drawn up and awaiting us ; the iron steps rattling, and the dirty straw displayed by the light of half a dozen links, the proprietors of which stood requesting the ladies to take their time, in a tone that sounded wonderfully like a threat. A nasty fellow of a coachman, whose rusty clothes seemed to have as much difficulty in adhering to him as the component parts of his coach and horses to each other, was pushing them back, with a hand that held a wisp of hay, while the other kept open the creaking door.

What an equipage for Emily ! As it stared me in the face, I seemed to *feel* that Jack Harris and his rampant crew were staring at it from behind me. I could hear their repressed laughter. I could imagine all that was passing in their minds.

Do me not the injustice, kind reader, to suppose
that it was for the Honourable Cecil Danby the flush
mounted to my cheek.   I know not how it might be
with me now, after the demoralization of an ill-spent
life.   But I was then only twenty and seven months.
I had still a heart, ay, and as full of magnanimity as
the leading article of a daily paper.

"You *must* allow me to accompany you home.   I
do not consider you safe," said I, whispering through
the chestnut curls of Emily.   "Do me justice.   I have
no presumptuous views in pressing my services upon
you.   But you are watched by those who would scruple
nothing in pursuing their aggressions.   If you choose
it, I will take my place with the coachman.   But you
shall not proceed so far as Southampton Buildings
unattended."

Emily answered not a word.   I could make nothing
of her silence, save that it gave consent.   Fool that I
was, not to suspect the truth,—that it proceeded from
her tears.

The moment I had placed her and the old lady in
the coach, I jumped in after them ; and, having flung
the link-boys their reward, whispered the address to
the surly old brute who was slamming the door.   At
that moment, the glare of half a dozen links, assembled to grace our departure, fell upon the faces of
the facetious group, of which Jack Harris formed a
part ; displaying, under varied forms of expression,
amazement, envy, and derision.

I did not dwell upon their insolence, further than by
grinding between my teeth certain imprecations, purporting to take a more developed shape hereafter; for,
though perplexed by the darkness, and distracted by
the jarring and jangling of the vehicle, the sobs of
Emily were audible from the shoulder of her companion, into whose arms she had thrown herself.

I had just self-command to forbear offering consola-
tions which would have aggravated her uneasiness.
My business there was to be a silent and unobtrusive

guardian. The old lady, or, since such was her name, Madame d'Acunha, was well satisfied to engross the conversation, by a torrent of words, of which the purport was revealed by the successive tones of rage, fear, and resentment, varying her ejaculations. Unless the truant, the delinquent, the absent-without-leave Monsieur d'Acunha, were far gone in apoplexy or some other lethargic seizure, I would not have been in his skin at their next meeting. She probably threatened quite as loudly the aggressors who had presumed on their unprotected situation. But of this, as no proper name served as index to her invectives, I was unable to judge.

All my thoughts, moreover, were engrossed by the grief of Emily. I fancied (what is not one able to fancy at twenty and a half?) that I could detect in her weeping, as clearly as in Madame d'Acunha's abuse, inflections of wounded pride, of suffering delicacy. I was even in hopes that my turn might come, and tears of penitent gratitude signalize her recognition of my modest merit. But her sobs subsided to sighs, and her sighs to silence, without a sound having escaped her lips indicating consciousness of my presence.

I could not stand this long. "You are better now, I trust?" said I, still preserving appropriate calmness of manner and attitude. Had I and old Madame d'Acunha been *tête-à-tête* in the coach, I could not have maintained a more decorous perpendicularity.

"As much better as I can be with the consciousness of having been troublesome to everybody, and a burthen to myself," she replied, with much emotion. "Mr. Hanmer warned me that I was imprudent in yielding to my passionate love of music so far as to venture to the Opera, attended only by those whose ignorance of the English language might expose us to difficulties. But habit renders bold. I have now so repeatedly occupied the same box without attracting notice or annoyance, that I ceased even to apprehend it."

" But since your father was aware of the danger," I observed, " why not himself attend you to the theatre ? "

" You have twice given me reason to suppose that you regard me as the daughter of Mr. Hanmer," was her mild reply. " Your kindness, entitles you to explanations which, as a stranger, I feared could not be very interesting. I am his ward. I have been but a few months in England. I am an inmate of his house. My name is Emily Barnet."

There was something in the explicit frankness of her explanation, which reminded me of Franklin and his boot-jack.

" I trust," said I, " you will not the less permit me to consider myself (connected, as I am, by peculiar ties, with Mr. Hanmer) privileged to officiate as your protector whenever or wheresoever my aid may be wanting."

" You have been most kind, and I am deeply sensible of the obligation," replied Emily, with some sensibility. " But forgive me for assuring you that any further acquaintance between us would be unacceptable to my guardian."

This was throwing down the glove of defiance somewhat cavalierly ; but I had no leisure to remonstrate. Emily's tears had prolonged themselves so unreasonably, that we were approaching Southampton Buildings. I perceived, moreover, that we were not only near the term of our journey, but dodged by a hackney-coach, evidently intent upon keeping up with us. Though careful not to breathe a hint of my suspicions, I congratulated myself silently on my foresight in not having allowed them to return home alone. At Mr. Hanmer's door, I was preparing to jump out, when Emily delayed me with an urgent request that, after depositing *her*, I would proceed with Madame d'Acunha, to her residence in Burton Crescent.

" Were she to alight here, to spare you this trouble," said Emily, " Mr. Hanmer would become aware that something unusual had occurred, and experience uneasiness for the future. Do me the favour, therefore, to take care of my friend home. She speaks no English, or would add her acknowledgments to my own."

So saying, she sprang out of the coach, the steps of which had been let down during her address. I had not even found time to offer her my hand ; and Pepper-and-Salt, with a tallow candle in his hand, was now on guard over us. All that remained was to get rid of the old lady with as much celerity as I had been got rid of by the young one.

But, while giving my attention to Emily's parting request, the artful dodger of a hackney-coach had escaped. No vestige of it in any direction. Having tracked Miss Barnet into the house, its mission was accomplished. For I don't suppose it signified much to Jack Harris at what number in Burton Crescent might reside the worshipful helpmate of the missing Monsieur d'Acunha.

"A pretty finale to my evening's amusements, upon my soul !" cried I, on finding myself jogging along the then gloomy and half-finished streets adjoining Burton Crescent. "I, Cis Danby, to be benighted in the wilds of Bloomsbury ! And for what ? To play the squire to an old cat in a rusty bombazine gown, with a complexion only half a degree less dingy !"

The mansion in which Madame d'Acunha had requested to be deposited appeared sufficiently respectable to warrant better habiliments and a more creditable equipage ; and now that I was alone in the coach, I could perceive, powerful even beyond its fustiness, the delicious fragrance of *vanille* which appears to form the natural atmosphere of the women of Portugal.

It was not, however, till fairly ensconced in the easy chair of my own room in Hanover Square (which, by the way, did not by any means correspond with Jack Harris's predictions), that I became fully sensible of the strangeness of my fortune in the events of the evening.

Petted by Lady Harriet—smiled upon by the marchioness — thanked — gratefully and affectionately thanked by Emily!—it was surely enough to turn a stronger head than the one which had never sat straight upon its shoulders since the bewitching epoch of its first cockade.

CHAPTER IV

In fact, there's not much interesting in't,
Unless it be in hot-press and good print.
PROCTOR.

Il semblait voler à des conquêtes, et n'avoir qu'à se mettre en frais de bonne volonté, pour inspirer autour de lui l'amour.
BRUCKER.

IT is time, methinks, that I afford some slight idea of the temple consecrated by my mother's devotion, and my own, to the worship of that memorable individual, the Honourable Cecil Danby. For though it was only the same double room on the third floor of the house in Hanover Square occupied by my nursery in my cockadehood, and by John and myself, conjointly, in our school-days, it now assumed a character of higher interest for posterity.

Lady Ormington, like the majority of silly women, had a passion for furnishing. Before the high-pressure-education movement came into play, writing ill-spelt letters and running up upholsterers' bills were among the least mischievous avocations of those whose game was loo, and whose virtue the charity that covereth a multitude of sins.

My rooms, gentle reader (or, on this occasion more especially, reader fair)—my rooms, as I found them on arriving for my first Oxford vacation, were hung with a highly-glazed white paper, matched with highly-glazed white furniture ; the whole being vivified by a gay pattern of blue convolvulus. Even the carpet exhibited, on its pale grey ground, the same design, and the Worcester china was what George Robins would call *en suite*. Nothing could be more summer-like and cheering. The furniture was of the darkest rosewood ; the shower-bath white japan ; but the triumph of the whole was the dressing-table, on whose spotless marble slab stood the crystal and gold belongings of the dressing-box, manufactured for me, by Gray, under the immediate directions of Lady Ormington.

The most refined coxcombry breathed in the arrangements of my sanctuary. Something, however, of the old bachelor was perceptible in the exactness of its distribution. The bootjack knew its appointed place ; and the nail-nippers would not have been at their ease unless laid side by side with the razor-strop. Unluckily, the small groom (for as yet tigers were not ; "we had not got the name, but had the thing"), who, as the characteristic curse of my younger sonhood, supplied the place of valet, did not always understand this as well as the bootjack and nail-nippers ; and, for the first three weeks Tim flourished in my service, seldom less than fifty threats of annihilation per diem were extorted by his negligence. I might possibly have put one of them into execution, had I contemplated any likelihood of replacing the little sinner within many inches of his meritorious exiguity.

Small grooms were just "come in," as they say of green peas, strawberries, and fashions. Women have, in all ages, been addicted to trifles of this description, such as pages, dwarfs, and marmosets. But it remained for our own times to attach to the six feet two of fully developed manhood, three feet or less, by way of henchman to its valour. I have heard of brats, born in a mews and in a stable bred, deliberately stunted, like puppies, and by the same spirituous potations, in order to accomplish them for tigerhood.

Tim—"my boy," as Falstaff used to call his page, and as we then all called our tigers—had won my affections by the pluck with which I saw him bear a severe fall from one of Lady Ormington's horses, to the back of which, poor atom, he had been lifted by his father, her ladyship's Irish coachman. I promoted him on the spot to tops and buckskins; and a few days afterwards not an eye in the ring but was bent with envy and admiration upon the natty little puppet who made so knowing a figure upon my bay mare. I was offered any money for Tim, by Sir Moulton Drewe. But as Lady Harriet Vandeleur had inquired "where I could possibly have picked up that love of a groom?" I would not part with him "for any money."

Tim soon proved himself invaluable—an enormous addition to my personal consequence. I stood higher in the world by three feet. I was one of the few who, by taking thought, have added a cubit to their stature.

"Yon's a varmint little chap o' yourn, sir," said Fetlock, the dealer, to me one day, as I was lounging in his yard with Sir Moulton Drewe. "Come o' the roight sort, I reckon. I s'pose he'll get to Newmarket in time. As good a whip, sir (Connaught Bill, the lad's father, I mean), as ever turned a family coach out of a yard; ay, and as showy with the ribbons in hand and his levee wig on as ever sat a 'ammercloth, is Connaught Bill. Many's the judge 'ould give his heyes for sich a presence as his'n. But I must say, sir, for her ladyship, Lady Ormington, your mamma, sir, that her ladyship knows a good thing when she's got it. I sold my lady them greys of hern, sir; and her ladyship wrote me out a cheque for the money on Drummond, sir, like a gemman. A long price in them times, sir, four hundred guineas. But I never heard no complaints; and when her la'ship was wanting summut neat for you, sir, last season, she sends to me, and, 'Mr. Fetlock, sir,' says her la'ship, 'you'll please to look out a good-looking 'ack for my son,' says she. 'Don't

stand to a guinea or two for price,' says her la'ship,
''cause the paying is *my* affair ; and I don't look to a
trifle, so as he gets summut as is not showy, but well-
bred and the roight thing,' says she. And, dang it !
that showed the roight thing, I take it, Mr. Danby,
sir. Your vulgar chaps, of nobody knows who, as
comes 'ere to my yard, with the tin ringing in their
pockets, the first thing they sings out for—'Fetlock,'
says they, 'haven't 'ee got summut *showy* — summut
as 'll cut a splash in the park ?' Lor' bless 'ee, sir, her
la'ship, Lady Ormington, be too much of a lady to wish
a son of hern to be cutting splashes in the park. I'm
main glad, I assure you, sir, to see that chap o'
Connaught Bill's in such good training, I be."

I have, I trust, brought my *lares* and *penates* sufficiently before my readers, to enable them to fancy me
when rousing myself, at the matin summons of Tim,
and stretching my manly limbs in my airy French bed.
On the morning after the opera affair, I slept as
soundly as if the bunches of bright blue convolvulus
over my head were so many poppies. I was even
moved to say something almost as uncivil as Solomon
said in his haste, concerning Downing Street and its
regulations, when Tim drew aside my curtains in the
dead of morning.

"Plase yer honour, tain't Downing Strate at all at
all !" cried the little fellow, laying a triangular billet
on my pillow. "Only Lady Hawyet's jontleman be a
waiting for an answer, sir."

Lady Harriet ! Yes, the three-cornered messenger
of bliss was come at last. Piqued, by heavens ! I
seemed to see an embroidered waistcoat in the per-
spective, and tore open the little treasure with the
eagerness of a child demolishing a flower.

Reader !—(between ourselves)—dost thou know the
little, conscious, fluttering, demi-semi tone of kindness
in which a woman addresses the man who is neither
acquaintance, friend, nor lover, but something more
than the one, less than the other, and whom she fears

perhaps as much as she wishes to convert into the
third ?   Art thou acquainted with the letter that
neither "dears" nor "my dears" thee ?—that calls thee
neither Sir, nor Mr. So and So; neither Henry, Harry,
nor Hal ; but, bursting at once into a strain of familiarity, as into a challenge, *in medias res*, gives thee to
understand that the sweet creature writes as she
would speak ; and would fain have thee read in the
same candid and eager spirit thou hast listened ?

A very great man committed himself by putting it
into print that he knew no greater happiness than to
sit by the fire and read good novels.   I could have
supplied him with a brighter notion : to lie in an airy
French bed, showered over with blue convolvulus, and
read such billets as I describe ; such billets, in short,
as the following, from Lady Harriet Vandeleur.   Am
I—Heaven and Watier's forgive my breach of trust !
—*am* I justified in making it public ?

" Come and dine with us to-day at Richmond.   If
you are at my door at four, Lady Devereux will give
you a place in her barouche.   We go early, that we
may do a little rural before dinner ; though I scarcely
know whether the lilacs and laburnums are sufficiently
in bloom to satisfy the demands of nightingales or fine
ladies.   By the way, what do you mean by defying my
prohibitions, and being seen with that dreadful Mr.
Harris—Harrison,—you know whom I mean, the
Oxford man, who wears flashy waistcoats, and takes
off his gloves to exhibit his rings ?   I have another
quarrel with you of the same kind.   But we will fight
it out at Richmond.   *Sans adieu !*"

The other quarrel, my exulting heart assured me,
regarded Emily.   Lady Harriet had heard of my
escorting a nameless beauty, a lady of equivocal
appearance, publicly at the Opera ; nay, had seen me
in her box.   Exquisite triumph.   I was to be called
to order by a reprimand.

" Plase your honour, Lady Hawyet's jontleman 'ould
be glad to know what answer for my lady ?" demanded

Tim, advancing towards the bedside, as he saw me about to commence a third reperusal of the billet. "Lady Hawyet's jontleman be werry partic'lar about waiting."

"I will send an answer presently," said I, already resolved that the "presently" should extend far into the morning ; and the answer, when received, reduce the little beauty to despair. Ten Lady Harriets and twenty pretty marchionesses would not have tempted me to Richmond.

Just as her ladyship's invitation determined me to absent myself, did Emily's prohibition excite me to return to Southampton Buildings.

A visit of ceremony—of inquiry—was indispensable. No need to alarm old Hanmer with allusions to what had passed. For a man of any skill, nothing so easy as to make old Six-and-eightpence the instrument of conveying my message to his ward, without consciousness of his mission. Between the claims of office-hours, therefore, and the remoteness of my Mecca in Bloomsbury, Lady Devereux's barouche (even had I been inclined for it) was out of the question.

I repeated this to myself fifty times while I was dressing. Always mistrust your own motives when you repeat a thing to yourself fifty times. Nothing more suspicious than to find yourself laying down the law to yourself with such damnable iteration ; more particularly those, who, like myself, have no time to lose in argument ; for time and tide, public offices and the green curtain, wait for no man.

I was forced to be in Downing Street every day by ten of the clock. Such was the compact between Votefilch and Lord Ormington, such the compact between Lord Ormington and myself ; the alternative lying between beggary and four hundred and seventy-five pounds a year. I was past the age for idylls and empty pockets. I had learned to talk with Voltaire of " *le superflu, chose si nécessaire !*" and consequently thanked my mother sincerely for the gift of an excellent

Breguet repeater ; owing to which, and my prudence,
I was seldom many minutes behind time.

Lord Ormington's voice, however insignificant in the
House to which he devoted it, was in his own as the
fiat of the gods. Even routine acquires an air of
forcibility, if powerfully persevered in. The regularity
of his hours and habits and the obstinacy of his reserve
endowed him as he advanced in life with the mysterious
importance conceded to the ebb and flow of the tides.
There is something portentous and awful in the
periodical appearance of heavenly bodies, or disappearance of mundane ones. I swear that the
nightly driving off of Lord Ormington's carriage was
beginning to inspire me with respect.

More than once, Lady Harriet had warned me
against irreverence towards his lordship ; and very
much more than once, had my mother checked me by
an anxious look, when I was hazarding against him
the sort of jest which an old man is slow to perceive,
but which, if he once perceives, he rarely fails to visit
with vengeance. She seemed horribly afraid of my
offending him ; and in process of time, I began to
participate in her deference.

My respect extended even to his colleagues. Branded
with the ignominy of cadet-ship, and consequently
doomed by the obsolete barbarisms of feudal law to
feed on husks in order that my elder brother might
luxuriate on the fatted calf, I was well pleased, since
my apprenticeship in public life was inevitable, to
serve it under such a master of his craft as Lord
Votefilch. He was a clever arbitrary man, a Napoleon
on a Lilliputian scale ; great in centralization ; having
an undeviating system of official subordination, and
keeping his youngsters admirably drilled.

There was a good deal stirring then in the administration of our foreign policy. "There were giants on
the earth in those days." Napoleon and Wellington
were making war ; Metternich and Nesselrode making
peace ; and *I* was making myself useful, by transcribing

in cipher, which I did not understand, despatches which *no* one understood. Yet, somehow or other, my vanity was interested in my vocation. I was the fly on the wheel. Whenever second editions were trumpeted through the streets by the newsmen's horns, I kept saying to myself, like that deluded insect, What a dust we are kicking up. After having simply mended the pens for the secretary who mended the style of Lord Votefilch's protocols, I looked down upon Sir Moulton Drewe and my cousin Squeamy as poor useless creatures, unworthy the noble soil of the land that pretends to rule the waves, while every year it yields up a foot or two to their presumptuous encroachment.

Joking apart, Votefilch was a great man for the times he lived in. Planted between a double battery, exposed in Parliament to the broadsides of a powerful opposition, and in office to the puzzlement arising from the shifting policy of such of the powers of Europe as were not already engulfed in the greatest despotism of modern times—the cannonarchy of Napoleon—his lordship stood firm as a colossus, or as a donkey,

> By his own weight made steadfast and immovable.

His patience had the skin of a buffalo. His temper was the sort of granite on which you may hammer for hours without eliciting a spark. It is difficult to rate too highly this species of impassibility in a public man. In official life, he whose shrinking susceptibility betrays his vulnerable heel, attracts such showers of arrows, that he has neither leisure nor self-possession for the accomplishment of his purposes.

Now the Right Honourable Secretary of State for Foreign Affairs had the highest esteem for the Right Honourable Lord Ormington. Lord Ormington was one of the heavy pieces of ordnance, invaluable to government in certain emergencies. When vexatious questions were pressed, he was always ready to rise and generalize with plausibilities, while the stunned party recovered its senses and gathered itself up for reply;—a sort of moral semibreve, giving breathing-space to the solos. Nothing but the importance of his services would have pleaded with Votefilch to admit into his office a young gentleman with hands so white and pretensions so towering as those of the Honourable Cecil Danby. For he was essentially a practical man ; an astronomer, not an astrologer ; one who regarded poetry as a mild species of insanity; quarrelled with the Woods and Forests, because they would not mend the roads with the ruins of Fotheringay Castle ; and could perceive no irony in Hamlet's assignment of the ashes of "Imperial Cæsar." It seemed a relief to his mind that emperors, when turned to clay, could be turned to account.

Gods ! how I ramble. Old fellows always do, from the moment they are pinned down into their gouty chair. Reminiscence is as trackless as any other land of dreams ; and the mind floats on, like the wind, whithersoever it listeth.

At five o'clock, on the day from which I started into these digressions, gentle reader, little Tim held my horse in Southampton Buildings while I left my card for old Hanmer.

"Since your master is not at home, say I will call again another day," said I, addressing Pepper-and-Salt, in a key that might have been audible in the King's Theatre, from Lady Harriet Vandeleur's box, to that of Madame d'Acunha. "All the family are well, I trust ? "

And the jerking gestures and stultified looks of the poor wretch, as he replied with grateful civility, that " he was werry much obliged to me. Messrs. Hanmer and Snatch were both of 'em remarkable stout," almost put me out of conceit with my stratagem.

I wondered whether Emily overheard us. It was indispensable she should see that, though obedient to her commands, I was not unmindful of her welfare. But whether I had her approval or not, I had my own. It was a real triumph to feel that I had sacrificed a pleasant party to Richmond, in order to effect my visit of inquiry to Southampton Buildings.

Four-and-twenty hours afterwards, I began to wonder what Lady Harriet Vandeleur thought of my desertion. I knew what other people thought of it. Though I had positively resolved to cut Jack Harris, to cut him irretrievably, with a bill-hook, with a pole-axe, with whatever instrument effected the surest dismemberment, the fellow walked straight up to me in St. James's Street with such an air of candour, that one might as easily have thought of cutting one's own face in the glass.

" My dear Cis," said he, " how unkind of you not to warn me at once, last night, that I was on tender ground. You know my regard for you, and that I would ride a lame horse five miles in a pouring rain, to avoid giving you annoyance. Yet you permitted me to make a jest of a person every way entitled to my respect ; even if not commanding it through her influence over your feelings. Accept my sincere apologies, as well as my congratulations on your happiness, in the acquaintance of the prettiest woman in town."

"Are you talking of Lady Harriet Vandeleur ? " cried I, pretending to misunderstand him.

" You are perfectly aware, my dear fellow, of whom I am talking. As to Lady Harriet, no one will ever talk of *her* beauty, so long as her countenance remains distorted by the envy and jealousy it exhibited last night, during your flirtation with the lovely Emily."

How the deuce did he know that her name was Emily ? I would not condescend to inquire. If I encouraged his familiarity, he would, ten to one, ask me to present him to Lady Harriet, or Lady Devereux, or some other woman to whom his audacity must have been insupportable.

The next time I entered the Opera House, I prepared myself to view, with a throbbing heart, the

scene of my interesting adventure ; more particularly
as I knew that Lady Harriet was gone to a breakfast
at Payne's Hill, and would be absent from her post of
observation.   That Emily would be absent too, was
equally certain, and a source of very different emotion.
It would, however, be something to place myself in
the seat she had occupied, and devote my thoughts
and recollections to her image.

To my surprise, however, not only had Madame
d'Acunha resumed her place by her husband (a burly,
square-looking, chocolate-coloured Portuguese, who
might have put to flight a regiment of Jack Harrises),
but Miss Barnet was again their companion ; not
seated in front of the box, indeed ; but the eyes of a
lover readily espied her.

"I have taken the liberty of intruding upon you to
express a hope, that you sustained no injury from your
fatigues the other night," said I, with all the awkwardness of a school-boy.   Finding myself graciously
received, I alluded slightly to having already relieved
my anxieties on her account.

"You are surprised, perhaps, to find me here
again ? " said Emily, with a blush inferring more than
words, that she felt in need of apology.   "But as we
have exacted of Monsieur d'Acunha not to leave us
again, and shall quit the theatre early in the ballet, I
had not courage to deprive myself of the Flauto
Magico."

I muttered something stupid, about being the last
person to find fault with any measure enabling me to
see her again.   But she did not seem to listen.
D'Acunha, to whom she presented me on my entrance,
interrupted us, with an offer of his place, that I might
have a better view of Tramezzani's remarkably bad
acting ; to which I replied by taking a seat at the
back of the box, beside Emily.   Her companions were
soon so thoroughly absorbed in the music, as to afford
me almost the enjoyment of a *tête-à-tête*.

She was looking just as usual ; not a plait altered

in her black gown, not a curl in the arrangement of her beautiful hair. It must have been her graciousness, therefore, which imparted a thousand new attractions to her beauty. I saw her smile for the first time. For the first time, her eyes assumed an expression of interest when I addressed her.

"You English people," said she, when the close of the act enabled us to converse with freedom, "can very little enter into the love of music engendered by the climate and early associations of southern countries. With you, music is a luxury ; with us, a necessary of life. I need not inform you that the establishment of my guardian boasts little to flatter the imagination. I have been three months a prisoner in England,—cold, barren, cheerless, solemn England ; and the severest convent of my native country, with the harmonies of its religious service and fragrance of its genial atmosphere, would have been, comparatively, a garden of Eden."

"Do not found your ideas of England upon the experience of Southampton Buildings !" cried I. "Our summers have their orange blossoms as well as your own, and our——"

"No, no ! don't pretend to tell me that you have as much taste for music as animates the poorest water-carrier in Lisbon," interrupted Emily. "I have rarely missed a representation at this theatre. Impossible to see a colder or less attentive audience. Perhaps you have too many other pleasures, to affix much importance to music. You come here with such a display of luxury, that it is easy to see you stand in no need of it as a consolation. It constitutes only one of the refinements of fashion. With us, it is more : it is part of our religion ; it is part of our foretaste of heaven ; a balm for sorrow, a substitute for the prosperities of life."

"Doomed to the society of old Hanmer, and the attendance of Pepper-and-Salt," was my silent and involuntary reflection, as I fixed my eyes upon the

G 2

countenance beaming with sensibility, that gave force
to her expressions. " Poor girl ! No wonder she
has recourse to the ' Flauto Magico ' to sweeten her
imagination."

" Are you likely to remain long in this country ?"
said I, with the benevolent project of effecting, through
my mother, some improvement in her position.

" Alas ! who can say ? My father is a Lisbon merchant, resident at Cintra. The grievous aspect of
public affairs in Portugal determined him to profit by
the departure of his friends, the d'Acunhas, to afford
me a home in England. Apprehensive, perhaps, that
their ignorance of the customs of this country might
endanger my comfort, he obtained a provisional shelter
for me in the house of his old acquaintance and cor-
respondent, Mr. Hanmer. Twenty years have elapsed
since my father quitted England. He was, therefore,
unable to appreciate—he did not exactly understand
—he—in short—for why should I not speak openly ?—
I have written to entreat that he will either recall
me, or find me a more suitable abode."

I was inexpressibly gratified by her frankness ; the
more so, that her previous reserve sufficed to prove
she did not lightly accord her confidence.

As we grew more intimate, I even ventured to tax
her with her reserve at our two first interviews.

" Would you have had me otherwise ?" cried she.
" Consider how bitterly my pride was hurt on finding
myself treated by a stranger as a subordinate of Mr.
Hanmer's establishment."

" I addressed you, surely, as his daughter ?"

" During my residence with him, I had heard
enough of Lord Ormington and his affairs, to understand that his lordship's son was scarcely ignorant of
Mr. Hanmer's being unmarried."

" Conceive how little interest I attached to the
private affairs of my father's solicitor. Believe me,
my offence was unintentional."

" At least let us now proclaim an amnesty !" said

Emily. " My pride has been sufficiently rebuked by finding myself in need of the kindness of one to whom it had been unjustly exhibited. Be your own indiscretion visited, in its turn, by a little compunction for having driven me to such a resource as a guarantee against intrusion. My situation at Mr. Hanmer's is a peculiar one. Without intending to wound my feelings, he gave me to understand, on learning our first interview—but we will say no more about it. War is over ! In place of disagreeable reminiscences, let us set about the improvement of peace."

I had always lived in the company which has the assurance to call itself the best. In that best, Lady Ormington was cited for the elegance of her manners. The world, that superficial observer, is apt to mistake aspect for deportment ; and the charm for which a woman is indebted to the amount of her milliner's bill, is often set down to grace of manner. I do not mean to say that my mother's were faulty. She could be charming enough when worth her while. But she never played to empty benches. Like the country manager who could not afford to give the snow-storm in his Christmas pantomime with white paper, when the audience was thin, she often "snowed brown," and was peevish and ungracious till further notice.

Lady Harriet, too, was a person remarked for what the great world calls high-breeding. *My* notion of high-breeding is the manner that raises others to your level, without at any moment allowing you to descend to theirs. But Lady Harriet, instead of placing other people at their ease, only contrived to show how much she was at ease herself, often at the cost of comfort to her associates. She was restless, too ; nay, worse, she was artificial. Her *naïveté* was calculated, her impromptus were *faits à loisir*. She could be courtly and refined, it is true ; but to be courtly does not imply to be well-bred.

In Emily's manner, on the contrary, I descried indications of that intuitive elegance, as inseparable from

certain natures as fragrance from certain flowers.
When offended, she was a queen ; when pleased, a
child.   Of the conventions of society, she knew
nothing.   All her ideas of decorum emanated from
instinctive modesty.   My coxcombry was as much
thrown away upon her as the beauty of some exquisite piece of mechanism on a savage.   But when
she approved, when by chance I gave utterance to a
sentiment that found sympathy with her own, the
moisture of her eye was instantaneous ; or if some
chance expression, some passing sarcasm, happened to
divert her, her pearly teeth became visible in a moment,
brightening the cordial smiles respondent to my efforts
for her entertainment.

For I *did* try to entertain her.   Every opera-night
I was as faithful to *my* post as Spagnoletti to his.
The d'Acunhas, aware of the annoyance to which
Emily had been subjected by the homage paid to her
beauty, favoured her wish to remain constantly in the
back-ground ; and between their passionate love of
music, and approval of Emily's modest retreat from
the public gaze, I had the field to myself.

I was now perfectly at home among them.   Though
ordinary-looking people enough, there was something
in their unsociable isolation in the midst of a great
metropolis that redeemed them from vulgarity.   Emily
gave me to understand that their affairs, as well as
those of her father (of whom she spoke with the
fondest affection), were involved in the precarious
destinies of their native country ; and that their
whole time was absorbed in business connected with
the finances of Portugal, save the half-dozen hours a
week snatched for the consolation of music.

They were at enmity, it seemed, with old Hanmer,
misunderstandings having arisen out of their mutual
position relative to the guardianship of Miss Barnet ;
and this was, I conclude, the motive of their silence
respecting my growing intimacy with his ward.
Though nothing passed between us on the subject, I

saw distinctly that my name was never mentioned to him, either by Emily or her friends.

Lucky for me that the Opera was only twice a week! The career of fashion and fortune I had traced for myself would unquestionably have been nipped in the bud. To pass more of my time in the society of a rational being, rational without homeliness, rational without a single drawback (save that she was only Emily Barnet, and I, the Honourable Cecil Danby), must have endangered my coxcombry as well as my heart.

Yet I don't know. The limitation of my pleasures only served, perhaps, to increase the risk. I could see *her* at no other time or place; while other sources of diversion were ever open. Emily alone, imprisoned in the dirty old den of my father's man of business, was as uncome-atable as a queen surrounded by her household brigade. Had it been any other person's man of business, I would have defied him. But old Hanmer would have assuredly communicated my visits to Lord Ormington; and Lord Ormington's displeasure, as I have said before, was not to be trifled with.

Meanwhile, the happiness of the hour sufficed me. At twenty-and-a-half one stands between yesterday and to-morrow, independent of either. To-day contains an empire; and heaven knows I had all things to put me in conceit with my reign. The liberalities of my mother rendered my allowance almost superfluous.

It was her duty, she said, to take care that my first season in town reflected no disgrace upon herself.

"Next year," said her ladyship, "if you do vulgar or foolish things, it is *you* who will be put to shame; for by that time you will have obtained a name. At present, people would only say, in alluding to your blunders, 'It is that silly son of Lady Ormington's!' I must beg, therefore, Cis, that you will be cautious in your conduct. You made me get you invitations to the duchess's loo-parties, to Lady Devereux's, to twenty other places, which do not open their doors

indiscriminately ; and, after all my trouble, you have
not shown your face at one of them."

"My face is highly flattered that its absence
should be remarked," said I, coolly. "It is more
than would have happened to its Honourable elder
brother's."

"Perhaps so. But John is at least consistent.
John does not care for the world, and never plagues
me for invitations. By the way, your brother is come
to town."

"Yes, I saw him yesterday in Albemarle Street. I
believe he quizzicalizes at the Alfred."

"I'll tell you what he does *not* do, Cecil. He is not
seen skulking down the back-stairs at the Opera, with
women in bonnets, whom he shuffles into a hackney-
coach."

"I am heartily glad to hear it," replied I, gravely ;
"for he is not a man who can afford to follow his
own conceits. If Danby were seen giving his arm
to a woman who looked like a housemaid, he would
naturally be mistaken for a footman."

"While *you*, I suppose, flatter yourself that you
are only taken for a *roué*. However, there is *roué*
and *roué ;* and I promise you, Cis, that obscure follies
of that description——"

"Follies of *what* description ?" cried I, interrupting
her. "Explain these mysterious allusions to bonnets.
By whom have I ever been seen loitering on any back-
stairs, save those of St. James's ?"

"By Lady Harriet Vandeleur, I conclude ; who
informed me you were degenerating horribly ; that you
did nothing you ought——"

"Nothing I ought ?" cried I, again interrupting
her. "Lord Votefilch considers me a model for the official youth of Britain. He has even given me sundry
hints, that if I did not write so bad a hand, and
spelt a little better, he would make me his private
secretary."

"I am sure you don't write much worse than other

young men," exclaimed my mother, peevishly. "However, I suppose you only say it to make me nervous. For I know, through Hanmer, who heard it from Lord Ormington, that they are satisfied with you at the office."

This was rather a discursive mode for the intelligence to reach my mother. However, I was getting tolerably accustomed to our family oddities.

Lady Ormington's sarcasms about ladies in bonnets did not frighten me from my usual resort. The charm I found in Emily's society was beyond all dread of vulgar censure; nor did I enjoy it the less for my conviction that mine was not disagreeable to herself. She made no effort to attract me. There was no eagerness in her manner of recommending herself; nor any pretensions, on my part, to the character of a lover. As we became more intimate, I refrained from even the demonstrations of admiration inevitable on our first acquaintance. I had my own dignity to maintain, as she hers; and though content that she should be aware of my deep devotion, chose to remain "*le plus debout possible pour être à genoux.*"

This did not injure my cause. Emily had every pretext for accepting my civilities as those of an acquaintance; and no sooner had she ceased to fear that a show of kindness might draw down upon her the crisis of a declaration, than she became perfectly at ease.

A child could not have let fall its words more artlessly than Emily, when describing the habits of her early life; her father's house at Cintra; her orange-gardens, her mountains, her thickets of myrtle, her choir of nightingales; her despair when apprised of the necessity of quitting all these, to dwell among strangers in a foreign country, a *northern* country, a Protestant country.

"And yet," she added, with a smile, "how far was I from surmising all the horrors of England, or imagining the mean narrowness of a house of business in

Southampton Buildings. I have heard my father
speak of Mr. Hanmer as enormously wealthy. Yet
what enjoyment does he allow himself? In what intellectual effort does he indulge? Books, music,
flowers, are as much unknown in his house as if such
things had no existence. *My* father, too, is a man of
business. *My* father is a mere merchant. But our
house is bright with pictures, our garden gay with
flowers. A day spent without music or reading would
seem a lost day to *us*. How is this? Are all your
professional pople as dull, cold, and inelegant, as those
I see? Is conversation considered, in all your socie-
ties, an idle waste of words?"

"The conversation in which *you* deign to take a
part would everywhere be appreciated," I replied. But
I could not but look with compassion on this plant of
a southern clime, crushed by the practical habits of
our middle classes ; checked for the joyousness of
spirit which, in every country but money-making
England, is cherished and encouraged; and censured
for carelessness of forms, the growth of an inferior
order of society.

All my care was to soothe the vexations of Emily,
and remedy her sense of isolation. I tried to connect
her, through *my* sympathy, with the sympathies of
others. I described London society to her, in all its
subdivisions; country society, in all its ponderous
complications. I told her what we were, what we
had been, what we ought to be. The merest trifles
illustrative of our social existence seemed to amuse
her. The details of my mother's establishment were
laid before her, as minutely as an interior by Mieris ;
nay, even my own apartments, with all their commonplace associations, were painted for her amusement,
as I have painted them for that of the reader.

It was curious enough that my object was to
reconcile *her* to England, and reduce her into one of
the million ; while the influence she exercised over
myself sufficed to detach me from the mass. Till I

knew her, I had acted upon the impulses of others; had existed but as a leaf upon a tree. I had now an individual identity, derived from an existence as dear as it was dangerous.

A disagreeable surprise was about to startle me to new perceptions. I have described the era of which I am writing as the age of slang. But those only who retain personal recollections of the coaching " peers of many capes," with their bang-up pastimes, the ring and the road, their vociferousness at public places, their brutality at the Fives-Court, their activity at O. P. rows and opera riots, can form an idea of the eccentric peculiarty of my brother's mild reserve and studious seclusion, in the midst of the general uproar. Danby was certainly not one of those who are fated to make a noise in the world.

" I have seen your brother!" said Emily one night, as I assumed my usual place by her side.

"I trust he had the honour of pleasing you?" said I, almost coxcombically. But my gaiety subsided at the thought that she had perhaps, in her turn, attracted his attention.

"May I ask," I resumed, " *where* Danby was so fortunate as to meet you?"

" You are very formal, very ceremonious to-night!" cried she, in some surprise. " Having heard that 'Mr. Danby' was in the drawing-room with my guardian, and being unaware that you had a brother——"

" You wished to ascertain whether I cut as awkward a figure as ever on the hearth-rug in Southampton Buildings."

" What would Mr. Hanmer have said, pray, on finding us such intimate acquaintance? No, no! I indulged my curiosity by a still more disgraceful proceeding. I was foolish enough to watch from my window the horse waiting in the street, till I saw its master jump into his saddle."

" Then you certainly did not see my brother!" said

I, interrupting her. " Danby was never known to
jump in his life—not even at a conclusion."

" Why play upon my imperfect knowledge of your
language ?   It *was* your brother ; though certainly
nothing in his appearance indicated the relationship.
But Mr. Hanmer mentioned at dinner that Lord
Ormington's son had been with him, preparatory to
taking his seat in Parliament."

" Parliament ? Danby in Parliament ?   Am I fated
to receive all my news of home through the medium
of Southampton Buildings ?" cried I pettishly, deeply
vexed at the prospect of worldly distinctions wasted on
this elder brother.

Why is it, by the way, that, according to the attestation of ancient history and modern gossip, from the days
of Cain and Abel, and Jacob and Esau, down to those
of the two Chéniers and the two Danbys, there has
existed so much fraternal discordance between almost
every pair of brothers ?   Is it that between two sons,
parental affection hath its ups and downs, like a swing or
a balance ?   Or does it arise from the inherent perversity
of human nature ?   I must confess I had, in early
youth, an antipathy to John.   Not because he was my
elder brother.   No ! my feelings towards him were as
those of Faulconbridge.   I would not have exchanged
fortunes with him, to have exchanged faces.   Ormington Hall and Hanover Square would have been poor
compensation for that frightful physiognomy, that
ignoble person, those stooping, narrow shoulders, those
long graceless arms, eyes that, conscious of defect,
quailed under those of others, and hair approaching to
the reprobated Judas hue.   Life was not worth living
for, with these defeatures.   I would not have been a
duke on such a penalty.

Emily's information, meanwhile, was as authentic as
it was strange.   Next day, Lord Votcfilch, in taking
some papers from my hands, congratulated me, that " his
Majesty's government was about to receive an accession
of strength by my brother's entrance into Parliament."

I said nothing ; I only smiled. But my smile, I conclude, was significant.

"We have very high accounts of the abilities of Mr. Danby," added he gravely, as if replying to my smile.

"From Lord Ormington, my lord ?"

"No, sir. His lordship recommended his second son to our attention ; but he tendered us, at the same time, the *services* of his elder. He brings in Mr. Danby for his own borough. There was no occasion for overlauding him. The obligation is conferred on *us*."

I bit my lips.

"It is from Cambridge we have heard so much in his honour," persisted his lordship. "Mr. Danby distinguished himself at the university ; and has accredited himself still more, by subsequently devoting his time, in defiance of all the temptations of society, to a course of severe study. Your brother, sir, has been reared in the old school. Your brother brings more into the market than mere talent.

'Ως ουδεν ή μαθησις, ην μη νους παρῃ."

Votefilch was vain of his own academic distinctions, and the old fellow was slily slipping on his crown of laurels under shelter of my brother's wing.

"I sincerely trust, my lord," said I, "that Danby may add another name to the catalogue of those who, to the honours of the university have added the more glorious distinctions of public life."

On the following Saturday his Majesty's lieges were acquainted by his Majesty's Gazette, that

"For the borough of Rigmarole, John Alexander Danby, commonly called the Honourable John Alexander Danby, was returned to serve in this present Parliament, *vice* John Julius Fudge, Esq., who had accepted the Chiltern Hundreds."

I suppose I ought to have felt proud at this announcement :—I felt angry. Fate was heaping a great deal too much upon the Honourable John

Alexander.   He was beginning to monopolize the good
things of this world.   After being exiled to the
nursery in his nankeen frock, and to lodgings in his
superfine blue one, to be thus suddenly snatched into
public notice !   Lady Ormington cared as little for
him as she had done three-and-twenty years before.
But Cambridge, it seemed, "bragged of him as of a
virtuous and well-governed youth ;" and his Majesty's
Cabinet ministers had been pleased to lend their long
ears to her vauntings.   Even Emily Barnet spoke of
him as if interested in his success.   For my part, I
should have cared as much for that of little Squeamy.

"You will go and hear your brother make his first
speech ?" cried Emily, whose heart was warm with the
sympathies of every generous affection.

"I wish I had nothing worse to do with my time
than dance attendance in the House of Commons, for
the chance of hearing the honourable member for
Rigmarole give utterance to a few words inaudible in
the gallery," cried I.   "However, Danby is just as
little likely to come and listen to an harangue of
mine, unless from the dock of the Old Bailey.   He
despises me as the young hopeless of the family ; and
we might pass for a fashionable couple, so complete is
our alienation.   Do not look so shocked," cried I,
startled by her grave countenance.

"Is it the abhorrence of cant and exaggeration,
which so often betrays you English people into abuse
of your relations and calumny of yourselves ?" said she
in reply.   "Bossuet tells us to beware of those who
exceed in goodness, as there is nothing more suspicious
than a pretension to exorbitant virtues.   But I see no
reason for falling into the opposite extreme."

This well-earned reproof vexed me, as seeming to
take part with my brother.   I was born without a
genius for family affection.   I am much inclined to
doubt whether such instincts exist ; or rather, whether
the love of kindred be not the mere result of education.
In mine, sympathy with any living thing, save Dash and

Bibiche, had never been even hinted at by my mother. I might have been reared in a tribe of Iroquois, with more exhortation to humanity. As to John and Julia, once or twice, when our respective nurses interfered with our fisticuffs, and inflicted upon Master and Miss Danby, on whom alone they were permitted to exercise their jurisdiction, the study of that pleasing lyric of the mellifluous Watts,

> Birds in their little nests agree,

my mother was sure to mar the business by carrying me off to Gunter's or Wetten's, and rewarding my domestic sufferings with maccaroons.

As to proceeding to the House of Commons to behold poor Danby vibrate like a pendulum between his two long arms ("two eel-skins stuffed"), while giving utterance to his maiden stammer, though neither the eloquence of Windham or Grattan, Curran or Canning, ever attracted me into that den of honest men, I might have made the sacrifice to my sense of what was due to the family name, had he deigned to express a proper desire for my countenance. But in this, as in all else, he maintained towards me the haughtiest reserve. As a matter of taste, politics delighted me not, nor politicians neither. At a dinner-party, they are crammed down one's throat by one's neighbours, as fish sauces are forced upon one by the butler. But I was not much of a dining-out man; and when political dinners occurred in Hanover Square, usually hurried *incog.* to Nerot's, and skulked to the theatre.

It was consequently an unlooked-for blow, when, one morning, as I took my accustomed place at the office, *i. e.* before the fireplace, with my hands under the skirts of my coat, I was beset with congratulations by the "seven other devils worse than myself," who shared with me the laborious task of cursing the climate and inquiring how went the enemy (I don't mean the enemy in Spain, but the enemy at the Horse Guards; I don't mean H. R. H. the Commander-in-

chief, but the time-keeper of London and Westminster).
For a moment, I fancied I was going to be married,
and longed to satisfy myself whether Emily or Lady
Harriet were the favoured fair ; more especially, as
each of them brandished a morning paper, to give
force to his felicitations, as the tragedians of England
smite their bosom or touch their sword, in allusion
to their conscience or their valour.   The newspapers
evidently contained the germ of my good fortune.
The newspapers had probably hitched me into some
announcement of " Fashionable Hymeneals."

I was wrong.   The newspapers announced the
apotheosis of the Honourable John Danby, not the
suicide of his brother.   The newspapers set forth that
his Majesty's government had to congratulate itself on
a powerful accession in the person of the member for
Rigmarole.   A new Chatham was born unto them ;
a " heaven-born minister," risen like a Phœnix from
the ashes of him of whom port wine and Austerlitz
had deprived the British empire.

> Could such things be,
> And overcome me like a summer cloud,
> Without my special wonder ?

Could I, Cecil the coxcomb, be wide awake, and Danby,
the Honourable John, the awkward, squinting boy,
have become a man of genius ?   My whole frame
tingled with irritation at the supposition.

" You are a made man, Cis, my boy," cried young
Lord Chippenham, one of my clerkly colleagues.

" I sincerely wish you joy, Mr. Danby," added
Halbert Herries, another of my brother-slaveys.   Congratulations were showered upon me, like bouquets on
an opera-dancer.

As I sauntered up St. James's Street at the close of
the day, and now that Lady Harriet's influence was in
abeyance I no longer made short cuts across the Birdcage Walk, matters went still worse.   The Cocoa-tree
stared at me with its leaden eyes, as I lounged along.

The Albion, albeit unused to demonstration, rushed to its bay-window to gaze. Boodle's shrugged its round shoulders as I passed. Even the chairmen of White's and Brookes's seemed to whisper to each other (for Connaught Bill and his cub had rendered my name familiar in their mouths as household words), "You's own brother to the new parli'ment man, what's to bate Charlie and Billy to everlasting smitherens."

To be immortalized by a leaf from the laurels of John Danby; to be brightened by a ray from his luminous countenance. Was such the reward of all my labour? Was it for this I had excruciated myself in boots, agonizing as the shirt of Nessus? Was it for this I had closeted myself for consultation with Stultz, with a degree of mystery worthy of Guido Fawkes and Garnet? Was it for this I had abjured hunting, for the sake of my figure, and shooting, for love of my complexion? Was it for this I had anointed myself with the oil of Macassar above my fellows? Was it for this I had delivered to Hendrie, under the patent of my seal, the original recipe for the Danby washball? To be overcrowed by an elder brother, a squinting elder brother, a man unknown to White's, ignored by Watier's; whom, had he pleaded the loss of his ticket to the door-keepers of the Argyle Rooms, not a humanized being, from Colonel Greville to the linkboys, could have identified as a man of (dis-) respectability.

I was afraid to dine at my club that day. All the world seemed in league to fling my brother in my teeth. Even at the Bedford, or some other slang house of my unaccustomed haunts, I might be recognized and pointed out as the Castor of Pollux the Politician. In the plenitude of my weakness, I determined to dine at home.

Never shall I forget Lord Ormington's face that day! Monk Lewis had just then brought into fashion, Tales of Wonder, treating of dead bodies taken possession of by the evil one, and playing a posthumous part in the

H

world.   Here was a Tale of Wonder more than
wondrous.   His lordship, usually as dull and dumb
as if defunct, appeared suddenly animated, suddenly
spiritualized.   The devil was in him that day ; he
was almost jocose.   He actually asked me to take
wine.

Strange to say, my mother waxed silent in proportion
to the fluency of her lord.   Her ladyship and I seemed
dumb-foundered, because Danby had taken to speaking, and Lord Ormington to talking.   With *me* she
was as pettish as if I had worn one of Jack Harris's
flashy waistcoats ; actually resenting the triumphs of
my father's favourite, as a delinquency on the part of
her own.

The most superficial observer might have discovered
that some very unusual occurrence had taken place in
the family.   His lordship's carriage was announced an
hour later than usual.   For once, he was bound to the
Commons, instead of the Lords.   A world of paternity
sparkled in his triumphant looks.   The pigtail of my
lord's own man seemed to vibrate with delight, when,
as he brought in his lordship's coffee, he whispered that
the chariot was at the door.

" I do not inquire whether you have read your
brother's speech," said Lord Ormington, as he was
about to quit the room, with far more of the nobleman in his air than I had ever yet seen him assume.
" I know that your have *not*.   I did not even expect it
of you."   And his manner plainly implied, " being
totally incompetent to apprehend its merits and
intention."   " But lest you should commit yourself
by ignorance of its purport," he continued, fixing his
eyes firmly upon mine, " know that it was on the Catholic
question ; that it carried away the House ; and that
I possess in the future representative of my family, a
son for whom the esteem of the kingdom will shortly
afford confirmation of my own."

Such was the first item of family intelligence which
Lord Ormington condescended to communicate to me,

otherwise than through the professional mouths of Messrs. Hanmer and Snatch, of Southampton Buildings.

————◦◦◦————

CHAPTER V

A very set
Smooth speech, his first and maidenly transgression
Upon debate : the papers echoed yet
With his *début*, which made a strong impression,
And rank'd with what is every day display'd—
The best first speech that ever yet was made.
BYRON.

Ce sont de ces nuances qui échappent souvent à l'analyse, et qui laissent pourtant une impression ineffaçable.
EUGENE SUE.

EMANCIPATION was the Irish giant of my youth, as Daniel O'Connell of my age ; and aptly indeed might Catholic Hibernia exclaim to Evangelic England, as the taunter in Tom Thumb—

You *made* the giant first and then you kill'd it !

It was a good giant, however, in its time, to have its head smitten off by the riders in the quintain ; a capital cockshy for parliamentary schoolboys ; an excellent coral to assist the dentition of teething statesmen.

Everybody familiar with the routine of public schools, is conversant with the list of magnanimities set apart by the masters, as themes for the twaddling of the inexperienced in *belles lettres ;* such as " Marathon," —" Regulus," — " The Revival of the Arts," — " The Clemency of Titus,"—and so forth ; concerning each of which well-worn topics, the Dr. Dronebys of successive generations are as conversant with every epithet and every argument, as if already stereotyped

H 2

in the pages of Blair's Lessons, or Stretch's Beauties
of History.

Even so must the Speakers of the House have
regarded for a quarter of a century the annual orations
on Catholic emancipation.   I can scarcely persuade
myself that the intolerance of England was spouted
out of countenance by the braying of these donkeys,
as the walls of Jericho were overthrown by the braying of trumpets.   But the canvass served as a sampler
to be flourished upon by the "promising young
men."   My brother's periods were about as much to
the purpose as Rode's variations ; and had I not
forsworn politics in the narrative of my adventures,
I would bring forward a little theory of my own on
this point, almost worthy the solemnities of a Quarterly
Review.

Stung to the quick by the triumph of Lord Ormington's son in the House, I was not sorry to find that
Lady Ormington's had distinguished himself in the
coteries by concentrating the pith of the Irish question.

"So your brother has immortalized himself by a
speech upon Ireland ? " said Lady Harriet Vandeleur,
addressing me across the Duchess of Moneymusk's
dinner-table, evidently for the purpose of provocation.

"*Poor* Ireland !" was my reply, accompanied by a
significant elevation of the shoulders, implying, " will
no one let her alone ? "   "The question of her legis-
lation seems to me to resolve itself into the proposition
suggested by Camille Desmoulins, concerning France
and the Convention : '*La Convention a trouvé la
France sans culotte ; sa gloire et son chef-d'œuvre seront
de la rendre culottée !*'   Whoever shall rid green Erin
of her rags, will work greater wonders in her behalf
than by allowing her to tell her own beads, or palaver
in her own parliament."

The diners-out applauded ; for they were displeased
by the triumph of a man like Danby, unknown to
fame through their premonitory flourish of trumpets.
But they dared not protest against him.   There was

no plausible "because" to preface their "dissentients." His speech was allowed to be a good speech. The universities were pleased, because it showed a spice of scholarship; the country, because it was indited in manly English; the town, because its wisdom was not altogether devoid of wit. As if wit were more or less than the *animus* of wisdom: legitimate offspring of a union between good sense and good spirits.

Still, amid all these plaudits, Thersites found something to rail at. The bile of sarcasm engendered by the repletion of society, brought a sneer to its jaundiced cheek. Single-speech Hamilton was quoted; and the speech of the honourable member for Rigmarole, when printed, was decided to be a prize essay. The knowing ones pretended to discover a cotton weft through the rich pile of the velvet.

When the subject was broached in my presence, I took refuge, like other false prophets, in mysticism. My French quotation having served my cause so well, I replied to all questions concerning the abilities of my brother: "*Entre l'apparent et le réel, il y a tout un abime!*" much as my boy Tim would have hinted that "the proof of the puddin' was in the ating."

One day, shortly after the sudden sprouting of the Danby laurels, I received a note from my Fee-faw-fum, Lord Votefilch, begging me to look out certain confidential documents, the whereabout of which in Downing Street was exclusively known to myself. The Opposition had thrown a hand-grenade into the ministerial camp; and it was necessary to clear away the wreck caused by its explosion.

Half an hour afterwards, having fulfilled his orders, I lounged for a moment into the gallery of the House of Commons. There was a great hubbub. That tumultuous assemblage, which calls itself a deliberative body, was considerably out of order; the light troops of the Opposition having been skirmishing like Pandours. When lo! a sudden lull succeeded to the raging of the billows,—"after the tempest a still small voice."

In a moment, you might have heard a pin fall. There is something awful in the self-stilling of a public assembly ; a tribute from the passions of the many to the power of the one,—

The power of thought,—the magic of the mind,—

that power which no man could hold, "unless it were given him from above !"

Even I, though thwarted by having my habits and privacy invaded by the dirty work of the nation, and who had arrived at the House in a bitter bad temper, even I could not refuse to hear the voice of the charmer when I found him charming so wisely that even the cunning old serpents of debate-shirkers crept out of their holes in the lobby ; while the murmurs of the Opposition died away, like a night-storm at the dawn of morning.

It is an interesting sight, for people sufficiently Catholic in their spirit to cast away party feeling and interest themselves in the lights and shadows of public life, to watch the gradual development of opinion consequent on a fine piece of oratory, in an enlightened assemblage. Such a public assembly as the parliament of 1810 was an instrument that responded visibly, or rather audibly, to the touch of a skilful player. He whose hand I found upon the chords, was a player less adroit than powerful ; the ear recognized at once the inspiration of genius. I was so placed that my eye commanded the Opposition benches, but not a glimpse of the speaker. I saw him only as a divinity is manifested,— in the devotion of his worshippers, and the despair of the devils he hath cast out. The brows of the leading Opposition members were contracted, their lips compressed ; but not a vestige of scorn, not a gesture of levity. They bore the sledge-hammer blows dealt upon them, with the surly self-respecting desperation of an Indian at the stake ; and one may generally estimate

the strength of an antagonist, by the attitude in which
his attack is parried.

Could I have allowed it to enter into the possibility
of things, that I, Cecil Danby, was ignorant of any
matter which it imported me to know, I should certainly have addressed myself to my nearest neighbour,
to inquire the name of this powerful debater, this intellectual Milo, who had silenced the bellowing of
John Bull, and was carrying him off upon his shoulders.
But for worlds I would not have committed a sin of
ignorance on such a point in such a place. The voice
of the speaker was new to me. Husky in the onset,
perhaps from infirmity, perhaps from excitement, it
gradually cleared, and—

Rose like a steam of rich distill'd perfumes,

as the soul of the orator expanded, and the moral
overpowered the material in his sensitive nature. My
heart thrilled as I listened. Half an hour before, I
was not sure that I possessed one.

There are as many modes of oratory as there are
ways to dress eggs; and there are even various modes,
each of which, others beside my friend Connaught
Bill might be pardoned for calling the best. The mode
of the N.N., to whom I was yielding breathless attention, was the very type of style for a high-born, high-
bred, highly-educated, and consequently high-minded
young man; "young Harry with his beaver up," ripe
for an Agincourt of the mind; "young Harry," fighting for his party without violating the still holier
bond of fellow-creatureship; "young Harry," feeling
himself a prince, without forgetting himself to be a
man. Good Lord! I am speechifying too! The parliamentary epidemic seems to exercise a posthumous
contagion; like the infection of the plague, communicated by the dust of the dead after a century's
interment.

Joking apart, I was carried away like the rest.

On the subsiding of the uproar of cheers consequent

upon this eloquent speech (which embodied a reply as forcible as elegant, to a ferocious attack upon the foreign policy of government), I found myself eagerly surrounded, warmly congratulated.

"I have thanks to offer to yourself, my dear Danby, as well as to your brother," said Lord Votefilch, when informing me, shortly afterwards, that my documents came too late ; "for I am convinced it must be *your* information which has placed our invaluable champion in a situation to come forward thus readily. The finest reply that has been heard within these walls these ten years. Not a living orator, sir, has a chance against your brother. The Napoleon of debate ! If a usurper, he knows how to make his usurpation respected."

I could have killed old Votefilch for the complacent crush of the hand, enforcing these effusions of his gratitude.

There was a dreadful struggle in my feelings. Had I been left to myself, had there been no one but Cis Danby and the victorious gladiator under the roof of St. Stephen's, I verily believe I should have thrown myself on his neck, as Benjamin on that of Joseph, and claimed fraternal fellowship with his nobleness. But the warmth of others chilled me. The exaggerated enthusiasm chanting forth the praises of Danby, only that its own voice might be audible, reduced mine to silence. My heart became as hard as Pharaoh's.

To escape the conflicting batteries of St. James's Street, I made straight for Buckingham Gate ; though with no intention, on *this* occasion, of surprising Colonel Morley knocking at the bower-chamber-door of his lady fair. I was on foot. It was a fine June afternoon. The shade and verdure of the Park ought to have refreshed me. But, by heavens ! through all the stillness of the Birdcage Walk, where scarce a gnat or a nursery-maid was stirring, I seemed to hear over again, like the roar of the ocean in a dream, the tumultuous plaudits of the House. I was brother-

ridden. The soul of Cain was within me; or rather
the soul of that Cain of civilization, the terrible
Franz von Moor.

The first thing that roused me from my meditations,
was a cheerly voice that saluted me as I was approaching Tattersall's, round whose gates a detachment of
tilburies, stanhopes, and led-horses were clustered.

"Anything *my* way, Mr. Danby, sir?" inquired
Fetlock, touching his hat, and joining me on my way
towards Hyde Park Corner. "As pretty a little bit
of blood in my stable, just now, Mister Danby, sir, as
you'd wish to see. Let you have it a bargain, as the
season's getting on : carry a lady, like an armchair,
sir ! The very thing for a gemman as knows what he's
about, Mister Danby, sir ; and 'twould give me pleasure
now (if 'twas only for knowing what pride her la'ship,
Lady Ormington, would take to see you so prettily
mounted), to let you have the mare on terms as might
be agreeable. A young gemman, like *you*, Mr. Danby,
sir, which leads the fashion among the tip-tops——"

"Good morning, Fetlock!" said I, seizing the opportunity of having reached the crossing by St. George's
Hospital, to send him to Coventry or to Pimlico, while
I proceeded into Hyde Park ; for I could not stand
being flattered by a horsedealer at such a moment.
It was like Correggio, sinking broken-hearted under
the load of copper coin, the ignominious guerdon of
his genius.

On reaching home, I found Lady Ormington so
desperately "nervous" (*Ang.* out of humour), that I
concluded she had already learned the new triumph of
her first-born. I was mistaken. She knew nothing
about the matter, and cut me short at mere mention
of the House of Commons.

"You know I don't care a pin for politics!" said she.
"Why plague me about such nonsense, particularly
when you see me so nervous? Just conceive your
aunt Agatha taking it into her head that she is well
enough to come to town."

"You know I don't care a pin for my aunt Agatha. Why plague me about such nonsense ? " retorted her graceless son. "But why may she not come to town when she likes ? "

"The season is more than half over. What can be the use of dragging Julia all the way up from Devon-shire, now that the birthday is past ? I am convinced they only do it to torment me."

"It is a long journey for so small a purpose, consider-ing how easily your ladyship is tormented," said I gravely. "I cannot, however, see why they should remain at Sidmouth during the dog-days. The sum-mer has set in more severely than usual ; and I under-stood it was only during the winter months Baillie ordered the old lady to a milder climate."

"It is no question of the barometer," cried Lady Ormington. "I see through it all. It is Julia's doing ! It is all this stupid speech of Danby's."

"You are in the minority in calling it stupid, my dear mother," cried I ; "and I have the pleasure of informing you, that half an hour hence the newsmen's horns will render it impossible for you to remain ignorant that you are again a grandmother."

"*Grandmother !*" reiterated Lady Ormington, aghast, the last person in the world to enter into a joke.

"Grandmother to a *chef-d'-œuvre* engendered by John's flirtations with the tuneful Nine," said I, laughing.

"Speaking again so soon ? What nonsense ! I have often heard poor Sir Lionel say, there was nothing the House detested so much as a callow member, chirrup-ing before it knew how to tune up its pipes. I am sure the reason these people have come up to town so unexpectedly is to enjoy his triumph ! As to Julia, from the hour she was born she has thought of nobody but her elder brother."

"Because nobody else seems to have been at the trouble of thinking of *her*."

"Lord Ormington wanted to have them all here to

dinner to-day. But I told him plainly I was too nervous for a family party. Besides, I have promised to be with the duchess early. She has got to go to the ball at Carlton House after her loo."

"Got to go!" Lady Ormington's syntax was scarcely so refined as that of her son.

"But why not take Julia with you to-night?" said I, with the amiable intention of provoking her.

"Are you out of your mind, Cis?" cried she, rising from the sofa, and placing Bibiche carefully in her basket. "Lord Ormington and his sisters would as soon let Julia set foot in a pest-house, as go to the Duchess of Moneymusk's. I do not interfere with the scruples of their decorumships, those two old maids. As they have been kind enough (in consideration of my wretched state of health) to undertake the task of introducing Miss Danby into the world, it would ill become me (would it, my pretty Bibiche?) to counteract their system of education. By the way, Cis, remember that Lord Ormington will take it amiss if you do not call on these people to-morrow."

I looked vaguely acquiescent; but I had cares at that moment far more critical than maiden aunts or a red-haired sister. I was about to make my *début* at Carlton House. Thanks to personal influence (certainly not that of Lord Ormington, who had no more interest in society than I with the bench of bishops), I had received an invitation from the Prince; and, till the startling event of my brother's success, experienced inexpressible delight at a circumstance which I knew would be wormwood to Jack Harris and Lady Harriet's colonel.

Oh! inimitable Mrs. Davenport!—Mrs. Davenport, whom Charles Lamb defined as "Garrick in petticoats," Mrs. Davenport, with whom expired the ripe familiarity of that empress of romantic gossips, Juliet's nurse; Mrs. Davenport, who, in the prime of thy mellow years wert then playing to perfection the part invented by Morton for thy transcendant talents, how

often has thy exclamation of " What will Mrs. Grundy
say ?" since recurred to my conscience, in the course of
my profitless career.   For those simple words contain
the germ of a thousand catastrophes, the heart of a
thousand mysteries, the secret of a thousand downfalls.
The ruin of almost every imprudent family may be
traced to the influence of a Mrs. Grundy.   The pre-
sumption of forward boys, the rashness of public men,
the speculations of private, are caused, nine times in
ten, by the ambition of eclipsing some intimate friend
or intimate foe, the Mrs. Grundy of our several destinies.

Apart, however, from the desire of astonishing my
rivals in love and coxcombry, I was overjoyed at the
prospect of entering that renowned circle, the school of
my art, the cradle of infant dandyism, the incipient
order that was to supersede the bucks, ruffians, and
bang-up gentlemen of the road, so long in possession
of the crown of the causeway.

"Away with such triflers !" cries the sage, flinging
aside our pages into the depths of his gloomy library,
as if the grubbers among the dry bones of history did
more to expedite the progress of the times than those
fluttering butterflies who oppose, at least, no dead
weight to the general impetus.   Like a straw thrown
up to determine the course of the wind, the triflers of
any epoch afford invaluable evidence of the bent of the
public mind.   *They* are always floating on the surface.
They are a mark for general observation.   Statesmen
and beaux are the only *really* public men.   Posterity
will see in Brummell and Castlereagh the leading
characters of the Regency ; the gilded, not the
golden age.

The creation of DANDYISM afforded the first indication to the public, that, in spite of Stultz and Truefitt,
the portraits of Sir Thomas and certificates of Sir
Henry, the Prince was growing old !   Had we written
the word then, it must have been thus, ——, or, at
worst, o——d ; for no one presumed to approach more
definitely that fatal hint.   If, when Louis the Four-

teenth attained his seventieth year, his courtiers defined *soixante et dix ans* as "*l'âge de tout le monde*," no
one at Carlton House now presumed to be less than
five-and-forty.

Nature, however, was no courtier.   Nature began
to hint that liqueurs were an unsafer beverage than
sherry, that jollity was a plebeian effervescence, wit
a more princely thing than humour, superciliousness
than noise.   And, lo! dandyism stole in on tiptoe;
and the vulgar began to record the prowesses of George
Brummell, as they afterwards enlarged on the feats of
Wellington.

It is all stupid and silly enough in the retrospection;
and Brummell is, at present, only known to history as
an adventurer who, after giving the law to princes,
died a lunatic, in a public hospital.   But our grand-
nephews will behold in George Brummell a great
reformer; a man who dared to be cleanly in the
dirtiest of times; a man who compelled gentlemen to
quit the coach-box and assume a place in their own
carriage; a man who induced the ingenuous youth of
Britain to prove their valour otherwise than by
threshing superannuated watchmen; a man, in short,
who will survive for posterity as Charlemagne of the
great empire of Clubs.

It would never surprise me to find the ashes of the
great ex-dandy fetched home from Caen, as those of
Napoleon from St. Helena, to be interred at the foot of
the Duke of York's column; on the identical spot
where he initiated the Prince into the mysteries of
Roman punch.   No doubt that, like the great man of
antiquity, George Brummell often threatened his ungrateful country that it "should not even possess his
bones!"   But flesh and blood are more susceptible in
their generation, than the enlightened ghost.

So Seneca—"Corruptibile corpus aggravat animam;
et deprimit terrena inhabitatio sensum multa cogi-
tantem!"

I digress, or rather I grow garrulous; and nobody,

nowadays, is allowed to be garrulous in print, save
literary ex-chancellors and parliamentary committees.
If Rabelais had written with the fear of the weekly
and monthly reviews before his eyes, he would have
grown as stiff and concise as a drill sergeant.

One word more, however, about the Brummell
school.   If effeminate, conceited, frivolous, in their
pursuit of pleasure, they pursued it with less peril to
his Majesty's lieges than the rufflers of more recent
times.   Melton, which owed its origin to their sport-
manship, still attests that they were good riders and
good fellows, though they smashed neither turnpike-
gates nor policemen.   They drank their claret without
forcing buckets of gin down the throats of the swell-
mob ; and like certain insect tribes which prey upon
each other, their victims were sought and found in
their own order of society.   It is not always that the
scum floating on the surface of a great capital, is of
so innoxious a nature.   Theirs was the foam of champagne, not the frothing of coculus indicus.

So much in honour of the circle into which I was
that night inducted at Carlton House.   I conclude I
passed muster respectably ; for, after a whisper with
which his Royal Highness accompanied his cordial
reception of my mother, I saw Lady Ormington's eye
assume   the   selfsame   supernatural   brightness   that
had emanated from her lord's on the day of Danby's
entrance into public life.

I flatter myself my tie *was* irreproachable.   It is
not every man who can wear a white waistcoat and
cravat, without looking either insipid as a boiled
chicken, or dingy as a Spanish olive ; but for those
qualified by nature by clear complexions and well-
planted whiskers, nothing like it to mark the inborn
distinction between a gentleman and a butler.   The
steward's room, and the Lord High Steward's room,
were just then assimilated in the fashion of their
garments.   Tights and Tituses were the order of the
day ; and the costume which the present reign has

restored to the English court, was the distinctive mark
of a fine gentleman.   It brings tears into my eyes to
reflect how that last remnant of the Chesterfield
school has since been vilified.   And why ?   Because,
of the mingled mud and spangles composing the
ground-work of a court, the succeeding generation preferred the mud.

CARLTON HOUSE (at the period of which I treat) had
not yet put on its judge's condemning-cap.   It was
the Carlton House of the Prince, not of the Regent ; it
was the Carlton House of the Whigs, not of the Tories ;
it was the bivouac of the Opposition, not the taber-
nacle of Church and State.   To me, there was nothing
very striking in its aspect ; the same degenerate
passion for trinketry and Lilliputian *virtù*, encumbered
its cabinets with china and its chimney-pieces with
fanciful clocks that rendered my mother's drawing-
room a Dædalian mystery.   Elegance, however, was
there, though over-gauded with superficial refinement.
Even gold may be degraded by super-gilding, or
attenuated to too fine a thread.

At my age, it was impossible not to be excited by
the spectacle of a *fête* so brilliant in its arrangements,
so remarkable for the beauty of its female guests ; and
gay music and glaring illumination produced their
usual exhilarating sensations, when the *coup d'œil*
burst upon my view.

But such is the ordering of every human destiny,
that, after the Egyptian custom, the death's-head, the
refrigerating *memento mori*, was not wanting at the
banquet.   Everybody was talking of my brother.   A
new speaker of importance is more estimated by the
adverse party than by his own.   The Whigs were
anxiously exclaiming, " Who *is* this young Danby ?—
Whose son,—whose scholar ?—Eton or Harrow ?—
Oxford or Cambridge ?—Did he distinguish himself
at the university ?—What private tutor ?—What
honours ?—What Club ?"

Nay, when some dowager or damsel, smitten with

the whiteness of my linen or blackness of my curls, was at the trouble of inquiring the name of the tall young man leaning against the door, I had the torture of hearing it answered; " Don't you know? A younger brother of the Danby by whom all the world is engrossed."

Ye gods!—to be accepted in society as supplementary to John Danby; to become tail of the comet to my squinting elder brother! I was on the verge of learning to despise conventional distinctions. The noble nature of Emily had so far regenerated my own, that the True—the Real—was acquiring value in my eyes. But now, all was over. The moment I found my position subordinate, came the ambition of rising. It was indispensable to my happiness not to be pointed out as the brother of the Honourable Member for Rigmarole.

But how to distinguish myself,—*how?*—The first of gladiators cannot conquer without a fight; and where was I to find an arena? Neither Bacon nor Milton, Burleigh nor Bolingbroke, could have made themselves remarkable by "a livery more guarded than their fellows" as clerks in the Foreign Office. Nay, as men of genius, they had been less serviceable in active life than such men as Hanmer and Snatch; as was exemplified by Walpole, when he pointed out a blunt paper-knife as a better instrument to divide the pages of a book, than a sharper blade. In my official capacity, therefore, my prospects of distinction were as remote as if lying on the oriental side of the Red Sea.

Even as regarded the lists of fashion, a Jack Harris might distinguish himself; because, to a low-born man, notoriety is fame. Whereas, for one of my position to make himself remarked by dress or equipage, were defamatory as the branding-iron. The highest distinction for a nobleman's younger son in such a clique as that at Carlton House, is to become undistinguishable. Woeful annihilation! a drop in the ocean, a grain of sand in the wilderness!

A sudden thought relieved my depressed spirits. What if I were to marry Lady Harriet Vandeleur, set the Thames on fire by our select dinners, and, like a hand at commerce, win the game by my skill at discarding? A Cecil and Lady Harriet Danby unanimous in their principles, able to command the best society, might, per force of tact, command the brigade of fashion. Eight thousand a year, though nothing in the hands of a gambler like Morley, less than nothing in those of a Squeamy, or a Sir Moulton Drewe, would become Pactolus, when flowing through the fertilizing regions of a brain like mine.

"After all," I reasoned with myself, on my return from the gorgeous *fête* which had proved such a scene of humiliation, "after all, but for that expedition to Southampton Buildings, I should have remained seriously attached to the piquant little personage whom Emily has taught me to regard as a doll. It would be a small sacrifice on my part to become her husband. The dozen years' difference of age between us must be estimated at six hundred a year each, and the jointure makes all equal. In affording me the means of shining, she commands my gratitude, and will, eventually, win my affection. Decidedly, I must set about recommending myself to the little widow ; a new Jason, devoted to the conquest of a Golden Fleece."

Next night came the Opera. I had already determined to drop my visits to Emily ; though not so suddenly as to cause an alarming vacuum in her existence. I would wean her, poor girl, from my society. My visit to the box should be a short one. On many accounts, indeed, this was desirable ; for the d'Acunhas were beginning to understand just so much English as rendered them bores. They *would* be asking questions and misconceiving the answers ; then, further inquiries, with new misapprehensions.

From Emily, however, I had nothing to fear in the way of questioning. *She* was happy enough to have me with her, without indulging in frivolous curiosity ;

I

nay, she *had* no curiosity. With *her* I was secure from
the vulgar gossip that beset me in company with Lady
Harriet ; tittle-tattle about births and marriages, pro-
motions and preferments. So far from knowing who
and who were together, Emily Barnet knew not even
who was whom. Had she been my wife, this would
have been a defect. In a friend,—a charming, intel·
ligent, conversational friend, it was little short of
a virtue. Her mind was thoroughly unsophisticated. She never read a newspaper, never heard a
scandal.

"I was at a magnificent ball last night, at Carlton
House," said I, by way of reply to Emily's remarks on
my air of languor.

"What *is* Carlton House,—a theatre?" inquired she,
with a *naïveté* that must have passed for assumed
with any one to whom the peculiarities of her situation were unknown.

"No ; the residence of the heir-apparent, the Prince
of Wales."

"The Prince of Wales? I have heard Mr. Hanmer
speak of him as a paragon," said she. "He is young
and handsome, is he not ?"

"Twenty years ago he was as charming as his last
night's *fête*. Never did I pass an evening so enchanting," cried I, with affected enthusiasm.

A heavy sigh must have escaped poor Emily ; for
d'Acunha turned his sallow saturnine visage round
upon us, as if to examine what was going on.

One of the most bewitching charms of Emily Barnet
consisted in a throat long and slender as that of Anne
Boleyn, which imparted a peculiar grace to her movements. It was impossible to see her under greater
disadvantage than I did ; always in the same place,
always in the same dress, always in the same attitude ;
no scope for the display of elegance of manners or
accomplishments of mind.

Yet, strange to tell, there was something in all this
that seemed to enhance the charm of our intercourse.

That dull silent box, with its solemn atmosphere of reserve, the mourning habits of its inmates, the peculiarities of their looks and language, imparted an almost monastic gravity to the spot, contrasted with the brilliancy of my usual haunts and the garrulity of my ordinary companions.   I felt as if under the influence of a spell the moment I crossed the threshold. It was like stepping into some picture by Velasquez; it was like creeping into the heart of some old Spanish romance.

But I was going to remark that I had noticed in Emily, among the few expressive gestures compatible with her invariable position, a peculiar mode of turning away her head, on pretence of looking towards the stage, between the wall and the intervening figure of Madame d'Acunha, whenever the discrepancy of our situations in life became apparent.   There was a deprecation in her desire to avoid my scrutiny at such moments, which, even had not the movement itself been exquisitely graceful, would have touched my feelings.   Never did she seem so lovely in my eyes as then; with nothing of her features visible but the fine oval of her soft cheek and dimpled chin, fair as monumental alabaster, and rendered still fairer by contrast with the glossy curls hanging loosely from her temples.   In that attitude does she recur oftenest to my memory.   I seem to see her still, averting her moistened eyes, and by slow degrees returning to her usual position; the long upturned eyelashes first becoming visible; then, the arched lips, the finely-chiselled nose, all that pure and noble physiognomy. Poor, *poor* Emily !

She detested England; how should she do otherwise ? and all her pleasurable anticipations regarded her return to Portugal. Her lamentations incessantly recalled, like Mignon's song,—

das Land wo die Citronen blühn.

Her visions were of silvery fountains and azure skies

of evergreen shrubberies and craggy mountains, of
music and song; not as pleasing imagery, or mere
accessories, but essentially interwoven with the business of life. So strong is the influence of early
associations.

"She *cannot* have formed projects in which we are
mutually interested," said I to myself, in an apologetic
tone, as I slowly descended into the nether world from
d'Acunha's box on the night in question. "She *cannot* suppose, poor girl, that there is anything in common
between the son of an English peer and the daughter
of a Lisbon merchant; between a Downing Street
diplomat and the ward of a snuffy old solicitor in
Southampton Buildings. She *cannot* imagine, when
raving about the groves and skies of Cintra, that I
am ever likely to wander by her side among its froggy
tanks and twisted-stemmed pomegranate-trees. Emily
must be aware that I lounge away a pleasant hour
with her, glad to refresh my eyes with her bright intelligent countenance, and as little serious in my attentions as she in her encouragement. She likes me,
because I am a little younger and more amusing than
old Hanmer or d'Acunha; but would infinitely prefer
some young Oporto winegrower of her own condition of life, to a mere idler about town like Cecil
Danby."

I said this to myself, dear readers (ambitious
plural!), with, of course, a secret conviction that
Emily would be proud and happy to perform for my
sake a barefoot pilgrimage to the shrine of St. James
of Compostella. But it was as well to keep up the
farce with myself of deserting her with the most
honourable intentions. After having pressed her
hand every time I placed her in her hackney-coach,
and brought her a sprig of some favourite flower every
time we met, I made up my mind to back out of the
business with a ceremonious decorum worthy the
king's champion at a coronation banquet.

I had quitted the box the moment I saw old

d'Acunha wipe his opera-glass, preparatory to placing it in its morocco case ; the signal for their preparing to quit the house. Heretofore, I had seized that moment to nail myself to my chair ; the happiness of my evening consisting in my transit from the clouds to the earth below, with Emily leaning on my arm ; her fragrant hair occasionally wafted across my cheek by the night air of the passages, her breath almost mingling with my own. But with my present views, it was high time this should end. So I walked quietly out of the box, as if intending to return ; and instead of returning, went straight down to Lady Harriet, and (thanks to the ample themes supplied by the *fête* of the preceding night) found occasion to be extraordinarily amusing.

A mere woman of the world must be generous indeed who does not allow herself to be diverted at the expense of her friends ; who, she is well aware, would feel little scruple in returning the compliment. Lady Devereux, wearied by her ball, was not at the opera. Nothing easier, therefore, than to describe to Lady Harriet the strip of plush on which her fair friend had mounted her diamond bandeau the preceding night, like the new order of a new Countess of Salisbury.

A peal of laughter from her ladyship and Lord Squeamy, who sat gibbering in the corner of the box, rewarded my sally. I next attacked the Duchess of Moneymusk, who, I declared, wanted only a philabeg at the Prince's ball, to look the image of a Highland recruiting sergeant. Again, Lady Harriet's laughter exploded. But I noticed that certain persons or personages who had been chattering away in the next box, became suddenly silent ; and had little doubt that her grace and her grace's Scotch bonnet were seated there in judgment upon my perfidy.

As it was my cue to take out Lady Harriet, and make an exhibition of our intimacy in the crush-room, I remained till the end of the ballet. The people of

the adjoining box were just before us in the lobby;
quizzes, decided quizzes—an old woman, escorted by
an ungainly-looking chap with his hat on, and a simple-
looking country miss.   I was struck, however, even in
the midst of my whispers to Lady Harriet, by the
melodious voice of the girl.   She possessed exactly the
same varied and refined intonation which had imparted
double eloquence to the speech of the Honourable
Member for Rigmarole.   And no wonder; for, on her
turning round, evidently shocked by one of Lady
Harriet's explosive laughs, exclamations were exchanged between us of "Cecil?"—"Julia?" and I
found that I had been following in the wake of my
maiden sister and maiden aunt.

"I hope you received my card?   I did myself the
honour of calling yesterday.   By the way, I *had* no
card, and simply left my name," said I, addressing Miss
Danby, sen.   But, with a sort of negative grunt, plainly
implying she did not believe a word I was saying, the
dear soul and her Bayard in the brown beaver hat
passed onwards.

Julia, however, lingered a little behind, in conversation with Lady Harriet, whom she had known, as a
child, in Hanover Square; and I was startled by the
singular sweetness of her countenance.   It was a face
such as Raphael or Titian would have delighted to
paint; the earnest expression of the eye and angelic
character of the mouth being exactly such as the old
artists used to lend to the celestial beings whose hair
bordered on auburn, as the natural accompaniment of
a transparent complexion.

More wonders.   The frightful sister was grown a
beauty, just as the stupid brother had progressed into
a genius.   The cockade was decidedly eclipsed.   What
was I, after all?   A mere B.A. of the art of dandyism,
a clerk in a public office, and desperately in love with
a young lady of problematical extraction, domiciled in
the vicinity of Bloomsbury Square.

The hare and the tortoise over again—always the

hare and the tortoise! However, the race was not yet won. I might still live to vindicate for the rash levity of genius.

CHAPTER VI.

Si melius quid habes, accerse ; vel imperium fer.
HORACE.

Quelque méchant qu'on soit, on ne réussit guère à faire le mal avec plaisir. Si ce n'est le remords, c'est la honte qui paralyse souvent les ressources de la perversité !—GEORGE SAND.

I WONDER why people are so fond of calling youth "ingenuous." No greater mistake. Youth has not *courage* to tell the truth, even to itself. As I said before, it is only after thirty that men presume to have a will or a way of their own.

Youth is an imitative animal. Youth is a monkey. The world is in conspiracy against it. The beasts of prey have the best of it. The monkey is condemned to a chain and a bag of nuts. Were the marmozet to wax grave, we should cry, "Stupid little beast, look at its airs of gravity! Give it a poke with your stick, and make it climb." The poor monkey is accordingly forced to be frisky, whether it will or no ; it dare not be natural—it dare not trust to its instincts.

But youth has another and still bitterer enemy than its masters—ITSELF. Of all the mockeries it has to dread, those most fatal in the creation of mistrust, are its own. The generous glow, the fervid impulse, are, in truth, vouchsafed by nature. But the curious in casuistry are requested to decide whether, of the spirits of good and evil assigned to each of us as companions through life, the good have not the ascendancy over our material, and the evil over our moral nature. The flush of joy, the thrill of horror, so instinctive in our early years, at the relation of wicked or virtuous actions, the gushing tears, or uncontrollable smiles, evincing our sympathies of affection, are far more independent of our will than we care to own. Whereas most of our evil deeds are the result of deliberation. But here we are on the brink of the bottomless pit of metaphysics ; and there are coxcombs enough in that transcendental department of the fudgerations of literature, without mustering among their number the Honourable Cecil Danby. My Pegasus is entered for higher stakes.

I only mean to say—for the longest preamble must arrive at the fact at last—that though I suspected myself of being desperately in love with Emily Barnet, whenever I tried to bring myself to confession, I deceived myself and the truth was not in me.

At my shaving-glass (tonsorial operations being peculiarly favourable to reflection ; nay, I am not sure that beards were not assigned by Providence to secure to every man five minutes' uninterrupted communing with himself in the course of the day)—at my shaving-glass I often interrogated my feelings ; and whenever, by a rising blush or gentle sigh, they suggested that Emily had claims on my affections, I pished and pshawed them into a more reasonable frame, as though I were old Munden enacting a peevish guardian in a Spanish comedy.

I said to myself, "Emily is a handsome girl enough " (my conscience whispering all the time that she was an angel !) ; "but every girl who smiles upon one, at *my* age, appears a divinity." I said to myself, "It is true that, niched into that wretched opera-box, Emily's manners appear tolerable " (my conscience whispering all the time that they would have done honour to a court !) ; "but, launched in good society, her deportment would probably be as awkward and unmeaning as that of other misses." I said to myself, " Certainly, her mind appears cultivated ; she has read foreign books that I know nothing about" (my conscience whispering all the time that the originality of her ideas was only exceeded by the depth of her acquirements !) ; " but it would be a bore to produce in good company a wife who seems to have been educated for a governess."

But this was not all. Bitter as were these treasons against Emily, I poured into the porches of my own ears a still more leprous distilment to injure the gifted being I was intent upon depreciating.

" After all," said Cecil Danby to me (flourishing one of Packwood's razors gracefully in his hand—and he deserved to cut his throat for his pains)—" after all, *who* will guarantee me that this girl is not an adventuress ? How do I know that the whole affair has not been a trap to ensnare me ? What assures me that old Hanmer, warned of my coming, did not station his pretty ward (perhaps some illegitimate offspring of the prim old solicitor) in his drawing-room, as a torch to singe the wings of the fashionable butterfly. Lord Ormington's younger son may be a bad match for one of the daughters of the Duchess of Moneymusk, or even for Lady Harriet Vandeleur ; but I flatter myself that, with *my* person and prospects, I am a catch for Miss Emily Barnet. As if those mum-chance, olive-faced d'Acunhas would have allowed me to sit there by her side, looking unutterable things and saying unlookable things, without apprising her guardian. If they did *not*, they are unconscientious, disreputable people—adventurers also. I am, however, the last man to be made a dupe of; and now that I espy the plot, will be cautious of throwing myself in the way of temptation."

Such was the " ingenuousness " of my " youth ;" and I will answer for it that few of those who " explore Cam's smooth margin," or the banks of the Cherwell or Isis, after being flogged through Eton, Harrow, Westminster, or Winchester — Horace, Homer, and the Greek Testament—are worth a maravedi more than myself in point of singleness of mind.

On the present occasion Cecil Danby kept his word
with me like a gentleman. Next opera-night not a
sign of him in the d'Acunhas' box. I even eschewed
the pit, lest the old Guimaraen plumb should adhere
to me, and invite me to accompany him upstairs.
This manœuvre had the effect of bringing Emily,
during the ballet, to the front of the box, where she
had never made her appearance since the first disastrous night of our meeting. I could plainly see her
eyes wandering over the pit in search of me. Nay, as
if I were not sufficiently distinguished from the mass
to be perceptible to the naked eye, she had even
recourse to old d'Acunha's glasses, which, Heaven
knows, I had never seen her use before.

.All this was in my favour. For I was of course
installed " close at the ear of Eve," close beside Lady
Harriet Vandeleur ; and my cause with *her* was not
injured by the attention excited by Emily's beauty.
People raved about her ; for she was both a beauty
and a mystery. Had one of the Duchess of Moneymusk's daughters been thrice as handsome, the world
would have said less about her ; as a planet, whose
rising and setting might be computed,—whose aphelion
and perihelion were matters for the almanack.

But Emily was a brilliant meteor, known only by
its radiance. All the world, that is, all the fashionable
world, knew her by the name of " Cis Danby's girl."
I was the only man admitted into her box ; the only
person ever seen to address her ; and a vague report
was prevalent (spread, doubtless, by the vulgar horde
who had dodged us home in the hackney-coach), that
she lived in an obscure street in the neighbourhood
of Bloomsbury Square. Was it *my* fault that the
world should form indiscreet surmises from such
grounds ?

The consequence was, that no one presumed to name
her disrespectfully before me, any more than they
would have done my sister. Though canvassed far
and near as the handsomest creature in town,

before *me* she was never mentioned. While talking that night to Lady Harriet, I saw her ladyship's eyes frequently directed towards the altitude where Emily's graceful head detached itself as by a halo, from the red curtain of her box. I could see that she was proud to have me with her, proud to render me faithless to so lovely a creature. No, not proud. Pride is a loftier feeling. She was vain ; vain that the battalion of fops surveying her box from the pit, should whisper to each other, " Aha ! Cis has changed hands to-night. Cis has forsworn the company of the gods. Cis has come down to the things of this world."

Cis *had* forsworn the company of the gods. But if Jove in his amorous de-deification disguised himself as a swan, the modern thunderer was proving himself a goose.

"I am quite anxious about Lady Ormington," observed Lady Harriet, suddenly addressing me, when she saw that my eyes were following the direction of her own. "She is growing ill and nervous again. I tried to get her to the Opera to-night. But she would not hear of it. I have not seen her so poorly these two years."

I hazarded certain filial allusions to the heat of the weather : not, however, because blind to the fact that Lady Ormington's illness was pre-ordained so long as Julia remained in town.

" I wanted her to go to our water-party on Monday," added Lady Harriet coolly.

"To a *water-party ?*" said I, satisfied that this was only a lure thrown out to make me petition for an invitation. " You might as well propose such a recreation to a Frenchwoman, the most hydrophobic of God's creatures ; or to Lot's wife, after her transformation."

"You are extremely witty to-night !" retorted Lady Harriet, drily--*very* drily.

" My mother is one of the many English women

who so band-box away their days as to lose, like Baron
Trenck, or Latude, or any other state prisoner, all
capacity for air and exercise. In her youth, things
so pretty were not made to stand," I continued,—
forgetting that the page of the register recording my
mother's baptism, might almost include that of Lady
Harriet.

"There will be no walking, and very little standing
in our expedition," she replied. "However, perhaps,
she was right to declare off, for your brother and sister
are of the party."

"Lady Ormington must feel proud of the miracles
wrought by her son's success," said I, bitterly.
"Danby's parliamentary triumphs seem able, like
faith, to remove mountains; for I remember once
your telling me you had given up an engagement in
Hanover Square, on finding he was to dine at home;
having no courage to confront a squinting man !"

"Mr. Danby has proved that he is worth listening to;
and where *that* is the case, *looks* go for nothing. I then
thought he was to make his way with us, like yourself, by superficial accomplishments. But who cares
for the figurehead of a ship which, charged with a
precious freight, is cutting its way bravely through the
waters ?"

"If we had but Gurney here to take you down,"
cried I, with supercilious impertinence. "Do you know,
dearest Lady Harriet, you would make a dangerous
rival for Hafiz, or Rosa Matilda of the *Morning Post.*"

"While Cecil Danby is to be rivalled only by the
ineffable Cecil Danby," said she, with perfect coolness ;
" *Crispin, rival de lui-même !* "

I was cruelly nettled : not by her sayings, but by
her doings. What in the world had induced her to
form this offensive and defensive alliance with my
brother ? Could John, frightful John, be superseding
Colonel Morley, absent without leave ? Her invitation to Julia was a natural consequence. For it was
well known in the Ormington clique, that Danby was

nowhere so vulnerable as through his affection for his
sister ; that those twain were as one flesh.   But why
desire to conquer him ?   *His* prospects were too good
to admit of his marrying for money ; and in the way
of mere flirtation, what woman ever threw away her
smiles upon a cub, because he had made a tolerable
speech or two in the House ?   Yet now I recollect—
but no !—there is no call upon me to reveal those
secrets of my times, in which I did not exercise a personal influence.

What right had I, meanwhile, to resent being excluded from Lady Harriet's water-party, when from
her last *al fresco* entertainment I had been self-banished?
I saw clearly that she had not forgotten Richmond,
because *I* was beginning to forget Southampton Buildings ; but chose that I should crawl my way, with
other creeping things, into her ark.   Her ladyship was
mistaken.

"It is a pity you do not persuade Lord Ormington
to join your party," said I.   "It would then include, to
the last fraction, the most high and puissant house of
Danby."

"Not exactly *to the last*," observed her ladyship
coolly.

"And what particle, pray, would be wanting?"

"The greatest in his own estimation," she replied.
But I managed to look so hopelessly puzzled, that she
was compelled explicitly to add, "*yourself !* "

"*I* am a nonentity," cried I, as if relieved from my
perplexity.   "Besides, all the world has heard of our
Greenwich dinner on Monday, which is to include all
the birds of the Heir (Apparent) and all the fishes of
the Thames."

Lady Harriet saw that her weapon had missed fire.
Unincluded in the clique of Carlton House, she fancied
that some party was *in petto* of which she knew nothing ;
and was piqued like a pouting child, who discovers
that there is a doll in the world larger than its own.

"*We* dine at Colonel Morley's villa, at Fulham," said

she. " I have not courage for the compound of villanous smells, punch, tobacco, and small beer which
infect one after a dinner at the Ship."

"*The Ship ?* " said I opening my innocent eyes.

" Did you not say you were going to dine at the
Ship ? "

" I mentioned Greenwich. Your ladyship, I perceive,
concentrates that nautical town into a fashionable
tavern, just as people consider the Pavilion, Brighton,
and Paris, France. If the tribe of Danby collected
round you at Fulham on Monday, are charitable
enough to send us their good wishes floating with the
return of the tide, I trust they will find me less publicly
installed."

" I am aware that you are fond of secluded retreats,"
observed Lady Harriet, raising her opera-glass towards
the d'Acunhas' box.

But I would not be browbeaten. If once a keeper
allows himself to be glared down by the animal he is
bent on taming, there is an end of him.

" Admit," cried I gently caressing my curls, " that
there is some pleasure in straying from the beaten
track, the vulgar, dusty, turnpike-road of fashionable
life, to luxuriate among " hedge-row elms and hillocks
green," youth, beauty, innocence, and delight. One is
apt to grow Paradisaical at the rural season ; when
the worn-out things of this world seem fit only for the
curiosity-shop. Buds and blossoms, haymaking and
love-making, go charmingly together, with the glass
at 78, and the reason at zero."

" I quite agree with you," replied Lady Harriet, too
much a woman of the world to be thrown off her
guard, even by this coarse attack, " when the hay-
makers are genuine Philly Nettletops, and the love
newly mown like the grass. But the shepherdesses
of Boucher, with their powdered wigs and hoops of
pea-green taffeta, or, worse still, the glazed calico
shepherds, and shepherdesses of a London ballet, are
to *me* as tawdry as all other counterfeits. By the

way, can you tell me the name of the illustrious unknown yonder, who seems to be watching us with so
much interest ?"

I did not expect that Lady Harriet would come so
decidedly to the point.

"That beautiful creature in mourning," said I, with
quickened respiration. "A Portuguese I fancy. The
gentleman at least, is a certain Don Vicente d'Acunha.
Perhaps you are acquainted with him ? It is amazing
the number of refugees from Spain and Portugal now
in London. The other night, at Carlton House, we
had the Duchess d'Hijar, the finest figure in Europe."

"And has the duchess also taken up her abode in
the fifth tier at the Opera, and the neighbourhood of
Bloomsbury Square ?" demanded Lady Harriet, losing
all self-command.

"You had better inquire of Danby, at your water-
party," cried I, scarcely able to control my irritation ;
"who is more intimate than myself in the house
where I had first the honour of meeting the beautiful
girl who appears so powerfully to excite your ladyship's interest. Drewe, my dear fellow, why have
you never sent the recipe you promised me for clean-
ing meerschaums ? Though I sentenced my boy to
a week's apprenticeship in the barracks of the German
Legion, Hudson assures me the fellow has no more
idea of handling a pipe, than I of hingeing a Lau-
rencekirk."

As I anticipated, Sir Moulton Drewe, who had
never heard a word of the recipe, and did not even
smoke, was so voluble in giving and requiring explanations, that Emily was safe. Before he half recovered
his astonishment, I was in the centre of the pit, squabbling with one of the Stanhopes about the comparative
merits of Vestris and Deshayes.

I begin to think there is a destiny in the said opera
(King's Theatre, Queen's Theatre, what is it, just now?)
for embroiling the affairs of bankers, managers, and
lovers. One of the cleverest fellows connected with

its harassing concerns, has often protested to me that
the London public would never enjoy a good opera,
till the present crazy barrack was burned to the
ground ; and I am of his opinion.   Fire is a universal
purification.   Perhaps, by the time the new Houses of
Parliament have risen, like blanched sea-kale from
their cinders, the Fire-King, of whom James and
Horace Smith made themselves the laureats, may take
to his embraces the great barn in the Haymarket,
which, on the night in question, I devoted to him and
all other Infernal Gods.

Yet, after all, there is something sacred and classical
in the old den.   The Opera-house is pretty nearly the
only place of public amusement of the Prince's time,
left standing.   Carlton House, Ranelagh, Lords, Commons, Whitfield's Chapel, Vauxhall, Fozard's Riding-
school, the Argyll Rooms, and the King's Mews, all
evaporated, all flown off *in fumo*.   This is the age of
demolition, the era of rubbish.   The very nature of
London buildings interdicts a pretension to the venerable ; for the moss of antiquity imparts no dignity
to brick and mortar.   "Nothing more deplorable than
the decay of a plaster wall," says a clever French
writer.   "Like a gauze dress, it is a thing not intended
for durability ; which, when it lasts, becomes a badge
of poverty and disgrace."

At all events, when the edifice which has drained
the resources of bankers, taxed the wisdom of lord
chancellors, and enriched the Gazette with nearly as
many respectable names as the battle of Waterloo,
shall down with its dust, like the wretched capitalists
whom it has involved in ruin, may some appropriate
historian arise to immortalize its archives.   When
those charming boxes shall have ceased to exist, whose
six-feet-square are enjoyed for sixty evenings of the
year, at the cost of little more than the salary of an
Irish bishop, when those stalls shall be broken up,
which, like that of Caligula's horse, are plated with
gold, may some Antoine Hamilton or Callot of the

twentieth century, dip his light pen in aqua-fortis, to
depict the lights and shadows of a spot consecrated by
such memories of beauty and genius, art and nature ;
human nature, of course; the only nature worth
writing of.

There was a time, ere poets, like the gods of poetry,
had departed, when the pastoral had still its votaries,
and kings wandered amid happy valleys and wedded
with shepherdesses. The world knows better nowadays. The pastoral has no longer a devotee, save in
one of Haydn's symphonies; and kings abide in castles
on the Thames, or palaces on the Seine, guarded by a
legion of honour and legion of cooks ; the only shepherdesses in whom they *now* take delight, being of
Dresden china, standing prim and crisp upon their
chimney-pieces.

But the amiable weakness of modern times that
approaches nearest to the hallucinations under whose
influence "King Cophetua wooed the beggar-maid," is
the passion of a lord for an opera-dancer. An opera-
dancer is the Perdita of the nineteenth century, and
the Crockfordites are her Florizels.

Some denizen of St. James's Street proposed to
extend the constitution of the country into king,
lords, commons, and opera. And why not ? The
choregraphic art is the nearest approach to a universal
language,—that *desideratum* of sages and centuries.
How else can we account for the mightiness of renown
which has bruited the name of Taglioni from Indus to
the Pole, enabling her to subdue the Hyrcanian bear
of St. Petersburg, and flourish in the court-circular of
the Celestial Empire? What statesman, what philosopher, what elder among the conscript fathers of art,
science, or jurisprudence, has attained a European,
American, Asiatic, and African reputation, like Fanny
Elssler? Which would England, which would Europe,
most deplore, the final exit of the Lord Chancellor or
of Cerito? By Terpsichore and all her caperings,
the ceremony approaching nearest the apotheosis

K

of the ancients, is the triumph of a popular opera-dancer.

I know not how I find courage for pleasantries upon the subject, unless as More and Anne Boleyn jested on the scaffold. For of all the adventures of my youth, that which commenced on the staircase at the opera, has left the most indelible impression on my mind. The evil issue thereof had its origin in the indiscretion of speech wrung from me, on the night in question, by the tauntings of Lady Harriet Vandeleur.

The following day, I was to dine with Lord Vote-filch, who had a villa on the Thames to refresh himself one day in the week by contact with the mud of nature, after immersion the remaining six in its clay. It was an ex-official dinner, or I should not have been invited. Lord Votefilch the minister, lived in St. James's Square, and gave dinners on Saturdays ; Lord Votefilch the man, at Putney, and gave dinners on Sundays. I had rather have belonged to the Saturday *pow-wow ;* for Votefilch the minister was a great man in the political circle ; whereas Votefilch the man was a mere mediocrity.

Besides (as Chippenham and I agreed when he invited us in an unceremonious way at the office), it is adding insult to injury for a *chef* to invite his youngsters to a family dinner, which he knows they dare not refuse. I wonder he did not beg us to bring our fishing-rods, like other clerks out for a holiday. Even then, we could not have allowed ourselves to be affronted.

To dine at Putney, at half-past six, then the general hour, necessitated a toilet at five ; and I consequently looked for a moment into Lady Ormington's drawing-room, at an hour at which I was little in the habit of testifying my filial respect. My mother used to receive tribes of visitors on Sundays. Fine ladies often do, as the consequence of their retreat from the mobs let loose upon the earth on that day of general debond-agement. Kensington Gardens was, if I recollect, just then the resort in fashion.   Kensington Gardens (a spot which oppresses my spirits as if the atmosphere confined within its masses of trees were mephitic as the jungles of Sierra Leone), has undergone fierce alternations of popular favour and scorn.   It is sure to be either so much in fashion and so crowded, that every blade of glass is worn from its sooty turf; or so deserted, that the palace looks ashamed to be standing there by itself, like a pelican in the wilderness.   At the period I write of, Bow Street runners used to be stationed at the gate, to prevent his Majesty's lieges from being mummied in their attempt to pass the wicket.   No! that was the preceding year.   At present, there was nobody in Kensington Gardens but the gate-keepers in their suits of green and yellow melancholy.   It was to the ring that the idlers devoted their gravel-grinding.

Lady Ormington and Co. consequently remained in their several habitations, sealed up, like patent medicines.

I had forgotten, however, that, in her dread of family dinners, it was her ladyship's cue to be nervous; and that she was consequently "not at home;" so that it startled me when on entering her china-warehouse, instead of the murmur of voices usual at that hour under its fresco ceilings of blue sky (a hateful fashion of that day, conveying the bitterest irony upon the dingy heavens without), I heard nothing but the peevish voice of Lady Ormington talking to herself or Bibiche, in tones that might have been mistaken for those of a sick parrot, quarrelling with itself over an almond.

Poor Bibiche! A legitimate descendant of the original Dash staring its unmeaning eyes out in Cosway's portrait of the Right Honourable Lady Ormington, Bibiche was whimsical, fretful, and unattached. I was never sorry when my mother worried the dog; for the dog had an immunity for worrying all my mother's fellow-creatures.

On the present occasion, however, it was not the
spaniel to whom her ladyship was murmuring her
woes. It was an animal of more consequence. It
was the heir of the House of Danby.

Saul among the prophets ! What on earth could
the rising young man be about in the sanctuary of
Bibiche and her lady ? I should as soon have expected to find old Droneby himself inaugurated among
the bronzes and mandarins at Carlton House.

Lady Ormington was evidently agitated. Her face,
when flurried, had a peculiarly ridiculous appearance,
like the marble basin of a flower-garden when ruffled
by a stormy wind, which I take to be the wire-wove
edition of a puddle in a storm.

The Honourable Member for Rigmarole, who was
standing up before the fireless fireplace, as Englishmen are apt to do (as one sees a sentinel still on
guard over poor dismantled Kew Palace), looked as
cool as if he had been iced. A lucky presentiment
forewarned me not to nod to him, as usual ; for a
moment afterwards I was honoured by him with a
Grandisonian bow ; one of those bows for which one
hears the foot slide formally on the carpet. The
honourable member saluted me as he would have
done old Votefilch ; and the salutation which, addressed to the minister, had denoted humility, when
addressed to the clerk of the F.O. was, of course, an
impertinence.

The colour rose to my cheek. Not the flush of
anger. No ! I was positively overawed by the
sang-froid of the Hon. John Alexander Danby.
Before I recovered my parts of speech, he had left
the room.

"A pretty business you have made of it," whimpered my mother, as soon as he was out of hearing.

"Business ? *I* guilty of business ?" cried I, trying
to recover my usual flippancy ; "and on the Sabbath ?
Fie ! "

"Don't be absurd, Cis. I am quite nervous enough

without your silly jokes. I tell you, you have irretrievably offended your brother."

" I rejoice to hear it. I was afraid he was only
slightly affronted, which would have given me the
very unnecessary trouble of trying to bring him into
better humour. The word irretrievable decides it. I
love an extreme case."

" *Pray* don't talk such nonsense. If you knew how
completely you depend upon Lord Ormington and
Danby, you would not indulge in these boyish caprices.
I tell you once for all, Cis (and you know that my word
may be depended upon in what concerns your interests),
your only chance of a settlement in life is by conciliating the goodwill of your brother."

" A *settlement*, my dear mother? The very word is
as hard of digestion as a Christmas pine. A *settlement*? Just what Stultz had the audacity to mention
to me yesterday! A settlement? Why, if I were on
the verge of committing matrimony——"

" For *once* be serious," cried Lady Ormington
angrily. " Your position is a most precarious one.
Take warning. Take heed. If Danby were to make
representations to your father of the injury he has
sustained at your hands——"

" Why, what, in Heaven's name, have I done to
him? I cheered his speech till it cost me my month's
allowance at Gunter's for Florence-drops to cure my
hoarseness. I may have said, perhaps, that he
dressed like a gentleman from the Inns of Court,
and so he does. Nay, if Herries, or any other
of my brother clerks, were to require a bow from
me in Pall Mall, buried to the ears in such a coat as
Danby's——"

" Cecil," interrupted Lady Ormington, with more
energy than I had ever seen her exhibit; " had your
brother addressed to his father, instead of myself,
his grievances against you——"

" He has been complaining, then?" cried I. " The
pretty boy has been here, with his finger in his eye,

declaring that unless I beg his pardon for having torn his kite——"

"Do not FORCE me to bring you to reason," cried my mother, with so sudden an assumption of authority that I sat down quietly, prepared to listen patiently to her expostulations. "With all your pretensions to good manners and good sense, Danby has shown, on this occasion, far more than yourself. He came here simply to appeal to me, as your best friend, as your only friend, to engage you to observe towards *him* the same forbearance and reserve he maintains towards *you*. It is his wish, his engagement, indeed, with me, that you should meet in public as friends; and maintain towards each other, in private, the mutual deference of elder and younger brothers."

"And pray, in what point of this extraordinary compact have I failed?" cried I, a sudden and terrible light breaking in upon me, a light which I own I wanted courage to humiliate her and myself by bringing to distinct admission.

"You have injured his reputation, you have wounded his feelings," persisted my mother. "Do you suppose that everybody is as indifferent to good repute as yourself? Do you image that because *your* heart is unsusceptible of attachment——"

"Come, come, mother. If you are going to set up John Danby in the pattern young man line, I must really beg you to let me off," cried I. "I dine at Putney——"

"With Lord Votefilch? How unfortunate. You will meet your brother!"

"Unfortunate, indeed. I have a great mind to break my leg, and send an excuse. Meanwhile," said I, "try to make me understand, in as few words as possible, *where* I have injured the poor fellow's reputation, and *how* I have wounded his feelings?"

"By representing him, last night, in Lady Harriet Vandeleur's box at the opera, as sharing your dissipations. You accused him of being engaged, as well as yourself, in some disgraceful *liaison*."

"Nonsense. I merely silenced Lady Harriet's inquiries concerning a young lady (unknown, I admit, in the fashionable world, but of the highest respectability), by informing her that Danby was as well able as myself to satisfy her curiosity——"

"Which you know very well that he was *not*."

"He *might* have been, since she is the ward of old Hanmer, of Southampton Buildings, with whom my brother keeps up quite as much intercourse as I do."

"Old Hanmer's ward? This completely alters the state of the case," cried Lady Ormington. "Why, she passes in the world for——"

"No matter! The world is an ass. The world believes anything that anybody in the world chooses to assert; yet nobody in the world ever utters a word of truth. And so, after all, Danby feels irreparably injured by being accused of an acquaintance with a charming girl, of good family, of——"

"You are aware, Cis, of Lady Harriet's style of repeating things. Between jest and earnest she attacked your brother about it in the crush-room, with Lady Susan Theydon on his arm, to whom, you are aware, he is paying attention."

"*Danby?* to Lady Susan Theydon? One of the prettiest girls in town."

"You will probably find her Lady Susan Danby before the season is over; that is, if he manages to get over with her mother (who is the most particular woman alive) the unfavourable impression made by Lady Harriet's allusions."

"I am truly sorry the thing has happened," cried I, in all sincerity; "for I can understand, that under such circumstances, he may have felt vexed by what was on my part a mere jest. But why couldn't John Danby come straight up to me, like a man, and ask for an explanation, without all these petticoat negotiations?"

"Because he is under a promise to me never to
to enter into disputes with you of any kind."

I shrugged my shoulders.

"Between my father, who negotiates with me
through his lawyers, and my brother, who treats with
me through your ladyship, I am beginning to fancy
myself a prince in disguise," said I.

"Rather, a beggar in expectancy," faltered Lady
Ormington. "But not a word more, Cecil! I have
said enough to induce you, if you have a grain of good
feeling in your composition, to make the necessary
reparations to your brother."

I was about to utter a bitter rejoinder, when the
butler hastily announced that Lord Chippenham, who
was to drive me down to Putney, was waiting at the
door.

Merciful powers. A toilet of five minutes at midsummer. What had society done to me that I should
insult it by appearing before it under circumstances
so unextenuating ? I dared not reflect upon the interpretation his Majesty's ministers might give to my
dishevelled locks. I thought of Copenhagen—of
the gallant Nelson—of the incautious wafer—and
trembled.

CHAPTER VII.

The proprietors are bitten by the rage of what they fancy to be improvement, and are levelling ground, smoothing banks, and building rockwork, with pagodas and Chinese railing. The laburnums, willows, and flowering shrubs are beginning to be tortured into what the gardener calls genteel shapes. Even the course of the river has been thwarted, and part of its waters diverted into a broad ditch to form an island,—flat, swampy, and dotted over with exotic shrubs.—BECKFORD.

"On y trouve bons compagnons, chère transcendante, vins très vieux, femmes très jeunes, des bougies à faire pâlir le soleil, tous les élémens avec lesquels se fabrique ordinairement la joie humaine."

ENGLAND is thought to excel in villas. A villa is an architectural whim, where every individual is allowed to display his taste or want of taste ; and the Dublin cit, accordingly, places his portico on the second floor, over the verandah ; the Parisian ornaments the sphinxes over his gates, with coquettish straw hats tied under the chin ; and in Holland, rows of tin aloes are ranged in stone vases along the wall. But in the environs of London, ye gods ! from Brentford to Stratford-le-Bow, from Paddington to Putney, what vagaries in brick and mortar, what barbarisms in Portland stone !

In all directions, for ten miles round the capital—villas—villas—villas. A villa is one of the first indications of prosperity on the part of a professional man. Thriving merchants, popular actors, popular dentists, popular lawyers, popular all sorts of things, are sure to have their Tusculum, their Eden, their 'appiness 'ouse ! A villa is the relaxation of a laborious life, the restoration of an unwholesome one ; and the days of many a cabinet minister have been lengthened in the land by his Gloucester Lodge or Footscray, his Ealing or Hayes.

But above all, a villa is an essentially aristocratic appurtenance.   Lords and ladies cannot dispense with a green and sunny nook, in which to go and hide their heads when they are glad or sorry ; in the sweets of a honeymoon, or sours of widowhood.

Among these there are doubtless a few such as

Youthful poets fancy, when they love.

There is Chiswick, matchless Chiswick.   There is Strawberry Hill, somewhat the worse for wear, but classic ground, every inch of it ;—Gunnersbury, where the flowers and fruit are formed, like those of Aladdin's magic garden of rubies and emeralds ; Sion, Wimbledon, Mount Felix, Ken Wood, Osterley.   *Where* conclude, if once we venture to begin, the enumeration of our suburban residences ?

In point of truth, the excellence we claim for the villas of London resides less in their site, than in the intensity of verdure engendered by our ever-weeping climate.   Their real attraction consists in the soft green turf, overshaded here and there by a clump of beeches, a shapely tulip-tree or drooping cedar, skirted at intervals by parterres of geraniums, or creepers trained in fanciful devices, throwing themselves like fountains of blossoms into the air ; while clumps of the choicer shrubs, allspice-trees, magnolias, or the gum cistus, exale their musky perfumes, like Moorish slaves swinging their censers of incense.

I speak all this feelingly, for one of the favourite subjects of my mother's grumbling was the want of a villa.   Ormington Hall was in Lancashire, a two days' —nay, for a nervous lady, a three days' journey from town.   What was to become of her at Easter and Whitsuntide ?   What was she to do during family mournings or other plaintive exigencies ?   Her sole resource was Brighton ; everybody's resource, from the prince to the haberdasher.   It was enough to put her out of conceit with being out of spirits, to have to exhibit her black crape or blue devils on the Steyne.

There was a time when I used to agree with Lady Ormington. It seemed a deuced hard thing to have no intermediary spot betwixt the Hall and Hanover Square ; some genteel purgatory between paradise and its antipodes. Every now and then, in the cowslip season, her ladyship used to be taken rural, and "babble of green fields." She would sigh over the advertisements of the auctioneers, grandiloquizing the glories of Richmond Hill, or the beauties of Shenley, till "the greenth and gloomth" of Horace Walpole were outdone. I really thought Lord Ormington would have to end with bartering his borough for the rangership of the parks ; or one of his Yorkshire woods for a grove of Canada poplars in the purlieus of Primrose Hill.

But now that my official helotism was beginning to familiarize me with the ministerial snuggeries ranged along the river from Vauxhall Bridge to that of Richmond, in white and sparkling rows, like the mineral teeth of a Desirabode, I was beginning to thank his obduracy. How befrogged I used to feel after one of those dinners of Votefilch's. Nothing but Undine could have swum it. Will-o'-the-wisps must have danced oftentimes after nightfall over his lordship's lawn ; and his ponds and tanks bore forcible resemblance to tureens of green-pea soup or basins of turtle. I fancied I felt fins expanding after a day in his charming fen.

The drawing-room windows commanded a view of an osier-bed on the opposite bank ; not rising out of the water, however, for that might have impaired a canaletto-like charm ; or intitled one to dream of "Sabrina fair," uplifting her "pearly arms" from the "pure translucent wave." But between the pewter-tinted Thames, and the dingy sallows, there stagnated, even at high tide, a strip of alluvial soil, barely concealed by patches of coarse rushes ; while, at low tide, were perceptible some twenty yards of that filthiest deposit of London and its suburbs, called Thames mud ; compelling one, at times, to hold one's nose, and inclining one, at others, to close one's eyes.

On one side of Maybush Lodge, there was a great soap manufactory, which indicted itself as a nuisance once a quarter, in order to be beforehand with its neighbours and pocket the informer's fine ; while, on the other, reeked a brewery. A distant view of a patent oil mill completed the charm.

But then the river,—

> The exulting and abounding river,—

the charming, bright, cool, refreshing river ; the river so propitious to the natatorial essays of preparatory schools no less than to the termination of the woes of certain deluded sempstresses, misled by the Tempter in the Eden of Cumberland Tea-gardens ; the river of coal-barges and lighters, funny-clubs and wherries ; where, three times a week or so, one has the satisfaction of beholding the victims of much punch dashed against the piers of the bridges, and dived for by the jolly young watermen, as though they were the pearls of Ormus or the wreck of the Royal George.

Oh ! happy river,—

> That rollest by the ancient walls
> Where dwells the lady of my love ;

whose flounders, like Mithridates, fatten on poison ; whose whitebait delight in gas, and whose eels luxuriate in pyroligneous acid : sooner locate beside the fœtid banks of a Batavian canal, sooner become a toll-keeper of Lethe's wharf, than breathe my summer breath within scent of thine unsavoury odours, within reach of thy pandemoniacal sounds.

Lord Votefilch's villa was one of the best of those compact white dwelling-houses, " seated," as George Robins calls it, " on a verdant lawn," like a solitary billiard-ball lying on its green table. The house was commodious within ; without, of Doric architecture. Nothing fanciful about it, nothing rustic. But it was as damp as a catacomb, unless during the dog-days, when its frontage lay exposed to a glaring south-western sun.

Maybush Lodge was the growth of royal favouritism. It had been created in George the Second's time by the old Duke of Newcastle; and during the long reign of his royal grandson had as regularly alternated with the Whigs and Tories, as if a part of the administration. What tales could its wainscots have unfolded, if wainscots were included in the category of wooden orators. What conspiracies (against the country) had been hatched in its premier-coop. What wars and rumours of wars had gone forth from its portals. How often had France been sent to the devil under its coved ceilings; how often the balance of power weighed in its scales, and found wanting! Poor Maybush Lodge. Green eyrie, to which the crook-beaked birds of prey retreat to feed their young with young ones torn from the nests of other birds, what heaps of whitened bones my mind's eye seemed to descry around the retreat of the plunderers.

To do mine host justice, no one could more gallantly lay aside the cares of state, or hang up more resolutely in his hall the toga of public life. There was a Lady Votefilch; a woman of a certain age and uncertain temper, whose former beauty one took for granted, though little trace of it remained, as the only means of accounting for the infatuation which had rendered so shrewd a man the proprietor of such a nonentity. There was a niece, too, either of hers or his, who resided with them, a certain Lady Theresa, the idol of my colleagues in Downing Street. It was a matter of special duty among such of them as were admitted to share the venison and household leisure of the great man, to fall in love with Lady Theresa.

I scarely know why. She was not old, not ugly, not disagreeable; negative qualities at best; but it was like finding a flower in the wilderness, to discover anything approaching to young, pretty, or agreeable,

among those bald heads and withered faces. The first
time I saw her sitting there among them, mute and
undemonstrative, I wondered what Chippenham, Herries, and the rest of them had found in her, to turn
their heads. But after a dinner or two at Maybush
Lodge, I began to examine her more curiously ; to
experience an interest in her merits ; to watch her
inexpressive blue eyes with the hope of detecting
some talent, sentiment, or emotion. She was the only
very human thing present. A bird which alights
upon the mast during a sea voyage is an object of
intense interest to the mariner, however dingy its
plumage or poor its note.

To make the agreeable to Lady Votefilch and her
niece, at the Sunday dinners, was part of the week's
duty. The major part of the task was easy enough.
Lady V was a vain foolish woman, not too fastidious
in the quality of adulation. To compliment her on
her beauty had been scandal in disguise. But she
was content to accept the far more easily levied
tribute of compliments upon her toilet. She cared for
nothing but dress. While the Right Honourable Earl
was inventing political combinations and speculating
upon European alliances, she was caballing with
Madame Le Brun, the Talleyrand of *modistes*, concerning revolutions in caps, and conspiracies against
turbans that be.

To such a woman, Cecil the son of Lady Ormington,
the Lady Ormington, could not but be an object of
interest ; and when she found I had tact enough to
refrain from dedicating my sighs with the general
monsoon of the Foreign Office to Lady Theresa, she
concluded that I recognized my insufficiencies as a
younger son, and begged Lord Votefilch to honour
my forbearance by a general invitation. He knew
better ; for he really wished to see me familiarly at
his table, and consequently restricted his civility to
giving me a formal invitation more freouently than to
the rest of his quill machinery.

Chippenham and I arrived late. When we made our appearance, dinner had been announced, and people were pairing slowly off with much form and ceremony, to traverse in couples twelve yards of Brussels carpeting, over which they would have stepped singly without embarrassment. Old Votefilch was conducting a fine-looking woman, known to me by name and history. Then came her ladyship, escorted by a stupid-looking man, who I saw must be somebody, or he would not have presumed to look so stupid. Lastly, came Lady Theresa, arm-in-arm with the lion of the hour, with Danby. It was Chippenham's privilege and place; but my dilatoriness had deprived him of his honours; and we were compelled to scuffle in with Herries and two great unknowns, to promiscuous places at table.

Though far from in my best of humours, I was soon interested in the conversation; which, at such tables, flows as naturally as if served round with the soup. The two nondescripts were official men of first-rate abilities, on their preferment; the glassy-eyed individual supporting Lady Votelfilch, was Lord Falkirk, a man who affected dulness as Pope Sixtus caducity, in order to influence, unsuspected, the conclave or privy council; and the tall handsome woman in white satin, was one of those showy intrigantes, those prima-donnas of society, who, whatever minister shall reign, are always to be found in musk-scented correspondence with Downing Street.

It was none of these, however, who imparted the colloquial charm to that chatty little party. It was the man who seemed determined to extinguish me by his superiority, in private as in public life. As the trunk of the elephant is constituted to pick up a straw after crushing the body of a man, Danby seemed bent on proving to his humiliated younger brother, that his small talk was as great as his speaking was effective. He could drive a tandem as readily as the car of Juggernaut.

To do him justice, I never met a more agreeable
man.   There was something fascinating beyond description in the melodious refinement of his enunciation.
His tone was easy, his language fluent ; and he was as
good a listener as ready in reply ; prompt in argument,
modest in pursuing an advantage.   Budge and Fudge,
the official aspirants, were evidently vexed to find
themselves thrown into the shade by so young a man.
But they were soon reconciled.   There is no disgrace
in being eclipsed by Jupiter.

Next to the chattiness of my brother, the thing
that struck me most, was the influence of time and
place on my collaborators, Chippenham and Herries.
Herries was, by birth and education, official.   He
was the Asmodeus of an ink-bottle.   His cradle had
been a despatch-box ; his swaddling-clothes were
sheets of government foolscap.   At the desk, he was
great, for the atmosphere of Downing Street was as
natal air to him ; and like Antæus, on touching
treasury-ground he became invincible.   I had always
stood in awe of Herries' superior abilities, when I
saw him issue from the Blue Chamber, with confidential documents in his hand, such as were intrusted by
Lord Votefilch to no sub. but himself.

But at Maybush Lodge, his distinctions vanished.
At Maybush Lodge, the peacock became a dingy jay
again.   I suppose it was because he did not feel himself
at ease ; but he was tongue-tied.   He joined in the conversation only to become an obstruction.   A fastidious
choice of expressions embarrassed his diction.   He
became heavy and verbose from trying to talk too
well ; missed the point of every story he attempted
to relate ; and filled up the pauses of his conversation
with an unmeaning laugh.

Chippenham, on the contrary, who was anything but
a genius, and who at the office passed for a ninny,
became talkative and agreeable among people of his
caste.   The subjects discussed were familiar to him.
His pockets were full of the small change current in

such society. He had twice as much to say as Halbert Herries ; or rather, with half as much to say, quadrupled it by his easy unaffected mode of expression. I perceived that with *him* Danby was quite ready to talk and listen ; whereas, when poor Herries addressed him, he fixed his eyes vacantly on the stammering man, who seemed baffled by the redundancy of his ideas or the insufficiency of his elocution. I was amused ; perhaps, a little gratified. In the office, Herries had the best of it. Whenever Chippenham, or I, or Percy, or De l'Isle stood convicted of the blunders inevitable to even the cleverest of novices, he used to over-crow us without ceremony. I was not sorry to see him silenced by my brother.

At that period, the Whigs and Tories of public life, whether dictating to the House, or disputing after dinner with the drouthiness of men whose real business in life is that of converting full decanters into empty ones, were now divided into a party maintaining that one Englishman could lick four Frenchmen, or that England " bangs Banagher, which bates the world ; " and a party beholding in Napoleon a man in command of the powers of darkness,—Demogorgon, minus his hoofs. The after-dinner politics of London consisted of " Are we to annihilate the French, or are the French to annihilate *us ?* " It is rather late in the history of the world to assign such overweening majesty to the edge of the sword. It was one of the evidences of the brutalizing power of war, that, from long contemplation of perpetual and bloody conflict, we were retrograding to the insensibilities of the dark ages. The law of the stronger was becoming our Alpha and Omega.

Precisely on this point, was the superiority of Danby's mind apparent. His ideas were not exclusively extracted from the returns of the War Office, or the statistics of Extraordinary Gazettes. Danby marched with the times, or, rather, marched with the pioneers who clear the way for the progress of the

L

times. It was upon the force of public opinion and
the strength of popular feeling throughout Europe,
that he grounded his calculations. His judgment was
not moulded by peremptory articles in Quarterly
Reviews. He was a scholar, and a ripe one. His
studies at Ormington Hall were not comprised, as I
had chosen to imagine, within limit of the Aldine
authorities. Herodotus and Thucydides were but the
plinth of the column of his universal knowledge.
The modern, living, breathing, circulating literature
of Europe, the pulses and arteries of the contempo-
raneous body of mankind, constituted the pillar's
strength.

French, German, Italian, nay, even the Sclavonic
languages, were familiar to him ; and, liberally supplied
with the best publications of the day, he possessed a
key to the gates of that mighty continent, from which,
as by a miracle, we were so long shut out. In the
progress of public enlightenment, he traced the progress of public events. It was from the excitement
of Germany, the indignation of Russia, the resentments of Holland, that he drew his horoscope of
France; and foretold the downfall of a triton of the min-
nows, a Gulliver among the Liliputians, a Cæsar among
the principicules of Germany, whom the liberals of
France detested as *un grand homme avorté en empereur,*
a conqueror whose foot was not only upon the neck of
humbled nations but upon that of public opinion, the
executioner of the Duc d'Enghien and of the liberty
of the press ; a man whose greatness was composed of
the wrecks of a great revolution, as the early temples
of Italy were framed of shattered fragments of the
noble architecture of former ages.

Newsvendors' horns were not his only organs of information. Wellington might be a great general ; but
Danby opined that a still more powerful instrument
was the combination of the many against the tyranny
of the one ; a balance of power, having France and
its cannon in one scale, and Europe, with the con-

sciousness of right, in the other. He foresaw clearly, and announced moderately, that the days of the empire were numbered.

Nothing more enrages a knot of middle-aged official men, who have been buffeting all their lives with the waves, till familiar with the strength of unseen currents and the peril of sunken rocks (the practical difficulties of public life), than to find a young fellow, necessarily a mere theorist, pretend to see further through the mist than themselves. It is useless to insinuate that, while engaged in the difficult operation of keeping their heads above water, *he* may have been stationed in the lighthouse, beholding,

—————— "as from a tower, the end of all;"

a warden, anxiously watching the operations of contending parties.

To the arguments modestly put forth by the young member for Rigmarole, accordingly, Budge and Fudge replied by interchanging glances of contempt. They knew nothing, not they, of the power and views of Russia. They cared nothing about Berlin. Germany was, to *them*, a country where a deluded population applauded Schiller's Robbers, or whimpered over the sorrows of Werther. They quoted Pitt and Fox, Windham and Percival; they talked about invariable principles, and the wisdom of our ancestors. But they wanted to hear nothing about the continent. The quarrel lay in a nutshell; the question was comprised in the Peninsula. It was there the oriflamme was displayed. It was there that the British cabinet was writing its leading articles in characters of blood.

But for old Votefilch, Danby would have been talked down. But the Right Hon. Secretary understood the art of extracting information, even under the semblance of disparagement; and took care that the young talker, who talked not for victory but out of the abundance of his heart, should have "ample

L 2

space and verge enough" for the manifestations of his
knowledge.

I saw Lady Votefilch shrug her shoulders in despair.
She had hoped better things of an elder brother of
mine (for herself), and better things of an elder son of
Lord Ormington (for Lady Theresa). Even I, as regarded my own feelings, should have been better
pleased to find him less earnestly occupied with politics
at that moment. I had made up my mind to a frank
explanation with him. My heart was more open
towards John than it had been since our days of
nankin frocks ; and I trusted to see him more reserved
in my presence. I had even hoped to find him angry.
It is a work of labour and sorrow to stir up the cold
embers of indifference.

Most young people fall into the blunder of attributing
to all other human natures the strength or weakness of
their own, or, as my friend Fetlock expressed it, "they
buy and sell by their own bushel." I, for instance,
chose to judge of Danby by myself ; my Self, like most
other young men, warm-hearted and generous while
glorying in the affectation of superciliousness and folly.
But there are spirits both brighter and blacker than
this sweeping denomination ; and Danby was of the
minority. I shall not explain whether of the elect
virtuous or elect vicious. But he was better or worse
than the common herd. When, taking him apart after
dinner, I entered warmly into my self-exculpation,
instead of expanding into the generous warmth I
anticipated, admitting himself to have been over-hasty,
and, like the hero of a German comedy, throwing himself into my arms and swearing eternal friendship, he
listened calmly, judged dispassionately, advised me to
be more prudent in the selection of my confidants, and
turned on his heel.

I was furious. I had accosted him, charged to the
muzzle with magnanimity ; my coxcombry laid aside—
my envyings and jealousies subdued—my fraternal
sympathies glowing. His coolness chilled me to the

heart's core. I had only despised the ugly John of former days. I *hated* the Honourable Member for Rigmarole, at whose bidding the stormy debaters were still.

Biting my lip till the blood started, I lounged across the drawing-room, and affected as much devotion to that classical antique Lady Votefilch, as the tall beauty, Mrs. Wrottesley, was bestowing upon the foreign affairs; and, on sufficiently recovering my composure to glance round the room, saw that Lord Falkirk was talking apart with my brother ; while Budge, Fudge, and Halbert Herries stood pretending to converse together ; their ears pricked up to catch a word here and there of the conversation. Even Chippenham, though smiled upon by the gentle Lady Theresa, was evidently wanting to get away and hear what Danby was saying. His influence had fixed its teeth upon them all. The power of the strong mind was manifest. Danby had snatched the tiara from their hands, and crowned himself Infallible.

We had scarcely even noted the transcendent excellence of a dinner dressed by the Francatelle of his day. We had not so much as found fault with (the common criterion of approval) the finest claret then extant in port-bibbing England. We did not perceive that the lawns of Maybush were steeped in delicious moonlight, or that the fragrance of a thousand flower-beds was stealing in through the windows ; and Lady Theresa and Mrs. Wrottesley smiled as vainly as the moon was shining.

There was but one way of breaking the charm. Lady Votefilch asked for " a little music." Forth came the harp, and up started Chippenham, who sang charmingly in every style. Not a more efficient method of delivering society from the ascendancy of a superior man than to call for that general extinguisher of light —" a little music."

The only bad result to myself was that Chippenham, to whom, on our return to town, I was inclined to enlarge upon the bore of the whole thing, was so pleased at having heard himself sing, that he forgot having heard my brother hold forth. I could have killed him for the good faith with which he declared that he had been spending a very pleasant evening.

He put the finishing-stroke to my ill-humour as we passed Hyde Park Corner (where a huge turnpike used in those days bid every man stand and deliver, ere he set foot in London), by inquiring whether he should meet me at dinner, at Morley's, the following day.

" *Not asked ?* How came that about ? "

Is there a greater impertinence than to inquire the motive of one's being omitted from some agreeable party ?

CHAPTER VIII.

Se amor non è, che dunque sento ?

PETRARCA.

How the first little rubs of life linger in one's memory ! I have had my share of grievances. I have drunk my fill of vinegar and hyssop. Yet I can recall to mind, even now, the irritation of smarting under the impertinence of Lady Harriet Vandeleur, the contempts of Morley, the vulgar quizzing of Jack Harris, and above all, the coolness of my brother.

There are moments when petty slights are harder to bear than a serious injury. Men have died of the festering of a gnat-bite ; yet, strange to tell, the only person on whom I visited my vexation of spirit was one who had never offered me offence ; Emily was the victim. Not even her pale anxious face, watching for me throughout the opera and ballet, exercised an extenuating influence. She looked as sad as a white

rose over a sepulchre. Yet I remained cruel—cruel
as a grand inquisitor or a jealous woman.

I never went near her. Poor Emily! Though I
had almost given up my project relative to Lady
Harriet, I could not make up my mind to condescend
again so readily. Besides, *she* was always attainable.
I might take her up again at any time. *That* was the
secret of my coolness. We grow indifferent to bless-
ings whose continuance is assured : the light of the
sun—the bursting of the spring—all the fairest phe-
nomena of nature. I should have taken the trouble,
perhaps, to ascend to the old box, had I surmised that
I was fated never to see her there again. For after
that night it remained empty. It was some comfort
not to see it polluted by strange faces ; particularly
such faces as one usually espies at that ignominious,
altitude. But it had been let for the season to the
d'Acunhas, who neither returned nor underlet it.

After the first night of missing them from the spot,
how I used to sit and watch that box. No astronomer
waiting the rising of his newly-discovered planet could
be more intensely anxious. My "upturned and wondering eyes" must have given me a strangely ridiculous
appearance. But, for once, I was not thinking of
appearances.

I bore it for a week—a fortnight ; still, not a vestige
of her. The season was drawing to a close. I had
taken no heed of its waning pleasures since I became
anxious about Emily. I was haunted by the pale
pensive face, of which I had merely said, at the time,
" Emily is not in beauty to-night. I will go and visit
her another time."

The last representation of the season took place.
Everybody who frequents the opera, and happens to be
in town, is sure to be there on the last night ; and I
made sure of seeing her. I provided myself with one
of her favourite magnolias. I felt my cheek burn with
eagerness as I took my station in the pit, with my eyes
uplifted as usual. I dare say Morley was in Lady

Harriet's box. I never looked. I was thinking only
of Emily.

But the box was again vacant.   That night it
looked like a tomb. I knew that my last chance of
meeting her was at an end. For six gloomy months
no opera. For six gloomy months that box, so long a
paradise, must remain a little, dusty, damp, ill-savoured
closet, given over to mice and spiders. I hurried up to
sit there once more. The box-keeper readily admitted
me ; and I took Emily's place behind the curtain. I
even laid down the magnolia before it on the crimson
cushion, as if she were there. The scent of vanille
lingered there still, as though its former inmates had
only just quitted the place ; and so powerfully were
they brought before me by the association, that I
kept expecting every minute to hear their voices by
my side.

I could stand this suspense no longer. Next day,
after office, I went straight to Southampton Buildings.
Nay, I inquired explicitly and without hesitation for
Miss Barnet. I was desperate.

My inquiry struck no amazement into Pepper-and-
Salt. He seemed almost prepared for it ; almost to
expect that one of Mr. Hanmer's clients should knock
at the door, and ask to see his ward ; and there was
a twinkle of satisfaction in the creature's eye, as he
announced that " Miss Emily warn't there no longer."

" Was she gone to Monsieur d'Acunha's ? "

" May-be she was, may-be she warn't ; he couldn't
say. Should he inquire of the head clerk ? "

It was, of course, more agreeable to me to inquire
of d'Acunha himself. So away I went to Burton
Crescent. A bill up ! THIS HOUSE TO LET ! Deeply
mortified, I turned my horse's head once more towards
the West-end. But on reaching Portland Road, I
had the weakness to turn, and to return. Perhaps
the person charged to show the house, might afford
information. I alighted, and requested to look at it ;
and the dry, withered, wooden thing in a green-baize

apron, man, woman, child, for it seemed to partake of
all three, immediately began to enlarge upon the size
of the "parlours" and the extreme convenience of
sinks and pumps; sufficiently innocent of this world's
sophistications, to believe that a person of *my*
manners and appearance entertained serious intentions towards a house in Burton Crescent, at a period
of the year when filberts and jargonelle pears were
coming into season.

I inquired after the last lodgers : it knew nothing
about them. It was "put in by the house-agent."
It "s'posed the last ludgers was furriners; for the
house smelt of backy enough to p'ison one." It even
wanted to tell me how much soap and how many
scrubbing-brushes had been required to obliterate the
d'Acnnhas.

I went home, thoroughly wretched. While my
illusions lasted, I had scarcely noted the progress of
the season. They were gone, and I discovered that I
was alone. All was over. There was not only no
Emily, but no London. At Watier's that night,
scarcely a soul. It had never occurred to me before,
that a government clerk was a denizen of Downing
Street ; that the rest of the world shot grouse, toured
to the lakes, or betook itself to the silvery sands of
the Isle of Wight ; while a clerkly pen must perforce
remain in the ink, and a clerkly hand on the pounce-
box. I began to think (as I sulked in the corner of
the sofa at Watier's, sole monarch of all I surveyed),
like a grumbling minister, who has been snubbed
by his sovereign, or by his sovereign's sovereign, the
House of Commons, about sending in my resignation.

The recollection of Lord Ormington's stiff condi-
tions touching the ways and means, luckily suspended
my resolution. I had not forgotten Lady Harriet's
advice to me, not to trifle with Lord Ormington.
Moreover, he was out of town. I had never missed
him. I ought to have inferred that he was gone ; for
parliament was up, and our officials comparatively out

of harness. Nothing remained but the clerks and the
desks : the rest of the wooden furniture had migrated.
But though the rumble of Lord Ormington's carriage
every evening had ceased, and the grumble of Lord
Votefilch's discontent every morning, I had been unconscious of my loss.

Such among my readers as may have been compelled
to outlast the season in London, from being in office,
in love, or in debt, must recollect the strangeness of
suddenly discovering, like Aladdin, that the magic
palace has disappeared. For the last month, we notice
with a sensation of relief hosts of travelling-carriages
departing. The dull and elderly go first. All June
and July, one sees family-coaches setting forth with
post-horses, as one is coming home from balls. And
then, there is triumph in remaining; for it is the select
few who are left, to do all sorts of pleasant things
never attempted so long as the mob remains undeci-
mated. It is a distinction to be one of the court-
cards kept in hand. Carlton House was never so
brilliant as during the dog-days. The last fortnight
of the season resembles one of those fine summer's
nights when only stars of the first magnitude are
visible ; when favourite constellations stand out in
relief ; the myriads of little stars having hidden their
diminished heads.

But this distinction imparts only a deeper shade to
succeeding darkness. On the day which rouses us to
the consciousness of being alone in hot, dusty London,
when the oblique rays of the autumnal sun betray the
coating of soot and dust incrusting the houses, when
the sparrows, grown tame, hop chirping impertinently
along the streets, when the city looks and smells like
a city of apple-stalls, when shopmen stand with pens
behind their ears on the door-steps instead of behind
their counters, when the suburban theatres and gardens placard the walls and palings with every variety
of coloured paper, announcing every sameness of
colourless entertainment ; then it is we suddenly

inquire where all the people are gone. And Echo answers " Where ?"

What a relief when the hollow nymph favoured *me* for the first time with this contemptuous reply, to reflect upon Lady Ormington's morbid appetite for the metropolis. It was an unspeakable comfort to think that our house was not going to be shuttered up like the rest. On the day I returned home from my expedition to the house agent's who had the letting of the "family mansion" in Burton Crescent, with information that the d'Acunhas had sailed by the Oporto packet, on the first of the month, for Portugal, and that, to the best of his belief, they were accompanied by a young English lady, name unknown, I could scarcely have borne to find myself in an uninhabited house. Even Bibiche was better company than my thoughts.

For my reflections were anything but rose-coloured. I was fain to confess that, with all my tact and cleverness, my season had been a failure. I had achieved nothing. My advantages had been great, the result— *fiasco.* My squinting brother was at the top of the tree. The last object that struck me, on the last night of the opera, was Jack Harris installed in the Vandeleurs' box ; not on sufferance, but smiled upon and encouraged by Lady Harriet and Lady Devereux ; evidently on the way to obtain waistcoat the third. Chippenham was the established pet of Maybush Lodge ; and Danby was gone down to Lady Warburton's family seat, as the accepted lover of Lady Susan Theydon. Everybody had paired off, saving myself.

When these humiliating conclusions occurred to me, I presumed to accuse Emily as the origin of my failure. Second thoughts whispered "Curse not Southampton Buildings, even in thy chamber." A painful presentiment already connected itself in my mind with the sweet face I had seen looking so sorrowfully down upon me from the opera-box.

The impression did not diminish as the autumn
drew on. The torment of London, *out* of the season,
is that one day telleth another, and one night certifieth
another : eternal sameness, the sameness of a sea-
voyage. Even the business of my official morning
was thrice as tedious as during the session of parliament. The gods were departed ; the master-spirits
gone who imparted relief to my labours. There was
no one left beside myself but Herries, — plodding
Herries ; one silent senior clerk, pretty much on a
par, in point of intellect, with Babbage's Calculating
Machine ; and two or three juniors, whose chief recreation, like my own and other natives', consisted in
gaping. The parks were enveloped in mist. The
town lay rotting like the fat weed on Lethe's wharf.
It was like a city of the plague ; nay, worse. In
the terrible descriptions of Defoe and Boccaccio,
there is something to excite the two strongest of
our sympathies, pity and terror. Autumnal London
excites nothing but *ennui*. I would as soon dig in a
lead-mine.

I record all this by way of apology for the infatuation with which I soon began to attach myself to the
recollection of Emily Barnet. I had fitted up my
second chamber as a sort of study, a study of anything
but books ; for I neither was, nor pretended to be, a
reading man. But I studied there something more
valuable in the perusal than printed paper. I studied
my Self ; I studied the past. My leisure was the
leisure of busy reverie. Whether seated, meerschaum
in hand, before my sparkling fire, or pacing my rooms
with listless steps, I was absorbed in living over again
the events of the last few months, arm-in-arm with
Cecil Danby.

And how wonderfully did poor Emily gain by the
retrospection. How sweetly did her words and looks
come back upon my memory. I could recall to mind
only what was thoroughly attractive, thoroughly
attaching. I had never heard a sentiment escape her

lips that was not noble and gracious. I had never seen her indulge in a look or attitude but might have served as the model for an artist. An atmosphere of poetry surrounded her, communicating a charm to all she touched, all she addressed. I recalled to mind the originality of her opinions, the freshness of her ideas, the vividness of her expressions, the tenderness of her attachment for her absent father; and no longer wondered that such companionship had estranged me from the vapid nothingness of the great world. Lady Harriet was equally brilliant—more brilliant. But in her, not a touch of nature. In her, not a gleam of the womanliness imparting so surpassing a charm to the conversation of Emily.

And this angelic being was lost to me for ever. I had ascertained beyond a doubt that she was gone. At the time I was harassing myself with expeditions to Bloomsbury, she was already on the high seas; on her way to the land of citron-groves, and the parent whose protection she should never have quitted. I should see and hear of her no more. Had she remained in England, perhaps we should have been equally alienated; for a Miss Emily Barnet could never be more than a Miss Emily Barnet to Cis Danby. Still, it was something to be within reach of such an embellishment to one's existence; like knowing that a volume of choice poetry is at hand, which we may snatch up and peruse, when we find the realities of life growing too hard for our digestion.

Sometimes my reveries assumed a less favourable colour. After excess of solitude, as after all excesses, a reaction of feeling takes place. I used to gratify my irritation by uttering blasphemies against my Egeria. She had come upon me so strangely, and departed so mysteriously, nay, she was so disconnected with the world of which I formed a part, that I began almost to doubt her existence. "Earth hath its bubbles, and she was of them." I thought of Melusina the sorceress, beloved by the Comte de Poitiers; whose face was that of an angel, whose body that of a serpent. I thought—But why recapitulate the foolish fancies of a lover or madman? After all, if I had fallen into the snare of an enchantress, there was some pride in having retained, after a college education, the generous weakness which admits of becoming a dupe.

I struggled hard to get out of the net. Fine sentiment was not the order of the day. The pallid muse of Byron, in her black-crape weepers, had not yet brought despair and anguish into fashion. There was no encouragement to turn Octavian, or let grow one's beard. After all, if I had overrated my destinies, if I had mistaken the salutation of the weird sisters on my arrival in London, if I had fancied that I was to be king of (the *beau monde*) hereafter, hereafter was a wide word. I need not yet despair of my enthronization. Jack Harris might have made his way faster. But his extinction would probably be rapid in proportion to his elevation, like the fusee of a rocket. Danby might be crowned with laurels ; but they would, perhaps, wither while mine were flourishing.

I determined, in short, to box it out with destiny, and put myself in a Cribb-like attitude for a milling-match with my fortunes ; and when at length even Lady Ormington's maternal sensibilities were insufficient to detain her in a city where nothing remained but Irish bricklayers and gentlemen compelled to live by rule, I dashed down to Melton, while *she* departed for the Hall ; and by dint of drinking and riding at the pace at which Satan might ride and drink when indulging in one of those "Walks on earth" which Porson and multitudes of imitators have immortalized in the "verse that eternally saves" (even Satan), I returned to Downing Street at the close of my six weeks' leave of absence, witht he tremor of my heart transferred to my hands.

Between agitation of mind and body I was now thoroughly done up.

I went through my duties like one walking in his

sleep. Unless when a packet arrived from Lisbon, I
found it impossible to interest myself in the progress
of public affairs. I had ascertained that the vessel
which bore the d'Acunhas from this country had
reached Portugal in safety. I knew that she was back
again with her fond father, back again at Cintra, back
again among those beloved haunts of cliff and shore
which she used to paint with such bewildering
enthusiasm. So much the better. All that remained
for me was to recommence life anew, from the point
at which I had been distracted from my career by this
luckless acquaintance. I had just attained my majority ;
an excellent epoch for a new start.

It happened that Chippenham, into whose society I
was thrown by the business of the office, was nearly
as much out of sorts with fortune as myself. After
falling into the snare set for him by Lady Votefilch,
which *he* called falling desperately in love with
Lady Theresa, his father, Lord Merepark, was kind
enough to extricate him by an assurance in writing,
that he was too young to settle, and that for many
years to come it was out of his power to make a settlement upon him. It is well known that next to a pipe
of port, there is nothing so difficult to settle as the
eldest son of a peer of the realm.

Chippenham had no means of helping himself. The
Votefilches dared not encourage him to bring down on
them the displeasure of a father having three boroughs
and a half at his disposal ; and all that remained for
him was to join with me in execrating the ruggedness
of the course of true love, and in exorcizing the little
god by the power of a bigger ; Bacchus versus Cupid.
I scarcely know the love that could stand out against
a couple of bottles of claret a day, topped up with
Garus punch.

The Flemish painters are greatest in their delinea-
tions of the most unsightly objects ; and Hobbema is
never more admirable than in a weedy ditch. I am
not so sure of a genius for depicting sloughs ; and will

consequently pass over the dissipation of two desperate
boys, in the enjoyment of too much leisure, cash, and
health ; and finding an apology for their vicious inclinations, in the pretext of having a secret sorrow to
escape from.   Nowadays, when a young man is
affected by a fever of the heart, or ague of the mind,
such as the feelings which drove us into folly, he goes
abroad.   The continent is a mighty safety-valve.   It
is surprising the quantity of vice that escapes in
that direction.   But during war, people were obliged
to stay and sow their wild oats in London ; and fertile
was the crop ever ripe for the sickle.   The coffee-
room at Stevens's could tell tales if it chose.   But
it had better hold its tongue.

If the brilliant coteries of the fashionable world
had been unable to efface the impression made upon
me by the fascinations of Emily, it was not likely that
the unrefined, unlettered heroines with whom I was
now in contact, should obliterate that charming recollection.   It required the madness of an orgy to render
me sufficiently blind and deaf to support their company, even for an hour.   I can understand the fable of
the Sirens having been invented for such creatures ;
only that in modern times one is forced to put cotton
in one's ears to avoid the disgust of their discourse,
instead of the fascination of their song.

Do what I would, however, laugh and listen, or
listen and sneer, eat, drink, and be merry, or merely
drink and be sad, the ever-haunting face and form
were before me.   My follies and vices appeared to
add new force to the vividness of the impression.
As the treasures of Herculaneum and Pompeii
have been preserved in pristine freshness by showers
of cinders, the lava, intended for the destruction
of the image cherished in my heart, served for its
preservation.

The only sacrifice, the only victim was myself.   After
months of vulgar dissipation, I found myself more
irritable in temper, more infirm in health ; and

thoroughly disgusted with my profligate companions. People were returning to town again. But whether they came or stayed away, I cared not. Parliament was about to unloose its thousand tongues. But whether they wagged wisely, or too well, was a matter of indifference. A cloud was upon my spirit. I was only half a coxcomb. I seldom appeared in Lady Ormington's coterie; never in those of her gay associates. I was becoming a lost man.

One day, it was but a few before the meeting of parliament, and I was beginning to anticipate Lord Ormington's presence superadded to my domestic displeasures, when I was struck by the elongated visage of Herries, issuing from the Blue Chamber at the Foreign Office.

"What is the matter, Hal?" cried Chippenham. "Is Grimgruffinhoff vicious this morning? Has he quarrelled with the syntax of your last despatch, or——"

To our great surprise, Herries, who was the meekest of mankind, replied by dashing down his papers on the table, with the addition of an interjection not to be found in any polite dictionary.

"My dear fellow, you seem strangely out of sorts?" said I, looking up from my desk, almost envying him the power of being in a rage with anything so small as a Secretary of State.

"And so would *you*," cried Herries, white with suppressed ire, "if, after having drudged here, as I have been doing for the last fourteen months without applying for a day's holiday, and being, at length, on the eve of asking for two month's leave, for the purpose of—of—no matter!"

"Well, well, we will take the purpose for granted. If, after all this, you say, we were to—what?"

"To be sent pitching across the Bay of Biscay, in the month of December, to deliver despatches to Sir Charles Stuart, which would be quite as safe in the hands of John the porter."

M

" Off to Lisbon ?" cried Chippenham—Percy—all of
us at once.

"Lucky dog !" added I, in a lower tone, and no
longer in chorus.

"Lucky ?" exclaimed Herries, angrily taking me up.
" I should like to see *you* resign yourself to such luck !
I should like to see Lord Votefilch send any one of
you on such an expedition. He knows better. There
would be fathers and mothers, or, rather, ayes and
noes after him, in no time. It is only because I have
no parliamentary interest to back me."

" Hush, hush !" cried Chippenham, who really liked
Herries, and saw that he was committing himself.

" Poor Hal !" added Percy provokingly. "It shan't
be sent to Lisbon. It shan't sail up the Tagus.
It shall stay at home and eat its Christmas turkey by
its own fireside."

For my part I said nothing. I was rapt in cogitation. What if I could obtain to be sent in his
room ? Not a moment to be lost ! I explained
myself to Herries. He was quite sincere in his
detestation of the appointment ; and he hastened,
hand-in-hand with me, to Lord Votefilch, representing
that I was exceedingly ambitious of replacing him ; that
I was slightly acquainted with the Portuguese language;
that my health, which was in a declining state, would
be materially benefited by a sea-voyage ; and that the
services of Mr. Herries were, just then, peculiarly in
request in the office, for putting in train the arrangement of certain official documents previous to the
meeting of parliament, which had been especially
recommended to his diligence by the Lords of the
Treasury.

My preamble went for nothing, for worse than
nothing, for an impertinent interference with authority.
But this last argument decided the matter ; I was
desired to hold myself in readiness to start for
Falmouth that very night. Not a human being was
in my confidence, as regarded my loves and likings;

and this sudden application was, consequently, a thunderbolt in the office. Herries thought me a fool; all the rest, mad. Had Lord Ormington been in town, the thing would probably have been prevented. As it was, I found it easy to persuade my mother that I had been selected by Goverument as a confidential agent for a difficult duty, and, though she wept a little and begged me to take care and not put myself in the way of the plague or the yellow fever, she was comforted when I promised to send her home, by return of packet, hanks of Lisbon chains and a "wilderness of monkeys." She still continued to murmur something about Lisbon being such a dangerous place, and to beg me to take care of the earthquake. But turning a deaf ear to her maternal anxieties, I hurried away to issue my last instructions to Tim, and a long farewell to the convolvulus chamber.

My preparations were easily achieved. I bequeathed to Lady Ormington the settlement of my Christmas bills. Government was my courier.

Facta etenim et vitas hominum suspendit ab astris !

> My chaise was at the door,
> My transport on the sea ;

And an announcement in the next day's Morning Post, that, "last evening the Hon. Cecil Danby left the Foreign Office with despatches for his Majesty's minister at Lisbon," contained all the adieux necessary to my disconsolate creditors.

Apart from the hope of seeing Emily again, there was something in the suddenness of the measure that imparted piquancy to my plan. As I rattled along the road, at the pace at which depositaries of despatch-boxes contrived in those days to be rattled, I could not help picturing to myself the surprise of Lord Ormington, on his arrival in town, at finding that, without departing from our compact, I had contrived to distance both him and Messrs. Hanmer and Snatch. It was a

triumph, too, to know that I should escape the
mortification of being omitted among the invited to
Danby's wedding ; which the newspapers assured the
world was to take place soon after Christmas. Parthian-
like, I was intent upon leaving wounds behind me, as
I posted along.

My enthusiasm, however, began to relax as the
hurry and excitement of departure gradually subsided.
At the moment of embarkation, I saw things in their
true light, which was far from a pleasant one ; and,
without sharing my mother's apprehensions of being
swallowed up, either in the Bay of Biscay or a second
Lisbon earthquake, began to perceive that the bright
eyes of my inscrutable divinity were leading me
strangely out of my latitude.

Not that the sight of the dark-blue waters inspired
me with the nausea so afflicting to the many. As
nurses reprove a squeamish child with the assurance
that "people sick in a carriage weren't born to ride in
one ;" I am of opinion that a sea-sick man was not
born to sail in his own yacht ; and am proud to
declare that the heaviest swell finds me enjoying the
robust health becoming a gentleman.

Still, the sea in December ! The Bay of Biscay at
Christmas. The perils and inconveniences of the ensuing fortnight were such as would have reconciled me,
without further argument, to finding myself back again
in poor Hanover Square. La Bruyère, or some other
of the fellows whose sayings one is always remembering,
observes that a woman must be charming indeed whose
husband does not wish himself unmarried at least ten
times a day. So, a sea-voyage must happen under
circumstances peculiarly favourable, if a man do not
wish himself on dry land forty-eight times in the
course of the twenty-four hours. I shall never forget
the fervour of my thanks to Providence when I found
myself at length going it easy on the smooth waters of
the Tagus.

"His Majesty's service." I could not of course

forget that I and my despatch-box were his Majesty's.
Though conscious that the magnet which drew me to
the shores of Portugal resided in a quinta at Cintra, I
was forced to go through the ceremony of delivering
my despatches, my notes confidential, and a day's
worth of private explanation, to the individual and
collective majesty of the mission, before I even named
the name of Barnet.

But how to do justice to the bore of being cross-
examined by an ambassador, a secretary of legation, a
private secretary, and three *attachés* : in the first place,
concerning the mysteries of their calling, as connected
with the fountain-head in Downing Street ; in the
next, concerning all that insignificant chit-chat of
London, which becomes so important the moment one
gets out of earshot of its babble. Next to the smell of
the quays at Belem, and the spectacle of their squalid
population, the investigation I was compelled to
undergo was the most disgusting incident of my
arrival.

Let it not meanwhile be supposed that, at the
mature age of one and twenty, I was young enough to
be beguiled into precipitate inquiries in my turn. For
worlds I would not have evinced the slightest curiosity
concerning anything or anybody in Lisbon. Among
my supercilious diplomatic brethren, I chose to be
better acquainted with all that was going on at the
seat of war, than Wellington or Beresford. I was so
good as to tell them what had been and would be
again ; and described to them the state of parties in
Lisbon with a graphic accuracy that obtained me
unlimited credit.

No occasion to explain how much of my time had
been spent, the preceding summer, in company with
those to whom the welfare of Portugal was as vital
air.

The rock of Lisbon was, in fact, scarcely more
familiar to me now that I had sailed under its clifted
heights, or the monastery of Mafra now that my eyes

had rested upon its majestic walls, than when described
by the glowing and eloquent partiality of Emily. Long
before we dropped anchor in the Tagus, I could have
painted, as after a circumstantial sketch, the towers of
St. Julien, and the castle of Belem ; the white walls
of the quintas and convents, peeping from among their
gardens of evergreens, the imposing palace of the
Ajuda, the venerable portal of St. Jeronymo, and the
lofty towers of the mother church, reflected upon the
surface of the waters.

I could almost have wished myself fated to know
them *only* by description. For Heaven knows the
bright and varied scene gained little by its accompaniments of sound or smell. A more ill-favoured, ill-
savoured community than the rabble of the quays of
Belem, is scarcely to be imagined ; and for many days
after my arrival, I was tempted hourly to invoke as
ideal the perfume of orange-trees and sound of guitars
wherewith my romantic friends had enlivened their
descriptions. The wrangling of beggars, the grunting
of pigs, and the *bouquet* of these and other unclean
beasts, including barefooted friars, appealed only too
energetically to my patience.

My sense of smell is at all times painfully acute.
The least ostensibly developed, it is by no means the
least susceptible of the senses. Strange that we have
no word definitive of its imperfection or extinction.
There are the blind and the deaf, there are even the
nearsighted and the dunny. But we want a name for
those fortunate individuals who walk through a fish-
market or a glue-manufactory without wincing or a
thymy woodland or choice conservatory without
rapture. For my own part, I protest that my most
vivid anticipation of the joys of Eden, consists in the
aromatic gales described by Milton, as

Able to cure all sadness but despair.

However excruciating the torture of my olfactory
nerves at Belem, I was amply rewarded at a subse-

quent period, when traversing some of those exquisite
valleys on the banks of the Mondego, shrubbed over
with lavender and rosemary, or balsamic thickets of
the gum-cistus; whose lofty bay-trees, cypresses, or
cedars, bathing in intense sunshine, impart an almost
Oriental spiciness to the atmosphere. But I had much
to undergo in the interval. My irritability, after three
days spent at an hotel reeking with garlic and tobacco,
and enlivened eighteen hours of the twenty-four by
the incessant drumming and fifing of a military parade,
was the precursor of illness. I have often known sea-
voyages produce deleterious effects on the constitution,
when they fail to affect it in the usual manner. But
in my own instance, I apprehended nothing. Never
having experienced an hour's ill-health, I scoffed at
the idea of sickness; and for the first three or four
days after landing, attributed my disorder to change
of climate, change of food, or fatigue.

I felt almost insulted when advised to see the
embassy physician. I was still more angry when the
said physician, having been peremptorily introduced
into my room, talked of bleeding and chicken-broth.
My indignation, however, was to little purpose; for,
three days afterwards, the ignominy of a tonsured
head was inflicted upon me, without my being conscious of the offence. Instead of making my way to
Cintra, I became delirious; in imminent danger from
the paroxysms of a bilious fever.

Poor Lady Ormington! How little had she suspected when, in our farewell interview, she bade me
beware of the plague and yellow fever, that her darling
was carrying with him the germ of a disorder equally
perilous. There was every chance that, instead of
marmosets and Lisbon chains, the packet which conveyed back to England intelligence of our safe arrival,
would also carry news that I was sleeping my last
sleep in the churchyard of Saint Jeronymo.

If it had, I doubt whether any of them would have
cared. But I was spared all efforts of sensibility on

that or any other point ; for during the ensuing three
weeks, my mind was in a state of torpor. I knew not
even that I suffered ; though, judging from the result,
my sufferings must have been severe. When my
danger eeased, my weakness was as that of a child.

One of my first impressions was a painful consciousness that, though thus thrust among strangers to
sicken, and all but die, I had experienced as much
sympathy and kindness among them, as I should have
done among my own people, and in my father's house.
This is a confession, by the way, which people are apt
to make as a reflection upon their relations ; whereas
it disgraces only themselves. It is a ease of rare
misfortune when we are not loved by our nearest of
kin, in proportion as we deserve to excite affection.
As to me—— But on this head I have enabled my
readers to judge for themselves.

The most imaginative bard of my time, he whose
poetry may be considered as the matrix of that of
Byron, has favoured us, by way of psychological
curiosity, with a picture of one of his dreams, the
result probably of opium, which a recent traveller* has
declared to be so exact a transcript of the scenery viewed
from Mount Lebanon, that, when halting under its
hoary cedars, he could find no truer description of the
landscape than the celebrated verses of Coleridge.

Are we to infer that, to the inspired brain of the
poet, that Oriental scene was literally manifested !
May there not even exist senses still imperfectly
developed by physiological science ? May there not
be mysteries of the soul indicated only by the divining-
rod of the initiated ; such as might pass for a supernatural visitation, did aught in our degraded nature
intitle us to communication with the invisible world ?

I can have no object in deceiving myself or others ;
and I swear that during my illness at Belem my
chamber was haunted. No spot or scene I ever visited

* Lord Lindsay.

in health and strength, is more vividly impressed upon
my memory, than those in which I seemed to live and
move and have my being, during the period in which
my physicians pronounced me to be labouring under
mental excitement. To me, Portugal was still *terra
incognita*. My experience of the lanscape scenery of
my own country was of the most prosaic nature;
Ormington Hall, situated in the ugliest county in
England,—Oxford,—Putney. I had seen nothing, I
knew nothing; nor had Art done much to expand
or refine my ideas of the picturesque. All I knew
was, that the prevailing colour of a landscape is green;
and that the prevailing colour of a sky had better be
blue.

But my perceptions during my state of *clairvoyance*,
lay in a land whose acclivities were clothed with the
pale foliage of the olive; whose rivers ran among over-
topping wildernesses of canes and reeds; whose lofty
bay-trees extended their deep, fragrant, glossy, glorious
growth like the tree of which David sang in his hour
of inspiration; whose rocks were overshowered with
the pink blossoms of the oleander, or the blue and
vaporous bloom of the rosmarinus; whose rich groups
of cork-trees, through which the gleam of marble
aqueducts appeared in the distance, afforded shade to
droves of buffaloes; whose fences were surmounted by
the spiky leaves of the aloe and intwined with con-
volvuli of very different hue from those of my poor
old blue chamber in Hanover Square.

Was this prescience? Was the influence of the land
already strong upon my spirit? Was the companionship that appeared to haunt me in those peculiar and
well-remembered scenes, also a delusion? Were the
words breathed in my ears by her who appeared to be
ever present with me, words of warning? I dare not
dwell upon these speculations! In this age of grovelling materialism, everything savouring of a pretence to
higher sources of intelligence is condemned as the impertinence of a fool or the vagary of a madman. Per-

haps I *was* mad. I will even admit that I was mad.
But this I know, that I would exchange the most
rational moments of my life for a single day or night
of that stage of lunacy, which seemed to transport me
to the banks of the Mondego, "with one fair spirit for
my minister."

So conscious was I, even then, of the ridicule
attached to my faith in this "supernatural soliciting," that my first inquiry on my restoration to
health regarded the degree to which my secret might
have transpired during my illness. I interrogated my
nurse. I questioned poor, faithful Tim, who had lain,
day and night, like a dog, at my bedside. I chal-
lenged, with a smile, my young friends of the embassy.
But in vain. The Portuguese nurse and Irish groom
admitted that I had raved like a man possessed. But
they knew not whether by angel or devil. As to the
attachés, they talked about my being light-headed ;
but they were not much disposed to knit up the
ravelled skein of my perplexities.

All I knew with certainty was, that my restoration
to health had snatched me from illusions worth an
empire ; and that the foul, filthy, sweltering, vermin-
haunted, drumming, strumming Belem which presented itself before me in fetid reality, was a very
inferior spot to the city of Morisco convents and
marble palaces which had risen out of the blue waters
of the Tagus in my Land of Thought.

Bales of letters had arrived for me during my
illness ; Christmas bills, reproaches on pink paper,
and (in black and white from Messrs. Hanmer and
Snatch) Lord Ormington's formal signification of his
displeasure that I should have solicited from Government an appointment necessitating my absence from
England at a moment so fraught with interest to the
Danby family as the approaching marriage of my
brother.

But this was not all. The pragmatical firm in
Southampton Buildings, patented by his Right Hon.

Lordship with the privilege of lecturing me in his name, was further pleased to intimate that, " should my visit to Portugal purport the renewal of my connection with a certain family, which by their means had been introduced to my acquaintance, they were instructed to inform me that my income would be peremptorily suspended."

A long shot, and wide of the mark. I had been more than a month at Lisbon, without attempting to obtain information concerning the persons thus harshly pointed out to my avoidance. I knew, indeed, that, as regarded the d'Acunhas, I might as well have walked to Whitechapel, inquiring all the way for a family of the name of Smith ; and with respect to Emily, felt a natural hesitation about pointing her out to the notice of the young gentleman in kid gloves who manœuvred the international relations between England and Portugal.

Lisbon and its environs abounded at that time in English merchants. The sealing up or corking up of France rendered the fierce potations of Spain and Portugal our sole resource against the humid climate of Great Britain. I determined to defer my inquiries till I could visit Cintra in person : the prohibition contained in the thirteen-and-fourpenny epistle of Messrs. Hanmer and Snatch having served only to determine me upon attempting an airing full a fortnight earlier than the measure was sanctioned by that remarkably obtuse body called the faculty.

CHAPTER IX.

J'étudiais cette femme avec un culte égal à celui qu'apportent les peintres devant les lignes pures et les chastes contours des Madones de Raphael ou de Cimabue. J'interrogeais en silence l'expression de son visage, afin de deviner ce qui se passait en elle. J'écoutais le son de sa voix; j'épiais un sourire, je la regardais marcher. Que vous dirai-je? C'était mon idole, la Madone que je m'étais choisie.—ALPHONSE BROT.

Jocundum cùm ætas florida ver ageret.
CATULL. *Epig.* 67.

FEW people pass through life without having experienced the rapture of convalescence. Socrates has described the delicious itching of the human flesh on the removal of manacles, as a sufficient reward for previous bondage; and it is quite as well worth while to be ill, for the satisfaction of finding oneself well again. The transition from the stagnant atmosphere of a sick-room, from lugubrious faces and presages of evil, to the blessed and revivifying light of day, with its snatches of fragrant breezes, its "lapse of streams and tune of birds," is like a foretaste of heaven.

Above all, I had every plea for exultation on finding myself for the first time transported beyond the confines of that fair-looking and foul-smelling capital of the land of oranges and lemons. I, who had come so far, who had defied my father and his solicitors, my creditors and their accounts, for the sole object of looking once more upon the most angelic of human faces, had, indeed, cause to murmur against the captivity which beset me on my arrival.

To attempt an excursion to Cintra on the first day of returning health was, of course, impossible. But Cintra was not about to move from its pedestal. In a week I might hold the hand of Emily in mine.

I am ashamed to say how many days that week

appeared to contain. From the moment I became sure of our approaching reunion, my impatience was redoubled. I felt as if the yearning of my heart must kill me unless speedily gratified. All the wild imaginings of my dreams had only stimulated my ardour. I began to appreciate the excellence of Emily as I had never understood it before. The earnestness of her character, its truthfulness, its cordiality, the total absence of pretension or pretence, were merits which the artificialities of the world rendered doubly attractive. I felt sure that, on entering her presence, I should learn at once, either from her expansive smiles or cold severity, whether she resented my conduct ; and whether her sudden departure from England had been equally a source of grief to *her* and to myself : and was resolved that, should I discover her regrets to have been as poignant as my own, I would not again sacrifice to worldly ambition a treasure which the hand of Providence seemed to have placed in my path. She should be mine, or——I had not yet exactly fixed upon the alternative.

While placing her before me in the character of an affianced bride, I retouched again and again in my memory the picture of her bright and beaming beauty, till I could have sworn that she was visibly present— my idol,—my love,—my wife ! How I had wronged her, how wronged myself, not to have snatched her to my heart long, weary months before, instead of leaving her exposed to the animadversions of the world.

Spring was breaking ere my convalescence was sufficiently advanced to admit of extending my drives. For some time, indeed, the physicians insisted on my not venturing out unaccompanied. Either the nature of my excitement or the suddenness of my former attack rendered them cautious. At length I was sufficiently strong to defy them.

" You may burn your books, my dear doctor ! " said I to my kind attendant, on the day of my purposed expedition to Cintra. " I have better remedies in store than the forests of cascarilla you are inflicting on me. Within a week, I promise you, I shall be no longer the same man."

"So much the better," cried Dr. A——, "so much the better ! But I had rather you did not promise it with so bright an eye, or so hurried a pulse. I have been writing a flourishing account of your amendment to Lord Ormington. Unless you lower your tone, sir, I must recall my bulletin till next packet."

I did not inquire of the official Esculapius whether he had addressed his intelligence to his lordship through the medium of Southampton Buildings. I was too happy at that moment to trouble myself about kith or kin. I had done like the gods invoked by Nat. Lee in his tragedy,—"annihilated both time and space to make two lovers happy." I had even overcome something *more* indomitable than time or space, my own listless nature, my own coxcombry. I had braved the perils of earth and sea, the displeasure of Hanover Square, and the fury of the Bay of Biscay, in order to enjoy once more the presence of that dearest of human beings.

Beautiful Cintra ! How I rejoiced to hail the rocky pinnacles that Emily had so often described. Oh ! that odoriferous breath of gardens, that vitality in the air, as of the young-eyed spring bursting into life and joy through a thousand blossoms. I bore the burthen of life too lightly, as I reached the first shrubby steep of Cintra, and looked up to the heights crowned by the convent towers of Nossa Senhòra da Penha. My heart was blithe as a bird. I was something better than Cecil Danby at that moment. I was a human being created to be happy and confer happiness, on the point of sharing my joyous thoughts and feelings with a better self.

I inquired—that is, my Portuguese attendant inquired, of a young *vinhateiro* whom we met trudging down the hill with a pole slung across his shoulder, and a modinha upon his lips, whether he could direct us to the quinta of an English gentleman at Cintra.

" *Inglese ?*" cried he, after the usual courteous
"*Viva !*" "There are so many English. There is the
general,—there is the commissary-general,—there is
the surgeon-general,—there are twenty others who
have quintas on the hill."

"No; it was not a gentleman connected with the
army."

"A fidalgo, then ?"

"No! not a fidalgo,—an old settler,—a merchant."

"The Senhor Barnet ?" shouted the man, with a
gladsome countenance, as if the name had a cheering
influence. "*Nossa Senhora !* Who does not know
the quinta of San José ?"

He seemed to take pleasure in directing the coachman to the spot. Our progress was between stone
walls, overtopped by the verdure of the ilex and bay ;
intersected here and there by the gates of different
quintas, enabling the eye to penetrate into the interior
of their trimly gardens and orange orchards. To me
every foot of earth we traversed was holy ground. I
thought of her surprise—her welcome—her eyes varying perhaps from the flash of joy to softening tears ;
her grateful recognition of all I had braved, all I had
forsaken, to see her again. As we gradually accomplished the number of turns and twistings suggested
by the *vinhateiro*, my breath came so short, my heart
beat so painfully, that I felt I could not much longer
support the excess of my emotion. A sad concession
for a coxcomb, to be shaken thus !

At length we approached a gate of somewhat statelier
appearance than the preceding ones. We were at San
José. The house, a modest mansion of white stone,
two stories in height, differed in no respect from the
neighbouring quintas, save in lying more exposed to
the road, the whole façade being visible. But of
all the human abodes I ever beheld, it presented at
that moment the brightest aspect. The house was
surrounded with almond-trees ; and the air seemed
brightened by the shower of pink and white blossoms,

thrown out into stronger relief by the dark back-ground
of evergreens formed by a lofty pine-grove.

The white mansion, encompassed by this wilderness
of blossoms, looked like a fair girl arrayed for her
bridal. It was afternoon. The nightingales, nowhere
more mellifluous than on the shores of the Tagus, were
revelling in those gladsome thickets. In just so sun-
shiny a place could I have desired to feast my eyes
once more on the face of Emily.

The gates were thrown open. But I would not let
the carriage drive in. Two gentlemen were sauntering on the broad gravel walk under the almond-trees
—elderly men, one of them probably the proprietor
of the quinta.

Alighting from the carriage, I inquired of the porter
whether that were Mr. Barnet, pointing to one of
the gentlemen, who had stopped short in his walk, and
was looking so earnestly towards me, that I thought it
better to hasten towards him, and explain the object
of my visit. Luckily for my nervous tremors he
came forward to meet me.

" I have taken the liberty, sir," said I, addressing
the old gentleman, hat in hand, with the most deprecating politeness, " to intrude upon you in the hope
that——"

" Is she coming ? " demanded he, interrupting me,
in a whisper, as if apprehensive of being overheard by
his companion.

" My name is Danby. I have not the honour of
being personally known to you," said I, concluding
that he mistook me for some other person.

" Is she coming ? " he repeated, in precisely the
same tone, and fixing the same intense look of inquiry
upon my face.

" You are under some mistake, I fear, sir," I replied.
" I had the honour of being acquainted in England
with your daughter, and——"

" Is she coming ? " again repeated the old man, in
precisely the same tone, and with a fixedness of aspect

that began to excite vague uneasiness in my mind. I
could scarcely doubt that I was addressing a person of
disturbed intellect. Even before I perceived that the
individual by whom he was accompanied was making
signs of intelligence to me to desist from the conversation. All the notice vouchsafed by Mr. Barnet to this
interruption consisted in turning towards him with the
same simple question, uttered in the same whisper—
" Is she coming ? "

" Presently, presently," replied his companion, in the
coaxing tone used to deceive children and maniacs.
" But you have had a long walk, sir. Supposing we
go in and rest ourselves ? This gentleman has promised
that he will come and visit you another time."

" Another time ? " muttered the old man, in a tone
of deep despair. " It is always another time ! "

Nevertheless, he quietly took the arm extended
towards him by his companion (who made signs to me
to await his return), and submissively attempted a few
steps towards the house. In a moment, however, he
stopped, as if some new idea had entered his mind, and
returned suddenly towards me. " At least, before I
go, let him tell me whether she is coming ? " said he,
in precisely his former tone and manner. Then
approaching me, and laying his hand familiarly on my
arm, he inclined his white face closer towards my ear,
to falter, in a lower whisper, " I will tell none of them,
if you will let me hear the truth. You said you knew
Emily. Is she—*is she coming ?* "

" I had thought to find her here, sir," said I, painfully agitated. " It is many months since we met. I
learned with satisfaction her safe arrival in Portugal.
The hope of meeting her, indeed, was one of my inducements to visit Lisbon."

" Then you will be my friend—you will go and seek
her for me," cried he, giving way to a burst of passionate feeling. " You knew Emily—you valued her
—perhaps you loved her ? But no ! you were not her
father. You could not love her as I loved her. You

N

could not have found the cruel courage to send her
away from you, that she might be safe in happy
England—safe from the terrors of war—safe from the
ruin which was overwhelming Portugal. Do you
know how it fared with my girl in England?—my
beautiful girl—my pride—my glory—the comfort of
my old age! They persecuted her—they vilified her
—they killed her for me, sir ! The curse of God light
upon them in everlasting fire for the deed! They—
they——but *is* she coming?" said he, suddenly changing
his infuriated accents for a mild earnestness that made
my flesh creep.

"If you agitate yourself in this manner, Mr. Barnet,"
interposed his companion in a tone of authority, "I
shall not be able to allow you a walk in the garden
again to-morrow. You are distressing this gentleman,
a stranger to you."

"No! not a stranger," interrupted poor Barnet,
again laying his hand upon my arm. "I can see by
his face that he is no stranger ; he is grieving for me ;
he is grieving for Emily ; he knows that it will be a
long time before they let my child come back to me
again. You see he dares not answer me when I ask
for her. The way with you all. No one—no one will
say whether she is coming. You told me your name
just now ?" cried he, stopping short, and again intently
regarding me.

"Danby—Cecil Danby !

"I should know it—I seem to know it!" he
exclaimed, shrugging his shoulders impatiently.
"Somehow or other I forget everything now. Nothing
seems to stay with me. My girl would not stay with
me. Poor Emily would not remain at San José.
They tell me I shall see her again—but *when?* Can
you tell me when?—*you*, sir !—Mr. Danby—Englishman—what are you? Is she coming, I say—is she
coming ?"

"You had better retire ; he is always thus excited
in the presence of strangers," observed his companion,

with the insensibility of a person accustomed to such
scenes. "I will rejoin you at the lodge as soon as I
have succeeded in restoring him to composure."

"How dare you call any one a stranger who comes
to San José to demand hospitality in the name of my
daughter?" cried the old man, turning fiercely upon
him. "Don't you know that Emily is still mistress
here? Don't you know that, when she comes back to
me, her first care will be to drive out of the house the
brute who has presumed to tyrannize over her poor old
father, to beat me like a child,—me, a grey-headed
man. She loved me very dearly, sir," he continued,
abruptly addressing me. "Though she left me, she
loved me very dearly. Come with me into the house,
and you shall see the picture she drew of me. It is
not finished, they say. There was not time to finish
it, when they took her from me. But she is coming
back to finish it. She ought to have been here by this
time. The flowers are come, you see," said he, pointing
to the almond-trees, "and the birds are singing,—and
the sun is shining,—just as if Emily were here again.
Bright, bright, it is all so bright and beaming, that my
poor head and heart ache with it. It is a very sad time
the spring! *Is she coming, sir*, that you are here to
meet her? Ha! ha! ha! We shall disappoint them
yet. They think they have buried her. But I know
better. I know,—I *know*—that she is coming!"

He had now locked his arm fast in mine, and a
request was whispered to me, by his attendant, that I
would accompany him into the quinta. The proposal
was a welcome one, for my own strength was
failing.

As we approached the house, the hall-door was
thrown open by two servants, who preceded us into
a large saloon, the green blinds of which were closed;
so that, entering it from the dazzling sunshine, I could
not, at first, distinguish the objects it contained. My
first impulse was to stagger to a seat. If the dreadful
surmises excited by the ravings of the poor maniac

N 2

before me should be grounded in truth ?—if Emily
should be really gone—gone for ever ?

One word addressed to the keeper, who was standing
at only a few paces distance, would have determined
the matter. But I had not courage to give it utterance. I had not courage to know the worst. A
deathly faintness came over me. I seemed to distinguish in the chamber the peculiar perfume of vanille,
indicative of her presence. Like old Barnet, I could
scarcely refrain from exclaiming, in a frantic whisper,
" Is she coming ?"

A few minutes afterwards (I conclude that minutes
only had elapsed) I found myself reclining in the same
chair, with a chilly sensation creeping over me ; on one
side the lunatic, with his unmeaning eyes peering into
my face ; on the other the keeper, who was holding
my hand in his, as if feeling my pulse. Great God !
was he going to exercise his horrible functions upon *me* ?

" He is recovering. I told you, Mr. Barnet, sir,
that you would harass him by your wild questions,"
said the man, addressing in a surly tone his unfortunate charge. " How can you expect that your friends
will continue to visit you, if you flurry and vex them
in this manner ?"

" He is not my friend. He is *her* friend. *Her*
friends will always be indulgent with me," ejaculated
the poor old man ; and he leaned over me with a look
so piteous, that I struggled to recover strength to
extricate myself from my dreadful position.

By degrees my eyes accustomed themselves to the
gloom of the darkened chamber. I could now perceive
that it contained a thousand indications of female
habitation. There were musical instruments—books
—flowers. There was an embroidery-frame upon the
table ; and a lory chained to a stand, sidling restlessly
to be noticed, as if impatient of the stillness of the
place. My fears began to subside. Why had I listened to the incoherences of a madman ? Emily was
probably in the house.

" These are Emily's books; this is Emily's work,"
whispered the old gentleman, leading me courteously
to the table. "If she were here, sir, she would show
them to you, and sing to you, and bid you welcome.
See ! there is the mark left in her favourite volume,"
he continued, showing me a sprig of withered myrtle
placed between the pages of Burns, a writer we had
often discussed together. "It is so strange that she
does not come and finish all these things. People do
not leave their work incomplete, and their mark in a
book, week after week, in this way. I can't tell you
how many days have passed, sir, since I heard the
sound of music. You know how she used to sing?
Never was there such a voice on earth. ' Nel
silenzio !' did you ever hear her sing ' Nel silenzio ?'
—Banti never attempted it after she had heard my
Emily. And now, not a note,—not a single note !
Nothing,—nothing,—*so* still that you may hear all
day the clinking of poor Yilko's chain.—I should
send it away, but that it was hers. The poor bird
seems watching for her. Every one is watching for
her."

I shuddered. I was beginning to feel an instinctive
horror of the concluding phrase so indicative of his
bewilderment. This time, he spared me.

" Supposing we go and look for her !" cried he,
with a vacant smile, as if struck with a bright idea.
" I know where they took her, when she was carried
away from San José ; and if we were to go and call
her, very likely she might come back. Ask the
gentleman to accompany me, Allan. He will not,
unless *you* ask him. No one does anything here that
you do not bid them," said he, addresing his keeper,
with a significant look.

" Will you promise me, sir, if we humour you, to
return quietly home, and take a few hours rest ?" was
the man's prudent reply. " You have not closed your
eyes these two nights."

" Would you have had me sleep, when Emily had

promised me a visitor ?" demanded poor Barnet, with
one of the cunning smiles peculiar to madmen. " But
I *have* welcomed him, you see, in spite of you. I have
shown him her books, her flowers, her bird. And
now I will take him to her ; that is, if you will
allow me."

" If you would so far indulge him, it would be an
act of charity," said the keeper, drawing me aside.
" For several days, Mr. Barnet's paroxysms have been
dreadful. To-day, he is more subdued ; and if I could
only bring him to shed tears, as he usually does after
that favourite walk, it would insure him a night's
sleep."

" I am myself, as you perceive, in so feeble a condition——" I was beginning.

"*Feeble ?*" interrupted the lunatic, who was eagerly
listening. "No matter. You shall lean on my arm.
I will support you. We will go together and visit
Emily. It is but a step. Allan, the key. You are
a good fellow, though brutal. You shall come with
us. There,—softly ! Don't hurry yourself, Mr.—
what did you say was your name ? Danby ? Don't
hurry yourself. She will wait for us. She was
always so good,—so patient. I never heard her chide
so much as a dog. She will wait—she will wait !"
Continuing to mutter praises of his daughter, he led
me through a suite of rooms, the keeper closely following ; one of which, from various articles of female
attire lying about, I concluded to be the chamber of
Miss Barnet.

" She is not here, you see," said the old man, pausing
a moment opposite the cold white bed. " She loved
this room, though. Look ! there is her father's picture hanging to the wall ; opposite the spot where,
when she was a little, little child, she used to kneel
down night and morning, and pray to God to bless
him. No one ever prays here for me now. God has
forsaken me. Ichabod ! my glory has departed !"

" You promised, sir, to take this gentleman to visit

her," interposed the keeper. "You must not break your word."

"Who talked of breaking my word? Am I not a gentleman still? My daughter has forsaken me. The French have burned my stores,—have ravaged my vineyards,—have ruined *me*,—have devastated Portugal. But I am a gentleman for all that. Don't hurry me, Allan. You know I cannot bear being hurried! I—I am a gentleman. I never thought of breaking my word."

And with stealthy footsteps, he made his way out of the room, and attempted to open the glass doors of a small vestibule communicating with the garden. Allan immediately took a key from his pocket, and enabled us to pass; then, after traversing a long gravel walk, skirted on either side by espaliers of myrtle, cut into fanciful arcades, we reached the extremity of the garden. Again, the keeper produced his pass-key, and unlocked the door of a boundary wall.

We were now in an orange-grove; a spot of little interest in the eyes of any inhabitant of Portugal, to whom the aspect of the glossy verdure, golden fruit, or richly-scented blossoms of that Hesperian tree, are as uninteresting as an apple-orchard to ourselves.

But it happened to be the first realization to *my* eyes of a scene so often and so vividly described by Emily, in association with the sports of her childhood.

"This was her play-ground, sir," said old Barnet, pointing between the smooth stems of the venerable trees; "and yonder——"

At that moment, Allan unlocked a third door in the exterior wall, and I found myself in a small green enclosure, the turf of which, rising here and there into mounds of a peculiar form——But why describe this?

The old man led me slowly, reverently, silently, to the remotest corner of the little enclosure; over which the boughs of a fine bay-tree, overhanging the

wall of the quinta, extended their shade. There was
a stone slab on the ground, placed there very recently,
for the rough clay around it had not yet attained a
vestige of verdure, and a few displaced sods still lay
withering around.

" This, as you are probably aware, sir, is the English
burying-ground," said Allan, breathing his hateful
whisper into my ear. " I am not often able to indulge
him with a visit. I dare not bring him here alone.
Look !"

The poor old man was down on his knees, with
his head bowed upon the stone ; tracing with his
trembling finger the letters engraven there :

Pray for the Soul
of
EMILY BARNET,
Aged eighteen years.
Died on the 17th of February, 1811.
Ora pro me.

Only three weeks in the grave. The earth scarcely
closed over that beloved face. Oh ! misery—misery !
—Had I hastened to San José on my disembarkation,
I had been in time to save her,—to spare the shattered reason of her wretched father ! Why, why,
thus tardy in my atonement? She had died of a
broken heart. That which the keeper, Allan, called
a rapid decline, was the anguish of a broken heart.
I heard all, soon afterwards, from the worthy man
whose aid was now once more called in to rescue me
from the grave. He had attended her. He had been
her friend,—her confidant. She owned to him on her
deathbed, that her sudden return to Lisbon was
caused by the infamous rumours spread concerning
her in England, by a noble family, who, resenting the
attentions of one of its members, had sacrificed her
without remorse.

" The spiritless man whom my father appointed my
guardian," murmured the dying girl, " forsook his
charge in the dread of these people's displeasure. He

sent me from his house. He even dared accuse me of levity,—of duplicity,—of shame. But that was not all. He—he for whose sake I bore all this,—he, by whose boasts I was exposed to such indignity,—*he*, too, shunned me in my disgrace. He deigned not so much as make one inquiry after her whom he had injured. But no matter. May God forgive him, as I do !"

When this was told me, I felt that not even the prayers of that sinless being could procure me the pardon of Heaven. Tears flowed from the eyes of my kindly attendant, as he adverted to her touching death-bed. All human skill had been unavailing. She refused to be comforted—she disdained to live ; but expired in peace and charity with all men—a saint—a martyr !

By a strange coincidence, he had closed her eyes on the very night he was first summoned to attend me. Two hours after witnessing the departure of that tortured spirit, he was at my bedside. He had scarcely resigned her clay cold hand, when my burning one claimed his ministry.

And I had known nothing of all this. I, who had come so far to behold her again, had heard the passing bell toll for Emily,—had seen mourning worn for her, —had—But no matter——

From that day,—

——quem semper acerbum
Semper honoratum (sic di voluistis !) habebo,

I became an altered man.

CHAPTER X.

Mon Dieu ! il s'accuse d'avoir été joli garçon, d'avoir eu de
charmans cheveux, une jambe fine, le mollet bien placé, le pied
petit, et une certaine tournure, dont fut jaloux plus d'un capi-
taine de dragons.   Le drôle !—BROT.

Μισω σοφιστην, ὑστις ουχ αὑτῳ σοφος.
EURIP.

I HAVE lingered long, much longer than I had
intended on this afflicting chapter of my reminiscences.
I ask pardon of my reader.   I know not what right
any scribbler may have to add one gloomy shade to
the dolefuls with which Nature has encompassed human
nature.

Most writers have a predilection for the dismal side
of things.   Historians are sure to dismiss a golden
age in half a dozen lines.   But when they come to a
bloody war and sickly season, to sieges, battles, a
drought, a famine, the plague, the cholera—see how
they run on.

For myself, be it plainly understood, my only
motive for alluding to this melancholy episode is to
excuse to the world what might otherwise appear an
unpardonable act of folly ; my having volunteered to
join the brigade of Beresford, and fought through the
remaining three years of the Peninsula war, as if born
the seventh son of a Welsh curate with an ensigncy in
a marching regiment.

I do not want to impose myself on the world as a
hero.   It is necessary, therefore, to explain *why* I came,
saw, and conquered.   Vain were the remonstrances of
my brethren of the *corps diplomatique ;* vain the
indignant letters of Lord Ormington.   Though, on
that occasion, he addressed me with his own hand, I
was steadfast in my purpose.   I cared nothing for his
threats.   I cared nothing for my future fortunes.   To

have confronted London—cold heartless London—
would have been greater torture to me than condemnation to the galleys.

My object was to die,—speedily,—bravely ; and so
escape the guilt of suicide, or the degradation of
insanity. When that heavy blow overtook me, I was
in no condition to wrestle with affliction. The only
wonder is, that I preserved sufficient reason to seek an
honourable career as the termination of my despair.

More people, however, expect to die of grief than
fall victims to their sensibility. *I* was not an Emily
Barnet. I was only Cecil, the coxcomb. After a few
months' desperate service, after volunteering in every
rash attempt, leading a forlorn hope or two,—and
fording a river under the enemy's fire, new desires
presented themselves. I still wished to die ; but to
die the death of the glorious. I hoped that a laurel
might wave over my tomb, as a bay-tree over that of
Emily. I trusted that, though my days were not to
be long in the land, the fame of them might survive me.

The man who cherishes a strong ambition, of whatever nature, is in no immediate danger of dying of a
broken heart. At the close of the year, instead of
having redeemed my pledge to the memory of the
dead, I was alive, strong, vigorous—a good soldier—
almost a good man.

Not a fellow at Watier's would have owned my
acquaintance. All that coat, hat, or boots could do to
disgrace a gentleman I was undergoing at the hands of
mine. Ragged,—patched,—wayworn,—sunburnt,—
who would have guessed in me the creature of the
cockade,—the fribble of the convolvulus hangings,—
the pet of Lady Harriet Vandeleur,—the darling of
the Right Hon. Lady Ormington ?

Be pleased, dear public, on arriving at the conclusion
of the last paragraph, to conceive me, placing my pen
behind my ear and my considering cap on my head, to
determine whether or not I shall fight my battles in
Spain and Portugal o'er again for your edification. I

am conscious that I could tell you a thing or two you
have 'never heard before. I have got some terrible
stories concerning sackings of convents and burnings of
churches, the desecration of my lord abbot's cellar, and
my lady abbess's oratorium. But, in my opinion, the
pipeclay novelists have taken the shine out of all that
sort of thing. When Gleig opened the trenches with
his "Subaltern," indeed, the ground was unbroken
and smelt wooingly, like all freshly-turned earth.
But now, it is the disturbed mould of a churchyard.

Were I to attempt a sketch of the storming of St.
Sebastian's, for instance, or the hateful business at
Bayonne, I should be having platoons of letters fired
at me from "Fair Play," or "An Old Soldier," and
perhaps have to fight some fire-eating Irish major at
the end of the correspondence.

All things considered, therefore, permit me to
parenthesize my years of heroism. I beg you to
believe me valiant as Lieutenant-General Sir Hurlo-
thrumbo Pipeclay, G.C.B., or the God of war, or Tom
Thumb, or any other great commander, or knight-
commander; and release me from the task of playing
commentator on my own Cæsarianisms.

Joking apart, there have been worse soldiers than I
was. I was enlisted in the cause only by the
accidental twirling of the wheel of fortune. At Eton,
the regimentals of the Guards, as they amused themselves at cricket in Windsor Park, had determined my
juvenile inclinations towards the army, in its least
martial form; and then, the negative of my governor
and governor's lady had defeated my intentions. But
when I enlisted for fighting's sake, without heed
of uniform, or thought of promotion, not even the
threat of disinheritance could turn me from my
purpose.• There must have been a fate in all this; or
I, the slave of Southampton Buildings and drudge of
Downing Street, should never have found myself
thanked for my services after the action of Toulouse;
which, according to competent authorities, had the

singular fortune to be gained by the English under Wellington, the French under Soult, and the Portuguese under the Hon. Cecil Danby. But this last little piece of bragging, is an interchange of especial confidence betwixt myself and my readers.

Three years,—three years of peril and privation,— elapsed between my landing at Belem and our triumphal hoisting of the *drapeau blanc* in the good city of Bordeaux. I cared little for the restoration of the Bourbons ;—who *did*, of those who devoted their blood and breath in the peninsula to that memorable cause? My feeling was the general feeling of the army ; to put down the French, to drive the French back into their territories, to bind them down, to confine their ambition to the country wherein it was their pleasure to decapitate a king and queen one day, as a punishment for the crime of being a king and queen, and create new sovereigns the next, to be dethroned on the third ; just as if, after destroying a nest of snakes, one were to thrust their eggs into the sunshine, for the perpetuation of the race.

Nevertheless, in common with some fifty thousand other blockheads, no sooner was the white flag flying, than I chose to fancy we had been fighting for the purpose of placing a fat, greedy, infirm old gentleman upon the throne, in place of an active, temperate, and enterprising one ; and, satisfied with having laid Napoleon on the shelf at Elba, began to fraternize with the French nation. During the week spent at Bordeaux, previous to my embarkation for England, I swallowed more oysters, perpetrated more conquests in the Allée de Tournon, and converted more Napoleons into Breguet watches, dozens of gloves, and boxes of eau de Cologne, than any other numskull in the British army or its auxiliaries.

La Rochefoucault has had the audacity to say that there are "few honest women who are not weary of their vocation ;" a sentence which has caused the prudes of successive centuries to bristle up their quills.

I shall, perhaps, provoke a similar porcupinism on the part of the heroes of my native country, by avowing my belief that few soldiers, in war time, but are equally sick of their calling. It is not danger and death by which they are disgusted, but privation and fatigue ; and, above all, the caprices of those " drest in a little brief authority," upon whose tempers, harassed by privation and fatigue, depend the minor grievances of the march or the garrison.

I am free to confess that never was I better pleased than on throwing aside the harness of war. My pride had yoked me to its endurance, so long as the bubble reputation floated before the cannon's mouth. But I quite agreed with the allied armies that it was time for those brazen rascals to close their mouths ; and, early in the month of May, one of his Majesty's transports landed me at Portsmouth, twenty times more eager for home and its enjoyments, than when released from Eton and all its birch.

How completely the ways and habits of Hanover Square were rased from the tablets of my brain, was sufficiently proved by the fact that I rattled up to the door, in my postchaise, no whit ashamed either of my plebeian vehicle, my ill-cut coat, my execrable Bordeaux hat with its voluted brim, or the bronze face it pretended to shade. After three years' absence, I felt privileged to be as uncouth and ill-favoured as I pleased.

Some months had elapsed since I had communicated with home. There was nothing to encourage me to punctual correspondence. My mother's letters, which were short without being sweet, rarely contained more than a bulletin of her own and Bibiche's ailings ; and every now and then, an outburst of reproaches at my having embarked in a branch of service in which I was never likely to be heard of. She even persisted in addressing her letters to the Honourable Cecil Danby, after I had attained the brevet rank of a field-officer.

Other correspondents I had none. The bitterness of misanthropy into which I had fallen, after the painful event which seemed to divide me from social life as completely as though I had taken the vows of a Trappist, left me no inclination to hear more of the London world than was to be gleaned from the newspapers which occasionally reached us. Nay, it had actually been news to me to read in one of those polite intelligencers, at Bordeaux, an account of the festivities at Ormington Hall, in honour of the christening of my brother's son and heir.

Nevertheless, on re-approaching the old mansion in Hanover Square, some natural emotions came choking to my throat. I had quitted it so suddenly,—so unadvisedly,—so like a thief in the night, and had since experienced such bitter resentment against it inmates, that I dreaded the moment of meeting. I almost wished I had written from Bordeaux, or even Portsmouth, to announce my coming. But I had been deterred by the apprehension of seeming to bespeak the killing of the fatted calf, in honour of one who formed such slender pretensions to the tenderness of the family.

When the chaise rattled up to the door, a disagreeable presentiment forewarned me that something was amiss. But it was not for *me* to trust to presentiments. Had I not entered the quinta of San José with my heart fluttering with joy,—like a bridegroom—like an enfranchised slave—like all that is most exulting among the children of clay?

At all events, there was no achievment over the door; no emblazonment intermingling the monsters of heraldry with skulls and cross-bones, to proclaim to the passing mechanic that an ennobled corpse was gone down to the worms. But since my father and mother were still alive, for whom was worn the black array that met my eyes as the hall door was thrown open? In whose honour gloomed those sable liveries with their black *aiguillettes*,—a lugubrious contrast

with the well powdered-heads of Lady Ormington's
standard footmen.

Neither the butler nor his delegates were known to
me by sight ; for Lady Ormington, like most ladies
curious in lapdogs, was hard to please in the article
of her slaveys. They were always too slow or too fast ;
or they snorted, or snuffled, or were guilty of some
other human infirmity. The three fellows who stood
staring at my postboy, being unknown to *me*, I was
necessarily a stranger to them ; and as there was little
to command respect in the discoloured valise and
dressing-box strapped to the dickey of that least imposing of all four-wheeled equipages, a yellow chaise
having a wooden cross on its green glass windows,
and "licensed to deal in post-horses," on the rail, I
had no reason to be indignant at the air of supercilious amazement with which these well-dressed, well-
disciplined varlets surveyed me, when I bade them
assist in uncording the luggage.

"I beg your pardon, sir, but pray is my Lord expecting you ?" inquired the butler, while the two
flunkeys gazed at each other for an explanation.

"Be so good as to pay the man and see the valise
taken off," said I, not altogether aware of the perplexities I was exciting.

"This is Lord Ormington's, sir, number eighteen,
I fancy there is some mistake," persisted the butler,
bowing back towards the house, and evidently about to
close the door in my face.

"I will thank you to have my luggage carried up to
my room, sir, to Mr. Cecil Danby's room," said I, by
way of explanation.

"SIR ?" ejaculated the man, receding in consternation, as I prepared to jump out, attributing his dismay
to remorse for his ungenerous reception of his master's
son returning from the perils and dangers of foreign
service.

"Is Lady Ormington at home ?" said I, following
him nimbly up the steps.

"Shut the vestibule door, John. Shut the vestibule door;" cried the butler in an authoritative tone, when he found himself *tête-à-tête* with me in the hall. "Shut all the doors!" And instead of replying to my question, he proceeded to whisper in the ear of the said John a message, in which I thought I could distinguish the words Marlborough Street. My identity was clearly a matter of suspicion.

"You seem to entertain some hesitation about admitting me?" said I. "Excusable enough; for you are all new since I quitted England. But there must surely be some person left in the household who can identify my person?"

"Young man," said the butler, whose mind was running upon his plate-chest, "it is a massiful thing for us that the family happened to be in town to defeat your nefarous pupposes. I am under the necessity of keeping you in custody till——"

"Blockhead!" cried I, out of all patience; "I tell you again that I am Colonel Danby, Lord Ormington's younger son!"

His reply was an insolent laugh, echoed, of course, by his familiars, John and Thomas. He even added something about his eye, which would be no ornament to these pages.

"As we happen to be in mourning, my fine fellow, for the only son as ever my lord had, with the 'ception of Mr. Danby the memberoparlment,—" John was beginning.

"In mourning, in mourning for *me?*" cried I, in spite of all my irritation bursting into a laugh. "And where was I killed, pray? Stay, as you appear to be a more idiotic one than the other, beg Mrs. Ridley, the housekeeper, to walk this way; or Mademoiselle Aglaé, if still with Lady Ormington. Even Bibiche would recognise me, and set your minds at ease."

Something in the decision of my tone, I suppose, convinced them that I was a man having authority; for Mrs. Ridley was instantly summoned, and, albeit,

little in the habit of toddling out of her still-room,
made her appearance smelling of lemon-peel, cinnamon,
and ratafia cakes, as English housekeepers are wont to
do when disturbed in their duties.

I spare my readers the recapitulation of her ejaculations, varying from horror to wonder,—delight,—
ecstacy.   At one time her joy threatened hysterics ;
and hysterics from fourteen stone and a half, is a
serious affair.   Suffice it, that under the housekeeper's
authority and a double salute of apologies from the
butler and co., I was removed into the dining-room,
my valise admitted into the hall, and the postchaise
dismissed.

"How ever we *shall* be able to break it to my lady,
is more nor I can take it on myself to say !" sobbed
the fat housekeeper.   "To be sure, Mr. Cecil, how my
lady *did* take on when you was returned missing, and
soon a'ter'ards killed !   And now, she'll take on again
every bit as bad, to learn as you be still alive and well.
Bless your soul, sir," she continued, drawing aside her
white apron to display her bombazine, "we've been in
mourning for you this month or more.   My crape's
a beginning to be a-rusty.   I'm sure I don't know
who'll dare speak about it to my lady, till Miss Richardson comes in."

"And who is Miss Richardson ?" cried I.

"Lor', Mr. Cecil, sir, pray have a care, or the men
might hear you.   Nothing's done in this house now,
without Miss Richardson, sir.   Miss Richardson is my
lady's companion, sir ; what Ma'mselle Aglaé calls her
dam' d'honour."

Poor Ridley pronounced the word so singularly,
that, in spite of the solemnity of her bombazine, I
laughed outright.

"And when is this '*dam' d'honour*' likely to make
her appearance ?" said I, "for I am impatient to be
admitted to your lady, and learn the latest particulars
of my decease."

We were interrupted by one of the footmen bursting into the room, with outcries for the housekeeper and sal volatile : the new butler, without much faith in her ladyship's sensibility, having walked straight to her dressing-room door and announced the visit of her ladyship's dead son, as coolly as he would have done that of her apothecary.

"Since the mischief's done, sir, maybe you'd best come up with me at once," said Ridley ; and scarcely knowing whether to laugh or cry, I followed her into the presence of my mother. The room smelt powerfully of burnt feathers. *Why* they had been committed to the flames I can scarcely take on myself to say ; for certes I never saw any one further from a fainting-fit than Lady Ormington. She reclined in her arm-chair. But her cheeks were red as pomegranates.

"Was there ever anything so shameful as the carelessness of the War Office, my dear Cis !" cried she, as soon as I had convinced her by an embrace that I was substantial flesh and blood. "Lord Ormington saw the return 'KILLED,' with his own eyes, at the Horse Guards ! This is the third instance I have known of a similar blunder. We have been in black ever since the returns. How glad I shall be to throw it off. The weather is getting very close for bombazine. But, gracious Heaven, Cis ! how you are altered. You are as brown, I might almost say, as black as a Spaniard. I hope you mean to shave off those horrible mustachios? You will drop the dragoon-officer now, I trust ? By the way, do the French women really wear the chimney-pot bonnets, imported by the Duchess of Oldenburg ? I cannot persuade myself that anything so extravagant is the right thing. And, after all, the duchess, though the emperor's sister, can't be called a criterion of fashion. But you don't ask after poor Bibiche ?"

"I don't ask after her, because I want no news. Her effigy yonder cries '*circumspice*,' as loud as the monument of Sir Christopher Wren in St. Paul's.

The naturalist has done her justice. Except at
Guildhall, I never saw a finer specimen of stuffing.
Only that she looks rather more animated than when
alive."

"Ah, Cis, you were always shamefully unjust to
that poor dog. It is only two months since she was
taken from me. I assure you I feel her loss severely.
There are times when I am obliged to throw a handkerchief over the glass case. When Miss Richardson
is out of the way, and I am sitting here alone, I often
fancy I feel her scratching my gown to be taken up.
Blane attended her through the winter. But he said
from the first, it was a lost case. She was in years,
poor little creature. She would have been thirteen
years old, had she survived till Michaelmas. In
fact, she died of old age. Blanc called it asthma,
but it was old age. They talked about asthma, when
Zaime, her mother, grew infirm. But *I* knew it was
old age."

It was painful to interrupt these important family
communications, with inquiries after Lord Ormington,
my brother, and sister.

"Danby? Much as usual, I believe. I rather
think Lady Susan is going to be confined again. I
wrote you word last year, didn't I, of the birth of his
son? They made a wonderful fuss about it, down at
Ormington; roasted oxen, and made bonfires, and all
that sort of thing, as if it were the first son and heir
ever heard of in the world. Lord Ormington took
especial delight in marking his triumph. Danby has
a house in Connaught Place. Just like him (isn't it?),
to go and settle at the extremity of the world. His
father, however, does not seem to think it far off, for
he is there every day of his life. I can tell you, Cis,
that if you wish to stand well with Lord Ormington,
you must not be wanting in civility to Danby and
Lady Susan."

"My dear mother," said I gravely, "before I quitted
England, you were constantly advising deference to

Lord Ormington and my brother as a matter of policy rather than of affection. I don't pretend that I ever found my heart overflowing with the family tenderness I have observed in other men. But whatever may have been exacted of me as a boy, as a *man* I will never affect a particle of concession towards either of them, beyond what their conduct claims at my hands. Lord Ormington used to communicate with me through his lawyers. As to my brother, he might have conversed with me through a speaking-trumpet, for any fraternal civilities that garnished his communication. So let it abide. What they have made me, they will find me. Thank Heaven, I have found friends in my profession, whose regard enables me to dispense with their niggardly kindness."

"We will enter into this another time," said Lady Ormington somewhat nervously. "But I entreat you, my dear Cis, don't let me hear you talk about 'your profession.' Your profession! Even if you had gone into the Guards, as you wanted, I should not have liked to hear you talk of the army as a profession; and——"

"Perhaps not," said I, ruthlessly interrupting her. "But after fighting my way through three hard campaigns, and by my own exertions attaining an honourable rank in the service——"

"The *Portuguese* service, which always sounds like the marines, or something of that sort."

"I should recommend no one but your ladyship to disparage it in my hearing," said I, with becoming indignation.

"There! Exactly the dragoon tone and cut," cried Lady Ormington, whimpering. "It couldn't be worse if you had been spending the last three years in country quarters."

Luckily for my patience, Lord Ormington at that moment entered the room; and I can scarcely do justice to the deep feeling of his welcome. I had not thought "the old man had so much blood in him;"

for there were actual tears upon his cheek as he
pressed my hands in his. I suspect the news of my
death had produced considerable self-impeachment in
the family. More than one of them felt they had
visited too harshly upon my head faults or crimes of
which I, at least, was innocent.

Again and again did he recount to me the particulars
which had reached Government of my having fallen at
Toulouse ; and very readily did I explain in return
that, having been taken prisoner, slightly wounded
in the hand, the exchange by which I was released
was not effected at the period of despatching the
returns.

" No need to recur to it now, since you are safe and
among us again," cried Lord Ormington, looking kindly
at my mother, as if sympathizing in the joy she must
experience on the occasion. But Lady Ormington was
absorbed in considering what summer dress would be
in readiness for her to put on when she threw off her
mourning on the morrow.

I could see that I had gained enormously in Lord
Ormington's estimation by the good reports of my conduct, as a man and an officer, which had reached the
Horse Guards with the announcement of my death.
Three years of active service had redeemed me from
the personal obloquy under which I had previously
laboured ; and the bronzed face and shabby coat which
so disgusted her ladyship were, in *his* eyes, the honourable badges of a noble calling. For my part, I felt
that no mortal had ever undergone in three years such
a transformation for the better as Lord Ormington.
I had reason to suppose the opinion reciprocal.

It was not, however, solely to my accession of merit
that the change in his feelings was due. I had ceased
to be his heir-presumptive. I had ceased to be an
object of jealous antipathy to him. The early marriage of Danby had been of his lordship's devising ;
and so gratified was he in the success of his plan, that
he seemed almost inclined to include me in his grati-

tude to Providence for having blessed my brother with increase in direct heirship to his honours.

It seemed a relief to him, moreover, when, instead of exhibiting envy or soreness, I frankly congratulated him on the birth of the grandson, the fame of whose spousal rites had reached me in lands beyond the sea.

"It *is* a prodigious fine boy!" cried Lord Ormington, with sparkling eyes; "Croft assures me he never saw a finer. And Lady Susan expects to be confined again about Midsummer."

In this triumphant announcement I saw only a promise of the duration of my favour. He proposed to me to accompany him to Connaught Place after dinner, and was satisfied with my excuses only when I represented that danger might arise to Lady Susan Danby from too sudden a presentation of the brother-in-law for whom she was in mourning. Meanwhile, not a word of Hanmer and Snatch, not a sarcasm, not a covert sneer. Lord Ormington was as companionable with me after dinner as though we had done nothing but dote upon each other from the hour I was born.

It is true we soldiers were just then top-sawyers in the world. We had so much to relate, which, though now a hundred-and-twice-told-tale, was then new and startling. All we had seen and suffered still wore its gloss of novelty. Our uncouth raiment and weather-worn visages attested our vauntings. The self-same anecdotes related by the soft silken Cis Danby of the F.O. three years before would not have assumed half authenticity.

Lady Ormington was doubly enchanted when she found that the sympathy testified by her lord was but a faint foreshowing of the fever of fashion I excited among the coteries of the season. I was the lion of the day; that is, the lion of private life, as the emperor and kings of public. After Blucher and Platoff in fashionable favour, came the Cecl Danby who had risen from the dead. The story of

my return, with variations *ad libitum*, was related
throughout the coteries, royal, noble, and ignoble of
the metropolis ; how the butler swooned and my lady
shrieked ; how Lord Ormington was forced to alter
his will, and the *"dam' d'honour"* to change her
apartment.

The *"dam' d'honour*," the Toady Richardson afore-
said, was, I believe, the only person who thought I
might have been just as well lying in the sands of
Toulouse as in the blue convolvulus bed. No longer
blue convolvulus, however. Profaned by the investiture of Toadyism, I represented to my lady-mother
the necessity of complete renovation ; and had now
the honour of sleeping in hangings of sea-green
damask, precisely the pattern of those which, the
following year, Bullock sent out to Longwood for
the use of a still greater hero.

"I must have you sit to Lawrence, Cis, before your
guerilla look is quite worn off," cried Lady Ormington,
"or Phillips. I should like Phillips to paint you in
the style in which he painted Byron, in his Arnaout
dress. You would make a beautiful brigand. Lady
Susan assures me you were more run after at White's
ball, the other night, than any of the Duke of Wellington's aides-de-camp."

"I am not aware of being hunted," said I, relapsing
into one of my ineffable smiles of former days. "Certainly, the dandies have just now a sorry time of it.
The hero fever is raging. We poor soldiers must make
hay while our sun shines."

I appeal to those readers of my own sex who are
able to call to mind the epoch in question, whether
the shabbiest and most rusty pair of mustachios might
not have taken the field against ten thousand a year ?
My brother had every reason to exclaim, as Sir Walter
Scott did to Moore, "Ah ! Tam, mon ! its lucky for us
we came sae soon !" The political distinctions which had
made a demigod of *him* three years before, would not
have stood their ground against a cornetcy of Cossacks.

It is true the Emperor and King, or, as the mob familiarly abbreviated them, "Proushia and Roushia," had inquired for him by name, as one of the most distinguished speakers of the House. But what was the curiosity of an emperor compared with the idolatry of Almack's, lavished upon one whom the lovely creatures protested had been the first in the breach at St. Sebastian's, and was not only killed, but buried at Bayonne. Women seldom trouble themselves to be *very* accurate in such matters. But who would not rather be blundered about by the enthusiasm of a hundred handsome women, than figure legitimately in the pages of Napier's History or Gurwood's Bulletins ?

What a moment it was !—Stars and garters, what a moment it was !—What an outbreak of public feeling celebrated the cessation of the European panic and the great blessing of peace ; peace that was to reconsolidate broken fortunes, suppress taxes, and heal the wounds of so many bleeding families ; peace that was to efface, if possible, from the records of God the damning fact that the progress of forty centuries of civilization and eighteen of Christianity had done no more towards humanizing mankind than comported with murders by thousands and tens of thousands, sanctioned under the name of WAR !

I was young then, and under the dominion of the enthusiasm of the moment. But on looking back dispassionately to my three years' apprenticeship in the art of heroism, I shudder at the ferocious enormities in which I played my part. It puzzles me to guess whether the tears of good angels, or the mirth of bad ones, must exceed ; while watching the progress of this wholesale butchery, this crime with a premium, arising from disputes whether such and such districts of the earth shall pay taxes to such or such a sovereign. At all events, from the said sovereigns down to a poor colonel of auxiliaries, like myself, all the world united to welcome the piping times of peace ; and the coteries of London, so long given over to the twaddling of

lords and schoolboys, knelt down to kiss the print in
the dust of a pair of jackboots.

WELLINGTON, whom they have since hissed and
pelted, was at that moment a divinity. St. Paul might
have preached in Hyde Park, and not attracted a
greater congregation, than crushed itself at the heels
of the conqueror, who *was* what Thiers describes
Napoleon, " *la plus grande gloire depuis César !*" He
might have overthrown the reigning dynasty, as easily
as a child blows down a pack of cards. I am not sure
that this last phrase may not be high treason, or con-
structive treason, or treason of some shape or colour.
But pardon me, O Lord Chief Justice and Bench of
Judges. I am only giving utterance to the opinions
of a coxcomb.

Not that the people had reason to complain of their
lords and governors. The afflicted king was as though
numbered with the dead ; and as to the regent, who,
to beguile the times looked like the time,—of all
modern princes he was the man to play the host to
the exotic royalties to whom we were affording king-
dom-room : graceful, silvertongued, a proficient in
foreign languages, and the hypocrisies of life.

It is true the shapely waist of " Roushia," and the
rough manliness of " Proushia," formed a disadvan-
tageous contrast to the unwieldiness of a prince who
had not been dieting on soup made of his own
boots : nor was the effigy of H.R.H. the Prince
Regent the one most calculated to win a lady's eye, of
those limned by Lawrence for the captivation of posterity. As my friend Byron said one night at Watier's
——But no !—had he intended it for publication, he
would have printed it himself.

For my part, it was neither Roushia nor Proushia—
Lawrence nor Byron—the regent nor Mr. Wilberforce
who arrested my attention. Reflect, indulgent reader,
that for three years past my eyes had beheld nothing
fairer, in the shape of the granddaughters of Eve, than
the suttlers of a camp, or coffee-coloured beauties of

the Peninsula. I never could abide the complexion of Spaniards or Old Point. I like a woman's cheek to be as the rose, before black roses were invented by modern science. I do not care to see the idol of my soul blush walnut-colour. To me, the transparent beauty of those English faces was something angelic. Like the Teutons, I could make no distinction between *Englisch* and *Engelisch!* I am not sure, by the way, that English women were ever before seen to such advantage, and I doubt whether they ever will again ; for they were *themselves.* No French torturers in stays, shoes, or curling-irons, were established in unsophisticated London. Their curls, shapes, complexions, were their own. They talked English, and they looked English. A French woman is as sweet as the sweetbriar, and nearly as *piquante.* But an English woman who affects the French woman, is like the donkey in the fable, leaping spanielwise into his master's lap.

I would give all that is left me in this world, my credit in St. James's Street, to live over again a day or two of that glorious month of June, 1814, to be smiled upon again as I was then, to go through those fêtes of White's, Watier's, and Carlton House, with the same partners, mothers (or in some instances grandmothers) of the poor vapid things I now see whisking round the ball-room, mere shadows of the brilliant beings who wreathed the laurels of Wellington and Alexander, the first to dash through the fiery-footed *valse à la Russe.*

Ahimè che memorie!—

Non ragionam di lor, ma guarda e passa !

CHAPTER XI.

At five-and-twenty, when the better part of life is over, one
should be something.   And what am I ? Nothing but five-and-
twenty, AND the odd months.—BYRON.

BREAKING up for the holidays is a pleasant thing,
whether to soldiers or schoolboys.   But after sick-
ening themselves with plum-cake, comes the reaction.
Homer and birch cannot be laid aside for ever.

The first thing Peace had leisure to discover was
that War must be paid for ; and long before the
triumphal arches of laurels had been cleared away, or
the stages for fireworks been removed from the parks,
the nation began to cry aloud that it was about to
appear in Basinghall Street ; that it was all up with
Great Britain.   After pretending to give the law to
the universe, she was all but amenable to the Poor
Law, and strongly advised to take the benefit of The
Act.   Tell it not in Gath, or, at all events, tell it not
in Gaul.   But so it was.

After the rumblings and grumblings of the Metropolis, how charming appeared to me the verdant
tranquillity of dear dull old Ormington Hall.   Instead
of imploring my mother to defer her departure till
September, I was as glad to go in August, as if its
grassy uplands had been scrubby moors, and its partridges, grouse.   The rookery disturbed me no longer.
I began to feel that the place was home ; that its
plantations and turnip-fields were not as other plantations and turnip-fields.   I had not yet forgotten how
often among the scorching plains and maize-fields of
the Peninsula, I had longed to flee away, and be at
rest, under the shade of my ancestral oaks.

Lord Ormington was pleased with the frankness of
these admissions.   He was beginning to treat me, if
not as a son, as an agreeable acquaintance.   Since my

resuscitation was an inevitable evil, the whole family seemed resolved to make the best of me. By tacit consent, not one of us ever adverted to any event antecedent to my expedition to Lisbon. My mother admitted that it was in consequence of the remonstrances of Lord Ormington, grounded upon those of Danby and the intelligence of Lady Harriet, that old Hanmer had thrust out of his hands the guardianship of his ill-starred Portuguese ward. But she disavowed all knowledge of the harshness of his conduct ; and was indignant when I assured her that the flight of the d'Acunhas from England originated in the terrors with which they were beset by the old lawyer. But I was not fully convinced. Experience has proved in many a well-known instance, that no means are considered unjustifiable to secure a family highly connected from plebeian alliance. Slander becomes meritorious, and falsehood virtue, rather than that a ball of their coronet should be tarnished.

I fancied—it was probably only fancy—that, after the birth of Lady Susan Danby's second child, *a girl*, he grew a little less cordial. But I had no reason to complain.

If reserved with me, he was mysterious with all the world; and we got on a wonderful deal better together, now that I knew a bean from a pea field, and mangold wurzel from Swedes, and condescended to potter with him in his rides and walks.

The house was full of company for the shooting season. Battues were not in fashion ; but the Ormington preserves had lost nothing during my absence. All this was better fun than among the guerillas. I scarcely understood the philosophy of Danby, who had declined my father's proposition to give up the family place to him on his marriage. But the peculiar distinction of my brother's character was moderation ; the highest quality, perhaps, of the philosophy of civilization. Sabine farms are thoroughly out of fashion. The first incentive to distinction, in

modern times, is prodigality ; and we have seen not
only the richest inheritors gallop through their
fortunes into beggary ; but the greatest men, who by
high faculties have achieved riches and honour, con-
demn themselves to years of misery, by an attempt to
rival the brilliant existence of people richer and sillier
than themselves.

I was not then able to appreciate the profound
wisdom of Danby's modest establishment.   It requires
a great mind to enter into the greatness of moderation.
All the mediocrities of public life, for instance, admitted themselves disappointed in the Honourable
Member for Rigmarole.   Since his splendid outburst,
he had not made a single speech deserving the honours
of the press.   It was only the practical men, like
Votefilch, who saw in him the unboasting Hercules
whose shoulder was ever to the wheel of the party ;
whose prognostications had been oracularly fulfilled ;
and whose greatest greatness of all, was the modest
good sense with which he contented himself with a
subordinate place in the eyes of the public.   For if the
power of acquiring be a great thing, the power of
abstaining from acquirement is a thousandfold greater.

I never saw happier people than Danby and Lady
Susan ; domestic, without nauseating others by a
display of domesticity, and wholly free from that
impertinent double-barrelled egotism which passes for
a virtue among the rigidly righteous of Great Britain.
They neither withdrew from society, to be made more
of by each other than society was likely to make of
them ; nor, in society, affected to see and feel for
themselves.   It was impossible to bear their faculties
more meekly.

Another, and scarcely less sober couple in our
family circle, were Mr. and Mrs. Halbert Herries, or,
as the newspapers would say,—"Halbert and the
Hon. Mrs. Herries"—Julia having been many months
the wife of my former colleague.   But my former
colleague was now under-secretary of state ; and his

bride, in addition to her hereditary ten thousand pounds, had inherited forty from her maiden aunts. The match was consequently a prudential one on both sides ; and Herries, originally as grave as a judge, was now as grave as a lord chancellor. I am not so sure, by the way, that the illustration is a happy one ; the chancellors *I* have seen on the woolsack — Erskine, Eldon, Lyndhurst, Brougham,—having been renowned for runaway marriages and convivial propensities.

My mother could not bear the marriage. She had written word of it to me in Spain, as a job of Lord Votefilch's ; and was constantly lamenting that her daughter had not married Lord Riddlesworth, a Catholic peer; or Colonel Morley, who, on finding Lady Harriet Vandeleur's jointure forfeitable by a second marriage, had looked upon Julia's ready money as ready payment for his debts. Even now, though she saw Mrs. Herries perfectly happy, and occupying a highly honourable position in life, she was always protesting against the precariousness of official distinctions, and the odiousness of office-men.

Her attacks appeared to fall innocuous on the happy couple. They were like people living secure in a thunderstorm, under shelter of a conductor. So far as Herries was concerned, the boy had proved so genuinely father to the man, that is, the clerk to the secretary, that I very much doubt whether he were so much as aware of any event occurring beyond the pale of Downing Street. Herries always looked puzzled when accosted by Lord Ormington with domestic or country news ; as if he longed to say, " I beg your pardon ; *that* belongs to the Home Department."

As for my sister, my red-haired sister, poor contemned Julia, I scarcely venture to speak of her, lest in making the *amende honorable,* I seem to fall into the contrary extreme. La Bruyère has said, " When an ugly woman is beloved, it is usually to madness ;" since it is a passion that must arise from the weakness of her lover, or some inherent quality superior to

beauty.   Mrs. Herries possessed a plurality of qualities
superior to beauty. She was both *aimable* and amiable ;
both loveable and excellent.   There was something in
the charm of her manner and intonation of her voice,
combined with the alabaster-lamp-like transparency of
her complexion, which most men found irresistable.
Wherever she went, the place by her side was eagerly
appropriated. No one possessed such general information, or said her say in so pleasant and unpretending
a manner.

   We had not spent a week together at Ormington,
before I began to repent my former injustice. Grateful
for the gentle cordiality with which, as Herries's wife,
she accepted as a friend the man who, as Julia Danby,
had rejected her as a sister ; I repaid her generosity
with the gift of my whole confidence.   Julia was the
only member of my family to whom I ever named the
name of Emily ; and never shall I forget my thankfulness when the tears of my neglected sister flowed in
sincere sympathy with my troubles.

   Of all confidantes, give me a woman !   For warmth
of sympathy, for active aid, for good faith, for trust-
worthiness, I say again, give me a woman.   Man (who
in the fable painted the subjugation of the lion), has
chosen to paint, both in fable and history, the incon-
sistency of womankind ; its infirmity of purpose, its
incontinence of tongue.   Away with fabulists and
historians.   Instead of being a noun substantive, man
is, after all, only an item of his clubs and freemason's
lodge. A woman is *herself;* that is, kind, generous,
and true.   I swear I would as soon run my head
against an iceberg, as intrust my sorrows to one of my
own cold, double-breasted, double-milled sex.

   Of my former friends and associates, some had
achieved greatness ; some had greatness thrust upon
them. Chippenham had achieved it by a natural
progress to the Upper House ; and having of course
inherited with his peer's robes the graces and faculties
of estate, he was now an ambassador, with her Excel-

lency Lady Theresa for his Countess. The Earl and Countess of Merepark throned it majestically at —— ; and his lordship was described in leading articles as an able and conscientious man. How far his union with Lady Votefilch's niece might have opened the eyes of Government to his sudden accession of abilities, it becomes me not to determine.

Among those on whom greatness had been thrust, I conclude I may enumerate Sir John Harris, K. all sorts of things, not omitting the Guelphic, and Honorary all sorts of things at Carlton House and in the Red Book. It would be difficult exactly to define his functions. He was supposed to invent wigs and collect Chinese lanterns ; sketch designs for yacht cabins, and cottage chimneys. But it was all supposition. His exits and entrances were noted, but nothing wherefore. He was tabooed, and had ceased to converse with the public at large ; occasionally letting fall something exceedingly mysterious to an earl or cabinet-minister, which was picked up and repeated at the clubs. For every one was overjoyed to quote Sir John Harris. Even *I* should no more have dared to "Jack" him, now, than to "George" H.R.H. the Prince Regent.

Many origins were assigned to this mysterious favouritism ; competition for a crackled teapot at Baldock's, in which Sir John had ceded with grace and solemnity ;—an inedited recipe for curaçoa punch *à crême de thé ;*—a pattern for a gored stock, which was said to impart to the most apoplectic throat the lengthened stiffness "long drawn out" of a stork. It was no manner of consequence. Sir John was born in a cork jacket, predestined to float, like other weeds, on the surface of the stream ; or, rather, he was one of those of whom it has been said, " Fling him, with a stone round his neck, into a horse-pond, and he will rise in ten minutes out of the water, in a court suit, bag-wig, and sword."

The first time I paid my respects at Carlton House

P

after my arrival, I determined to take the initiative in
cutting so great a man. But sweet Sir John knew
better than to afford me a pretext for prating of his
early whereabout, and held out his finger with almost
as much condescension as if *he* had been Emperor of
the Celestial Empire, and I a mandarin of the third
button. I took him as I found him. It was not for
Cis Danby to quarrel with the pretensions of a coxcomb ; and as I have always held success the test of
merit, I was bound to consider Sir John Harris, K.A.,
K.B., K.C., K.D., K.E., K.F., K.G., and so forth
through the alphabet, the Admirable Crichton of
modern chivalry.

There was some excuse for the beknighting, just
then, of so many very simple citizens. The deluge of
foreign titles which swept over the surface of society
had created such a craving appetite for titularity, that
(as Napoleon observed of one of his sisters, who sulked
with him for withholding from her the dignities of
queen, " Would not any one suppose I had defrauded
her of her share of the realms of the king our father ? ")
the Prince might have observed of certain animalculæ
crawling about the court, who insisted on the honours
of knighthood, " Would not any one suppose that all
the apothecaries in my dominions were born in spurs ?"
There was even one clerical knight, a crooked scion of
a noble house, who always reminded me of Sir Hugh
in the " Merry Wives."

As to myself, I had to run away almost on my knees
(like the mayor of Newcastle from George III.) from
the be-Guelphing sword of the Regent. I gave out in
the coterie of Carlton House that I should be disin-
herited by Lord Ormington were I to assume any
other designation than that conferred by my birth-
right ; and secured under lock and key my insignia of
the order of the Tower and Sword, as though it had
been the badge of a hackney-coachman.

This scrupulosity may now appear overcharged.
But I appeal to all who visited Paris or London in the

year of grace 1814, whether a ribbon in the button-hole were not then the nearest approach to the letters T. F. (*Travaux Forcés*) branded on the shoulder of a convict.

What was *I* to attain by being Guelphed? My hereditary distinctions placed me in the category of gentlemen; and my professional ones had certainly done nothing to place me in that of heroes. I had fought my way bravely. So had thousands and thousands of others who put in no claim to the glories of the spur. Soldiership had done more for me than fifty knighthoods, by softening the influence of a profound affliction, and hardening the effeminacy of foppery. I had now attained as much philosophy as was compatible with my four-and-twenty years and a monstrous good-looking face; and Byron, with whom at Watier's and elsewhere I had picked up an acquaintanceship almost amounting to friendship, often expressed his envy of my unaffected apathy.

We heard the chimes at midnight together; and he saw me stand fire without flinching. That was a strange epoch in the history of the female society of Great Britain. The knight who suddenly flings aside his armour, is more defenceless than the simple clown, habitually *in cuerpo;* and the Englishwomen, who, during the visit of the Allied Sovereigns, laid aside their prudery to make a virtue of hero-hunting, certainly went lengths in the excitement of the hour which it would be difficult to match in the history of less highly-reputed countries. Had Byron lived to complete "Don Juan," he would have put anecdotes on record in some of which *I* was an actor—in some, himself—such as might have made the tales of the Queen of Navarre blush, or turn pale with envy.

This it was that rendered Ormington Hall such a relief to me. Those frantic three months in London, with their orgies, ruinous to health and fortune, had so thoroughly disgusted me, that I was too happy in sauntering with Lord Ormington over his farms; still

happier, when chatting by the fireside of Danby and
Lady Susan at Forest Lodge, a pretty place they had
hired on the Bracknell side of Windsor Forest.

They saw little or no company ; for my brother was
as studious and almost as silent as ever.   But when he
did converse, people held their breath to listen.   Like
the flowering of the aloe or gestation of the lion, the
product was proportionate to the delay.

I suppose it was on account of Danby's taciturnity
and Lady Susan's extreme gentleness, that their boy,
now nearly two years old, took so decided a fancy for
his soldier-uncle.

I dissuaded him from crawling on the carpet, by
instituting a school of discipline ; and with my cane
and word of command got him through his exercise,
till Lord Ormington, albeit little addicted to mirth,
used to burst into fits of laughing at his martial airs.

Lady Susan was engrossed by her girl ; Danby, in
compiling an edition of Bolingbroke.   Little Arthur
consequently fell to my share as a companion.   While
enjoying the last gleams of autumnal sunshine under
the magnificent beech-trees overshading the lawn,
originally a part of the royal forest, Lord Ormington
and I seemed to enjoy ourselves more in that little
domestic snuggery, than at his own princely domain.
For *him*, I suspect, there were disagreeable reminiscences attached to the old Hall.   For myself, I do
not scruple to own that the growing friendship of
Danby was the great embellishment of my existence.

Yes, I, Cis Danby of the cockade, was actually
proud of him ; proud of frightful John ; proud of the
urchin exiled to the nursery that I might play the
peacock unmolested.   Through him I seemed to feel
as if the Danby family were grappled, not only to the
passing time, but to future ages ; and though celebrity
has been defined by a clever French writer as the
advantage of being known to those you will never
know, it is an advantage which greater men than
myself are far from despising.

I had commenced life by a false step. At the instigation of a passionate impulse I had abandoned a
promising vocation. And though the military career
thus wildly embraced had spared me life and limb for
new adventures, I never yet saw an existence prosper
which commenced by a blunder. Sailors have a superstition against voyages that begin with putting back.
I confess I share the prejudice.

Lord Ormington probably discerned, after I had
been six months resident in England, that I was giving
myself up to listlessness, like a man whose destinies
are accomplished, when mine, in fact, were scarcely
begun. For he took occasion one day gravely to
inquire whether it were true that I had declined an
apointment in the household of the Regent.

"To the letter," replied I. "Sir John Harris was
commissioned to offer it me, a few weeks after my
appearance at the levee."

"You did wrong," replied Lord Ormington drily.
"You must be aware, Cecil, that the peculiar circumstance under which you threw up your appointment at
Lisbon have closed against you the doors of diplomatic
distinction?"

"Not more than I desire," was the reply. "I
have no yearning after the mysteries of the despatch-
box."

"May I ask, then," resumed Lord Ormington, "what
are your projects? It will never be in my power to
do more for you than I am now doing. By your
mother's marriage settlement you are intitled to ten
thousand pounds. I have no intention of increasing
the provision.

"Why should you, when it fulfils my utmost
ambition?" said I coolly. "Campaigning luckily
took me out of the hands of the Philistines and the
perfumers; and I have now come to consider four
hundred a year a fortune for a prince of the blood."

Lord Ormington looked vexed.

"I must still presume to suggest," said he "that

you would do well not to trifle with the good-will ot
the Regent. You are in a situation to require the
support of your friends. You want occupation, Cecil ;
you want a purpose for your young energies. There
is good in you, if you would only turn it to account."

This was a great deal for Lord Ormington. I
remember the time in his days of mystery, when,
previous to uttering so long a sentence to any one (to
me he uttered only monosyllables), he would have
barred the door, and placed sentinels outside. I contented myself with inquiring what " good " he thought
would result from my holding a place about the person
of the Regent ?

"Are you serious, or is this a return to your old
habits of irony ? " demanded Lord Ormington. " Is it
nothing to be reckoned among the friends of the heir-
apparent to the throne ? "

"Fortuna vitrea est : tum, quum splendet, fran-
gitur," I replied. " *Who* wishes to be caught
up and whirled round by the sails of a windmill ?
When I quitted England, I left the Prince of
Wales surrounded by all that is ultra among
the liberals ; his very terrier barking Whiggery.
I find the Prince Regent surrounded by all that is
narrowest in Toryism ; his very cockatoo screaming
' Huzza for Castlereagh ! ' "

" His Royal Highness has wisely conceded to the
spirit of the times," replied Lord Ormington gravely.
"The fable of Dame Partington and her mop is
applicable to both sides of the question. You could
scarcely expect the sovereign *pro tempore* of these
realms——"

" I expect nothing, either *of* or *from* him," was my
somewhat cavalier interruption. But from that day, I
perceived that his lordship lost no opportunity of im-
pressing upon me the ignominious obscurity of being a
younger son, unless upheld by talents or industry. I was
quite of his opinion. But ignominious obscurity, *id
est*, inglorious ease, was now my idol. For the life and

soul of me, I could not reunite the shattered links of the chain of ambition.

It was the era of great achievements. Laurels were as plentiful as hawthorn hedges; and the trumpet of Fame was as almost as familiar as the horn of a mail-coach. As Byron used to say, the only distinction was to be a little undistinguished. Napoleon, if he had an antechamber of kings, had also created a mob of heroes: and under such circumstances to raise oneself above the crowd was a Herculean task. I resolved, therefore, to content myself with my modest peninsular renown, till it should be worn threadbare; then, trust to the chapter of accidents for its renovation. I tried to pass off my indolence under the plausible name of content.

That winter, all the world—more especially that foolish portion of it which calls itself the fine world—was hurrying to Paris. Among others, my mother took it into her head to experience an eager longing for a glimpse of the Louvre. She had not visited Paris since I saw the light there, shortly after the assembling of the States General.

To my surprise, Lord Ormington opposed no obstacle to the project. But as Sir Lionel Dashwood had been her ladyship's cavalier on the former occasion, he seemed to consider it a matter of course that *I* should be so on the present.

He did not even put it to me in a hypothetical form, whether I should accompany Lady Ormington; but gave me succinct instructions concerning the mode in which I was to draw upon his bankers in her behalf. His liberality was excessive. But I suspect he would have given double the money for the satisfaction of getting rid of us, to divide his time exclusively between Julia and John. As he pleased. I gave him ample credit for the two thousand pounds he placed to ours at Drummond's, and departed.

Let it be taken for granted that we arrived safe at Paris. My readers have, I trust, done justice to my forbearance in the daubery or description line. If not, I give them notice that my palette was got up with an assortment of the finest oil-colours from Newman's, expressly to inflict a sketch of the Convention upon them, enlivened with the proper varieties of national costume and British or foreign uniforms, and the particoloured brilliancy of the Lisbon quays, crowned by a sunny sketch of high-mass in the cathedral.

It depended on myself to develop all this in a couple of dozen pages, emblazoned like a missal with scarlet, cobalt, and gold. But I forbore. I reflected that the florid was going out of fashion. Scarcely a scribbler who wields a crow-quill but has got up a bit of fine writing of this description, for the use of boudoirs and the delight of the tallow-chandlers' wives.

For the same reason, I now refrain from embellishing my life and times with a picture of Paris emerging from the iron tyranny of Napoleon ; which may be found in better English in the pages of Scott's " Visit," or " Paul's Letters to his Kinsfolk ; " besides being married to immortal verse in the Correspondence of " The Fudge Family."

It matters little that all which these or other English authorities saw or desired to see of Paris, is comprised within the Boulevards and the Palais Royal. They and the public were satisfied,—and so am I.

As to Lady Ormington, whom I escorted to the banks of the Seine, with the conviction that her elegant valetudinarianism would resign itself as quietly to a *bergère* in the *Hôtel de Breteuil,* as to an easy-chair in Hanover Square, I was awed on detecting the influence of the *genus loci,* the moment she found herself within view of the Tuileries. She seemed to recede the whole twenty-four years of my existence, and become one and twenty and a beauty.

No sooner installed in that temple of frippery, than she cried aloud, like the Pythoness, inspired by the afflatus of the tripod. Poor Toady Richardson wore herself to a cambric thread with rendering the hourly tribute of flattery exacted by her patroness, upon her rejuvenization. I scarcely knew where this second childhood of coquetry would stop. For though her ladyship had attained her forty-sixth year, old women, from Cardinal —— downwards, were at a premium at the court of the corpulent sovereign whose brightest reminiscences had of course attained their majority.

To us, his rotund Majesty was singularly gracious, affording us what was in his eyes the highest mark of distinction, excellent dinners. Worthy soul! I beg his Majesty's pardon—worthy body! A course of twenty years' roast mutton and batter pudding had developed his royal sensibilities towards the true enjoyments of life. Prolonged divorce from the stewpans of Paris had taught him the eminent superiority of the *Almanach des gourmands* over the Almanack of Saxe-Gotha; and while hundreds of antediluvian princesses and ci-devant duchesses were trying to restore the Holy Inquisition of Bourbon etiquette, his Majesty ate, drank, and said grace after meat; conceiving that, in a world full of marrow and fatness, where Providence assigns ortolans and *foie gras* for the food of man, there can be no pretext for fretting after idle distinctions of precedence and estate. I love a straightforward epicurean, who makes no compromise with his pleasant vices; nor disfigures with a sneer the unctuous lips, imbibing to satiety the good things of this world.

I was surprised, by the way, considering the enormous ravages of the guillotine, and the number of unfortunate nobles said to have died in emigration, in England, not of starvation, but of bad cookery, to find the Faubourg St. Germain flourishing in all its pristine stiffneckedness. It did not appear to me that its hotels could have contained more dowagers or bishops, had Robespierre never encumbered or disencumbered the earth.

Among these, Lady Ormington was an idol. They had worn her for twenty years in their heart of hearts;

and the old Cosway print, deepened in its tints by a
quarter of a century's smoke and dust, was still extant
in more than one mansion of the Rue de Grenelle.

It was a great delight to these fossil grandees to
turn the tables upon the duchesses and countesses
hatched under the wing of the Empire, in Madame
Campan's dovecot at Ecouen : and by such as these,
the Allies were welcomed as friends, and the English
as Allies. The moral of the case was nothing to *me*.
I was content to be made much of in those charming
boudoirs, and told twenty times a day that any one
might have guessed from my appearance that I was a
Parisian-born. I made the most of that happy
accident. Like the bat, I was a bird with the bipeds,
and a mouse with the quadrupeds.

My former affectations were budding anew. Like
a tree that has been cut down instead of grubbed up,
the old root sent forth a plenteous growth of under-
wood. Everything vigorous or manly seemed to have
retreated from public life ; and the recent vicissitudes
of royalty inspired such a dread of the instability of
human enjoyments, that "*dum vivimus, vivamus*" was
the motto of many wise men besides the pious Dr.
Doddridge.

I will not pretend to exculpate myself from the
epicureanism of the hour. No one enjoyed more exquisitely the dinners of Bouvilliers,—the gleanings of
Corcellet's stores.—the *Feen Welt* of the ballet,—the
pleasantries of the Opéra Comique. Above all, I was
enchanted with the French women. I do not blush
for my taste. When John Clare, the Northampton-
shire poet, was transplanted for a month into the
sorceries of London life, the thing that charmed him
most was the bewitchment of the French actresses at
the Tottenham Street Theatre.

As to me, I had never before seen a Frenchwoman.
The peevish *emigrées*, who used to waste their time
fretting over their fall, at Ormington Hall or in
Hanover Square, scarcely deserved the name. As

well call an oyster-shell an oyster ; as well consider
the wooden puppet in a showman's box, the Punchi-
nello, whose squeaking witticism's convulse the mob.
A Frenchwoman, properly so called, means not only a
Parisian, but a Parisian in Paris. A Parisian must
have her appropriate atmosphere, like the tender
tropical plants, to refresh whose roots the watering-
pot is warmed over a slow fire. Her leaves do not
expand, or her flower-buds effloresce, unless sure of a
quantum suff. of sunshine. But *in* Paris, what a
bewitching creature ; what a brilliant butterfly, what
a richly-scented blossom. Nothing real about her, it
is true ; but the pretence, how delightful ! One
would put up with deception for ever, to be so charmingly bamboozled.

A *Parisienne*, properly so called, is a creature full
of intelligence and grace ; for her own enjoyment
sake, incapable of the yea-nay, dawdling, unmeaning
nonentityism of London fashion. Her countenance is
bright with purpose. She wills resolutely, and, lo !
her will is accomplished ; her rapid and strongly-
accented utterance imparting irresistible energy to her
decrees.

Perhaps I was the more sensible to the charm of
this vivacity, because recent experience had put me
somewhat out of conceit with my countrywomen.
The very good ones, I had begun to consider fine ;
the very bad ones, coarse. The society of Byron had
not improved my morality. Lady Harriet Vandeleur
(whom I found established in Paris, as the idol of the
new court) used to revile me with sacrilege against
my exceedingly loving countrywomen. No need to
inform her ladyship that *she* was precisely one of those
who had rendered me hypercritical.

Had I followed the bent of my inclinations, which
nobody does in this world, least of all in the matter of
falling in love, I verily believe I should have dedi-
cated my affections to some choice specimen of the
Rococo. My early education seemed to have created

me for a passion *à talons rouges*. I adored the high
polish of those Sèvres-like Marchionesses, scarcely
more alive than the effigies of their grandmothers
from the pencils of Mignard or Rigaud.

Of one or two of these, I was the pet and favourite ;
better pleased to share their regard with their lapdog
and abbé, and be called "*mon enfant*" by their colourless lips, than "*mon cœur*" by the vociferous fashion-
ables of the Chaussée d'Antin.

But I was not to be my own master, that is, master
of who should be my mistress. I could weep, now, to
think of all I lost. What a winter I might have
spent in the warm, snug boudoir, of the charming old
Princesse de Trémont, of whom Boufflers had been the
lover, fifteen years before I was born. What pleasant
talk we should have held together ! What an insight
I should have obtained into the philosophy of life.
Instead of this (dare I confess it ?—but I vow I had no
more to do with the matter than one of the Chinese
bonzes on her chimneypiece), instead of this, I became
a martyr to the caprices and exactions of the young and
fashionable Comtesse Anarcharsis de la Vrillière.

Thérèse (I thought myself a happy man the first
day I was permitted to call her Thérèse !)—was the
daughter of one of my mother's most favourite friends.
One of Lady Ormington's first cares on arriving in
Paris, was to inquire for the progeny of her darling
Duchesse de St. Barthélemy, who had fallen a victim
to the revolution ; and great was her indignation on
hearing that the young duke was wearing away his
unpopularity in foreign travel, having figured at the
court of Josephine as equerry, or grand something or
other in the way of courtiership.

But in addition to the degenerate duke, the lovely
duchess had left a little girl, born about the same
period as myself ; and there had been some sort of
romance about a Paul and Virginia interchange of
nursing. Little Thérèse, my contemporary, was now
of course, according to the Parisian calendar, an old

woman that is four and twenty ; and pleasantry apart, a marriage at sixteen *is* apt to reduce four and twenty to decrepitude.

But Thérèse, if an old woman, was a woman of fashion ; one of those angels without wings to whose delicate features the ethereal pencil of Isabey has assigned diaphanous immortality.

Go to Versailles, gentle reader ; and in the picture of the baptism of the king of Rome, you will discover, seated in the tribune, surmounted by a coronet of diamonds, a face scarcely equalled in sweetness not only from those days to these, but from the days when Rome had Emperors, till those when the Eternal City was required to yield tribute to that very transitory little king. If it do not give you the idea of Miranda, "admired Miranda," sunning herself in the smiles of Prospero may you never turn a page of Shakspere again.

Thérèse was not quite so pretty as that picture when I had first the honour of her acquaintance ; but she was a lovely creature still. To me, there was something peculiarly interesting in her faded languor. I saw she was what is called *passée ;* and not possessing a Frenchman's intuitive knowledge of such matters, instead of attributing her loss of bloom to the natural progress of events, chose to surmise a secret sorrow, "a worm i' the bud."

I fancied, according to my English creed, that in woman, four and twenty is the meridian of beauty ; that, should these clouds of sorrow ever pass away, the obscured luminary whould shine forth again, more effulgent than ever.

I could not have flattered the pretty comtesse more than by this construction. Thérèse would rather have been thought "interesting," than fair as Hebe. Thérèse chose to play her part in the world in sable drapery, or at least in French grey. Thérèse was *la femme incomprise !* The phrase is now common, exhausted,—effete. Everybody understands the *femme*

incomprise ; and a woman might as well pretend to
be an Egyptian mummy for any interest likely to be
excited by so exploded a pretension. But it was
specious enough then.

Monsieur le Comte de la Vrillière, the lord, if not
the master, of the unappreciated lady, was a very
great man in his way, and a very large man in everybody's way. •

Yet the count's figure, instead of being heavy and
clumsy, like most unwieldy persons of my own country,
was sinuous and graceful as one may conceive the
Apollo Belvedere fed upon oilcake, and weighing
eighteen stone. He was rotund as an air-cushion ; or
as two handsome men rolled into one.

Impossible to be better got up. His grey hair and
whiskers were arranged with as much care as if am-
brosial curls. His coat was as scrupulously symmetrical as though his waist were as slender as his means
were great. His boots were as well varnished as if
the members they encased were not capable of playing
the part of the oriental ox and treading out the corn.
But in spite of all this (the truth must out !) he was
not the man to win, or retain a lady's heart. His
appetite was "more to bread than stone ;" and more
to a succulent dish of cutlets, with *sauce à la Soubise,*
than bread. The result may be inferred ; and a pro-
tuberance below the region of the heart is more unsightly to the eye of woman, than the hunch of Æsop
or hump of a buffalo.

There was nothing else particularly odious in La
Vrillière, except that he breathed hard after dinner,
and possessed at all hours of the day a sort of inso-
lently prosperous air, which must certainly have exposed him more than once in his life to peril of assassination from the brooms of street sweepers. It is an
act of great self-denial in beggars, to put up with a
man so well to do in the world.

But if an object of hatred to the kennel, he was
one of surpassing affection to the court—the court,

tale quale. He was just one of the men of whose
moral and physical preponderance Napoleon knew so
well to dispose. He possessed the very length, breadth,
and thickness for a Préfet. His respectability of person
and purse was the one thing needful to fill an Hôtel
de la Préfecture, in a southern department; and during
the last five years of the Empire, accordingly, Monsieur
le Comte Anacharsis de la Vrillière had eaten his
truffles fresh from the sod, with a stipend from government of eighty thousand francs a year, and the opportunity of dedicating his income towards upholding, on
behalf of the emperor, the dignities of the state.

His marriage was of Napoleon's making. Anacharsis
de la Vrillière was a man of high descent, who, beg-
gared by the revolution (which found him with a very
good head on his shoulders, and, strange to tell, left it
there unmolested), had managed by dexterous appro-
priation of his talents to the shifting exigencies of
public life, to win back all he had lost, like a cunning
gamester, taking his revenge on fortune. Directory,
Consulate, Empire had successively found his Ko-too
at their disposal. POWER was with *him* the right
divine; and like most of those,

> Who, as the veering wind shifts, shift their sails,

a trade wind blew him into port. He was, in short,
one of the thousand Tartuffes of political life engendered by the schisms and vacillations of the days of
Talleyrand.

Among the rewards lavished upon him by a sovereign in no position to deal hypercritically with the
moral qualities of his partisans, was the hand of
Mademoiselle de St. Barthélemy. As a rich orphan,
she had been of course Campanized; for as Frederick
of Prussia chose to institute a Newmarket for the
improvement of his race of grenadiers, by alliances
between six-feet-two of hero with six-feet-nothing of
heroine, Napoleon of France, aware that the era of
brute force was at an end, chose to elevate *his* ad-

herents by uniting men of ten thousand a year
in ambition with women of ten thousand a year in
possession.

Hence the discrepant union between the soft, sentimental Thérèse de St. Barthélemy and Monsieur le
Comte Anacharsis de la Vrillière,—*Conseiller d'État—
Chevalier de la Légion d'Honneur,* &c. &c. &c.   Hence,
la femme incomprise !

For how was it possible for an individual of such
dimensions, an individual who if fossilized, would have
afforded grounds to Cuvier for a new theory upon the
degeneration of mankind, to enter into the hysterical
affections and catalepses of a sensitive creature like
Thérèse,—a sylph, an aerial being, liable to evaporate
on the touch of a mortal so materially material as
Monsieur le Préfet ?

La Vrillière perfectly understood, on the first proposition of the match by his friend Cambacères, the
substantial advantages attached to the possession of
this unsubstantial bride ; and, to do him justice, had
never ceased to demonstrate his consciousness of her
merit.   He was a model husband.   The pin-money of
Madame la Comtesse was as punctual as the dividend
of the Bank of France.   A new equipage every second
year, — diamonds reset every third, — and annual
étrennes, which made many an envious eye of the
Faubourg "pale its ineffectual fires," attested his conjugal devotion.

When installed at her Préfecture, the fêtes of the
countess, her toilet, her household establishment,
created all the precedents of the province.   She enjoyed, as the phrase runs, everything that money can
give.   But, alas ! it too often happens that people who
enjoy everything in the power of money to give, enjoy
also a redundance of leisure, which begets an appetite
for things that money will *not* give.

Madame la Comtesse de la Vrillière sighed for a
sentiment.   Madame la Comtesse wanted to be
" Thérèse."   Her indulgent husband, huge as he was,

did not fill up the vacuum in her soul. He did not love her; and who would waste their affections on the unloving? She preferred being a victim. She chose to be *la femme incomprise!*

Chateaubriand, the grandfather of the romantic school, and Madame Cottin, its eldest daughter, had obtained possession of her mind. She had never recovered "Atala" and "Réné;" and had wept a Hellespont over "Claire d'Albe" and "Malvine." She would rather have been the impassioned Mathilde, blistering her feet with Malek Adhel, in the Syrian sands, than Madame la Préfette at ——, or Madame la Comtesse, in the Rue du Montblanc. *Néobstand*, as her favourite writer would have said, I suspect she was almost in hopes of a reverse of fortune, when Napoleon took refuge on board the *Bellerophon.*

It suggested itself to her sanguine imagination that the fat préfet might possibly be incarcerated for life at Ham, or Mont St. Michel, or Blaye, or la Force, or, perhaps, driven into exile or emigration (the idea of poor Anacharsis being *driven* anywhere!) to die at Cayenne or some other peppery colony. In that case, she determined to become a Sœur de Charité; one of the interesting victims of romantic life whose costume is least unbecoming.

But, to her surprise, almost to her indignation, the first person to whom the thanks of his Majesty Louis XVIII. were tendered for the promptitude of his oath of allegiance, was M. le Comte Anacharsis de la Vrillière, now Chevalier de St. Louis. And, lo! the daughter of the ancient and loyal house of St. Barthélemy was folded to the bosom of the Duchesse d'Angoulême, till she was ready to cry for vexation and mercy.

Not the smallest opening for heroism. No hope of persecution—no chance of a reverse. On the contrary, the family diamonds were reset a year sooner than usual; and on establishing herself anew in the Rue du Mont Blanc, a fresh suite of furniture saluted the repining eyes, whose only quarrel with the rumpling of the rose-leaf in her destinies was that it did not turn out a thistle or prickly pear.

Such was the position of the countess when I arrived at Paris. On the entrance of the allies, the count still occupied his prefectorial functions in the south ; or the *femme incomprise* would most likely have been appreciated by some general of Cossacks, or Hessian field-marshal, Mohicanly starred and feathered. But just as my mother began to look up the scattered remnant of her former friends, Monsieur le Comte et Madame la Comtesse Anacharsis de la Vrillière were welcomed to the exceedingly soft bosom of the new court.

Lady Ormington was everjoyed at the meeting. There had always been intense sympathy between her and the Duchesse de St. Barthélemy. They had drunk of the same ether, and wept over the same page of the Nouvelle Héloïse ; and on discovering that the daughter who inherited the duchess's name of Thérèse inherited her nature as a swooner of swoons, and sympathizer of sympathies, Lady Ormington began to feel that she had recovered a congenial soul in this younger and fairer quarter of herself.

Lady Ormington made a bad throw off, however, with her new idol. On her first introduction to the princely hotel in the Rue du Montblanc, with its damask hangings, gilt-bronze arabesques, carpets of Sallandrouze, and tables of malachite and lapis lazuli, she was *naïve* enough to congratulate its lovely owner on being thus surrounded with the prosperities of life. Aware that Thérèse I. had lost her head, she seemed to think that Thérèse II. must be minus a heart ; actually presuming that the wife of a man weighing eighteen stone, with an abdominal prominence, a great white forehead, and a great red face, could possibly be reconciled to her unpicturesque matrimonial destinies by the possession of varnished rosewood or damask of Lyons. Never was the *femme incom-*

prise more thoroughly misapprehended than at that moment.

But Lady Ormington was open to conviction. It did not take long to satisfy her that she looked upon one of the most unfortunate of her sex ; that the expressive countenance of the young countess was indebted for its pensive paleness to wounded sensibility ; that her widowed soul was pining in the isolation of conjugal mismatchment. Her ladyship was peculiarly qualified to enter into these delicate distinctions. She had been enacting the same tragedy,—comedy,—farce (what shall I call it?) for the last quarter of a century ; only that, not having been educated by Madame Campan, *her* phraseology was by no means so Lamartinian, or her tones so plaintive.

In point of fact, she could not make out so good a case. Instead of being driven by a despotic emperor, at the point of the bayonet, into the arms of Lord Ormington, she had thankfully accepted him for better for worse, three days after his presentation to her, at a country race-ball ; and was consequently sadly to seek in the epithets with which the Comtesse Anacharsis was entitled to qualify her barbarous sacrifice.

If I wanted to fill a volume, instead of desiring to improve the minds of man and womankind by the promulgation of this my autobiography, I would favour the world, in detail, with a few of the pet phrases of poor Thérèse. But as they are precisely such as all French novelists have assigned to an indifferent wife whining her monotonous quail-call after the missing moiety of her soul, I respect the common-sense and uncommon decorum of Great Britain.

When Lady Ormington first acquainted me with her treasure-trove in the Chaussée d'Antin, I turned an unwilling ear. There was about as much sentiment in my soul as in a jar of Jamaica pickles. "Campaigning at the king of Bohemy" had alloyed my double-refinement. At Paris, I had fallen in with a knot of Peninsular friends, excellent fellows, with whom it was much more agreeable to lounge at Very's or the Opera, than to sigh the perfumed sighs of a lady's boudoir. The only *Parfait amour* which I was disposed to pronounce nectar came out of the cellars of Chevet.

I never saw an Englishman yet, with a genuine vocation for these Platonic heroines ; who seem to consider the purity of the mind so much less sacred than that of the body, and admit no bond of conjugal fidelity on the honest affections of the heart. Whenever Lady Ormington used to talk to me of the lovely wife of the corpulent ex-préfet, I made it a point to answer her with rhapsodies about a *matelotte Normande* at the Rocher, or a dish of *tournedos* at the Frères Provençaux.

I was fated, however, to make acquaintance with the countess in a manner to convert acquaintanceship into something of a tenderer likely nature.

It happened, that, one day, as I was trying, in the Bois de Boulogne, a horrible brute, such as the French horse-dealers of those days used to call a horse, the beast turned restive ; and after seeing the leafless trees of the Bois run away from me for five minutes or so, a desperate crash seemed to bring heaven and earth together ; and after the crash, as might be anticipated, —chaos !—I was lying insensible on a heap of flints in the road leading to the Pavillon de Madrid.

The next sensation of which I was conscious, was that of awaking in heaven ; that is, awaking in a sort of dreamy Elysium, surrounded by fleecy eider-down, muslin curtains, the fragrance of *frangipanne*, the sobs of waiting-maids, and by way of antidote to all this delicious poison, the overhanging face of a doctor by whom I had been dephlogisticated in unknown quantities ; looking exceedingly like a horned owl in a Vitchoura and pair of spectacles. I had never heard of such bipeds in the Elysian fields ; and consequently took it for granted that I was still in the arrondissement of the Champs Elysées.

I was not fractured. Only miserably contused.
Only destined to rise from my couch, piebald as the
brute which laid me there. To rise, however, was for
the present out of the question. I was assured so
by the gentle accents of an exceedingly plaintive
voice; and to judge from the predictions of the
spectacled owl who hooted affirmation of her intelligence, no chance of truffled turkeys or iced Champagne
for full six weeks to come! Agreeable intelligence
for a man who had dinner engagements to the end
of the Carnival. There was however no help for it;
for when I raised myself from my pillow to remonstrate,
I fell back and fainted.

On my second recovery, the withered face of the
owl was replaced by one whose soft oval seemed thrown
into more beautiful relief by the glossy bands of raven
hair in which it was enframed. But even the oval
face had been nothing without the foreign aid of two
pearly tears that stood upon those pure and placid
cheeks. Tears; tears of sensibility, and shed for *me!*
From that moment, the soft touch of the slender
fingers attempting to minister to my aid, communicated a gentle thrill to my bosom. I was obliged
to make haste and recover, in order to thank such a
nurse.

In return for my thanks, she "gave me for my
pains a world of sighs;" acquainting me, that as she
was returning through the Bois from her villa at
Suresne, she had met a horse without a rider, and
found a rider without a horse; that her good Samari-
tanism had determined her to pause by the wayside,
and pick up the desolate stranger; who being too fine
a gentleman to wear anything in his pocket save a
few loose Napoleons, was still *Non Nominatus* in the
mansion where, being a stranger, they had taken
him in.

Never shall I forget the effect of the announcement
by which I replied to this delicate note of interrogation. No sooner had I declared myself to be an

Englishman, by name Cecil Danby, and by domicile
resident at the Hôtel de Breteuil in the Rue de
Rivoli, than my charming preserver uttered a sound
which I conclude was what the novelists call " a
faint scream," a thing I had always been particularly
curious to hear, from the moment of my acquaintance
with the pages of Monk Lewis and Mrs. Radcliffe. I
have a great mind to be poetical about it myself.
Nothing would be easier than to liken it to the subdued cry of a bird during an eclipse of the sun ; with
which, if my readers be unacquainted, I am sorry for
them, for there is nothing so plaintive in or out of
nature.   Suffice it, however (for I have an abhorrence
of stage trick), that the eider-down bed was that of
Madame la Comtesse Anacharsis de la Vrillière ; the
soft twining fingers, those of the *femme incomprise.*

Lady Ormington was instantly sent for, and said,
did, and cried all that it was necessary to say, do,
and cry on such an occasion.   Madame la Comtesse
had not been so near the brink of a sensation for the
last five years.   Even the ex-préfet was enchanted to
render service to the offspring of one whom he remembered a reigning belle at the Trianon when he was himself aide-de-camp to Monseigneur the Comte d'Artois.
In short, I seemed to have been thrown from my horse
expressly to oblige them.

What a convalescence it was.   How different from
that struggling back to life at Belem, when conscious
—no, not conscious, *anticipative*—of a great joy awaiting me, which I wanted only strength to clasp in my
arms.   Now, I perceived that it was my business, for
my own sake and the sake of others, to prolong my
indisposition to the utmost verge of convalescence.
"Better is the foe of well," quoth the proverb.   I did
not want to be better, or better off.   I was as content
to be returned "killed" on this occasion as on that
which recommended me to the goodwill of Lord
Ormington.

Monsieur le Comte was just then pre-occupied with

important business at the Council Office. It was all he could do to pant into my room once in the twenty-four hours with inquiries after my health; entreaties, very needless ones, that I would consider his house and all that it contained my own; and assurances that the royal family had made minute inquiries into the condition of one in whom they were so deeply interested as the son of their good Lady Ormington.

In reply, I looked as grateful and feeble as I could; and would have allowed the horned owl to exhaust the last drop in my veins rather than abridge my sojourn in that charming abode. It is all nonsense when northern imaginations pretend to luxuriate in descriptions of the gardens of Alcina, or gardens of Armida, or gardens of the Hesperides, or any other gardens, poetical or prosiac. The very word "garden" has a damp, aguish sound to an English ear, a sound as of water-engines and gravel-rollers. If anybody wishes to paint the bower of Circe in a way to make its perils *really* alluring to a son of the fog, he will make it a snug boudoir, having a patent fireplace, ponderous curtains, three-piled carpets, a luxurious divan; and, by way of nurse, a Thérèse.

I wrote word so to Byron. He and I were always squabbling, upon paper, about the poetry of nature and poetry of civilization. It was a hollow pretension on *his* part (he, who could not abide Wordsworth), to declare in favour of

> The silence that is in the starry sky,
> The sleep that is between the lonely hills.

The sleep in which he *really* delighted was anything but lonely; and as to the starry sky, like myself, he was fonder of the fluted damask of a luxurious tester. Starlight vigils may be charming for those who, like Poussin's shepherdess, "lived in Arcadia." But, between ourselves, dear reader, for people who live in the nineteenth century and pay parish rates, it makes one's teeth chatter to think of them.

I have a strong inclination to prove in black and white, in Childe Harold's handwriting, that the episode of Haidee was planned and executed as a sort of moral counterpoise to the pictures with which I favoured him of my blessed existence in the Chaussée d'Antin. Byron evidently shipwrecked his hero as a set-off to my spill ; imagined the cave as a contrast to my boudoir ; and devised the fried eggs as an antithesis to my *violettes pralinées*. He even sketched the skittish Zoe as an impertinent set-off to my charming little Manette. St. Spiridion be praised, there was no Lambro in the case. Monsieur le Comte Anacharsis de la Vrillière, conseiller d'état, ex-préfet *in esse*, and pair de France *in posse*, was as little akin to the old pirate-patriot as I to Hercules.

Champfort has told us, and people have learned to give credit to his sayings, that "to oblige is to attach ourselves ; " and if it be true that *l'on s'attache par ses bienfaits*, Madame de la Vrillière had every excuse for predilection in my favour. Her kindness and charity far exceeded that of the Samaritan ; whose bald-headed effigy, pouring a bottle of balm of Gilead balsam into the wounds of the man by the wayside, used to figure as a sign to the apothecaries' shops.

Youth and beauty apart, Thérèse was a kind creature ; and, if misunderstood, really deserved interpretation. But it was herself to whom she was most an enigma. For she tried to coax herself into all sorts of absurdities and affectations, when nature had designed her for the same honest calling as the great majority of her sex.

I dare say I did my part towards confirming her error. It was difficult not to wish she might continue to undervalue her happiness as the wife of a man with so good an account at his banker's, and so good a disposition to gratify the whimsies of a Parisian wife. For her morbid discontents were manifested in sitting beside my sick couch, reading to me, talking to me "far above singing," yet singing, too, whenever I ex-

pressed a wish to hear the gentle cadences of Romag-
nesi breathed by the favourite pupil of Garat. It was
from *her* I learned those charming stanzas addressed by
Madame de Walewska to Napoleon, a model for all
tender reproaches; and I could not help flattering
myself that there was what the French call *intention*
in the countess's energetic manner of enunciating the
concluding verse :—

> " Viens, donc, essayer les douceurs
>   D'une passion sans orage.
>   Que tu sois fidèle ou volage,
> Rien ne désunira nos cœurs !
> Pour te plaire, mon âme ardente
>   Découvre un nouveau sentiment.
>   Oui ! sans t'aimer moins vivement,
> Je t'aimerai *mieux* qu'une amante."

I, too, had discovered a new sentiment as regarded
the beautiful creature who thus generously devoted herself to my consolation. Though aware of the ground-
lessness of her repinings, though convinced of the
grievous wrong she did herself and those belonging to
her, by lavishing on a chimera the affections due to
her larger and legitimate moiety, I fell as much in
love as if her woes were as real as those of Andro-
mache, and I King Pyrrhus of execrated memory.

There may be some among my readers who see
nothing in all this to laugh at; who consider, with
Lady Ormington, that it is torture for a woman of
" exquisite sensibilities," a woman organized to " die
of a rose in aromatic pain," a woman for whom the
moon has influences that " cause every nerve to vibrate
to an unseen centre in the soul," a woman for whom
" music hath a language mystic as the lyre of Apollo,"
to be united for better for worse with a soulless, sordid
being, whose sensibilities were invested in the five per
cents., and whose tenderest point was his digestion.

Were I blessed or cursed with wife or daughter, or
did I possess a right to exercise the tyrannies of legitimate proprietorship over any fraction of the gentle

sex, how careful should I be to inspire her with a taste
for some definite pursuit ; rational, if possible ; at all
events, a pursuit. Men are too apt to sneer at the frivolities of women's accomplishments ; to find fault with
daubings of water-colours, embroiderings of tiffany,
collections of autographs, emblazonings of missals. My
brethren ! take the advice of a bachelor deeply studied
in such mysteries. Failing the maximum, accept the
minimum. Till your better or worse halves acquire,
by force of education, an aptitude for higher occupation, discourage nothing that yields harmless employ-
ment to their leisure. In a class of life where neither
household nor nursery exercise peremptory demands,
beware of the lapse of listless hours. Beware of the
peevish retrospections of reverie. Beware of the want
of excitement arising from want of occupation. It is
in the unenclosed waste that the thistle wings its seeds
of mischief. It is in the neglected hedgerow the night-
shade ripens its deadly fruit.

Had Thérèse been only able to conjure up an innocent enthusiasm for any of the busy idlenesses of life,
she would have seen in the rotund Anacharsis the
indulgent friend who cheered her occupation ; sauntering into her boudoir, to confide his little grievances of
public life, and listen in return to histories of colours
that would not blend—canvas that would not dry—
camellias that would not bud—or any other of the
trivialities that become important when prattled about
by rosy lips to willing ears.

But her play and work were alike done for her.
Her embroideries were bought ready stitched, her
camellias ready grafted. Her very album, instead of
being extracted from her friends, drawing by drawing,
sonnet by sonnet, with pain and anguish, like so many
teeth, was laid on her dressing-table, one new-year's
morning, filled with artistic performances. In a word,
as the French say, after wasting a whole dictionary,
there was nothing left for her to do, but mischief.

Pretty much the same thing that made my friend

Byron, at four-and-twenty, a misanthrope, converted Thérèse at the same age into a *femme incomprise.*

Be it observed, that no sooner had the noble poet a real grievance to complain of,—a wife who rejected him, and a child from whom he was exiled,—than he ceased to adorn his verses with anguish and remorse ; and Childe Harold, really aggrieved, became the laughing, devil-may-care Don Juan. I have a shrewd notion that had the corpulent ex-préfet taken to beating his wife, *she*, too, would have renounced her green and yellow melancholy, and become what nature intended her, an open-hearted, energetic creature, full of warm feelings and resentments. Nay, had he become a bankrupt or traitor, in spite of his bulbous outline, she would have turned out a devoted wife.   But the poor soul wanted excitement.   She wanted something to prevent her cowering over her boudoir fire all winter, or dreaming in her conservatory at Suresne all summer,

> ——gathering sweet pain
> About her fancy till it thrill'd again.

Unluckily for *her*, perhaps unluckily for me, she found that something in Cecil Danby.

In what whims and vagaries we used to indulge. Word by word, sigh by sigh, I translated the "Giaour" for her ;—Byron not having as yet undergone at the hands of the French those rinsings in cold water, by which they have managed to extract all colour out of his poetry, without effecting its purification.

Like Othello, I told her campaigning tales, that would have filled volumes of Railway Novels ; and by dint of plenty of orange-groves and quintas, modinhas and seguadillas, made her free of the Peninsula.

While recounting my

> Hairbreadth 'scapes in th' imminent deadly breach,

my adventures in conflagrated convents and slaughtered villages, her pale cheeks used to become gradually suf-

fused, and her mournful eyes animated. My story was
reflected in her face as in a camera obscura.

She was a capital listener ; " an excellent thing in
woman," and rare as excellent. An intelligent countenance bent upon one while telling a story is positively colloquial. What are the vulgar ejaculations of
wonder and satisfaction with which commonplace
people interrupt a narrator, compared with the speaking blush, the flushing glance, which, though no interruption, cries, " Bravo !" or " Alas !" in accents not to
be mistaken ?

But the thing that delighted her most, or the thing
which she *said* delighted her most, was my confidence
in her, my reliance upon her friendship. *I* understood
her, she said. With *me* she was not *la femme incomprise*. She even indulged in certain little Goetheisms
about kindred souls and elective affinities. It was not
my cue to apprise her that I did *not* confide in her ;
that I told her only what I would have told to the
fellows at Watier's, and the brother-officers of my
brigade ; or that I *had* bosom secrets (memories of a
departed love, and grievances against a nominal father)
which I would no more intrust to her keeping than to
the hands of the marble Atalanta, skimming in cold,
indecent self-exposure along the gardens of the
Tuileries.

Lady Ormington was often with us ; so often, that
we called it always. And it might have been always,
for there was nothing in her presence that imposed
silence upon our mutual professions. Our Cupid was
one of those humbugging little boys who, because
wingless, *i.e.*, because heavy and stupid, chooses to call
himself Friendship.

If I may be allowed to insinuate so much in a
whisper, I suspect that, had my indisposition been
prolonged another fortnight, his wings would have
sprouted. To keep up with the overstrained exaltation of Thérèse, was very much like the feat accomplished of late years by Paganini, of playing on the

fourth string a fantasia better performed on the whole instrument. I was flattered, however, that the cold, supercilious Comtesse de la Vrillière, insisted on being called Thérèse by an ex-colonel of Portuguese dragoons. But I blush to write myself down so incomparable an ass.

CHAPTER XII.

Malo me fortunæ pœniteat, quàm victoriæ pudeat.
QUINT. CURT.

Honte à celui qui, déshérité de religion, ne voit dans la sainte confiance d'une femme, qu'une âme à dépraver.
MICHEL RAYMOND.

LET my readers be so obliging as to recall to their minds, unless the remembrance be already there present, that all this occurred the year preceding the battle of Waterloo, when Englishmen maintained in Paris very different ground from the position afterwards conceded to them. As yet, the Cossacks had the crown of the causeway; and even Louis XVIII. dared not exhibit towards us any preference over his Muscovite pioneers to the throne, or his Parisian supporters thereupon.

It behoved me, therefore, to do nothing to enrage Anacharsis, the great or big, as I had no means of securing his wife from his displeasure. Jealousy of her preference was not likely to disturb his peace of mind ; but he would not have put up with being made ridiculous.

Except in humble life, French husbands are as rarely betrayed into the honest resentment of jealousy, as into any other breach of politeness. To a great extent, self-esteem is their protection ; to a greater, that " un-

taught innate philosophy" which prevents them from
being

over exquisite
To cast the fashion of uncertain evils.

I suspect, however, that more than one of those whom
I saw welcoming to their houses, with the utmost
cordiality, men whom, for their honour's sake, they
were bound to lay under the sod of Père la Chaise, were
enduring the agony of the Spartan, with the gnawing
fox hid under his cloak.   No anguish more bitter to
bear than that arising from some capitulation of conscience, which, unsuspected by the world, is ever before
us, like phosphorescent light shining amid the gloom.

This is a long digression ; more particularly as the
barouche of Thérèse, with its beautiful pier of bays, is
waiting to convey me to the Bois de Boulogne.   Every
day, after I left her house, did she insist upon
administering to my airings ; my mother's carriage
being a close one.   Just as the poor Duchesse de St.
Barthélemy and Lady Ormington had driven, day after
day, on that very spot, past the selfsame haha of the
Muette or wall of Bagatelle, five-and-twenty years
before, did Thérèse and Cecil enjoy every afternoon,
in addition to each other's society, the delicious fragrance of the wood, carpeted with violets and wild
anemones, and displaying between the tall stems of
the chestnut-trees whose great resinous buds were just
opening to disclose the pale green leaflets within,
thickets of blackthorn, bright with snow-white blossoms ; affording some excuse for the exulting notes of
the linnets and chaffinches, making such a deuce of
a fuss about the return of spring.

All that sort of pastorality is charming in its proper
place.   Nobody likes it better than I do, within the
fourteen lines of a sonnet ; in the prose of Sir Philip
Sidney, or the occasional poetry of the Lady Melusindas
of the Book of Beauty.   But I hate a woman who *talks*
daffodils.   The time is gone by for Florian's shepherds.

As for Gessner, should his works ever be republished in this country, they will be illustrated by Cruikshank or Phiz.

With these vulgar prejudices, it will be believed that I was ill prepared for the eglantinian sweetnesses budding from the gentle soul of Thérèse, as soon as the primroses put forth their leaves. I dare not say how great a bore I thought her. Having outgrown my first childhood, and not achieved my second, I could see no necessity for being bound to the rack of fine sentiment, while there was so good an opera in Paris, and such capital cooks.

By her own will, Madame la Comtesse would have had me Haroldize to the brink of misanthropy. *I could not.* For the life and soul of me I could not. If the memory of her whose hair I wore as a pledge of unavailing affection were incapable of exalting my imagination, not all the countesses of the Chaussée d'Antin could screw me up to concert pitch. I had recommenced my bachelor life. Breakfasts at Tortoni's began the day, to conclude with a gay supper at the Mille Colonnes ; and the Montagnes Russes, the Salon, and fifty other brilliant follies, filled up the interval.

I had, in fact, no longer any decent pretext for loitering away my days in the boudoir or *calèche* of Madame la Comtesse, seeing that they were also those of Monsieur le Comte ; and though by dint of being called a monster of ingratitude fifty times a day, on pink satin paper, I had begun to consider myself a charming young man ; even Lady Ormington was fain to confess that I had every excuse for my apparent remissness, in the hint afforded by my gracious friend, the Duc de Berri, that I was endangering the peace of mind of the corpulent ex-préfet, by exposing to the disapproval of Madame d'Angoulême the conduct of his wife.

I scarcely know whether it were prudence on the part of her ladyship, or whether some mysterious forewarning announced to her the return of the em-

peror, but, one fine day, I found post horses to our
travelling carriage, our affairs wound up by the united
exertions of Toady Richardson and Lady Ormington,
and our passports and everything else in readiness for
departure.

I burst into remonstrances. I began to plead dinner
engagements, and all sorts of engagements, as an
excuse for doing what I liked. But my mother had
an argument for immediate departure, against which
there was no contending. She protested that Lord
Ormington was alarmingly ill, and had *ordered* us
home.

It was not till we were fairly ensconced in the little
parlour of the Old Ship at Dover, a hostelry which
well deserved its name, for its rooms were cabins, that
she told me the truth ; that she had employed subter-
fuge to withdraw me from a spot where my fortunes
and virtues seemed to be following the example of the
courage of Bob Acres.

I was in a most unfilial rage. The moment was ill
chosen to acquaint me that I had been made a fool of.

In the first place, I had the reminiscences of the
steam-packet fresh upon me. A good man introduced
fire-proof into the terrors of Tophet, must suffer,
if possible, greater anguish than the wicked. How
much more the healthy man on board a steam-packet,
exposed to—but why nauseate my readers ? In the
next place, I had the irritation of finding myself
dipping in the dish with the "*dam' d'honour.*" In
the third place, after the exquisite course of gastronomy
I had been following, I was reduced to the aboriginal
food of the Britons ; not exactly the hips, haws, and
acorns of the Saxon Heptarchy ; but worse, far worse,
the beef-steaks and apple-pie of an inn. The waiter
asked me whether I pleased to take malt liquor ;
while an agreeable vapour of sulphur issuing from the
dingy fireplace, served to add a local colouring to the
emphasis of my execrations. All was as the devil
would have it.

People prose about the influence of education on the human mind. Talk to me of its power over the human stomach. The mechanism of the organs of deglutition may be trained and tutored, till it becomes fine as that of Breguet's watches. More than once, on returning to England after a long sojourn in France, I have sustained a serious illness from the crudity of the tough meats and parboiled vegetables. The thick sauces, spiced into blackness, the horrible astringency pervading every made dish, has brought on a cruel derangement of the epigastric functions. Were I a fire-eater, I would make money by showing myself at a fair ; and swallowing cayenne and new port, without " poison " labelled on dish or decanter.

Nowadays, the transition is less striking ; the best French cookery being got up, and down, in London. The junior branch of the Bourbons did nothing for the stewpan ; and under Louis Philippe there was serious talk of establishing a *bureau de pompes dînatoires* on the model of that of the *pompes funèbres*, where official or private dinners might be regulated according to the tariff.

But at the period of which I am writing, the empire still dominated in the national institutions of the land.

Posterity has rendered justice to the legislative wisdom of Napoleon. The empire has been called the triumph of this and the triumph of that. The soldier twists his moustache, and talks of the *victoires et conquêtes* of the *Petit Caporal*. The political economist praises the organization of his financial system. The legist quotes his code ; the *curé* his restoration of the church ; the man of science, the man of letters, the artist, his protection of the academies.

In point of fact the real triumph of his reign was its gastronomy. The greatest exploit accomplished by the grand army was its march from one end of Europe to the other, with cookery-books in its pocket. Let them sing of the victorious eagle flying from steeple to

R

steeple. Reality is more sublime than romance. The real perch of the eagle was from spit to spit.

This is not vague assertion. The tone of an epoch is indelibly impressed upon its literature. Look at that of the empire. Look at the sleek periods of Joüy. Does not *perdreau truffé* exude from every line? Look at the pages of Desaugiers, of Beranger. Could any age that did not keep a good table produce such drinking-songs. Grimod de la Reynière is one of the conscript fathers of literature, the originator of a style; as much a creator in his way as the authors of Fleur d'Epine or Vathek, Waverley or Childe Harold. Even the music of the days of Napoleon has a ring of champagne glasses in it. The Opéra Comique has never had anything so joyous as Joconde, or the Calife de Bagdad.

Half the horrors of the prevailing school of French literature, on the other hand, are attributable to the decline of gastronomy—to a moral indigestion consequent upon a physical. Old Burton assigns the engendering of melancholy to the vacuum abhorred by nature, in terms too matter-of-fact for these matter-of-lying days; and just as the monstrosities of Monk Lewis's Tales of Wonder were traced by the acumen of the reviewers to suppers of raw pork, the flagrancies of Eugene Sue arise from the gritty dinners of Véfour.

How different from the days when the table of the Archi-chancelier Cambacérès was a vatican that fulminated its bulls (in the form of *bœuf à l'Italienne*) to the uttermost ends of Europe; when the Maréchal de France, returning ravenous from his campaigns to the domestic hearth where simmered the *pot au feu*, offered, like Alexander, a premium to the man who would create a new dish.

From conquered countries, too, they brought back the booty of new ideas. From Moscow, the *Charlotte Russe*; from Italy, the *poulet à la Marengo*. What did they bring from Algiers? A taste for raw dates, or a recipe for stewing locusts.

For my part, had it been my fate to become top-sawyer of any possible community (and kings and princes turn up so oddly that one is never sure of not waking some morning Tribune of the Argentine Republic or Cacique of Poyais, — just as a certain Belgian student used to say, on leaving the key of his lodgings with his porter, "If any one calls to offer me the throne of Belgium, say I shall be back in an hour ")—had it been my fate, as I observed before this very long, though apposite, parenthesis, to become governor of a people, I would have issued *my* ukases on the principle upon which the gentleman won his wager of making a donkey ascend the steep staircase of an eight-story house in Edinburgh ; *i.e.* by pulling it back stoutly by the tail every time it reached a flat ; on which signal, with a becoming sense of its duties, the jackass pushed forward.

When Parmentier, the chemist, introduced the potatoe into France, that obstinate nation, which had swallowed the *corvée,* the *gabelle,* and the *guillotine,* refused to swallow the new vegetable. But Parmentier understood the national character.

With the sanction of the Directory, he planted half a dozen acres in the Plaine des Sablons, close to Paris ; and had the plantation watched night and day by soldiers with fixed bayonets, ordered to put to death any feloniously-minded citizen presuming to lay a finger on that precious growth ! To steal a potatoe was hanging matter.

Within a year nothing but potatoes would go down. The silk attire interdicted by sumptuary laws became doubly endeared to the belles of old England ; and the food guarded by the artillery of government was regarded as manna from heaven. Old Parmentier died happy in having potatofied France ; and I have perpetrated a long story in attestation of the wisdom of my system of codification.

CHAPTER XIII.

Memini etiam quæ nolo, oblivisci quæ volo !—CIC.

Il y a des voix qui ne mentent pas. Les âmes sont à jour dans
les grandes occasions, et le doute tombe quand elles se mon-
trent.—MICHEL RAYMOND.

NOTHING awkwarder than the first evening spent
together by the different members of a family united
after long absence, who feel it necessary to disguise
from each other, in polite hypocrisy, the extreme relief
they have experienced in living apart.   Lord Ormington, my mother, and my Self, had enjoyed ourselves
fifty times as much as if we had been dwelling together
in domestic infelicity in Hanover Square. But it would
not do to say so.

Luckily, Lady Ormington had a grievance or two
to complain of.   I have already mentioned that Lady
Harriet Vandeleur was only a few years her junior.
Yet the gay widow was accepted in Paris as a beauty ;
while *she* was consigned to dowagerhood !   It was vain
to represent to Lady Ormington that, in France, so
long as a woman is on her preferment, she is sure of
being preferred. She returned to the charge with "Yes,
I know they all wanted to marry her—that is, marry
her fortune. Still, I must say I think it extraordinary
for a woman of one or two and forty to be surrounded
with partners in every ball-room ; and a woman of
four or five and forty to be surrounded with
chaperons."

"You must have noticed, however," said I, "how
rapidly Lady Harriet's little group of suitors diminished
when some good-natured English friend revealed the
fact that she has only a life-interest in her fortune.
Admiral de la This immediately asked for a ship, and
sailed for the Mediterranean. General de la That

repaired to his command in the south, six weeks previous to the expiration of his leave of absence."

Lord Ormington seemed vexed that, instead of these pribbles and prabbles touching our own country people, we had not brought home a word or two of authentic intelligence of the political position of France. Living as my mother had done at the Château, and seeing with its eyes, *she* of course did not hesitate to assure him that the nation was Bourbon to its heart's core ; that the white flag was as dear to its affections as the white tablecloth it so closely resembled ; and that were Napoleon to land again in France, he would be torn to pieces by the populace.

She spoke more prophetically than she knew of. At that moment he *had* landed ; and they *were* tearing him to pieces with the warmth of their affection. The arms of Talleyrand were already round his neck ; the authorities of the capital at his feet.

All that his lordship had to offer in return for her accurate political intelligence, was the information that Danby's " Life and Times of Bolingbroke " was pronounced by the *Quarterly Review* as good as if written by Bolingbroke himself ; and those who were fawned upon by the *Q. R.* of those days were deified by the vulgar, just as of old some slave, whose hand was licked by a lion of the arena, to whom he had been flung as a victim.

" I must say," observed Lady Ormington, " I think it a stupid thing of Danby to write a book. What good can it do him ? A man writes for money or distinction ; and Danby don't want to be made a baronet, or to increase his income. Where can be the *use* of writing ?"

Lady Ormington saw, heard, and felt with the eyes, ears, and understanding of the least intellectual coterie in the world ; and did not perceive that the human mind must bring forth fruits after its kind, in due season. Nevertheless, to do her justice, she was almost as courteous to Danby, as her lord to *me*. This arose, on

her part, from a considerable modification of her
partiality for the boy of the cockade; while her lord was
as passionately attached to Danby and his offspring, as
I to the grave at Cintra.

The feeling of grand-paternity is, I sincerely believe,
(next to the love of a young child for its mother),
the most instinctive of human affections. It is the
earliest indication of the simplicity of second childhood.
One of the most difficult points to determine in the
course of our mortal career, is the commencement of
the decadence of our faculties. Decay of body speaks
in a language no one can misunderstand. The cane, the
crutch, the spectacle case, the wig, the set of minerals,
are too peremptory in their parts of speech to admit of
turning a deaf ear. But with respect to the decline
of our faculties, we deceive ourselves and the truth is
not in us : and we go twaddling on,—from the woolsack,—the pulpit,—the bench,—the bar,—without
suspecting that we are seen to drivel.

Even I, though perfectly aware that at the clubs I
am called " old Danby," am puzzled to know whether,
in these my memoirs, I am beginning to prose. If I
had a grandchild, I should know it was my *cue* to be
in my dotage. I should find myself repeating the
witticisms of little Harry or little Jane, instead of
reverting to Lord Votefilch, or Thérèse.

Independent of the use of grand-paternity as a
moral vane, there is something peculiarly endearing in
a little creature who wears our image and super-
scription, without entailing upon us those duties of
reprehension and flagellation, which render the office
of papa and mammaship anything but a sinecure.
Grandchildren are the shadows we cast before us into
future centuries ;—our link to posterity,—our invest-
ment in the future,—a bark of Columbus, which we
have launched for a voyage of discovery upon the great
ocean of time.

Independent of the favour which Lord Ormington
could not but accord to a little fellow so handsome and

promising as my nephew, he regarded him as a sort of page bestowed by providence for the duty of upholding his peer's robes in the eyes of a succeeding generation; a speaking-trumpet, through which he hoped to proclaim his own consequence to the Britons of the reign of Albert I. It was not incumbent upon *him* to scold the boy when he broke a Dresden teacup, as he had been forced to do poor squinting John, to satisfy the antipathies of my mother. He could allow the little fellow to be as wilful as other fine children of three years old, and not feel himself accountable for Arthur's sins to Solomon or Dr. Watts. On any symptoms of nursery rebellion, he might allow himself to say, like Herries, on being told of a corn riot at Hull or Truro, "That is the affair of the Home Department."

It would have been difficult not to spoil that boy;

> For from the birth of Cain, the first male child,
> To him that did but yesterday suspire,
> There was not such a gracious creature born!

His deep, loving, blue eyes,—his clustering curls,—his graceful symmetry,—had attracted the notice of more than one artist of eminence; and I find myself spared the necessity of enlarging upon his graces, by the descriptive words of one of our modern poets.

That little one, that gentle one, that simple child of three,
I'll not declare how bright and fair his little features be,
Or how silver sweet his infant tones as he prattles on my knee.
His little heart's a fountain pure of kind and tender feeling,
And his ev'ry look's a gleam of light, rich depths of love revealing.
When he walks forth, the country folk, who pass him in the street,
Will shout for joy and bless the boy, he looks so mild and sweet.
A playfellow is he to all, and yet with cheerful tone
He sings his little song of love when he is left alone;
His presence is like sunshine sent to gladden home and hearth,
To comfort us in all our griefs and sweeten all our mirth!

On visiting Forest Lodge, where Danby and his

wife were spending the Easter holidays, I found that, now Bolingbroke was in print, and the Honourable Member for Rigmarole at leisure, the little fellow was becoming as great a pet with his father as he had long been of his uncle and grandfather. Lady Susan again promised to become a mother. Yet with her, as with the rest of us, Arthur was all in all.

The spring was far advanced ; and that modest home of my brother's was, in springtime, a bower of Eden. Of all places where the *gioventù dell' anno* assumes a smiling appearance, none more propitious to its charms than a venerable forest. The transition from the hoar antiquity of those ancient trees, to the tender verdure suddenly enclothing them with shell-like leaflets or snowy blossoms, is like a bright and auspicious rejuvenescence ; how exquisitely exemplified among the old oaks and beeches of Windsor Forest.

> The wild flower laying
> Its fairy gem beside the giant tree,—

the wood-sorrel with its crysophrase verdure,—the ophrys, with its balsamic odours,—the wild hyacinths, glimmering like sapphires in the brakes

> Where the snake casts its bright enamelled skin,

served to variegate the scene, whose gradually deepening bowers seemed formed of such transparent foliage that the light came down, scarcely subdued through the ——Reader ! I humbly ask your pardon. I feel that I am forgetting myself and you. I promised, like Plato, to banish poets from my republic. Take therefore for granted, that, eclogues apart, the hoary moss grew as good as new ; and that even the venerable holly-bushes, the least life-like of the trees of the forest, were looking, as one says to some crusty old bachelor from whom one expects a legacy, as young and fresh as a four-year-old ; when Danby and I sallied forth for our daily saunter, either on foot or pony, gossiping as we went, of far countries, or far times ;

for an uneasy feeling seemed to connect us with the passing hour.

Danby was just the fellow to trouble himself about Polynesian researches, and speculate concerning penal colonies ; to dream of noble cities established at Swan River on the principle of that scapegoat from the galleys and marshes, Havre de Grace ; or to foresce a future nation, great as that push-on keep-moving people the Go-aheads, rising in Vancouver's Island, *like* the Go-aheads, out of the excrement of the mother country, — Jonah's gourd generated by a dungheap.

I, on the contrary, had my pretty little anecdotes to relate of the frivolities of the Tuileries ; which saw in the great kingdom it was recalled to govern, only a country which grew its own truffles, and bottled its own Clos de Vougeot ; or of the anger of the nation which had betrayed an emperor in the hope of establishing a republic, only to crown a king.

Danby philosophized in good set terms upon these data. I forget what he said about it. One always forgets things that are said in good set terms. The wisdom that is let fall, is always surest to be picked up ; as the gorgeous Buckingham at the court of Anne of Austria, gained more credit by the jewels he wore, ill set, that they might be scattered to attract notice, than by the finer brilliants displayed in his cap. I remember thinking, whenever Danby was conversing with me, that it was a pity so much good prose was wasted. His well-turned periods would have filled a capital page in his History of the Life and Times of Bolingbroke ; neither out of date nor out of place. For the natural history of kings and countries is the same in all ages, like the natural history of fleas or lions, garden bugs or buffaloes.

I scarcely know whether Danby derived most satisfaction from his success in public, or in domestic life. The two feelings were so consolidated in his heart, the popular author of the *Quarterly* and the happy

husband and Father of Forest Lodge, were so inex-
tricably Siamese twinnified into homogeneity, that an
injury sustained by either had been death to the sensibilities of the other.

Scarcely possible for a man to enjoy a happier frame
of existence than Danby's; solaced not only by "the
concealed comforts of a man locked up in woman's
love," or the triumph of floating double, like "the
swan on still St. Mary's Lake," upon the placid stream
of life; but because tranquil in body and mind, with
the mighty repose of the Farnesian Hercules, secure
in his tranquil strength because holding in his hand
the golden fruit of the tree of knowledge. A very
great mind is seldom restless. It is into the depths
of still water that the divers plunge fearlessly, certain
of bringing up pearls such as Cleopatra might have
matched with her "pendants worth a province;"
while the roaring ocean throws up only tatters of
weed or fragments of wreck.

My eyes were still dazzled with the gorgeousness of
the Parisian ball-rooms, when I took refuge in his
calm, holy, philosophical retreat "on the skirts of the
forest;" with the sensation of relief one finds in a
soft, grey, mild, autumnal day, after the scorching
radiance of summer. The spring was not so forward
but that we were glad to gather round the fire of an
evening, after Arthur had held up his pomegranate-
bud of a mouth to be kissed, before he was marched
off to bed. The lounging-chairs were drawn round.
Danby's great white dogs (resembling those we see in
the frescoes of Paul Veronese), instead of stretching
their lazy length on the hearthrug, used to plant
themselves among us, gazing upon the glowing logs,
as if listening through their canine reverie to my
brother's reasoning upon the half-cut periodical or
half-digested evening paper. There we used to sit and
gossip. It was impossible to feel envious of the superiority of such a mind, which, like the sun, shone only
to cheer and fertilize. I saw, without humiliation,

that I, who had roamed the world, and beheld man in
his various patterns and mouldings, who had visited
the galleries of art and majestic institutions of foreign
countries, knew less of what I had seen, than Danby,
upon hearsay, or printsay. While apparently bounded
by the narrowness of his monotonous domesticity, *his*
intellectual horizon was illimitable ; while I, carrying
with me wherever I wandered the littleness of my
own soul, had scarcely elbow-room for thought, so
bounded was the compass of my views.

There is something, to be sure, in the consciousness
of stability. It is only when the vessel is lying at
anchor, that her appointments are smartened up and
rendered ship-shape. Danby was not only at anchor,
but in a harbour fair as those of Naples or the Golden
Horn. The flowers had no choice but to expand in
the sunshine, where not an angry breath had leave to
blow. I, on the contrary, was a scatterling on the
mountain-side ; blown about by the tempests, snowed
upon, rained upon. Like one of those floating webs
of gossamer one sees upon the evening air, as if evermore in search of the setting sun, I lived in a state of
vague expectation of being caught by some bush,
and endowed with a local habitation. I trusted to
Destiny (the blind goddess compared with whom the
blind god is a lynx), to accomplish something for me
worthy my imperceptible deserts.

Like more people than choose to own it, I have
passed through life waiting for some one,—watching
for something, — I scarcely knew what ; like the
"letters by the post,"—those "airy creatures" which
a man who wants an excuse for staying at a place he
ought to leave, is sure to be expecting. *My* post,
alas! has brought me no letters. Day after day,
month after month, year after year, I have been still
waiting,—still watching :—my aimless destiny unac-
complished ; eternity flowing through my hand like
the limpid waters of a fountain through the unconscious, unenjoying lips of some marble Triton. But

let us return from my prosaic poetry to the poetical
prose of Forest Lodge.

I swear I never felt more joyous than when rising
every morning from the breakfast-table presided over
by Lady Susan, cheerful, elegant, fair, kindly, par-
ticipating with intimate cordiality in our anticipations
of the sport or business of the day, disdaining nothing
that we enjoyed, enjoying nothing that we disdained.
What an embellishment is such a woman to the
wilderness of life. Even I, who in the strife and
turmoil of the world's vices had almost lost the power
of distinguishing good from evil, whose conscience was
deaf and dumb, impassive amid the fret and seething
of human passion as a rock planted in the bed of a
river, even *I* was deeply touched by the holy and
hallowing influence of this gentlest of wives and
mothers.

There was an old cedar-tree on the lawn at Forest
Lodge, under whose drooping branches I have seen
her sit on sunny afternoons, with her youngest child
sleeping on her knee ; the babe, the mother, the
massive shadows of the venerable tree, all so still and
motionless, that it required no great stretch of imagination to fancy oneself looking at the Riposo in Egypt,
painted by some great master.

Why is it I dwell thus loitering upon the picture of
their domestic happiness ? Or why did I enter so
fervently into the refined simplicity of their existence,
that not even the enthusiasm with which it was
pointed out to my admiration by Lord Ormington,
sufficed to disgust me ? One evening, after I had
spent half a dozen happy days among them, and was
beginning to be as much at home as the sturdy hounds
maintaining their place in our circle, the boy was
come to toy away among us those last few minutes
before bedtime, so endeared to all children by the
inherent frailty of our nature, rebellion against the
constituted authority of the nurse, and ambition
of conquering a few moments more of interdicted

enjoyment. There he was,—little joyous fellow,— passed lovingly from knee to knee, questioned by each of us in succession, with the view of eliciting the treasures of a spirit bright as the souls of children, whereon still lingers the effulgence of the eternal dayspring from whence they so lately emanated.

His father's hand lingered among the curls of that little head, as if striving to develop in the happy face he drew down towards him as the boy clambered upon his bosom, unnoted indications of the faculties brightening its fairness. Lady Susan kept calling to her husband to be careful of Arthur's footing, as the father and child sported thus lovingly with each other. Lord Ormington said nothing; but sat watching them, proud of the beauty of the boy, the distinctions of the man; and prouder of both that they were so closely and manifestly his own.

"And so, sir," said Danby, with his eyes fixed on the boy, as though to devour every movement and gesture of his graceful nature, "and so, sir, you have been in the boat to-day with uncle Cecil?"

"Ay, but naughty uncle Cecil wouldn't find Arthur the nest!" said the child, hiding his little head in his father's bosom. "Uncle Cecil promised Arthur to go and find a nest among the rushes, and then he brought Arthur home again because there was no nest. Uncle Cecil broke his word. Papa and mamma never break *their* words."

"Never mind, my boy. We will try again another time," said I, turning to explain, in a few words to Lord Ormington, that a day or two before I had found a reedtit's nest among the rushes of the reservoir; but that not having marked the spot, I had been unable to find it again on my expedition with Arthur. "The sun was gone in," said I, "and I thought it too chilly for him to remain longer on the water, while punting among the reeds."

"I was not cold, though," persisted the disappointed child. "You know, you promised me I should see a

pretty little nest hung among the rushes, with two
green eggs in it, and a little bird flying about to take
care of it.   But there was no nest, and no bird, and
no eggs.   You broke your word."

" You might have caught cold," said I, to soften his
little pouting resentments.

" No, no ; I guess all about it.   I heard Coulson
tell my nurse the other day, that mamma was very
wrong to trust Arthur in the boat with you ; and
that he shouldn't be surprised if harm came of it.
What did Coulson mean, uncle ?   Nurse told Coulson
to take care how he said such things, for that I should
come and tell you again.   What did Coulson mean ?
He said you always pretended to be glad to see me,
but that you would be gladder still to see the last of
me."

All this time, Danby was vainly endeavouring to
stop by his caresses the prattle of the child.   But, like
all darlings, Arthur chose to be heard to an end.   I
know not which of us looked most uncomfortable
before that end was attained ; my brother, or Lady
Susan, or Lord Ormington.   For this same officious
Mr. Coulson was no other than mine ancient enemy of
the pigtail, Lord Ormington's own man.

Danby ended where he had better have begun, by
carrying off the child in his arms to bed ; trying to
drown in the noise of a playful altercation about kissing mamma, and grandpapa, and uncle Cecil, the extreme awkwardness of our position.   I thought he
seemed to hesitate as he approached me in my turn,
as if doubting my inclination to bestow upon the little
fellow my usual kiss ; whereupon I stretched out my
arms to give him a fervent embrace.   Danby's eye
met mine as I pressed my lips to his soft white forehead ; and I could detect a glance of grateful feeling
towards me for not resenting the boy's innocent
offence.   How often the sensation of pressing my lips
to that round, smooth, warm, and glossy brow, recurred afterwards to my recollection.

When Danby and the boy had quitted the room (Lady Susan following them with some parting charge to be delivered to the nurse about the little girl), a dead silence ensued between Lord Ormington and myself. Those few witless words of Arthur's had summoned up betwixt us the ghost of old. times, the spectre of our mutual antipathy. I verily believe that both of us counted the minutes till my brother's return. But when once Danby got into the nursery, so many endearments were bestowed upon him to cajole him into staying, that one was never sure of seeing him again.

It was not till summoned by the announcement of dinner, that he and Lady Susan made their appearance ; and then, their manner was so constrained, that I plainly saw they had been talking over the best mode of covering the impertinence of the servants and the indiscretion of the little fellow. I had never felt their kindness oppressive before. For it evidently purported to efface whatever painful impression might have been made upon my feelings.

Next morning, matters were worse. Our pursuits had been hitherto so simultaneous, our plans so unstudied, that I felt more at home in Danby's house than in Hanover Square. But now, Lady Susan was so earnestly attentive, that I determined to return to town that very afternoon. Lord Ormington was off already ; not in consequence of the little *contre-temps* that had occurred, but because previously engaged to spend at Dropmore the two remaining days of the Easter holidays.

"Stay, at all events, till to-morrow, Cecil," remonstrated Danby. "I am obliged to go to Windsor to look at a pair of horses the coachman is plaguing me about, and Susan will be left alone."

This was only a kind pretext for detaining me four-and-twenty hours longer; but, being as eager to accept the olive-branch as he to offer it, I stayed. After luncheon, he mounted his horse and rode off; while I

offered my arm to my sister-in-law, for a saunter in
the forest, into which there was an entrance through
the shrubbery.   It was a bright spring day.   The air
was astir with life.   All nature seemed in activity.
The birds were darting about with straws in their
beaks ; and I fancied I could see the leaves expanding
under the bright sunshine.   Lady Susan was a charming companion.   There was no effort in her conversation, nothing overstrained in the tone of her mind.
She was so simply pious and calmly wise, that one
accepted her remarks without challenge.   She seemed
so serenely penetrated with the truth of what she
advanced, that one felt she *must* be in the right.

It is a pleasant thing to saunter with a gentle intelligent woman along the mossy paths of an old
forest, on a budding spring day, with a dear child in
whose impulses of health and animation you take
mutual delight bounding on before you in search of
violets ; or with his little hand resting on the sturdy
back of a fine old hound, such as Snyders would have
turned dogstealer to paint.   I was exceedingly happy.
We talked of Danby.   She had a thousand traits to
relate of the homage tendered to him by the master-
spirits of the age ; and I listened with pleasure to the
tender intonation of her voice, as it recorded praises
of her husband.

Her situation did not admit of taking very long
walks ; so that we returned home much sooner than
suited the restlessness of the boy.   Lady Susan was
obliged to threaten the wilful fellow with the privation
of some promised plaything (a wheelbarrow, I think,
which his father was to order for him at Windsor),
unless he submitted.   Before we reached the garden,
however, I had compromised the business, not by a
threat, but a bribe.   I had previously agreed to ride
and meet Danby ; and promised the boy to take him
before me on my saddle to surprise papa.   No sooner
had I made the offer than I repented ; for I saw a
deep flush suffuse the cheek of my companion.   But

Arthur's expectations once excited, were not to be repressed ; and Lady Susan gave her consent, partly, I suspect, lest the disagreeable incident of the night before, should seem to influence her decision.

The horse was brought round. Arthur, his little eyes beaming with delight, was lifted up to me, after I had taken my seat, and, though I saw that his mother, who stood at the hall door to see us off, looked anxious and nervous, the exultation of the spirited little fellow, whose voice was ringing and eyes glittering with gladness, communicated itself to me. I set off as joyously along the Windsor road, as though it were my own first ride, and not my nephew's.

"Papa, papa, — what *will* papa say? How we shall surprise dear papa!" was all Arthur could utter, while enjoying the novel sensation of seeing the hedges fly past, as we speeded along at a gentle trot.

"You see, Uncle Cecil, they *could* trust you to take care of me," said Arthur, as we reached Sandpit Gate. "Coulson was a foolish old man, wasn't he?"

I had expected, according to Danby's arrangements, that we should meet him before we proceeded so far ; and now, proposed to return. But the boy would not hear of it.

"Let us wait here, Uncle Cecil ; pray, *pray* let us wait here. Papa will not be long. Papa never breaks his promises!" cried Arthur.

We waited accordingly. Five minutes elapsed, but no signs of Danby. I began to get fidgety, and so did the mare. But the boy begged earnestly ; and there was something so endearingly earnest in the clasp of his little hand, that I could not find it in my heart to say "no."

"What, won't you stay another minute if Arthur loves you very—*very*—much?" was uttered in a tone of infantine cajolery there was no resisting. It was the plea of a child conscious of his hold upon the affections of many.

S

As the afternoon, though bright with April sunshine, was growing chilly, I would not loiter longer at the gate, but proceeded at once into the park. When lo! as if the demons themselves had ordered it, scarcely had I reached the first clump of beech-trees overshading the road, when an orderly of the Blues, either on important duty, or run away with by his charger, passed us at full gallop towards the lodge.

The mare, irritated by long detention at the gate, fretted by its unusual burthen, or frightened at the clang of military accoutrements, became suddenly restive. I was unprepared for the first plunge, and the child was nearly thrown from the saddle. Clutching his dress tightly in one hand, I strove to restore his balance and retain my own. But the cries of the little fellow, and the eagerness with which he clung to the mane, served still more to terrify the accursed brute.

Why enter circumstantially into details? I have little fear of incriminating myself in the eyes of the reader, by the appearance of carelessness or want of skill. Any human being who is really human, will believe that I did my best, my earnest best, to forestall the catastrophe.

Even after all these years, it is so bitter to my feelings to revert to the event, that I have difficulty in tracing even this slight description. Unspeakable was the agony of my feelings when, at the lapse of a minute, I felt myself losing hold of the boy, who had already received a dreadful and crushing blow from the horse's head, as it reared and plunged in insane fury. There seemed only the alternative of having the precious child dashed from my imperfect grasp upon the road, and probably trampled under the horse's feet; or of saving him, by flinging him upon the soft grass.

I acted according to the suggestion of my poor judgment. The next moment, I congratulated myself on what I had done; for the beast, lightened of its unaccustomed burthen, set off at full speed. I had not had such a race since the business in the Bois de Boulogne; and remembering the sequel of that memorable event, was prepared to find a sudden crash put a term to my luckless exploit. Two horsemen, whom I passed on the road, made matters worse, by attempting to stop my horse just as I had all but regained command over its mouth. It started off, however, anew; nor was it till five minutes afterwards, that I found myself, breathless almost as the panting animal, attempting to explain what had happened to Danby, whom I met scarcely a second after the brute had given in. I found it difficult to make him understand me. Arthur, little Arthur, on horseback— thrown—lying on the road?—Impossible!

Both were in a state of agony beyond the power of language to describe, as we returned towards the spot. No person had passed to afford help. The two horsemen had followed me, and were still in our rear. The child lay where he had fallen. From a distance, we saw the white motionless speck upon the green turf. He was probably too much terrified to move. God grant he might be too much terrified to move. Oh! moment of agony and terror! *How* shall I proceed?

We reached the spot, and still he stirred not. He lay quietly on his side upon the grass, as he might have laid himself down to sleep. Nothing unusual in his attitude; nothing to inspire further alarm. Further *alarm?* Could there,—*could* there—be a greater than the panic which congealed the whole current of my blood, as I watched Danby, more dead than alive, bend over him, lift him gently from the ground, then fling himself, with the burthen prest to his bosom, wildly upon the grass.

A single glance had revealed all to *him* as it now did to *me*. The little fellow's arms hung down nerveless, as his still warm body was strained to his father's heart. Drops of blood were trickling from his lips. His eyes were still open, but fixed and

s 2

lustreless. Spare me, kind reader ! He never stirred again !

What a return home. What an evening. I cannot render justice to the noble conduct of my brother. No being of a higher sphere could have judged more equitably, or borne himself more patiently, though tortured to an indescribable pitch of anguish. I would fain throw a veil over the frenzy of the parents, as over my own. Poor promising infant,—poor murdered boy. His blood was on my head ; and when, after laying the body on the little couch, I divested myself of the garments dabbled with that innocent blood, I could scarcely have felt more guilty had I been his assassin, instead of a mourner who would willingly have sacrificed life and limb to bring him back to his distracted mother.

An express was despatched to Dropmore. In less than three hours, Lord Ormington arrived. We were assembled beside the bed where lay the body of the child ; already white and rigid as marble, a sweet smile overspreading his little features, as though grateful for having escaped so early and so unsullied to a more genial sphere. Still there was horror mingled with that touching beauty. On the white pillow where lay that little head, was a purple streak. The fair curls were clotted and stiffened over the forehead, whose warm touch of the preceding night still lingered on my lips ; and the distracted nurse who stood by aggravating the despair of poor Danby by her comments, kept pointing out, in cruel detail, the injuries her nursling had sustained.

It was well that they were able to prevent Lady Susan from entering the chamber of death, still strewn with his playthings. Danby had the little cold white hand pressed within his own as he knelt beside the bed, when Lord Ormington entered the room. Never shall I forget the haggardness of his face as he approached us. Never shall I forget the piteousness of the old man's look as he cast his eyes upon the

smiling countenance of the dead. The sobs that burst
out of the depths of his heart, sounded as if forced
from a breast of iron. He did not affect to repress
his feelings. His glance towards myself when I
attempted to moderate his grief lest his mournful cries
should reach the chamber of Lady Susan, was like the
glare of a beast of prey.

I could hear imprecations muttered between his
clenched teeth. Let me not record the horrible words
intermingled with his curses. If he called me murderer, if he called me———no ! I *will* not repeat them.

> Questuque, cruentus,
> Atque imploranti similis,

I throw myself on the compassion of the reader.

———◆———

CHAPTER XIV.

> Qualis ubi alterno procurrens gurgite pontus
> Nunc ruit ad terras, scopulosque superjacit undam
> Spumeus, extremamque sinu perfundit arenam :
> Nunc rapidus retro, atque æstu revoluta resorbens
> Saxa, fugit, litusque vado labente relinquit.—*Æneid.*

> Metaphysics,—mountains,—lakes,—love unextinguishable,—
> thoughts unutterable,—and the nightmare of my own delin-
> quencies.—BYRON.

I HAVE no right to inflict upon others more than
this faint outline of a family affliction such as falls to
the lot of few ; such as *could* have fallen to the lot of
none more capable of sustaining it with heroism,
than my brother. He was able to thank Heaven as
for an act of mercy, when, the following day, Lady
Susan was pronounced to be safe, after giving birth to
a dead son. *Another son!*

I will advert no further to this piteous epoch of
my life. Had it not been for the generous sympathy
of my brother and sister, I could not have survived
the cruel insinuations of Lord Ormington, or the still

more agonizing reproaches of my own mind. I saw
the scowl of the ancient domestics directed towards
me. I perceived the revived hatred of Lord Ormington. I, the changeling, was become his heir again ;
or rather, according to his malignant suspicions, had
made myself his heir ; I, the interloper in his family,
the exterminator of its dearest hopes. A tigress,
bereft of its young, could not have been more ferocious
than the grandfather of that lamented boy.

Enough ! Be my sufferings, whether from grief or
indignation, surmised by every generous heart. I
ceased to be Lord Ormington's inmate. I could no
longer sit with patience at his board. My income was
so secured that nothing brought us of necessity into
contact. I determined to quit England. Lauding
the gods that one portion of the continent at least
remained open, though France was once more closed
against English intrusion, I hurried from the sound
and sight of familiar things.

The excitement of military enthusiasm, which on a
former occasion had roused my mind from the stupor
consequent on deep affliction, might renew its bene-
ficent influence. The talons of the Eagle of France
were matched once more against the paw of the Lion.
Great armies were in the field ; a great cause was at
stake. I flew to Brussels. I fought as a volunteer at
Waterloo—unsuccessfully—for the object of my soldiership was release from a life of torture. In place of the
death I sought, a wound, not even dangerous, though
involving a long, tedious, and painful recovery, served
only to increase the measure of my sufferings.

My name was mentioned with honour in the
despatches ; and even at one's last gasp, one is never
sorry to see oneself in print. I had once expected to
obtain less honourable mention in that Alpha and
Omega of public life, the Gazette.

> Indupedita suis fatalibus omnia vinclis.

Fortune seemed determined to make a hero of me.

I may permit myself to observe, by the way, that we Waterloo men were unconscious at the time of the magnitude of our heroism. We did not foresee that our deeds were stereotyped for the use of posterity. As regarded myself, my soul was too embittered for the soothings of vanity. The surgeons who watched over my recovery, noting the feverish varia- tions of my temperament, often went away desponding. They even apprised me, so soon as I gained strength enough to be intrusted with the ordering of my destinies, that nothing but the absence of excite- ment, moral or physical, would perfect my convales- cence. They recommended change of air and scene, interdicted my project of rejoining the army in Paris, and advised me either to return to my natal air, or take up my abode, during the autumn, in some tranquil spot in one of the Rhenish principalities.

The project was a tempting one. The Rhine was not then the vulgarized and Charing-cross-like tho- roughfare it has since become. It was not dese- crated by steamboats. It was not infested by the plague of frogs and flies, the hopping, buzzing English, who have caused the savour of beefsteaks to reek from all its valleys. There was not so much as a Guide- book to rob one of the pleasant uncertainties of travel. The wanderer took his chance ; the very chance that renders a wandering life agreeable. If he chose to go and eat a bad dinner at the Golden Lamb, when the Wine Bush was the best inn in the place, no need to revile himself for obstinacy. He could plead ignorance. The good or evil renown of either had never reached him at his dinner-table at the Alfred.

It is one of the curses of the times I am fated to survive to, that Europe, Asia, Africa, and America, have become itinerarized. From the banks of the Wye to the shores of the Hudson, we know everything we are to see in foreign parts, as distinctly as if we had viewed the scene in one of Burford's panoramas. Not a dark point in the landscape—not a suspicious lane—

not an inn of dubious reputation. John Murray has
much to answer for, besides the burning of Byron's
journal. He has not left us a mysterious nook in
which to niche a romance; and were poor Mrs.
Radcliffe to revive, she might as well attempt to conjure up horrors about Islington Hill, as about the
Apennines. No doubt we shall soon have folding
maps of the moon, Mogged or Tegged for the touring
season.

Unprepared for the beauty of the scenery awaiting
me, I can scarcely describe the effect produced on my
mind by the aspect of the shattered walls of Ehrenbreitstein, now, alas ! as trim and smooth as Woolwich
barracks. I resolved to pass a week or two at Coblentz ;
chiefly for the purpose of contemplating its sublimity
of desolation. An inexplicable sympathy attracted
me towards everything on which the breath of adversity
had seemed to blow.

Coblentz was one of those unhappy frontier towns—
half frog, half tadpole—half French, half German,—
which Napoleon Gallicized, which the triumph of the
Allies re-Germanized, the reappearance of the Emperor
re-Frenchified ; and which was consequently now ex-
piating by the infliction of a Prussian garrison, the sin
of having thrown up its hat a second time in honour
of the Emperor. As a counterbalance to this misfortune, Coblentz may boast of being one of the favoured
towns, to which nature has assigned a prepossessing
countenance ; the features being comely rather than
sublime, and, above all, the complexion wholesome.

A confluence of streams is pretty sure to embellish
a landscape ; and between the majestic cliffs on one
shore, and the spreading pastures and feathery poplars
of the other, betwixt the grandeur of the Rhine and
sweetness of the Moselle, the scenery is agreeably
diversified. We catch a glimpse of the noble scenery
of Nassau, to which Coblentz officiates as a sort of
park lodge, embowered amid evergreens and flower-
knots ; while to the opposite shore, the green hills

come sloping down, as if to find in the Rhine the
natural boundary of that hideous country which calls
itself *la belle France.*

As the Prussians then occupied as victors the town
which now pays its modest taxes to the Black Eagle,
they had possession of the best quarters in the place.
I had, however, the luck to find quiet lodgings in
a narrow street almost adjoining the Benedictine
suburb ; and still more fortunately (as a particularly
hot dog-star was raging), it was on the shady side of
the way.

Lieber Gott ! On what trifles are our destinies
balanced. Had it been on the sunny side, I should
have had no occasion to include the Rhine in these my
reminiscences, or have remembered Coblentz only for
the cool rush of its waters, the rustle of its poplars,
and the pure whiteness of the frosted silver from the
mines of the neighbouring duchy, which it manufac-
tures with such tasteful adroitness.

But as it was a fierce July, and my sitting-room
window secure from a ray of sunshine, I placed as near
to it as possible the table whereon were deposited my
desk and books, and the easy chair in which I used to
enjoy my meerschaum and reveries. There, my arm
in a sling, and my spirits almost equally infirm, I used
to sit from morning till twilight, studying the German
language in the pages of Goethe and Kotzebue, till I
grew as blue and sentimental as a forget-me-not, and
began to Kant most abominably.

After having cudgelled my brains so successfully
with conjugations and declensions that, without much
recourse to the dictionary, I could make out Wilhelm
Meister or Werther, I began to notice, in the lucid
intervals of my wool-gatherings, that the opposite
windows, which were closed all the morning for the
same reason that caused mine to be left open, namely,
the aspect of the house, were adorned with flowers,
the fragrance of which was distinctly perceptible from
my chamber—mignionette, heliotrope, verbena, gera-

niums, besides various plants less grateful to the smell,
but to the eye more beautiful, as well as to the pocket
more costly.

There were five windows, the ledges of which, pro-
tected by an old-fashioned *grillage*, were filled with
flowers.

I had every reason to be satisfied with my opposite
neighbours ; for in addition to the sweetness of their
hanging gardens, there lived in one of the windows a
piping bullfinch, whose performance of one of Mozart's
prettiest waltzes was a constant source of amusement.

After enjoying the sweetness of its song and the
heliotropes, for a day or two, it suddenly occurred to
me, that birds and flowers afford strong indications of
female vicinity.   The handsome solid hotel, straight
into whose face I was compelled to look sixteen hours
of the twenty-four, must contain at least one charming
specimen of the sex, addicted to the poetry of nature
as developed in bullfinches and rose-bushes.

As soon as I had taken this for granted, I became
anxious for the hour when, on the disappearance of the
sun, the blinds were thrown open ; and the apartments,
whose cooler morning aspect was towards the court-
yard, became partially disclosed.   My dinner-time interfered once or twice, I fancy, with the happiness I
ambitioned of discovering by what fair hand the flowers
were watered and the birdcage supplied with fresh
groundsel.   But after three days' watching, I contrived to jump up from dessert just as the snow-white
dress of a retreating figure was apparent, vanishing
from the window.   That night I scarcely slept ; so
great was my disappointment at having missed a sight
of the charming unknown intermingled in my dreams
with the fragrance of delicious flowers, and the music
which, to my thinking, is the realization of fairy
song.

If I died of hunger next day, I was determined not
to quit the window till I had seen the face of the pro-
prietress of the piping bullfinch. I was convinced that

she must be beautiful, I *felt* that she must be beautiful ; and it is a delightful incident, at four-and-twenty, to be the opposite neighbour of a beautiful woman, who waters her own mignionette and blows the chaff from the seed-trough of her own birdcage. Particularly in Germany. Such situations are made for Germany. I turned over the leaves of nearly the whole edition of Goethe and Kotzebue, for a quotation germane to the matter, and found more than enough to fill half a dozen commonplace-books.

At length, after several days of irritating anxiety, my wish was accomplished. And what an accomplishment. What an ethereal creature, what a pure and gracious being met my view. Fair, not as daylight, which is *not* fair ; but fair as moonlight, and like moonlight, serene and touching. I never saw a skin that so completely justified the old and hacknied comparison of the lily. I never saw eyes that so thoroughly exemplified the equally worn-out simile of blue as heaven. The beauteous vision might be compared rather to one of Ossian's shadowy heroines, than to mere flesh and blood. She was attired in a floating filmy dress of muslin ; and between its silvery whiteness, the aërial form of the wearer, and the profusion of flaxen hair accompanying that seraphic face, I could have persuaded myself, when she vanished from the window, that I had been gazing on an angel. I began to think it strange that the people who had offered so many vulgar pretexts as an excuse for the high price of my lodgings, should never have thought of naming the advantage of living opposite to the Herr Bau-Berg-und-Weg-Inspector von Schwanenfeldt and his beauteous Wilhelmina.

My dear reader is by this time sufficiently familiar with me to know that I am afflicted with no propensity for falling in love ; and that I could have waltzed through half a dozen seasons at Almack's, or played billiards through an indefinite number of frosts at country houses in the Christmas holidays, without

endangering my own peace of mind and heart, whatever I might do to those of other people.

But one cannot always resist the force of situation.
The propinquities of that snug apartment in the Rue
Montblanc, for instance, and the charm of lodging
opposite the flower-beds of the wife or daughter of a
Prussian Bau-Berg-und-Weg-Inspector, afford juxta-
position of the most dangerous nature. I felt myself in considerable danger of a fit of the senti-
mentals.

There must have been infection in the air ; for the
following day the flowers were watered a quarter of
an hour earlier than usual, and the bullfinch was
allowed to perch on her finger and was chirruped to
with a degree of innocent tenderness that might
have undevilled Mephistophiles. A sweet girlish
smile irradiated the heavenliest of human faces as
she kissed the beak of the happy bird previous to
replacing it in its cage. Bewitching being ! How
I thanked the lucky accident which had directed me
to pause at Coblentz previous to repairing to the
baths of Ems and Schlangenbad.

It is doubly pleasant to fall in love in summer-time,
when earth and air seem also inspired by the tender
passion. The birds sing, the roses blow ; and one does
not feel quite so ridiculous when inditing one's first
stanza to the moon.

Blessed moon ! how grateful was I to its brightness,
when, at the close of half a dozen anxious days and
feverish nights, my eagerness to obtain an uncon-
strained view of my lovely neighbour was rewarded by
an hour's unintermitting contemplation of her angelic
countenance, upturned towards the effulgent lamp of
night. Unconscious that she was watched from behind
the curtain of the opposite window, die Unbegreifliche
sat, wrapped in her dressing-gown and pensive meditation, at her own. The street was narrow ; the summer night tranquil, not a breath astir. I fancied I
could detect the sighs that heaved her gentle bosom ;

nay, I could almost have sworn that I saw a tear glitter in her eyes as she gazed on the unsullied brightness of that glorious orb. But that my right arm was still in a sling, methinks I should have rushed to my writing-table and hazarded a declaration of the feelings gene-rating like a summer storm in my overcharged bosom.

But I forbore. Conscience, or prudence, or some other highly commendable scruple, reminded me that there was a tenth commandment; and that the fair being on whose alabaster forehead the moon was shining so serenely, while the flowers mingled their ambient odours with her breath and mine, was not the daughter, but the wife of the worshipful Herr Bau-Berg-und-Weg-Inspector von Schwanenfeldt. I had no more right to covet that aërial creature, than the man-servant, or maid-servant, or postwaggon-horse wherewith the inspector jolted off, evening after evening, to booze away his hours with the commandant of the garrison, old General Maximi-lian Schlachenwachenhausen at his head-quarters at Thal.

Wilhelmina was only a few years my junior, yet in aspect still a child. Something in the secluded domes-ticity of the German women seems to secure them from the touch of time. They are the youngest of their years of all the daughters of Eve. There was an almost scriptural purity in the looks and gestures of the inspector's wife. I said to myself that night, after the moonlight scene, when I had held my breath and Wilhelmina her peace for two hours by the clock of the Rath-Haus, Heaven send that this singular adventure end not like the fatal passion of the *Junge Werthers* for his Lottchen. I began to hate myself for the levity with which, only two years before, I had allowed myself to jest with Byron over the Hoff-mannisms recited for us by Schlegel and Madame de Staël. I had laid unhallowed hands upon the ark, and atonement might be demanded of me.

I hazarded no attempt, however, to present myself

to the acquaintance of the lovely Wilhelmina. Content
to breathe the same air with her, to inhale the fragrance of the same flowers, to worship the brightness
of the same delicious planet, my heart was too withered
with its sorrows to aspire to a dream of greater happiness. I had no right to refresh my blighted feelings
in the dews of a spirit so young, so pure, so heavenly.

I could not but flatter myself that my sympathy
had not wholly escaped her notice. She could not
but have seen me transfixed beside the open window,
hour after hour, day after day ; with my eyes riveted
on her own, as a Persian gazes on the sun, or as
Leander may have watched the light emanating from
the torch of Sestos' daughter. For she lingered longer
and longer with her bird and flowers. I almost fancied
tears of sensibility trembling in her large blue eyes, as
she bent them on my window, whenever, in the wanton-
ness of vanity, I delayed to make my appearance
simultaneously with her own.

Though I still swore to myself, almost on affidavit,
to respect the virtuous home of the Herr von Schwanenfeldt, there was nothing to forbid my enjoying the
visionary pleasure of lending a soul to that beauteous
form, supposing all that was passing in that gentle
bosom, and dwelling upon the perfections manifested
to me as those of some heavenly visitant. I might, at
least, permit myself to dream of Wilhelmina. And
dream of her I did ; till my sleep was far happier than
my waking.

One day, as I sat musing beside my window with a
volume of Schiller in my hand, I suddenly descried,—
oh, joy ! oh, triumph !—the door of the birdcage
slightly ajar. I do not mean to reflect upon any one.
Heaven forbid I should insinuate that Wilhelmina
had any share in such inadvertency. But I say again,
that the door of the cage was slightly ajar. If the
little flutterer would but take advantage of this
negligence to pay me a visit. On this hint of my
ardent imagination, I instantly began to chirrup in a

tone as nearly similar to that I had heard emitted by
Frau von Schwanenfeldt, as was in the power of my
manly voice. I saw Master Bully duck his little black
poll, and wink his cunning little eyes, as if meditating
a flight. I chirruped again ; he sidled on his perch.
I chirruped again ; he hopped down. I chirruped
again ; he reached the threshold of the cage door.
Again ! he lighted on the bough of an hibiscus, then
on the window-ledge. At length, he flitted across the
street and lighted on my own.

Magna Dii curant, parva negligunt.

I could scarcely breathe. The slightest movement
and the little startled truant might make his way
back again, and defeat my projects. Again I chirruped
invitingly, though preserving the most rigid immo-
bility. And this time, Bully piped up his waltz, as if
to acknowledge the commencement of our visiting
acquaintance.

From the days of the Fox and the Crow, this
species of vanity has been fatal to the perpetrator.
He was taking too much pains with his song to perceive the Bandana I flung over him, till fairly taken
in the toil. I was not bound to know whose bird it
was ; and, having possessed myself of a Berlin basket
that stood by way of ornament on one of the *consoles*,
incarcerated the little anonymous runaway, till further
notice.

That day, instead of waiting at the window the
moment when the gradual retreat of the evening sun
enabled the major-domo of the Herr Bau-Berg-und-
Weg-Inspector to open the blinds of his master's state
apartments, and the Frau Bau-Berg-und-Weg-Inspectorinn to sprinkle her heliotropes and mignionette, I
kept quietly in the background ; my ear on the alert
to catch the first exclamation of horror, proclaiming
her discovery of the departure of her faithless favourite.

Exclamation of horror ? Ah ! Wilhelmina ! Her
shriek might have brought down the tottering rem-

nants of the shattered wall of Ehrenbreitstein. Instead of a faint scream, this fragile sylph-like being exhibited the impassioned energy of Siddons, when, as Elvira, she used to strike terror into the brazen soul of Pizarro. I was paralyzed. I trembled to think on what I had done. Bully, in his basket, trembled too.

Within half an hour, came round the Rathsdiener, with his bell, announcing to the good burgesses of Coblentz, that vier Kronthaler would be given in reward to whosoever should bring to the residence of the Excellent Bau-Berg-und-Weg-Inspector von Schwa-nenfeldt, a bullfinch answering to the name of "Schatz-chen," and no questions asked.

This did not exactly suit my views. *My* object *was* to be asked questions. By-and-by, came the town printer, with a copy of the Steckbrief that was to make the walls of Coblentz eloquent with the loss of "Schatzchen."

I seriously recommend novices in the prigging line to be cautious of entrapping a piping bullfinch. You may leave a watch unwound, so that its ticking betray you not. A pocket handkerchief has not a word to say for itself. But the fright I was in, lest that infernal waltz of Bully's should prematurely pipe up, is beyond description. I was afraid of closing the windows, lest so unusual a movement in July might beget suspicion. I was still more apprehensive of closing the basket too hermetically, lest I should stifle suspicion and the bullfinch together. Schatzchen must pipe in the land of the living, at least till the post-waggon carried off the Herr Bau-Berg-und-Weg-Inspector to Thal.

There must be something peculiarly emollient in the atmosphere of Germany. Here was I, Cis Danby, blackened by the smoke of Waterloo, after years of previous defacement by the smoke of London, grown tender as a pheasant poult, maidenly as a snowdrop, simple as a cowslip; about to make my *début* with a flaxen-haired divinity in white muslin, with a piping

bullfinch on my finger. I would not have had Watiers
catch sight of me at that moment, for the rent-roll of
Ormington Hall.

Thut nichte! As soon as dusk and the post-
waggon arrived (but the post-waggon arrived first, for
a July twilight is eternal as the youth of the lovely
matrons of Teutonia), I arrayed myself as though I
had just stepped out of the pages of one of Auguste
la Fontaine's novels, or Kotzebue's comedies; dishevelled my hair, and inserted my wounded arm into
a sling as black as midnight ; then, after a glance or
two at the mirror, and a glance or two at Schatzchen,
who was beginning to cower pensively in a corner of
his basket, as if greviously in want of hemp-seed or
Wilhelmina, tottered down stairs leaning on the arm
of O'Brien, my valet ; rang the bell of the Inspector's
mansion, and requested an audience of the Frau Bau-
Berg-und-Weg-Inspectorinn Wilhelmine von Schwanenfeldt.

If there exist in this nether sphere the slightest hint
of those sympathies which the pages of Goethe and
Wieland describe as familiarly as if disembodied spirits
were as common as town criers or Prussian sergeants ;
if, I say, there exist such spiritual influences, the lights
must have burned blue, at that moment, in the chamber where the Bau-Berg-und-Weg-Inspector was engaged in a game of dominoes with the redoubtable
General Maximilian von Schlachenwachenhauscn,
knight of the second class of the Black Eagle.

I never knew what sensibility was till I witnessed
the meeting between Wilhelmina and her bullfinch.
Familiar from my infancy with the passion of Lady
Ormington for lapdogs, I had looked upon such pen-
chants as the bran, sawdust, shavings, or any other
soft material, filling up the interstices between harder
objects commingled in the great packing-case of the
human heart. But I had not conjectured the intensity
of love that might exist between five feet six of human
nature, and a feathered favourite to whom a patch-

T

box would serve for coffin. I doubt whether affection
half so true ever existed between five feet six of heroine,
and six feet nothing of hero. Scarcely had I opened
the basket in Wilhelmina's presence, when the bird
roused itself as by enchantment, shook its plumes,
noddled its jetty crest, and at the merest accident of
her chirp, flew to her finger, trying by a thousand
little cries and flutterings to render her sensible of its
joy in seeing her again. Kisses,—real kisses,—were
interchanged between them ; and when, at length,
Bully attempted a slight carol of his waltz, tears fell
from the large blue eyes of his lovely mistress, like
summer rain from the azure skies of June.

I leave it to a reader of even moderate humanity to
conceive my sensations when, approaching me in a
paroxysm of bewilderment, she seized my hand and
pressed it fervently between her own. Wild with the
joy of receiving her lost treasure, the Bau-Berg-und-
Weg-Inspector's wife knew not how to express with
sufficient fervency the excess of her gratitude.

What a woman. What a gem of sensibility. What
treasures must exist undeveloped in that gentle bosom.
Such sei! If a bulfinch could thus excite the fervour
of her emotions, what would be her tenderness, what
her truth, what her elevation of soul, when roused by
the influence of a sympathetic passion. I would not,
I *could* not bring myself to believe that Herr Bau-
Berg-und-Weg-Inspector von Schwanenfeldt had
touched the finer chords of her nature. He was a
hard, square, bony, rectangular man ; highly respected
by his tribunal and his tobacconist, but making too
much use of his nose both to talk through and feed
with rappee, to render him a fitting partner in life for
a fleecy cloud, inspired by soul so finely organized as
to expand into ecstasies at the song of the bulfinch. I
had, in short, very little doubt of finding a second
femme incomprise.

After Schatzchen had been reinstated in his cage,
with fresh groundsel, sugar, seed, and sand, on a much

higher system of philosophy than causes the pedagogue
to brandish his birch over a returned truant, it followed of course that, as four rix dollars could not be
proposed as my recompense, I must be civilly entreated.
So as Wilhelmina could offer me nothing else, she
offered me a seat.

Her bosom still heaved with emotion, and tears
glittered in her large blue eyes, like dew upon a gentian.
The moment seemed propitious for the avowal of my
long and ardent desire to make the acquaintance of my
charming opposite neighbour ; and I accordingly commenced a recapitulation of certain phrases indispensable
to the occasion, which I retained as part of the shib-
boleth of Thérèse.   But I was careful not to mount at
once too high into the clouds, remembering that " *Chi
troppo s' assotiglia si scavezza.*"

Never shall I forget my disappointment at the blank
look of wonder accompanying Madame von Schwanenfeldt's shrug of the shoulders, intimating that she
understood neither my French nor my explanations.

I was beginning to read German indifferently well ;
but to ask for my breakfast was the utmost I could
accomplish in speech.   As to clothing fine sentiments
in appropriate language, I might as well have attempted to dress a wax doll in the wrap-rascal of a
Connaught cadger.   I had nothing that would fit the
occasion.   My best German was worthy only to order
an omelette for myself, or corn for my horse.   I should
barely have known how to pronounce

Empfüll bavon bein Herz,

or any other bit of tender eloquence.

Gott steh' mir bei.   What was to become of me.   Was I
to find my way to the affections of Wilhelmina by
piping a waltz, like Schatzchen ?

But though incapable of talking, I was not incompetent to listen ; and listen I did, with exquisite
delight, to the expressions of exaggerated joy and

T 2

gratitude poured forth by Wilhelmina, bright and
sparkling as the waters of Selters leaping from their
rock. She tried to impress upon my mind by the
united force of diction and pantomime, her agony at
the first discovery of the cage-door being open and the
bird departed ; her hopes that it might still return to
one who loved it so dearly ; her fears lest it should
have fallen into the hands of cold or careless persons ;
and all this was uttered so fluently, yet so energetically,
with so much aid from sighs and tears, eyes uplifted to
Heaven, and white hands clasped with impassioned
fervour, that I felt as if a page of the choicest poetry
were unfolded for my delight. My soul was kindled
to enthusiasm by the rays of inspiration brightening
the countenance of that celestial creature.

At last came the moment for leave-taking. I had
delivered myself of my errand, and was as destitute of
means of allusion to heliotropes or moonbeams as if
just landed from the Sandwich islands. All I could
do was to heave an enormous sigh, place my right hand
emphatically on that portion of the left side supposed
to be consecrated to the tender affections, look as
cruelly charming as I could, and go about my business ; all which I executed with proper emphasis and
discretion.

I do not think even the drowsiest of Kotzebue's
comedies would have secured me a night's rest that
night. I tossed and turned on my pillow as restlessly
as the narrow dimensions of a German bed would
admit, and thought myself greatly to be pitied for
rising with as severe a headache the following morning
as if I had swallowed a flask of Kirschwasser at the
Herr von Schwanenfeldt's, instead of deep draughts of
that Elysian nectar which converts men and women
into divinities, just as of old it brought down gods and
goddesses from Olympus.

Now that I am stricken in years I can appreciate
the ecstasy of a restless night of that description—a
sort of delirious *imbroglio* of flowers, moonlight, per-

fumes, blue eyes, pearly teeth, lily hands, bulfinches, Goethe, the devil, and Dr. Faustus. One hour of such boyish infatuation were worth whole ages of my present grovelling materialism.

A worse infliction than the headache, however, awaited me on the morrow. O'Brien, my valet de chambre, made his appearance with much such a smile as he used to wear some years before as Tim my tiger, when undrawing the convolvulus curtains on especial occasions. The boy was father to the man, the tiger to the valet; and his eyes were twinkling with inward laughter as he laid a billet of considerable promise on my rumpled pillow. Could not one swear to the letter of a pretty woman by shape and scent, as one does to those which have passed through quarantine?

Need I say that I tore it open as became the petulance of Cecil Danby. Perhaps I need not add, to a public so intelligent as that I am addressing, that not one syllable it contained could I make out. Written German was more incomprehensible to me than German spoken; and Wilhelmina's billet looked something between one of my Greek exercises and the hieroglyphics of a doctor's prescription. What it prescribed to *me*, I knew no more than William the Conqueror.

What was to be done? It was a dreadful exigency. The servant waited for an answer. To call up my landlord and consult him about the contents of a billet from the Frau Bau-Berg-und-Weg-Inspectorinn was out of the question. Promising to send an answer, therefore, I sent for a carriage, and made the best of my way to my librarian's, with whom abided an intelligent young Frenchman, to whom I had already had recourse in several dilemmas; and to him, tearing off the signature at the bottom, and with a face blushing celestial rosy red, as mine had seldom blushed since Eton, I exhibited my billet-doux. Like Pharaoh, I requested an interpretation.

"I congratulate, you, sir," said he, in a tone that left me little doubt of my good fortune. "Considering the briefness of your sojourn in this city, you have achieved more than many of my countrymen who have resided years at Coblentz."

I trust he did not perceive the self-complacent air with which I ran my eye along my own graceful outline, till it rested on the point of my boot.

"You are invited," he continued, "to dinner to-day at two o'clock, by one of the most respectable magistrates of the city — the Herr Bau-Berg-und-Weg-Inspector von Schwanenfeldt, who resides in——"

"Yes, yes—I know," cried I, interrupting him. "I was aware that it was an invitation to dinner, but could not exactly make out the hour. At two, you say?"

"At two—the usual dinner-hour in Germany. You will find charming people, sir, in Monsieur de Schwanenfeldt and his wife. The lady is one of the loveliest women in the Rhenish provinces."

Again I might have interrupted him with "I know —*I* know." But I preferred asking for the last edition of Jean Paul, by way of pretext for my intrusion ; and hurried home to answer the invitation by polite verbal acceptance.

I was about to behold her, then—to behold her surrounded with the duties and joys of her innocent life ; not only with the bullfinch and the heliotropes, but with husband and children.

I did not much fancy the idea of dining at two o'clock, or rather of going out to dinner at two o'clock. How was I to make myself irresistible in the broiling middle of a July day? There was nothing for it, of course, but boots and half-dress. I must trust to nature to accomplish her own miracles. Schatzchen would be there to plead for me ; if, indeed, there needed any other voice with Wilhelmina than that of her gentle heart.

It required some courage to confront the Herr Bau-Berg-und-Weg-Inspector and his Teutonic croaking. But had I surmised that, instead of German, he would

accost me in Germanized French, such as would have
convulsed any audience of the Boulevart with laughter,
if delivered by Brunet or Potier, I should scarcely
have found courage to attempt my self-introduction
to the middle-aged gentleman who, with the pedantic
solemnity of a retired schoolmaster, thanked me
for having " *rabborté lé bétit why-so te Matame zon
ébouze.*"

Wilhelmina was attired as angels ought to be
dressed on gala days ; *i.e.* in a clean white muslin
dress, with a sash of dark-coloured riband that displayed to admiration the turn of her delicate waist.
No ornaments—nothing but a single rose fresh from
the garden, which looked as if it had caught among
her ringlets, as she made her way through the entangled
branches of a shrubbery. I could have indited quires
of hexameters to that happy rose.

Conceiving that it may be as disagreeable to my
reader to peruse as it was to me to listen to the
" bladidudes " of the Herr Bau-Berg-und-Weg-Inspector, I shall briefly state that he was not much
more boring and disagreeable, nor *much* more of a
Schlafmütze, than privileged by matrimonial patent ;
and that we sat down with a dog-day sun flaming into
the room to a dinner that savoured of the quarters of
the Royal Irish, when campaigning among the renowned
onion-fields of Portugal. Our soup consisted of snip-
pings of cabbage, served in the water in which they
were boiled, with little suet dumplings floating on the
top. Our fish was a cold pike, with sweet sauce garnished with rings of onions. To these (washed down
by a gargle of Rhenish *ordinaire*, which, like the
famous Nauemburger, serves to indicate where vinegar
grows wild) succeeded a dish of exceedingly fat *bouilli*,
accompanied, Germanwise, by four sauce-boats, containing pickled cherries, a *purée* of onions, another of
Meer-rettig, and a black nameless compound that looked
and smelt like senna-tea.

My nerves were somewhat shaken on perceiving

with what heroic fortitude Wilhelmina not only divided
her fish with her knife, but afterwards, immersing the
clumsy blade in the vinegar so as to blacken the
surface, insinuated it fearlessly into her mouth. For
a moment I was apprehensive of the worst consequences. But as *she* survived it, so did I. Of the fat
bouilli and senna-sauce she ate voraciously ; and when
the third dish was placed on table, consisting of a stew
of wild boar swimming in stewed apricots, and looking
like everything that was nastiest in nature, I shuddered at the unctuosity of lip with which this etherial
being absorbed the mess.

Next came an *eierspeise,* which she imbibed with
equal satisfaction, accompanied by an ill-roasted joint
of veal, well basted with butter ; then, two or three
soup-plates of leguminous compound, that looked as if
ladled out of a weedy ditch. Then wafers, then
salad, then leveret, that must have forgotten the date
of its killing ; then cheese, that must have forgotten
the date of its pressing ; then fruit, then *zucker-
brod,* then sugar-plums, then coffee, then kirsch ;
to say nothing of half-a-dozen *hors-d' œuvres,* such as
pickled herring, Brunswick sausage, slices of raw ham,
pumpernickel, caviar, and other creature-comforts of
equal delicacy.

Gott im Himmel! To see the idol of one's soul fill
the lips that Leonardo would have delighted to paint,
lips like the half-open bud of a Boursault rose, lips
that seemed formed only for murmurs of tenderness
and joy, the plaint of Margaret, the song of Thekla,—
to see those lips dilate to receive a vile, circumferential
slice of Braunsweiger Bratwurst.

The horror of the Arabian husband who beheld his
wife Amina steal to the churchyard and indulge in
her foul repast of human flesh could not have exceeded
mine. I should as soon have expected the Venus de
Medicis or Belvedere Apollo to sup on cheese and
onions, as that heavenly creature. My only consolation
was the belief that this sylph, this Undine, this fay,

this sprite, was perhaps trifling with my sensibilities, and trying the force of my attachment.

We repaired together to the drawing-room ; the *persiennes* of which were closed to exclude the afternoon sun, so that I had no pretext for alluding to the flowers. The flowers, nevertheless, would have been a most agreeable accessory ; for the Herr Inspector entered the room with a grevious flavour of second-rate tobacco reeking from his garments.

But though my faith in Madame von Schwanenfeldt's divinity was somewhat staggered, she looked so lovely, there was such a glance of deprecation in those heavenly eyes, even when eating sauer-kraut, that I began to revile myself for the want of amplitude of soul, that could make no allowance for national customs, or the force of early habit ; more particularly when, on Schatzchen's striking up his accustomed song, Madame von Schwanenfeldt turned towards me with a smile of tender intelligence that might have "woke a soul under the ribs of death," or the rock of Ehrenbreitstein.

The Herr Bau-Berg-und-Weg-Inspector, a little boozy with wine and tobacco, perceiving that I made no movement to take my leave, proposed that, later in the day, when the sun became less fervid, we should proceed together to a garden of Eden, on the Nassau road (which after-experience proved to be some abominable tea-gardens), and that, in the mean time, Wilhelmina should favour us with some music.

Music executed by the object of our affections has always struck me as the acme of human felicity. To listen to some *chef-d'œuvre* of Mozart or Cimarosa, or even some touching romance, from the lips of Wilhelmina, would transport me above this visible diurnal sphere.

After the much-approved fashion of performers and inn-keepers, of asking you what you will have, though pre-determined to inflict the pig-and-pruin-sauce which your soul abhorreth, Wilhelmina, on seating herself at

the piano, inquired what she should give me. I
ventured to propose, "Non so più cosa son,"—"Voi che
sapcte,"—or some other of the master-pieces of Mozart.
When lo! to my utter horror, she bust into a crashing,
thundering sonata, of the high-pressure instrumental
school ; just then, for the curse of pianofortes and
society, beginning to bring heaven and earth and the
two extremities of the instrument together.

Wilhelmina's piano was execrable to an ear accustomed to the full-bodied tones of Broadwood and
Kirkman ; and she had not skirmished up and down
the keys five minutes, before I felt as if I had
swallowed a glass of vitriol.

Not so the Herr Bau-Berg-und-Weg-Inspector.
Exalted to the seventh heaven by this astounding
rattling of keys and chaotic confusion of sharps, flats,
and naturals, he saw fit *not* to beat, but to stamp time
to the music, till the flooring seemed giving way under
the horrible iteration of his blows. The measured
tramp of the *commendatore's* ghost in Don Giovanni
was not half so appalling.

I felt myself in considerable danger of committing
Inspectoricide. My evil spirit was roused by all this
banging :—

Duris ut ilex tonsa bipennibus
Nigræ feraci frondis in Algido,
Per damna, per cædes, ab ipso,
Ducit opes animumque ferro.

I do not affect to be an amiable man. I *know*
myself. As Byron sings,

I had been ill brought up, and was born bilious ;

and beg my readers to take into consideration that the
thermometer was at 84°, my frame undergoing the
digestive process of dumpling soup, raw veal, and
divers other equally hard matters. The room was full of
buzzing flies, my head of the fumes of Asmannhausen ;
and I admit that I felt capable of the manslaughter of

the Herr Bau-Berg-und-Weg-Inspector, who was so hospitably entertaining me. But for Wilhelmina's azure eyes and floating ringlets, methinks I could have found it in my soul to include *her* in the massacre.

Before the close of the stormy sonata, however, Schwanenfeldt was called away to a client; whereupon, after receiving my thanks for the extraordinary exertions she had made in my favour, Wilhelmina quitted the piano, evidently satisfied that she had accomplished a miracle.

Having gazed earnestly and circumstantially round the room, to ascertain that the thumper who had kept time for her elaborate performance had no longer any time at her disposal, she seated herself on a sofa near the window, which I had often seen her occupy, and with smiling serenity took out her work.

I trust the reader does me the justice to conclude that I assumed a place by her side.

> Vos, ô patricius sanguis, quos vivere par est
> Occipiti cœco, posticæ occurrite sannæ!

CHAPTER XV.

> So regeln wir die Mond- und Sonnentage
>   Sitzen vor den Pyramiden,
>   Zu der Volker Hochgericht
>   Ueberschwemmung, Krieg und Frieden,
>   Und versehen kein Gesicht.
>
> GOETHE.

My poetry is the dream of the sleeping passions. When they are awake, I cannot speak their language—only in their somnambulism.—BYRON.

DEAR reader, wert thou ever in Germany? I do not mean didst thou ever steamboat it up or down the Rhine, or swallow the natural physic of the waters of

Baden or Aix-la-Chapelle; for who hath *not?* I mean,
didst thou ever abide in the soft bosom of a *recht herz-
liche* German family; drink of their beer, smoke of
their tobacco, and chew metaphysics with them; the
exaltation of their minds justifying itself to yours by
anxiety to lose sight of degradation of body so preposterously gross and nasty. By Jupiter! if the spitting-
box and beer-bottle do not incline a man to refine with
hair-breadth casuistry upon some psychological theory
capable of propelling the soul into the clouds at the
rate of the Nassau balloon, Satan himself would not
make a metaphysician of him!

But I say again, dear reader, wert thou ever in
cordial, kind-hearted, boozy, foozy Deutschland?
Kennst du das Land? not where the Citronen blühn; but
where the lindens shed their summer bloom; where
the round-polled acacia, like a green mop or sham
orange-tree, adorns the beer-garden; where weeping-
willows, hanging over a pond enlivened by fancy ducks,
wring poesy out of the soul of the fair student; where
learning hath run herself to earth, where poetry
hovereth in the air, where the drama, as the transcendental school would say, "kindleth eternally her terrible energies, like the Destinies spinning a thread of
asbestos; where classical lore hath found an inner
temple in which the law to lay down—the divinities
re-enshrining, wherewith he hath run away charged,
like some old Corinthian, from the sack of his city,
with his household gods upon his back; and where all
that is coarse, uncivilized, and matter-of-fact in human
existence, with all that is heroic, sublime, creative,
soul-refining, purpose-exalting, hope-exciting, for evermore united is?"

If not, thou art incapable of appreciating, guess
what? I give it thee in ten, I give it thee in twenty,
as Madame de Sevigné wrote to her daughter. It is
neither Goethe, Jean Paul, Beethoven, the Sonnets or
Glyptotheca of Ludwig I., nor the policy of Metternich, nor the Hegelian philosophy, nor any other of

the grand or glorious incomprehensibilities that " with
the moral hieroglyphics of the land of spiritual influences interwoven or co-existent are." If not, I say—
for thou art so slow of surmise that I must fain disclose my mystery—if not, thou canst little appreciate
the influence of the knitting-needle in the history of
domestic life.

A casual observer might spend six months in
Germany, particularly in Rhenish Germany, and
carry away an impression that the men were never
without pipes in their mouths or the women without
knitting-needles in their hands. I once saw the body
of a drowned woman taken out of the Rhine, round
which five anxious individuals were clustered, labouring to minister to its resuscitation. Not one of them
dreamed of removing his pipe from his mouth while
the work of life and death was proceeding under his
hands. Nay, I once saw a fair Tedescan exposed to
the soliciting of a lover eloquent as Mephistopheles,
impassioned as St. Preux, tender as Romeo, enterprising as Lovelace, who proceeded the while with her
lambs-wool stocking as industriously as the witch of
the Caucasus.

I do not say who it was ; the name of the parties
is nothing to the purpose : but she plied those two
long, black whalebone knitting-needles as if the fate
of the universe hung upon her stitches.

But unless any unkind person—and the world to
which I write is as bitter as Rochefoucault's maxims
or the elder daughters of Lear—should ascribe the
imperturbability of the heroine to lack of merit in the
hero, I beg to add, that I have seen in the Hof Theatre
of Vienna a gentle creature weep Danubes of tears over
the sorrows of Thekla or the woes of Amalia ; then,
almost ere the curtain fell, certainly before the bodies
were cleared from the stage, quietly re-assume her
confounded knitting-needles as though they contained
balm for her wounded feelings.

As to me, if Cleopatra had invited me to sail with

her on the Cydnus, and under her purple canopy
chosen to amuse herself with knitting, even though
the stocking or brace were destined to Cecil Danby
in lieu of Mark Antony, I should have dropped asleep
while watching the hitching of her fair hands and
jerking of her elbows.

By all this, my public will be induced to conjecture
that I had some difficulty in keeping my eyes open
under the influence of the evening sun, the buzzing
flies, the two o'clock dinner, the Rhenish wine, and
the detestable stitchery upon which the blue eyes of
Wilhelmina von Schwanenfeldt were riveted while I
tried to make it intelligible to her that the individual
seated by her side, and usually divided from her by the
width of a street, was nearer akin to her in all the
brighter sensibilities of the soul than the stamping
Herr Bau-Berg-und-Weg-Inspector, or any other native of the land which wrote Werter and luxuriates
in sausages and small beer.

I poured out my soul in a happy mixture of French,
English, German, Latin, and gibberish ; and as she had
sufficiently comprehended the same when I tried to
make her understand that I did not eat apricot-sauce
with my wild boar, I thought she might prove equally
intelligent when I talked about the stars and the
flowers, Schatzchen, heliotropiums, kindred souls, the
music of the spheres, the immortality of love, and all
the other little bubbles with which the Cupids of the
banks of the Rhine tip their arrows, as Camdeo, on
those of the Ganges, tippeth *his* with bees.

At every fresh outbreak of sentiment Wilhelmina
gently raised her eyes from her knitting and fixed
them upon me, large, dilated, and blue as one of
Wedgewood's saucers ; letting them fall again upon
her quilt like a wax doll at the instigation of the
wire which silently governs its glassy eyes.

The imagination is a sad gad-about, the *"folle de la
maison."* There are moments when, like Ariel, she puts
a girdle round about the earth ; and others when, on

the contrary, she causeth the said earth to whiz round like a knife-grinder's wheel. When she chooses, she can make eleven thousand angels dance on the point of a needle ; or concentrate all the events of a life, all the heroisms of an Alexander or a Wellington, into the millionth part of a second. But I question whether the powers of the imagination were ever more put to the test than by myself, when supplying an interpretation to those silent looks of Wilhelmina.

Like an astrologer star-struck and bewildered, I sent forth my soul, as it were, in quest of hers ; and at moments fancied I had overtaken the bright fugitive, and was intermingling my thoughts with its aspirings. I grew more and more eloquent, more and more impassioned. I began to feel that I was making an impression. I had got the ear of the house. I warmed with my subject and my situation ; I grew emphatic as Clavigo ; my very German flowed clearer and clearer. It was impossible that even the serenest of knitters could stand it long.

I saw that I was reaching a crisis. Provided the tribunal, or particular business, or particular friend, or small account which had carried off the Herr Bau-Berg-und-Weg-Inspector, detained him half an hour longer, I felt persuaded that my next visit to the garden of Eden on the Nassau road would be paid on the express proposition of the gentle creature, still a world of affection in my debt for having stolen Schatzchen in order to bring it back again, endangering my precious neck and precious soul as a purloiner of piping bulfinches.

I fixed my eyes upon her heavenly face. She grew restless ; her colour came and went ; the knitting vibrated in her hands. I was about to imprison them in my own (which would have been easy enough, for I was sitting much closer to her than etiquette could justify), when, lo ! suddenly flinging down the knitting-needle contained in her left hand, she placed it before her mouth, and, within an inch of my beating heart,

executed a sonorous expectoration as loud as the
report of a culverin. The product she deposited at
my feet.

Und damit holla! Let us draw a veil over the crimes
of beauty. The sequel of this climax of my disen-
chantment would be described by a dramatist in
three words, appended to the part of Cecil Danby :
" Exit in distraction." I trust my public is too indignant to wish for more. I should, in fact, have
passed over Coblentz in solemn silence but for the
consciousness that, every summer, an enormous proportion of the academic youth of the three kingdoms
enjoy its vacation between Rotterdam and Strasburg,
in danger of being betrayed into bad English and bad
logic by the delusions of modern Almaine ; and still
greater, of adventures with blue-saucer-eyed heroines
who exchange kisses at the window with a favourite
bird.

Such a conclusion to such a love-passage as mine
would as efficiently exorcise the ethereal spirit of Love
as fumigation and bad Latin Sathanas, from a man
possessed ; and to avoid such a disruption of the soul
(for Love, once forcibly expelled, leaves, like the
gigantic ghost which expanded from the Castle of
Otranto, the structure in ruins), I am in conscience
bound to admit that, not choosing to be spat upon
like a Jewish gaberdine, I ordered post-horses, and
took myself off into Switzerland the following morning.

The land of the mountain and flood was indispensable to re-romanticize my spirit to the pitch from
which it had been precipitated by—— But enough
of her ; I will not defile my Bramah by writing her
name again !

If a spark of latent poetry exist in the breast of
man or woman, it *must* be called forth by collision
with the rocks and stones wherein, instead of finding
sermons, Byron found his third canto of Childe
Harold ; and *I*, regeneration after being Wilhelmina-
fied. Torrents and precipices, the lonely lake, the

silent glacier, enchanted me; and I took up my quarters at Vevay, resolved, for one short winter, to see what I could make out of the society of a man cited as the pleasantest in London or Paris, but with whom, at present, I kept up a very slight acquaintance —to wit, the Honourable Cecil Danby.

The spring found me still loitering near the lovely shores of Lake Leman, still spell-bound at Clarens,

Sweet Clarens, birthplace of deep love!

It was to join me at Geneva that Byron betook himself in the same direction. One of the wicked wits of the wickedest and wittiest of times has said that "there is something in the misfortunes of our dearest friends not altogether displeasing to us." I trust there was nothing in the mortifications which just then overtook poor Byron from which I was capable of extracting comfort. But if they did not afford me pleasure, I own they excited my amazement. I had left him the spoiled child of London, *the* poet and lion of the day, the bridegroom of an heiress, who was also a beauty and a *bel esprit*, and the idol of her whole sex. He rejoined me, at the close of little more than a year, a pariah, a banished man, a monster rejected by the moral caprices of Great Britain. In *his* case, the reaction was as sudden as absurd. So extraordinary a man as my noble friend could not expect to be treated in an ordinary manner. But the pit and gallery of society, the vulgar groundlings, had exceeded permission in flinging rotten apples in the face of their favourite actor.

Lord Byron afforded one among a thousand proofs that the most fatal charge you can make against a man is an indefinite one. It might be very inconvenient to Jupiter to embrace a cloud, but it is quite as unsatisfactory to have to fight one. People looked unutterable things when they alluded to the sufferings of Lady Byron. A horrid mystery overhung the separation of the unhappy couple; and such as the

U

survivors of that period as remember the ostracism of one of the finest fellows breathing, will scarcely recall to mind without indignation, that the putting asunder of those whom God had joined is now admitted to have arisen from the mere estrangement too often engendered by pecuniary embarrassments.

To Byron himself, such a result of his duns and bailiffs seemed so incredible, that he could not believe himself to labour under the stigma of having married an heiress to pay his debts, and maltreated her as a punishment for their non-payment ; but seemed to fancy he must have attempted assassination in his sleep, or committed forgery without knowing it. It is some comfort to those who cherish his memory, that " the late remorse of love," *though* late, has not been wanting.

The two men of my times to whom alone I concede the title of sublime, Napoleon and Byron, were both deserted by their wives. It is a fault for which, I fear, themselves must stand accountant. Both were men who would have been good, had they not chosen to be great. But the thirst of distinction, if indulged to excess, becomes fiendish as the thirst for blood. The defence of Napoleon's kindly nature, so warmly appreciated by all who approached him nearly, I leave to the eloquence of his biographers. On that of Byron, which manifested itself without remission towards me and my distresses, I must be permitted to expatiate.

I do not pretend that in many things he may not have been mean, selfish, savage. But I know, that of all my acquaintance, there is not one who, if reared by such a mother, rejected by such a wife, and coaxed into egotism by the flatteries of such a host of toadies, would not have come forth from the furnace fifty times as hard, as hot, and deteriorated with fifty times as much alloy, as he with whom I spent so many hours upon the shores of Lake Leman ; the man who devoted his blood to the cause of Greece, and who was finally bled to death at Missolonghi.

Both of us were in the feverish frame of mind arising from a sense of injury. Byron's exaltation showed itself in unnatural mirth; mine, in profound despondency. But his frantic laughter and my frantic tears sprang from a common source. Would that the bitterness of Cecil Danby could have qualified the waters of Helicon to fertilize so fair a field as that which overshadows with laurels the name and grave of my noble friend. But while Byron was plucking the stars from their spheres to form a circlet that might supersede his crown of thorns, a wreath of nettles was the utmost I could accomplish. *His* ardent soul soared into the majestic altitudes of heaven, while the sublunary eyes of Cis Danby were evermore riveted upon the waste places of this world.

As I said just now, in speaking of my poor lost Arthur, we bring with us into this shabby little planet, a reflection of the heavenly light from which our souls emerge. But the longer we live the more the earthly particles obtain the ascendancy over its brightness, and blot out the spark divine. Our clay becomes mud, and the effulgence of our spirit,

> Base and unlustrous as the smoky light,
> That's fed by stinking tallow.

I crave pardon for the homeliness of the simile. But Shakspeare and Molière are privileged. Like the long-eared gentleman of antiquity, who converted everything he touched into gold, those immortal bards have rendered classical even tallow-candles and *tartes à la créme !*

Metaphors apart, as I outlived my grief, I found myself growing a vile materialist. The brute began to predominate in my nature. Nor was there anything in the society of Byron and his " co-mates and brothers in exile " calculated to sweeten my imagination. Most persons of very refined minds with whom I ever came in contact, are coarse in their enjoyments as a country squire. The only transcendental Platonists of my acquaintance are beer-bibbing German students ; at mere recollection of whose habits, one's gorge rises.

As to the noble Childe, I could relate anecdotes of his diversions when maddened by persecution and misrepresentation, which the Dean and Chapter of Westminster would reprint in golden capitals, as an apology to posterity for the prudery which excluded his ashes from a church where Buckingham hath a grave and Dryden a monumental inscription.

But Byron has suffered enough at the hands of his friends. I was near coming it Heraclitus over the world, when those Conversations saw the light. To see the public accept such a portraiture as that of Byron, embracing "a lubberly postmaster's boy," and fancying it " sweet Anne Page ;" to see the flashing, dancing, irritable Byron set up to be lectured and documented, pearls and diamonds snatched from his mouth, and toads and frogs substituted in their stead ; to find *him* play the part in the dialogue, which dunce does in the " Tutor's Assistant " of modern tuition, where the little boy inquires with much *naïveté*, " Mamma, does the sun go round the earth ?" and mamma replies, " No Georgy !—the earth goes round the sun. Georgy will be a good boy, and know better another time." Grant me patience or wit to indite a new edition of the fable of the " Fly on the Wheel."

Byron himself, instead of " turning out his silver lining on the night," delighted to expose his blackest lining to the day ; nay, to adopt a temporary sable lining, for the express purpose of making a sensation. But this is no excuse for the perfidy of his associates.

In his lifetime, I often expressed to him my wonder at the total deficiency of elegance of mind characterizing the women who obtained an ascendancy over him. The Beatrice of his worship was always some sorry creature. His butler, old Fletcher, has immortalized, for the edification of posterity, his lordship's extreme susceptibility to female domination. But my

business is to narrate my own adventures, not those of
George Gordon, Lord Byron.

For my part, I never fell a victim to a camlet
petticoat. *My* notions of beauty are essentially
aristocratic. I adore the women of Vandyke. In the
shrine of my imagination, woman stands upon a footcloth of velvet, lest her redundant satin robes should
touch this nether earth. Though drawn up perhaps
by a string of orient pearl, or a hand of alabaster,
laced by azure veins, those garments of glistening
sheen must evermore rustle around her, to impart a
double charm to the graceful waist and gorgeous
stomacher. The nut-brown maid is to me a homely
creature ; and your "neat-handed Phillis," with her
"savoury messes," a mere kitchen-maid. I have no
taste for the rural in animated nature. Its nails are
dirty, it wears black stockings, it eschews the tooth-
brush, it scratches its head, it does a thousand revolt-
ing things. Such green sward charmers should never
be viewed nearer than in one of Gainsborough's
pictures, feeding rabbits.

At the villa Diodati, during that delicious autumn,
we indulged in a thousand chimeras, theories, and
fantasticalities of this description. We rowed and we
rode, we sighed or were sighed to, we learnt Italian
or taught English, with all the ardour incidental to
the most intellectual companionship enjoyed amid the
most exquisite scenery. After despatching to Geneva
evening after evening poor Polidori (who was of an
age and features to fancy that well-dressed people
assembled in any well-lighted room constituted society),
Byron and I used to go and enjoy ourselves under the
canopy of heaven when there was moonlight, or
remain ensconced in a comfortable room when there
was not, comparing our notes of the London world.

Gad ! how we talked them over, the young women
who had wanted to marry us, and the old ones we had
wanted to unmarry, the suppers at Watier's, the dinners at Holland House, the breakfasts in St. James's

Place. I cannot conceive how Byron, conscious as he was of the deep sympathy of the few, could trouble himself about the antipathy of the many. All the master-spirits of the age went hand in hand with him. All the first-rate women and first-rate men despised the absurd calumnies which encircled him, innocuous as serpents hissing round the pedestal of a statue. It was only the very silly people whom we paraded for our diversion in the glasses of our magic lantern, who fancied themselves raised above his head by distinctions about as honourable as the elevation of a chimney-sweep on a gate-post.

Shelley, essentially a poet, a man who had kept aloof from the deteriorating vulgarisms of conventional life, was sometimes amazed at the platitudes which derived piquancy in *our* imaginations from associations of which he knew nothing. He would have been shocked, perhaps, but that his mind was endued with the indulgence of true greatness.

On quitting Diodati, we travelled together to Venice. It is something to have visited Verona, the birth and burial-place of Juliet, with the creator of Zuleika, Leila, Medora, Gulnare. Everybody knows, who knows a great poet, that poets are the least poetical of God's or the Devil's creatures, unless when hanging over a sheet of wirewove, crowquill in hand. However, we really *were* struck by the splendour of the amphitheatre ; and if I did not quite sympathize in Byron's interest in the stone horse-trough which passes as the tomb of the daughter of the Montecchi (or, rather, of the daughter of Bandello and Shakspeare), our hearts melted at dinner that day over a flask of Monte Pulciano and a dish of ortolans.

That autumn witnessed the brightest efflorescence of Lord Byron's genius, and Manfred was fermenting in his soul,—immortal Manfred. No wonder if he became sometimes uncognizant of Cecil Danby.

Once settled at Venice, matters grew worse. The too celebrated Marianna shared his attentions with the

Witch of the Alps.   Leaving him to the undisputed
enjoyment of his lodgings in the Spezieria, I took up
my abode in a grand gloomy apartment of the Pelazzo
Gritti, on the Canal Grande; surrendering myself a
prisoner at discretion to the enchantments, animate
and inanimate, of that city of poetical illusions.

Dear reader, I perceive your consternation.   Do me
justice! *Did* I bore you with Mont Blanc on the
shores of Leman, or the Drachenfels on those of the
Rhine, that you suspect me of an intention to crush
you under the weight of the Rialto, during my sojourn
on those of the Canalaccio?   With Beppo on your
shelf, and (unless you wear a surplice or a muslin
frock) Don Juan hidden behind an edition of Chesterfield's works, Heaven forbid I should inflict upon you
so much as the description of a gondola.   Everybody
worth speaking of, or speaking to, who ever dipped
pen in ink, has had a daub at Venice ; Shakspeare and
Schiller, Byron and Beckford, Lewis and George Sand,
have projected their shadows on the lagune, or rather,
images that *came* like shadows, but have not so departed.

I may therefore hold myself exempt from dwelling
upon mildewed palaces.   Canaletto has shown you all
you need to know of the aspect of the spot—

Where Venice sits in state, throned on her hundred isles ;

and Prout and Stanfield have added an appendix to
his canvas.

Fancy yourself, therefore, in Venice.   After all the
painting and printing of the last three centuries, this
is surely no great stretch of imagination.

But you must fancy *me* also in Venice ; a good-
looking misanthrope, as black in hat, coat, and countenance as a gondola.   While Byron was polishing his
periods, or lisping Italian with Countess Albrizzi, and
Venetian with Marianna—

> Contemplando, fisso fisso,
>   Le fattezze del suo ben,
> Quel bel viso, lisso lisso,
>   Quella bocca e quel bel sen ;

I went sauntering about, fancying myself into a Pagan
in the mosque of St. Mark, and more than a Christian
in the Church of San Giorgio Maggiore ; a pigmy on
the *scala dei giganti*, a giant amid the solitudes of the
Lido.   I even breathed the sighs exacted of every
traveller who respects himself, on the Ponte dei So-
spiri ; and had serious thoughts of inditing a sonnet to
Liberty, after viewing the *pozzi* and *piombi ;* but that,
conceiving Byron would not let slip so golden an opportunity, I judged it more convenient to say "ditto
to Mr. Burke."

The tranquillity by day, the vivid animation by
night, consequent on the opening carnival, were however anything but favourable to those same metre
ballad-mongers, who require a night as silent and
solemn as the frost-bound stillness of some northern
city, disturbed only by the hoarse denunciations of the
town clock, telling the time austerely as that which,
in the unfathomable abyss, proclaimeth to the souls in
torment that eternity rules the hour.

I don't know how Childe Harold managed to get
on with his stanzas ; but, as far as I am concerned,
I never felt less romantic than in the city of romance.
The lights of the coffee-houses dazzled my eyes, whenever I tried to grow pathetic with Jaffier on the
Rialto ; and I had not been a month in the place,
before I saw as clearly as that Byron was making an
ass of himself for love of a linendraper's wife, that I
should quit Venice without an adventure.   When lo !
one evening, of all the days of the year the festival of
St. Stephen, being that which immediately succeeds
the feast of the Nativity, and nearly of as much
account among the minions and dominions of the
Austrian house of bondage, I was gondolaing it lazily
home to the Palazzo Gritti, when, on nearing the
platform of St. Mark, my ears were startled by the
tumultuous joy of the multitude assembled in honour
of this popular holiday.   The strumming of guitars,
the explosion of petards, the shouts of the merry popu-

lace, seemed to send their demonstrations gladsomely into the sky.

Startled by the vivacities of the hour, I determined to alight for a nearer survey of the Venetian commonalty. A crowd in England (as I have some thought of standing for Finsbury, let me beware of calling it a mob !)—a popular assemblage in England is the dullest-looking thing in nature. Its dinginess seems arrayed in sackcloth and ashes, diversified here and there by the diabolism of a chimney-sweep, black with the sins and soot of a seacoalfire-warmed generation, too selfish to sweep its flues with machinery. In gazing on a mass of this description, one might fancy, indeed, that the House of Hanover ruled over a nation of dustmen.

In Italy, on the contrary, a rainbow in the sky has fewer gradations of hue than a crowd upon the earth. Nothing of the monotonous dreariness of the pallid north. Blue bright as the skies, scarlet glaring as their suns, match with the vividness of the bronzed cheek, coal-black hair, and pearl-white teeth of the aborigines. All is gay and brilliant as a parterre of tulips. The aristocracy of Venice probably assumed its black array to distinguish itself from the particoloured garments of the Scaramuccian οι πολλοι.

As I stood at the foot of the Campanile, wrapt in my cloak, and fancying I could discern in the frosty air a lingering trace of the incense dispensed by the processions of the day, I perceived that the crowd, thicker in my vicinity than at the further extremity of the platform, was attracted by a company of jugglers or posture-masters, who were exhibiting their feats "supported," as we say on the entablatures of our hospitals, "by voluntary contributions."

I don't happen to care about posture-masters, or jugglers, or any other privileged distortionists of the human frame. I hate learned animals, or unlearned tumblers, just as I hate conversation-men at a dinner-party, because they pretend to achieve more than

was chalked out for them by nature. I consequently
did not so much as raise my eyes over the shoulders
of the crowd, to see what sort of feats these wonder-
workers were perpetrating. I heard the people shout
as if Cæsar were before them, putting aside the crown.
But Lord ! what will not the people shout for ?

While I waited there, contemplating for the hun-
dredth time the beauties of the Loggetta, which seemed
to gather a new and more romantic charm from the
softening shades of evening, like a fair woman peeping
through a veil, musing upon the fall of the winged
lion, and other casualties of Venice, and repeating between my teeth the flight of the French rhapsodist,

> Voyageur, à qui Venise
> Se dévoile après le jour,
> Si ton âme ailleurs est prise,
> Que je plains ton autre amour !

In the midst of my meditations my ear was startled
by an altercation in a harsh jargon, differing strangely
from the birdlike sibillation of the Venetian *patois*.

Few things attract my attention sooner than an
unfamiliar dialect. To *me* there is something as mysterious in its influence on the ear, as in that of hieroglyphics on the eye. I fancy hidden treasures of
knowlege concealed in its perplexities, and new de-
velopments of sentiment incoiled in its phrases ; and
though the promise is usually fulfilled, like most of
the promises I make myself, by the discovery that all
human tongues serve to convey the same trivialities,
and that the words which sounded supernatural as the
soliciting of the Weird Sisters only enabled Jack to
exclaim, that he was hungry, or inquire after the health
of Jill, the same feeling would be renewed, were I at
this moment in the centre of a circle of Tschusans,
hearing them and asking them questions.

I was roused from my reverie to wonder what the
squabblers on the Piazza were quarrelling about. One
of the voices was rough as the coating of a pine ; the
other, sweet and unctuous as its kernel. The contra-

basso was that of a "salvage man," a hard-looking,
masculine fellow of forty, Saracenic in beard and pro-
portions, arrayed in a pale blue jerkin, with white
trowsers, and a shaggy sash of red silk twisted round
his middle; while the girl he was addressing, a fragile-
looking thing, light as an antelope and flexile as a
cane, was attired in a yet more fanciful costume,
a spangled, close-fitting bodice of green velvet, her
black hair braided Albanian-wise, and falling upon
her naked shoulders; while muslin trowsers, of ample
fold, formed her sole defence against the nipping air of
a Christmas evening. The case was clear; these people were part of the company of funambulists.

The dispute ran high. The girl kept retreating
towards the foot of the Campanile; and the man,
evidently the master, following her with what sounded
like menaces and imprecations. If mistaken in the
meaning of his spoken accents, I could not be in the
expressive idiom of the foot that stamped on the pavement, or the swarthy fist that clenched itself in her
face. Still less could I misinterpret the gasping sounds,
half sob, half groan, that burst from the bosom of the
damsel.

To have inquired of either the cause or purport of
the dispute, would have been much the same as to ask
the question of the granite lions of St. Mark. But I
kept close at hand, determined to interpose in favour
of the girl, should it appear advisable. She was shuddering with cold; and the withering effect of the
atmosphere seemed to pinch her features and dilate
her large dark eyes, orbed with resentments such as
ought to have kept the blood circulating in her poor
blue cheeks.

Never did I behold so graceful a creature. Angiolini might have borrowed attitudes from the instinctive movements of her gracile frame. Every
menace, every impulse that uplifted her arm, was a
study. At length, some bitterer word than the rest
so excited the fury of her task-master, that a brutal

blow of his fist almost felled her to the earth. I
started forward to retaliate : sure that, however faulty
the girl, *he* was fifty-fold more condemnable. When,
lo! with the velocity of lightning, she plucked from
her girdle a stiletto I had not noticed among the
accompaniments of her Greek costume, and was about
to avenge herself in a manner more summary than
lawful.

As her best defence, instead of laying low her antagonist, I snatched the poniard from her grasp, and
prevented the commission of a crime which would
have sentenced to the axe of the executioner the most
beauteous head I ever looked on.

She was about to turn upon me, more infuriated
than against her tyrant, when a huge phlegmatic
Schwab of an Austrian soldier, who had witnessed the
affray, seized her by the shoulder; adding certain
Germanic expositions of the law, somewhat more com-
prehensible to me than the outcries of the two rope-
dancers.

Whenever justice takes people's business into her
hands, every human being present begins to talk at
once, as if the goddess of the scales had as many ears,
as Rumour tongues. In order to enable the animal
in the white and blue uniform to lend one of his exclusively to myself, I slid into his hand as much of his
emperor's particularly base coin as it would contain ;
and persuaded him, in bad German, that I was the
only credible witness of what had occurred.

The girl, regarding me as an enemy, drew away
with an intensity of scowl that must have disfigured
beauty less remarkable than hers ; while I gathered
from the explanation of the Austrian soldier that these
people were *Zigeuner* belonging to a gang of Hungarian tumblers, who had come to Venice from the fair
of Trieste, to gather a few sequins during the Carnival
ere they returned to their settlement in the Carpa-
thians. The brute whom I considered the girl's
master, was not only her master, but her father ; and

the crime which I had contemplated as assassination, would consequently have been parricide. The girl still shivered and chattered, not only with her teeth but her tongue; and her words probably conveyed further threats of violence; for the soldier kept assuring her, that unless she amended her intentions, he should be under the necessity of conveying her to the guard-house on the Zecca, where, in consequence of the holiday, she would be locked in for the night.

"Do!" cried she, with clasping hands and earnest eyes. "Do lock me in for the night. I implore, I beseech you!"

"Without fire or candle on St. Stephen's day, child," replied the soldier, "is no such treat as you may suppose; to say nothing of the sentence that might perhaps await you in the morning."

"Better than the fate that certainly awaits me, if left at liberty to-night!" cried the girl, her bosom heaving with emotion; "to be starved, beaten, and thrust out here in the cold, exposed to the insults of the boatmen, and all the other brutes who stand to see me tormented. I am his daughter. I am bound to work for his maintenance and my own. I know it. But it is written 'Thou shalt not muzzle the ox that treadeth out the corn.' There is no law for the stripes wherewith I am goaded. I have been toiling since sunrise. I am exhausted with cold and hunger; while *he*, as you may plainly see, has been drinking and carousing. I told him just now, when he was about to place the lanterns at the corner of our carpet, that, like other slaves, I must have food and rest; above all, that he must abide by me, lest I should be used as I was last evening on this very spot. He derided me; is that like a father? He struck me; is *that* like a father? He——"

"And you would have dashed your stiletto into my side, had not the stranger yonder prevented you?" interrupted the man, who perceived that the sympathy of the standers-by was enlisting itself with the oppressed.

" You would have stabbed me. Is that, I ask you, like a *daughter ?* "

"It is like *your* daughter, for you murdered my mother. Never deny it ! You murdered her. Though acquitted for want of evidence, did not the tribunal of Bröny bid you go and repent ? "

" I strongly recommend you to take this girl into custody," said I, addressing the soldier, after watching, as well as the deepening shades of evening would permit, the ferocious countenance of the *Zigeun.* " Here is my address at the Palazzo Gritto. I will appear as your witness to-morrow. I am convinced that, if you leave her at liberty, there will be blood- shed before morning."

" There will, there *shall !* " added the girl in her former sweet voice, so strangely at variance with the frightful purport of her words. " I surrender myself your prisoner ; and unless you accept me as such, this night shall see the last of him or me.

The fellow in the crimson sash protested, however, vehemently against the arrest ; promising to bestow paternal coercion upon the damsel, if left to his care. For a moment, the soldier, whose purpose of enjoying the *fête* was grievously interrupted by the duties of office, had evidently a mind to comply. But a crowd was beginning to gather, inquiring, in a thousand Venetian lispations, the meaning of the affray ; and the good sense of a popular assemblage, not bamboozled by what is called eloquence, is pretty sure to decide in the right. The Gondolieri and their feminine gender insisted that the girl ought to be taken to the royal and imperial guard-house on the Zecca, and thither she was accordingly conveyed. Her father would fain have followed, but there were her two fellow-exhibitors, the learned ape, and the poodle dog who showed tricks on the cards, to be taken care of ; to say nothing of the piece of faded church-tapestry which officiated as their footcloth, the lanterns belonging to its four corners, and the chest which contained the wardrobes of all four, and served as a stage to the performers. These demanded his protection quite as much as his refractory child.

I alone, therefore, followed the soldier and the girl. I even insisted on her being conveyed in my gondola; for the populace, at the sound of the word "assassin," was crowding fearfully upon her.

When we entered the gondola, instead of taking her seat on the bench, she flung herself headlong on the carpet, and sobbed audibly. It was dark. But I could feel her writhing on the floor at our feet. I began to wish that I had hit upon some less rigorous mode of extricating her from the hands of her despot; and even offered a second handful of coin to the soldier to let me land him on the quay of the Canal Reggio, or anywhere else he pleased, and set free his unhappy prisoner.

But the man told me in good set German that my proposition came too late; that the wench must be imprisoned that night, appear before the magistrates on the morrow, and perhaps be sent to work in the Idrian mines before the week was over. He had no longer a choice in the matter. Hundreds had seen her taken into custody; hundreds would be ready to bear witness against him, should he fail in his duty.

On one point I was myself resolved; that I would not surrender to her the dagger which I still held under my cloak. The temptation might be too strong for that young and impetuous creature, imprisoned in silence, solitude, cold, and hunger, on a winter's night. Time enough to return it to her at the tribunal, the following morning. The soldier who had refused my second gratuity as a bribe for her escape, accepted it as an argument with the sergeant on duty, that she should be gently used, and provided with food and covering in her cell; and Franszetta, for such I discovered from her father's imprecations to be her name, so far recognized my care for her

preservation, as to seize my hand and cover it with
kisses.

There was something in the movement, as she lay
there crouching at my feet, so resembling the mute
endearments of one of the brute creation, that I felt
towards her at that moment as one feels towards an
affectionate and grateful hound, whose caresses are his
only mode of demonstrating attachment.

After seeing her safely deposited by my friend in
the white uniform, in the hands of an Austrian bombadier, who looked like a wooden Goliath and smelt
like a tobacconist's shop, I dashed into my gondola
again, and bade the men make off in haste to Byron's
lodgings in the Spezieria. I knew he was to dine with
the Contessa Albrizzi, and conceived that he would
meet there certain of her Venetian acquaintance, who
might put me in the way of befriending the Signorina
Franszetta, by means of more fluent Italian and better
law, than I could possibly pretend to.   Besides, if the
truth must out, I was not sorry to have a little adventure to recount, and a heroine to boast of, in return
for the eleven thousand with which he had favoured
me in the course of our confidences.

" A tumbler, a gipsy, a stabber in the dark ; yet
pure as Lucretia, and beautiful as a houri ?" cried he,
proceeding with his toilet, while I, with as much embellishment as honesty would permit, proceeded with
my narrative.   " Come, come ! you are practising on
my ingenuousness.   Or you have been drinking
healths to St. Stephen in choice alkermès in one of the
booths of the Piazzi.   Assassinate her father, with half
the gondoliers in Venice as witnesses of the act ? These
things are not done under the leaden mace of Austria.
Even the *Zigeuner* know better.   Remember this is
the 20th day of December, Cis, my man, not the 1st
of April."

Put on my mettle by these insinuations, I chose
also to be on my metal.   I produced my stiletto.   It
was a short blade, formed like, though smaller in

dimensions, a Malay kriss.   The blade was of a lustreless complexion, and had a peculiar musky smell, like that emitted by the rattlesnake ; and on the hilt, which was of virgin gold, was a single rough carbuncle.   Nothing could be ruder than the workmanship of the little weapon.   But it looked antique, like one of the early efforts of a tasteful, but unenlightened people.

Byron was curious in arms ; and he examined this circumspectly, by sight and scent, from hilt to point.

"Tell me in what Armenian armourer's shop you made your purchase," said he, "for I would gladly have its fellow.   I have not seen such a poniard since I left the East.   I once had one made, almost on its model, for a fair London friend of mine, who has since, I suspect, often longed to send me with it to assist in solving the grand problem."

"I have half a mind to do as much myself," cried I, "as a punishment for your incredulity.   Come with me, however, to-morrow to the police-office on the Zecca, which is closed on account of the *fête* to-night ; and you will see Franszetta delivered up to justice, and perhaps assist me in extricating her."

That night, I met him at the Fenice, whither he had accompanied Countess Albrizzi and a party of Paduan friends ; and he still persisted in quizzing me upon my adventure, as if no one but himself had ever swum in a gondola or caught a heroine.

But even I, after spending the night in dreaming of Franszetta, her grace, her beauty, her arrow-like activity, her impetuous ferocity of character, even I woke in the morning, convinced in my turn that the whole had been the baseless fabric of a vision.

The dagger lay on my table, in refutation of the suggestion.   Again I examined its serpent-smelling blade, and cabalistic-looking carbuncle ; and as I passed my sleeve over both, half expected to see some slave of the dagger start up, in the form of an eastern *genie*, to reprove my unbelief.

x

There was no time to wait for his appearance. I had slept so long to dream of the wild-eyed Franszetta (whose name, by the way, I beseech such of my readers as read aloud, to pronounce Franchetta) that I had brought it nearly to twelve o'clock; the time for opening the tribunal.

Byron had promised not only to bear me company, but to assist me with the advice and authority of a grave old gentleman in black, who wrote himself *procuratore* or *avvocato*, and was recommended to him by the Armenian fathers for the care of his secular affairs. We were both in high spirits ; he, in anticipation of a novel and perhaps exciting scene; I, in the expectation of a second glimpse of the strange being in whose destiny I was interesting myself.

I was not, however, altogether satisfied to exhibit the charms of my gipsy to so accomplished a *conosciatore*. The wildness of eye and gesture of Franszetta could not fail to enchant a man with so much music in his soul. Still greater would be the fascination of her reckless desperation, her wayward humour. Byron was attaining that epoch in the life of a sinful son of clay and clubs *blasé* with the softer pleasures of the heart, when nothing is so exciting as the turbulence of a virago. It was not long afterwards that Margarita Cogni obtained an ascendancy over him by smashing looking-glasses and pulling his raven curls till he roared again.

I had a presentiment that Franszetta would become his idol ; and my mien was grave in proportion to my fears, as we ascended together the stone steps of the police-office, to which the double-bodied eagle of Austria was affixed, like a bird of prey to a barn, by way of warning to addleheaded birds still on the wing.

There stood the soldier, there the sergeant. There sat the official in his black silk robe. Before him an open book, containing his registry of committals. In every corner of the office lurked the smell of tobacco, and the dirty dogs of *sbirri,* by whose garments and head-gear it was dispensed. But in the way of female prisoner, as the French say, *pas plus que sur ma main !*

Byron laughed heartily; and, but for shame, I could have as heartily cried. The Signor Dottore, meanwhile, who wore as solemn a countenance as if "from Padua, from Bellario," took the wiser course of interrogating the wooden sergeant and his equally stolid witness, the soldier. It appeared that on the preceding night Franszetta had been locked into her cell, wherein was a rug-bed for the use of prisoners, and the provisions I had bespoken for her; together with an iron lamp, for which irregular and illegal enjoyment she was also indebted to my gratuities.

In the morning the lamp stood there, untrimmed, the supper untasted, but the bed not untouched; for the sheet was found attached to the stanchions of a window, grated in proportion to the ordinary dimensions of prisoners in guard-rooms, and not purporting to shut in a fairy or a rope-dancer. The inner frame of the window was broken; and there were ensanguined traces on the glass and sheet, as if the enterprise had not been accomplished without difficulty.

But *had* it been accomplished? *Had* she escaped? The chamber from which she had made the attempt was on the third or highest floor of the old guardhouse of the Zecca, abutting against the canal. The street reached only to the stone ledge surmounting the rustic basement; and from this height she must have sprung into the canal, or crept along the ledge with a degree of skill and intrepidity worthy of Fenella.

Byron suggested that not even a cat could have done it; while the soldiers swore as stoutly, that by dropping into the canal in the dead of the night, at such a degree of cold, she could not have intended escape, but suicide. One thing was clear; that the course of justice was defeated, that the prisoner was gone, and my sole consolation lay in the fact, that

before we quitted the royal and imperial post-office,
the brute with the Saracenic physiognomy made his
appearance, growling and blaspheming at the announcement of his daughter's disappearance ; plain
proof that, whatever evil had betided her, she was not
in his power.

The fear of being laughed at, which operates so
disgracefully upon our actions in this weakest of
worlds, prevented my following up my inquiries as I
wished to do, and perhaps ought to have done. I had
quizzed Byron so unmercifully about his passion for
the linendraper's wife, that I felt satisfied he would
cruelly retaliate upon mine for a mountebank, if I
evinced even ordinary interest in Franszetta's destinies.

So I went my ways home, and pondered upon these
things. I have always felt deep sympathy in the gipsy
race,—

> Tribe of the wandering foot and weary breast ;

which, whether derived of Ishmael or Cain, surviveth
in all the countries of the old world, to attest that it
is not upon the Jews alone that the hand of election
or reprobation hath set its seal. Independent of
the beauty and grace of this strange girl, independent of the interest attached to her sad position,
I earnestly desired to see her again ; to interrogate
her, as well as my imperfect German would admit,
concerning the usages of her people, and her erratic
habits of life.

I felt, therefore, like a child robbed of its toy, on
discovering that I was to see no more of her. But
for the stiletto, I should have almost begun to doubt
whether I had ever seen her at all. There it was,
however, safe within my vest ; the warmth of my
bosom bringing forth its musky odour, till I could
almost have fancied a nest of snakes was coiling around
me.

Altogether, my mood was somewhat mystical and
Hoffmannish. I had heard the preceding night, for

the first time, Rossini's opera of "Otello;" in *my*
opinion the only really serious opera he ever produced.
With the exception of a few passages in the
"Semiramide," nothing of his ever touched me so
nearly.   The scene of Desdemona's tapestried chamber
in the second act, at the Fenice, was a facsimile of the
one I occupied in the Palazzo Gritti; and albeit no
one who knows Venice, where

> Tasso's echoes are no more,
> And silent rows the songless gondolier,

would expect to find a line from Dante conveyed to
him by a fine bass voice from the Canal Grande, I
confess that after hearing the

> Nessun maggior dolor
> Che ricordarsi del tempo felice
> Nella miseria,

breathe so touching an interruption to the woes of
Desdemona, I felt that I should never pace my dark
and somewhat fantastic chamber after the drowsy bell
had stricken midnight, without expecting some such
mournful ejaculation to startle its stillness.

   That day, I dined with Byron at the Pellegrino;
and bore at the hands of my friend a series of whips
and stings, which he, who made no secret of his susceptibility to quizzing, ought not to have inflicted.
Nay, he was so wondrous witty in twitting me with
Mignon, and branding me with the name of Wilhelm
Meister, that I was obliged to silence him by declaring
that, if I had stolen my love-passage from Goethe's
romance, *he* had pilfered from it his opening stanza in
the Bride of Abydos.

   He was almost angry; for, sooth to say, we were
drinking deeper than was the practice of either; and
I was glad to divert his attention from my charge
by bringing forward a favourite theory of mine concerning the said *Lehrjahr:* that in Mignon and
Albertine the poet intended to typify Celestial and

Terrestrial Love, just as Shakspeare personified the two extremes of the *Geisterwelt,* the sylph and gnome, in the Ariel and Caliban of his Enchanted Island : a psychological antithesis of the happiest kind.

"Upon this hint he spake ; "—and when Byron *really* spoke, I deny any man of sense, in his senses, to do aught but listen.

It was late when I got home from a second representation of the thrilling "Otello ;" of which, how· ever, we heard only a fragment ; but it was a fragment that contained the "*Preghiera,*" the "*Sono innocente!*" the "*Perfido-ingrato!*" and consequently

Sent the hearers weeping to their beds.

I repaired to mine, not weeping perhaps, but shuddering, partly with cold, partly with discomfiture. My last charge to Berto (a burley Fiessian who served me as gondolier and groom of the chambers), was to pile up the fireplace with logs, to cheer me through a night which I felt was to be sleepless. My mind seemed in a state of somnambulism. My pillow only redoubled my sense of restlessness. With the desperation of all nervous persons, I left my curtains undrawn, that I might command, as I lay, the whole extent of my chamber, and admire the design of its tapestry, whereon was expressed, with becoming sadness, the death of Adonis, exhibited in his last agonies, giving up the ghost in the depths of a wood gloomy as the pine-forest of Ravenna.

Right opposite to my bed, whose venerable draperies were of dingy velvet, graced by a valance of Venice point, stood a huge mirror upon an old-fashioned toilet-table, Venetian also, both in point of point and of glass ; and to the right of the bed, at some twenty paces betwixt it and the mirror, a table, whereon, previous to betaking myself to rest, I deposited Franszetta's stiletto.

I was in the strangest mood of mind. All the bewilderments that wine, music, and romance, introduce

into the interstices of a somewhat spongy brain, were
seething in mine. I was possessed by that demon of
Doubt which seems suddenly to subdue the mind, and
deprive all things, earthly and unearthly, of their
stability. Every object, in and out of nature, became
suddenly a matter of inquiry and misgiving. The
society of Byron usually operated upon me like a dose
of opium ; *not* as a narcotic, but the origin of a trance
wherein the body becomes transfixed, while the soul
acquires preternatural activity.

In just such a state of *clairvoyance* was I now. My
spirit "o'er-informed its tenement of clay." I began
to see or imagine those things in heaven or earth,
which in Horatio's philosophy were undreamed of.
Before my mind's eye, flitted the forms of the trembling
Desdemona of the Fenice ; of Mignon, out-Mignoned
by the busy fancy and fervid eloquence of Byron ; and
of Franszetta, as she stood on the platform of St.
Mark's, rage flashing in her eyes, and the stiletto in
her hand.

To my nympholeptic and delirious fancy, the atmosphere seemed instinct with aërial beings.

The night was bitter and cutting as the Arctic
Circle or a conjugal retort, and cheerless as it was
chilling. But for the crackling of the fire upon the
hearth, I could scarcely have borne the sad wailing of
the wind, driving showers of sleet against the windows,
seeming to sob at intervals, like the moans of a soul in
torment. The very tapestry was heaved from the wall
by these searching gusts. Everything looked portentous; everything sounded like an omen. The very bell
of St. Mark's, as it struck the hours, had an appalling vi-
bration that night, as if conscious that evil was betiding.

I was beginning to feel that even the chirrup of a
cricket on the hearth would be a comfort to me, as
token of the presence of a living thing. When, lo !
right across the mirror, on which the brightness of
the firelight was reflected, flitted a shadow ; the
shadow of a human form.

In our conversations at Diodati the preceding autumn, our little circle of illuminati had so often indulged in speculations touching the world of spirits (speculations that gave rise to Byron's Fragment, Polidori's Vampire, and Mary Shelley's Frankenstein), that I own I indulged a little in the superstition reproved by St. Paul. People are fond of attributing such imaginings to scepticism; as if the reappearance of the dead were not an especial article of Christian belief. For my part, I hold, with the highest of authorities, that fear is the beginning of Wisdom; and that those who begin by deriding the spilling of the salt, will end by mocking the overthrow of the altar. This is no excuse for my own frailty. I do not blush to admit that, at sight of that passing shadow, my breath came as short as that of the lover of Honoria, horror-struck in the demon-haunted forest.

My second thought, or rather my first, for some seconds elapsed before I had courage to think at all, was that some person was concealed in my chamber. My next impulse, to start up, and rush to the table where lay the stiletto of Franszetta.

It was gone!

Though certain as I lived, that the last thing I had done after Berto's quitting the room and my bolting it for the night, was to place it on the table, from which I had scarcely since withdrawn my eyes,—it was no longer there.

I was now assured that some one was in the room, probably with a murderous purpose. Yet, instead of proceeding to an immediate examination, by beating the curtains, the draperies, and the angles formed by one or two ponderous cabinets, I contented myself with taking from the latter my pocket-pistols, which, after Byron's fashion, I kept charged; and laying them beside me on the bed, to which I retreated. By lying quiet, I might encourage the miscreant to come forth and meet his fate.

The bed, I must tell you, dear reader, as you may never have been a lodger in the Palazzo Gritti, stood in a recess, with a space round it, to admit the passage of a servant. Between me and the wall, therefore, was an ambush. The curtains were drawn. I had perhaps only to tear them aside, and discover the ferocious eyes of an assassin glaring upon me. Yet I refrained. I felt as if acting under the pressure of supernatural agency. I kept my eyes fixed upon the glass, expecting to see the shadow traverse it as before. But though I strained them with watching, nothing appeared. I fancied however, so full of fancies does one become in situations of this kind, that I heard the breath of a concealed person; nay, a sigh, a deep sigh, uttered so close to me, that I was able, as it were, to *feel* the invisible presence.

There was no bearing this. I was about to snatch up the pistols that lay on the bed, and discharge one of them by way of warning; when, lo! on extending my hand, *they were gone also!*

Great God! what was the meaning of all this? Was I losing my senses, or was I about to lose my life? It was useless to affect bravado. It would only hasten my fate, to rush forth, detect, and challenge my enemy. All I had to do was to recommend myself to Heaven, and be as still as death. Still enough, perhaps, I was destined to be shortly.

Some five minutes elapsed, which my agitation converted into twice as many hours, when I became convinced that the respiration which I still distinctly heard, proceeded not from behind the ponderous curtain, by which the sound must have been stifled, but from the open side of the bed.

My immediate impulse was to thrust forth my hand. As instantly did it encounter an object, a clay-cold cheek, the touch of which thrilled through my frame like a bolt of ice.

The flickering fire-light at that moment threw up a tongue of flame; enabling me to perceive a female figure, seated upon the velvet hassock beside my bed, that enabled me to climb into its lofty altitudes; a female figure, of exceeding loveliness.

I beseech my reader to cry aloud, in the tone of Mrs. Siddons in Lady Randolph—

"WAS IT ALIVE?"

——◦◆◦——

CHAPTER XVI.

And then she gaily wander'd through the world
    Wherein her fancy led her, and would stray
(The sails of her bright meteor wings unfurl'd)
    Through many a populous city, and survey
The chambers of the sleeping ; oft she curl'd
    The locks of young chaste maidens as they lay,
And lit new lustre in their sleeping eyes,
And breathed upon their cheeks the bloom of Paradise.
                                          MOULTRIE.

Τις δ' οιδεν ει ζην τουθ' ο κεκληται θανειν,
Το ζην δε θνησκειν εστι ;—EURIP.

Somnia, terrores magicos, miracula, sagas,
Nocturnos lemures, portentaque Thessala.
                                          HOR.

PROSY people, a race against which I entertain what Beckford (in speaking of the antiquary who talked him to death about the under-drainage of the amphitheatre of Verona), calls "a capital aversion," people, I say, who are habitually prosy, are sure to select some moment when one's heart is on tenter-hooks, to pursue the slow winding of their ball of cotton. Just when we have made some agonizing discovery, or are expecting the consummation of the event that is to complete our happiness or plunge us into irremediable woe, in proses the bore, with a long-winded story about nothing, causing us to send him, by mental execration, to a spot whereunto the best railroad going would require half a dozen ages for his conveyance.

No doubt my readers are at this moment favouring *me* with some such gentle apostrophe. I therefore cut short a very interesting article upon apparitions and spectra, which I had intended to insert at this place, to heighten the interest; and by what the Yankees call "piling up the agony," prove that I am a tolerable dab at fine writing, a species of composition good only " *al dilettar le femine e per la plebe.*"

Where was I? At the clay-cold cheek methinks, or rather at the deathlike chill which congealed the very marrow in my bones, when I discovered the strange motionless figure stationed at my bedside. Certes the apparition had taken no *very* alarming shape ; being that of a fair Venetian, not of *bel sangue*, not a *nobil dama*, not a Mocenigo, or Gradenigo, or Albrizzi, or Benzoni, or Grimani, or Balbi. But one who would call herself " VENE-ZIANA !" and think it title enough, if her costume did not sufficiently announce her to be a child of the Lagune.

I had been only a month in Venice ; a month devoted to its churches and palaces, its Titians and Giorgiones, rather than to pursuits likely to expose me to assassination from a female hand. I had loved nobody, and consequently nobody had a right to hate me. But perhaps the *fazziolo* might be a decoy? The pistols and stiletto might be in the hands of an accomplice.

This notion vanished in a moment as the figure, turning slowly round, disclosed to me the beautiful features of FRANSZETTA ! Franszetta domiciled in my house—cold, sad, cheerless. The welcome I offered sufficiently expressed my sympathy.

" No nearer, 'celenza !" cried she, recoiling from my
advance, and brandishing her weapon in a style almost
as resolute as she had displayed the preceding night
on the Piazza. " Should I be here, think you, but
that I know myself capable of self-defence ? Lie
quietly down. The night is cold as if man and not
Providence had made it. The Euganean hills will be
white before morning. But blessed be God, we have
a good roof over our heads. With your leave, I will
throw on another log ; and then resume my place,
and say out all I have to disclose. For I would fain
retain my confidence in your goodness. Such frankness as mine ought to beget honest dealing in
return."

" Quick, quick, then, with the fire," cried I, " for
I have a thousand questions to ask, touching your
escape last night, and the means by which you effected
your entrance here."

" Neither exploit is much to boast of," she replied,
obeying my behest, and after despatching her task,
resuming her seat on the hassock. " It needed only
for your domestics to keep as careless a watch as their
master, who, with his eyes fixed just now on my
stiletto, suffered me to snatch it from the table un-
observed."

She took the poniard from her bosom as she spoke,
and pressed her lips to the blade, passing it along them
with a slow and tender movement, as we caress that
which is dearest to us in the world.

" It was to claim this of you that I came," said she.
" Before this hour to-morrow, I shall have quitted
Venice. A vessel is sailing for Fiume. From thence,
I will push my way back into our country, under the
guidance of some of our people, who, in Istria and
Dalmatia, have settlements in almost every village.
But I would not depart without my stiletto. No, no !
I would not go without my stiletto. It is all I can
call my own in this world. It has been my friend in
danger, my friend in desolation. It was the dying

gift of my poor, poor mother. Admit, 'celenza, that I could not leave Venice without my stiletto ?"

" It were more gracious if you said you would not leave it, without seeing again one who has shown such eager dispositions to befriend you, Franszetta," said I reproachfully.

" Why lose our time in mutual compliments ?" replied Franszetta, " I want you to tell me exactly what passed to-day at the police ; whether they supposed me drowned or rescued ; and what manner of threats were uttered by my father ?"

I told her all. I described, with as much fluency as my halting German would allow, the unconcealed rage, not of the parent who had lost his child, but the juggler who had lost his apprentice.

" You are a shrewd guesser," cried Franszetta, almost with a laugh. " It were indifferent to him to leave me at the bottom of the canal, or on the stones of the quay. For in his heart he loathes me. No wonder. When a child loathes its parent, there must be loathing in return. And Heaven will forgive me the sin of hating *him ;* for my mother's blood is on his hand."

" *Poverina !*" said I, directing towards her an involuntary glance of pity.

" The ape, and Grelotte, and I, between us, earned him two hundred scudi at the fair of Trieste," continued Franszetta, resuming her usual tone, " and he expected us to have done as much more at Verona. We were then to have pushed on to Milan ; and so home, across the Tyrol, and Styria. But I could stand it no longer. I have to thank *you,* 'celenza, for saving me from embruing my hands in blood. For after that, I fear, even Fridszin would not have forgiven me."

" And who is Fridszin ?" said I, prepared by her manner of pronouncing the name, for the answer that was to follow.

" Fridszin is my lover," said she ; " my husband

soon, if I can accomplish, in safety, the long and
terrible journey before me. We are *Zigeuner*, 'celenza ;
that much you know already. There are many such
in the country where I saw the light. The Hun-
garians of the Krapaks call us Tsigàny ; and give us a
name at least, though they allow us neither hearthstone nor rooftree. The hut in which I was born at
Bröny, is an excavation in the sand-cliffs, near Krem-
nitz, part of a large settlement, one of the largest in
Hungary, and favoured with higher advantages ; for
our people are attached to the imperial mines."

" And is Fridszin a miner ? " I inquired, eager to
enjoy again the melting intonation with which she had
pronounced the name she loved,

" He is not so favoured," replied Franszetta. " To
be a labourer in the gold-mines, you must be a born
vassal of some magnat. Fridszin is a poor orphan
lad, who works in the imperial glass-manufactory, at
Bröny. We used to play together when children ;
rolling and sporting together in our tattered garments
on the green sward, and sharing all that is assigned by
Providence to the enjoyment of all, the blue skies,
the clear waters, the fields, the flowers, the summer
weather ; and as we progressed into the cares and
labours of life, our hearts grew together into love, as
branches of the same tree bear flowers at the same
moment. I loved him very dearly before I knew it ;
and after I knew it (for the moment he asked me the
question, I discovered my secret), I felt only the
prouder of loving one to whom I was so dear. I
knew how to value the happiness of being loved ; for
all spring and summer (poor child of misery that I was),
I was forced away from home, to wander from fair to
fair, and town to town, with Grelotte and the ape ; and
that my father cared no more for me, and tended me
no more than he did my two companions ; nay, less !
for when the ape was sick, he was anxious, saying the
beast was too delicate for the rude climate of Hungary.
Whereas, when aught ailed *me*, I was left to grow

well again as I listed. Right glad was I, when poor
Grelotte, who had been reared with me, used to come
and lie at my feet of nights, and lick my hands at my
waking. I weary you, 'celenza! I want you to know
why I so love Fridszin. I want you to know that,
during those dreary nights and comfortless days, it
was my solace to think that my poor mother was not
lonely during my absence ; but that Fridszin laboured
to make her life easier ; always in and out of the
hovel, devoting his leisure hours to work for her, and
be unto her as a son."

" In reward for which good deed, a grateful daughter
plighted her faith to him."

" Would you have had me regardless of his devotion, *his*, the kindest and truest of human beings.
Yet my father hated me for what he called my poor-
ness of spirit. Fridszin was but a poor friendless
boy ; while *I*, he said, possessed means of acquiring
riches for myself and those belonging to me. So
much the better, I thought, whenever I thought of
Fridszin. But what was worse than hating *me*, my
father used to revile my mother for having sanctioned
our affection. And so, the older I grew, the wider
the breach between me and him who had the privilege
of inflicting punishment heavier than I could bear.
It was all this," continued Franszetta, in a more
resolute tone, "that made a woman of me. I am but
a child," said she, suddenly extending towards me her
slight delicate hand and arm. "You perceive that
this is the limb of a child ; yet, I have the heart and
soul of a lioness."

" The ferocity of one," cried I, laughing. "Children
do not stab, my pretty Franszetta. Children do not
swim a canal in the dead of night ; or clamber up
through the window of a Venetian palace."

" Into a young man's bedroom ? Say it out," continued Franszetta coolly. "What I have courage to
do, I have courage to hear repeated ; and my conscience is clear on both points. I have so little fear

either of myself or you, that I give you leave to say your worst. A kinder thing were to curb your mocking humour, and listen. For the night advances, 'celenza. Perhaps you want to sleep ?"

I assured her I had not the least disposition to close my eyes ; but was careful to avoid irritating the wayward creature by a single expression of kindness.

"This is the first time," said Franszetta, suddenly starting from her cushion, and gazing round her with wonder and delight, " that I was ever in the sleeping room of a palazzo. I have been called into courtly halls at Pesth, Presburg, Trieste, a hundred places, to amuse the poor, listless, gaping nobles, with my feats of activity ; and to judge by their rapture at my tumbling, or the antics of Grelotte and the ape, they must lead a dreary life. But beyond their fine clothes, and menials in gaudy suits, or the pieces they flung me in payment, what knew I of their ways ? Nothing in their cold colourless existence tempted me. If such be the dreariness of the rich, God keep me poor."

The language in which Franszetta conveyed these ideas was of far higher tone than all this commonplace. But I was absorbed in the contemplation of something more picturesque than her language ; namely, her buoyancy of figure and elasticity of step, as she flitted round the apartment, verifying by her touch the nature of the objects it contained ; the hangings, the tapestry, the books, the various glittering objects scattered upon the toilet-table. But no sooner did she find herself opposite the large swing-glass to which I have before adverted, than her delight became ecstatic. It was probably the first time she had seen the full reflection of her own fair person ; for she stood there a moment transfixed, then broke into gestures and attitudes, each of which might have served Canova as a study for a new Ballerina. I never beheld anything more remarkable than her power of compressing her pliant form, cowering, as it were, into a ball ; then, suddenly recovering her grace and vivacity, assuming a succession of postures stolen from some undiscovered treasury of nature.

She seemed to lose all thought and recollection of *me*, or where she was, or what had brought her there, and give herself up to the enjoyment of her calling, and admiration of her own feats and graces, of which she was for the first time an eye-witness. There she stood, sometimes poised on the point of a single foot, her delicate white arms tossed gracefully above her head, in a *pose* that a Bayadère might have envied; the light of the fire shining fitfully upon her figure and its reflection in the mirror, so as to impart to both an appearance equally unreal. And there I lay, my breath suspended, wondering whether the whole scene were not the fantastic coinage of a dream, and satisfied that, by attempting to ascertain its reality, I should drive the reckless Franszetta to some desperate act. All I had to do was to wait the issue as she chose to construct it.

The stiletto was in her hand; and she seemed to take especial delight as she brandished it in the rapid movements of a sort of national military dance, to watch the flashing light caused by the reflection of the fire upon its blade, and the blade upon the mirror. After all, there was more of the child than the woman in her antics and perceptions. She could not have numbered more than sixteen years. In wilfulness only was she a woman.

At length, panting and exhausted, she flew back to the bedside, flung herself on the cushion, and threw back her head to rest upon the coverlet, so as to afford me a full view of her laughing face, brightened by exercise, and excited by the triumphs of her skill out of all recollection of her sorrows.

"How warm it is here, how soft, how tranquil, how bright, how happy!" cried she, as if pursuing her previous train of reflections. "How different from the biting air of the Canal Reggio last night; how

Y

different from the smoky cavern of our home at
Bröny."

"But were such a residence as this your own, *Lieb-
chen*," said I, "you would scarcely find amusements in
tumbling and pirouetting all night, when reasonable
people are in bed and asleep ? "

"Perhaps not," she replied, with quiet self-possession. "For then, I should be a *dama*, living here with
my lord ; not the affianced wife of Fridszin the *Zigeun*,
and sworn upon my mother's dying bed to be a faithful one. My poor mother !" she exclaimed, the expression of her mutable countenance changing in a moment. "Oh, if you knew how precious her memory is
and ought to be to me ! I told you before, 'celenza,
that she was murdered. The monster from whom you
rescued me last night felled her to the ground with
an axe, as she was pursuing her household labours by
her own hearth-side, merely because she insisted on
keeping me with her now that I was a woman grown,
instead of seeing me dragged from fair to fair, and
shown for hire, within hearing of things to which no
woman's ear should hearken, and exposed to perils
more fatal to woman's happiness than steel, or wave,
or cold, or hunger. He killed her, 'celenza. I saw
her fall. I bore her poor body to the miserable bed,
where I and my little brothers had been born to her ;
miserable bed, where she had shed her bitter tears in
silence when I was absent, and where sleep was vouchsafed her only because those who labour hard from
sunrise to nightfall must find rest at last. There she
lay, writhing like a crushed snake, her life-blood ebb-
ing away ; my little brothers kneeling at a distance
on the floor, not daring to approach, lest they should
be wet with her blood ; nor to hasten to the factory
after Fridszin, as I bad them, lest they should encounter by the way the desperate man, who, after mur-
dering his patient, humble wife, had rushed out into the
darkness, in a mood to kill and slay for very madness.

"I saw her die, 'celenza, die slowly and in torment ;

for how could I assuage her sufferings,—I, a poor ignorant girl of fifteen! Shall I tell you what she said to me during the two miserable hours I hung over her?

"Not if the recital distress you thus, Franszetta," said I, perceiving, as I took her hand in mine, that it was cold as death; while on her smooth forehead stood dews of profound emotion.

"She said that her life had been a life of bitterness, of blows, of toil, of want, of woe; that no sunshine had shone upon her, save from the faces of her children. But that now she was going to her Maker, to her exceeding great reward. 'My comfort on this cruel deathbed,' said she, 'is, that my soul is pure from stain. Amid all my trouble, all my weariness, vice never found a crevice to enter my dwelling. Wherefore I know that I shall rejoin my mother and my God, in a land where there are no tears, no trials.' And then, 'celenza, then, as I tried to stanch the blood welling from her wounded throat, she uttered charges to me too sacred to be breathed by any voice in any ear, save by a mother to her daughter; and bestowed upon me her dying blessing, and the stiletto which her dying mother had, with the like benediction, bestowed upon herself; an eastern relique of our tribe, who, they say, are from the land of the Saviour. Only a minute before she died, she bad me be an honest wife to Fridszin, as she had been to him who was sending her to her grave, if I had hope to meet her in heaven with the love and trust we had shared together on earth. And when I leant down, 'celenza, to kiss her poor lips, in token of my solemn pledge in life and death to obey her, the breath was gone from them! I had no longer a mother; only the holy commandment she had given me, and the poor, bruised, bleeding body, which had sacrificed all to keep me spotless with a spotlessness like hers. Oh! surely, surely, the angels of God must have taken to their charge so bright, so true a soul.

"And now," cried Franszetta, starting up, after a pause of deep emotion, during which her thoughts appeared to be absorbed in prayer, and standing erect upon the floor, with her arms crossed over her panting bosom, and her brows wearing an expression of mingled anguish and intelligence,—" and now, 'celenza, tell me whether, with this poniard in my hand, this heart in my bosom, I have aught to fear from being alone in your chamber at midnight ? "

"Nothing. Compose yourself," said I, awed by perceiving the veins upon her temples swollen with emotion, and her whole frame tremulous, as with the passion of a Pythoness. "Sit down again, Franszetta, and tell me gently what has since betided you, and what are your projects."

" It was spring-time when all this chanced," said the girl, her voice sinking again into a desponding murmur. " For I remember that when I went my way at daybreak to the high-bailiff's at Bröny, to call upon the authorities to bury the dead and deal the rigour of the laws upon the murderer, as I hurried along the green turf bordering the road, I trod upon the first primroses of the year. I saw their pale stars even through my tears ; and so long as I live, and so dearly as I love the spring, shall never look with pleasure upon those flowers again.

" 'Celenza ! they buried their dead—but they dealt no justice on the living. None had seen the blow. Even I and my little brothers knew only that we had found our mother bleeding on her hearthstone ; the door of the hut open, all in disorder. That to which I bore witness, as having heard from her lips, they rejected. For the laws of Hungary discountenance so monstrous an act as for a child to swear away the life of a parent. But such laws never contemplated the existence of a father like mine. And so, as it mattered little to the bailiwick whether there were a *Zigeuner* woman or child the more or less in the world, saving so far as they were troubled with their correction, the tribunal admonished me to go home with my father and study to be a dutiful daughter to him in his bereavement. A dutiful daughter to *him!*"

Would I could convey an idea of the thrill of horror and despair expressed by the gestures of Franszetta, as she seemed to contemplate anew the terrors of such a sentence. I could almost fancy I was returning with her into the desolate hut, from which the body of her mother had been removed.

"I obeyed—I had no choice. I went home, though she was no longer there," murmured the poor girl, making no effort to repress the tears that fell in heavy drops upon her bosom, as she reseated herself by the bedside. "There was no kind voice to soothe me, no fondling hand to comfort me; only the two boys crying beside the cold ashes on the hearth. But there, even there, was the trace of——O God!—my poor, poor mother!"

Half stifled by her suffocating sobs, a grievous pause ensued. At length I took courage to inquire of Franszetta whether her father had ventured, at such a moment, to renew his violence?

"He *dared* not!" cried the girl. For he knew that the eye of authority was upon him, and that the neighbours were resolved, on any act of cruelty against us, to inflict summary punishment upon him. Besides, his bread depended on my skill or his own labour; and he loved his ease as he loved the *raki* flask. So on our return home, 'celenza, he spoke me fair; and, laying all that had chanced to the score of drink and passion, swore that, if I would pursue my calling as a tumbler only another year, he would place the boys in the school of the bailiwick during our absence from Brőny, and at the end of my apprenticeship grant me half my gains by way of dowry."

"And Fridszin," said I, interrupting her, "did he accede to this proposal, instead of claiming you as a wife?"

"Alas ! 'celenza, on the very eve of my poor mother's death, he was sent off by the commissioners to Vienna, with a cargo from the imperial factory, under escort ; and was not to be back till summer. He had been chosen at a minute's warning by the director, as trustworthiest of the workmen ; with the choice of forfeiting his place, or departing without a word of farewell."

"Poor fellow—poor Franszetta ! "

"Even had he been there, what could he have done? I was a minor, my father's bondswoman ; and was it likely he would consent to lose me by a marriage with a penniless workman, when so great was my renown, that the Leopoldstadt theatre had bidden money for me, to figure in one of their magic stage-plays? From ten years old I had been exhibiting all the summer months at Raab, Presburg, Ofen, and elsewhere. My father's business was to frequent fairs with his dulcimer, and Grelotte and the ape, showing conjuring tricks, and mending stringed instruments ; and so long as they were only three, their gains were so small, that he often said he would almost as soon work in the mines or turn the plough. But from the moment he thought of carrying *me* with him to display the feats of activity he had taught me as a pastime for winter nights, his copper earnings became silver ; and he was in hopes that, as I grew older and stronger, the silver might turn to gold. You know not all I can do, 'celenza, when the blood is not stagnant in my veins with cold, as it was last night on the Piazza, or my muscles unstrung with hunger. Nay, I know not myself. There is a spirit within me that sometimes carries me, as it were, into the air : and the flower could no more give you a reason why it blows than I how I conjure up the postures that bring down the plaudits of the standers-by. They come to me as my life came, by the will of Heaven!"

"But since you are thus successful, Franszetta," said I, "whence the abject poverty you complain of?"

"Because, after passing the day in the square of some great city, a show to the people till it shames me to know myself a woman, and · soon to be a wife, at night the bag of money I have worked so hard for is melted away at the wine-house. Not a *tratteria* in Trieste or Venice in which that man has not squandered his means, while I was famishing in our wretched lodgings. Yesterday, you heard me refuse to dance after dark, because, the night before, when I had been breaking my very heart-strings to tumble for the sailors of the Zecca, the heavy bag of silver I collected never so much as entered our dwelling. Dice and drink emptied it before morning."

"You are right. Such a father has forfeited all claim over you," cried I. "But how, my poor girl, *how* are you to escape from Venice without his knowledge?"

"How did I escape from the guardhouse last night without that of the bombadier. How arrive in your chamber, without alarming your servants? Think you that Nature endowed me with such force of muscle and agility of limb, without suggesting them as a means of defence? You, a noble, and bred in enervation and luxury, cannot dream the strength of arm, heart, and soul, of one of the people. You know not of what I am capable."

"You are a little miracle of courage, as of strength and feeling," cried I, with a sentiment of profound sympathy. "But so young, so unprotected—"

The smile on Franszetta's lip displayed mingled archness and bitterness. "Strive and thrive!" cried she. "Nothing was ever achieved by moaning. In these Venetian weeds, 'celenza, *who* will recognize Franszetta the dancing-girl? Did *you* know me at first, when I sat shivering here by your bedside? I have flung aside those villanous spangled slippers and velvet jerkin, for good and all. I would not so much as part with them to the salesman of whom I purchased my *fazziolo*, but tossed them into the canal on my

way hither.   If words of mine could only say how I
abhorred them !   Never shall I forget my sense of
loathing when my father took them out of the chest
into which they had been thrust at the time of my
poor mother's death, and I saw that, from some of the
rags thrown in with them, they had contracted stains
of blood."

   "And when do you expect to reach Bröny ?" said
I, to change the current of her thoughts.

   "When GOD pleases !" replied Franszetta.   "He
permitted my poor mother to be slain in her innocence.
It is not always prayer or virtue that obtains the protection of Heaven.   But that good mother is now
among the angels ; and I feel that she will plead for
me, and that it will go well with her child."

   "And when you arrive at home, you will become
the wife of Fridszin ?"

   "If he consent to resign all for my sake, and flee
the country ; for it would be death for me to await
there my father's return. Nay, Fridszin must do more.
He must carry off my little brothers with us.   Not
for my life's sake would I leave my mother's sons at
the mercy of that man."

   "But since your labour will scarcely enable you to
support yourselves ?"

   "Providence is over all ! If we are in need, a
burthen is the lighter borne, the more there are to
bear it."

   "At least, Franszetta, you will not deny me my
share in the good work.   I owe you some compensation for the bitter plunge into the canal Reggio, to
which I condemned you last night."

   "You fancy, then, that I had to swim for it ? Did
it never occur to you, that the old Gallician sergeant
could be moved to mercy as well as yourself?   Do you
hold with my country people that ' *Német ember, nem
ember ?*' Must you be the only Christian in the world?"
And the saucy girl clasped her hands over her *fazziolo*,
and laughed till her white teeth became visible, at my

look of stupefaction; in this, as in every other mood and guise, displaying the mutability of a playful child.

Not, however, to dwell too lengthily on perfections that must have been seen to be appreciated in their rapid changes, suffice it that my contributions towards her travelling-purse were as liberal as my means allowed. Luckily perhaps for my prudence, my treasury was chiefly stored with Hammersley's notes; to Franszetta, about as available as the bill of my day's dinner at the Pellegrino. But in addition to some twenty ducats, I forced upon her acceptance two rings of price (one of them the gift of my sister Julia), to which she could have recourse on an evil day. All this it was an easy matter to deposit in a little leathern bag which she wore within her girdle, already stored with a few gold coins, gifts, on various occasions, from magnats and noble ladies, before whom she had exhibited her feats.

" I accept your goodness without scruple, 'celenza," said she, " for I see that you are rich, as well as generous." She had been surveying with wonder and delight the ornaments of crystal and gold displayed on my toilet. " You have scattered benefits upon me out of your abundance, nor have they fallen on an ungrateful soil. I shall bless you on my desolate journey. I shall bless you when I reach my miserable home. I shall bless you when I fold my little brothers in my arms. I shall bless you when I am folded in those of Fridszin. I shall bless you in my prayers, when I kneel upon my mother's grave! I know not your name. I know not your country. You have a language which is neither that of Italy, nor Germany, nor Hungary. But your heart seems to inherit from the same fatherland as mine; and *that* makes me speak to you so freely, without fear of your greatness, without fear of your riches, without fear even of your youth and gallantry. When you appeared so suddenly yesterday on the

Piazza, a stranger in Venice, and speaking the language as imperfectly as myself, I hailed you as a
protector sent by GOD and my mother to my defence.
There was a something so noble in your air, so kindly
in your voice, something I seemed to recognize as
though heard and seen a thousand times before.   Do
you suppose, 'celenza, there are no brothers and
sisters in the world, save children of the same parents?
Do you imagine that there is not more sympathy of
nature betwixt you and me, than betwixt me and the
father who beats me with stripes, and would glory in
seeing me brought to shame? "

"I am thankful to you, pretty Franszetta," I replied,
"for adopting me as a brother.   But thus far it is a
brother's duty to warn you : that you will gain little
credit in the eyes of men from having passed the night
in my chamber : and that when discovered here in the
morning——"

"What care have such as I for credit in the eyes
of men?" interrupted Franszetta, with something of
her wild recklessness of the preceding night.   "Think
you that a mummer of the market-place can be curious
in matters of fair renown, like your *nobil dama*, who
goes to the ball of the Cavalchina with her gallant,
and fancies that, because masqued from her equals, she
is hidden from the eye of Heaven?   No, no!   The
eyes of my mother, and of Him with whom she
abideth for evermore, know that I have done no
wrong ; that were I to die this night, my soul would
depart from me pure as when it struggled into this world
of care.   As for being discovered here—but no matter.
Sleep in peace, 'celenza.   You are weary.   The embers
burn low.   The night draws out.   Sleep in peace.
When morning approaches, I will wake you, that you
may let me forth before your people are astir.   Nay,
I will sing you to sleep, as I used my young brothers,
when they were restless."

In my desire to hear her lullaby I pretended to
comply with her proposition ; and promising myself

to remain awake, laid down my head upon my pillow,
while Franszetta commenced in her own language a
doleful chaunt, like the gradual swelling of the wind on
an autumnal evening.   Never did I hear anything so
wild, so mournful.   It seemed to bring before one the
fluttering down of withered leaves, and the gathering
shadows of night. I tried hard to adapt English words
to the rhythm, with a view of describing it on the
morrow to Byron, and the following stanzas were the
result of the attempt :—

CHANT.

Rest to thy pillow,—rest,—
    I watch beside thee ;
No care shall wring thy breast ;
    No ill betide thee !
Love guards thy pillow,—LOVE,—
    The unrepining !
Heaven's moon is bright above,
    Heaven's stars are shining :
Peace,—peace,—forget,—forgive,—
    And be forgiven ;
That all who love and live
    May wake in heaven !
Dream of thy dear ones,—dream,—
    The past retracing ;
Thy native valley's stream,
    Thy love's embracing ;
No sound shall mar thy sleep,
    No fears perplex thee ;
Angels their vigils keep,
    Thy GOD protects thee !
Peace,—peace,—forget,—forgive,—
    And be forgiven ;
That all who love and live
    May wake in heaven !

While gathering the sounds of a dirge as sad as a
Highland coronach, all seemed suddenly to cease, and
Berto was calling upon me to rise, and talking about
shaving-water, when I opened my eyes again.   I
started up.   I looked on the footstool.   I gazed round
the room, into which the sparkling rays of a winter

morning were pouring their brightness. I tore open
the heavy curtains intervening between my bed
and the wall. Not a vestige of my midnight visitant !

"Why did you let her out before you woke me ?"
cried I, addressing my attendant, in utter consternation ; whereon Berto, who, from my precipitate
movements, evidently thought me possessed, presumed
to suggest that I was still dreaming.

"But the girl !" cried I—"the girl who was sitting
beside me when you entered ?"

"No one was sitting here, eccelenza !" he replied,
looking somewhat demure at such a supposition. "All
was closed as usual. I entered the room with my
pass-key. Now I think of it, the curtains of yonder
window were undrawn, and the blinds half open,
though I remember well that all was safe when I left
you last night. I suppose your excellency unfastened
them."

And again he began to talk about shaving-water.

I was half out of my wits. Was it possible that the
event of the night had been an illusion, that I had
dreamed of Franszetta's visit, of her strange history ?
If so, would that I could have slept for ever, to retain
before my eyes the graceful froward being fluttering
before my glass, like some sylph new lighted on a
flower.

Rising in haste, I examined the dressing-case, which
we had seemed to open together the preceding night.
The ducats were gone, the rings were gone, but nothing else. Though on the toilet-table lay scattered
numberless objects of value, gifts from those towards
whom I would not be guilty of the perfidy of bestowing
them on another, not the smallest of them was missing.
In her mysterious flight, the gipsy girl had taken with
her only what was legitimately her own.

It would not amuse my readers to hear recited the
oaths I bestowed on my own somnolency, or upon Berto's
awkwardness, all the time he was ministering to my

toilet; oaths which would have driven O'Brien out of his senses. I felt convinced I should never behold that bewitching creature again. I had known from the first, that she must go at sunrise; but I had a few kindly words to whisper to her. I wished to establish some future medium of communication between us, in case disaster should overtake her; in case, for instance, that on her return to Brōny, Fridszin should not have arrived, or should be unwilling to fulfil his contract. Ass that I was to fall asleep, because a beautiful girl was singing me to rest.

I resolved not to say a syllable on the subject to Byron. I had not courage for the railleries he would launch like a shower of arrows at my head. I dressed myself in haste. It was, at least, some comfort that the wind was directly contrary for Fiume. The frost was severe. What rubbish one talks in England about the genial skies of Italy! Out of the Two Sicilies, where is the winter less tedious, or less searching, than our own?

I had promised Byron to accompany him that day to the Convent of St. Lazarus, where, between the pauses of a dissolute life, he was pursuing his studies in the Armenian language, by way, he said, of a "rock to break his mind upon." Hitherto I had declined the honour of a morning in this synod of learned pundits, among whom I should be thoroughly out of place.

I abominate monasteries. Two things peculiar to the cloister are my especial detestation; the smell of human fustiness, and the aspect of human hypocrisy. The faces one sees in such places, are as much made up as that of Lady Harriet anybody. Rouge and patches are not the only foreign aids of ornament by which people falsify their visages. Humility, piety, patience, may sit just as discordantly upon the countenance, as white lead or painted eyebrows. The soft deprecating accents of an old monk are my ideal of the voice of Satan.

Byron was partial to these Armenian fellows. He and other enlightened English, who have loitered beside the Rialto, have done their best to recommend the learned recluses of San Lazaro to the favour of the world. With all my affection for B., I could not enter into his predilections. That bleak ride on the Lido, the convent in question, and the linendraper's wife and family, seemed to me far less inviting than a Pellegrino dinner, or our box at the Fenice.

We breakfasted together, and proceeded to his gondola. Tita was in attendance ; the morning bright. But my spirits did not respond to the cheerfulness of the hour. Byron was full of mirth. If Father Pasquali, the learned friar to whom he was hastening, could have overheard the confidences of his noble pupil concerning his opera adventures of the night before, he had probably been of opinion that Byron was quite right to select so severe and sobering an investiture for his faculties, as the intricacies of an Armenian grammar.

Previous to repairing to the convent, we were to leave a letter of recommendation I had received from my brother for Count Mocenigo ; and as we were entering the grand canal, the slackened pace of the gondola attested that something unusual was occurring. Byron swore it was only some raft or fruit-barge, and called to Tita to push on, an invitation which procured for us the explanation that they were taking the body of a young girl out of the water.

" Dead ?" said I, with some interest, looking forth towards the crowd of gondolas clustered round the spot.

" Impossible to say, eccelenza," was Tita's reply. " See, they have placed her on the steps of the Mocenigo palace. They are feeling her hands. They shake their heads. *Corpo di Diana!* 'Tis all over with her ! "

" It is a poor peasant girl," said Byron, to gratify whose curiosity, rather than mine, Tita pushed towards the spot, " and beautiful as an angel ! "

At this declaration I looked again. Two gondoliers were at that moment bearing down the body, to place it in a boat for removal ; one of them an old, grey-headed man, the other young and powerful, whose arms were encircling the feet. Both were so placed, with regard to us, that I saw only the face of the old man, and the stalwart form of the young one ; and the same idea at that moment struck both Byron and myself. What a realization of the famous picture of the interment in Atala. *There* was Chactas, *there* the dead virgin they were bearing to the grave.

In another moment a cry burst out of the depths of my heart, which suspended the observations of my companion. The sun was upon that mournful group, and a sudden turn of the bearers brought the face of the dead full under its brightness. The reader has forestalled the fatal truth. That cold, white face, that raven hair, from which the chilly waters were dripping as they bore her along, those delicate and slender limbs were those of Franszetta !

We followed the boat to the Ospidaletto, to which it was destined. We saw the best efforts of art directed towards her resuscitation. In vain ! There were severe bruises, there were traces of outrage. The belt containing the money had been torn away. The stiletto was not in her girdle. She had not, as I had first supposed, fallen into the water in escaping from the Palazzo Gritti. She had shared the fate of her mother. The girl was murdered !

Could anything have increased my affection for Byron, it would have been the brotherly manner in which he entered into my affliction, assisted me in attempting to stimulate the investigations instituted by the criminal tribunals, and joined with me in yielding such poor tokens as occasion permitted, of respect to the memory of the dead.

Poor Franszetta ! poor high-minded Tsigány ! Little didst thou suppose, amidst the girlish drudgery of thy wretched hovel at Bröny, that the noble poet of England, the man whose name was European, would attend as a mourner at thy obsequies. It was Byron who suggested an inscription for the stone I placed over her remains, copied from some tomb he had seen at Ferrara :—

FRANSZETTA IMPLORA ETERNA QUIETE.

A long silken tress, shred from her head ere they placed her in her coffin, moist with the chilly waters of the Lagune, is all that remains to me as a token of the reality of that most strange adventure.

I never dwell upon the recollection of Franszetta as a child of clay. She lives in my memory as pure among the pure, because uncorrupted among the corrupt ; an angel with her mother, who is in heaven. Eheu ! Franszetta !

CHAPTER XVII.

The grand Prior of Aviz, shrinking back in his chair, exclaimed piteously,—"I shall never be able to stand this ; my eyes would become fountains, and we have had weeping enough lately." So saying, he retired without further ceremony.

BECKFORD.

Εν τῳ φρονειν γαρ μηδεν, ηδιστος βιος.

SOPHOCLES.

BYRON would not hear of my returning to my desolate quarters at the Palazzo Gritti ; he protested that no human fortitude ought to be exposed to so gratuitous a trial. But this arrangement only hastened my departure from Venice. My consciousness of the inconvenience imposed upon him by my sojourn in his apartments in the Spezieria determined me to expedite my departure from the city. Its familiar haunts were now accursed in my sight. The Piazza, the Zecca, the Canal Grande, and, above all, that haunted

chamber in the Palazzo Gritti, were full of Franszetta.
Strange mortals that we are! The events of eight-
and-forty hours, an acquaintanceship of two dreary
winter days' duration, nay, of less, was fated to de-
stroy my peace of mind for many ensuing months,
and endow me with memories of sadness enduring as
my life.

I succeeded in persuading Byron that the most
friendly part he could play by me was to assist in
hastening my journey; and before the middle of the
month, was rowing back again from San Giorgio
towards Fusina, repeating almost the same words I
had uttered at Cintra seven years before, that in all
my wanderings, all my pursuits, misfortune was beforehand with me.

I was bound for Rome, a city of the past, and consequently a place of tribulation; appropriate sojourn
of those who mourn and refuse to be comforted. At
first, Byron insisted on bearing me company in my
tour. But he had previously pledged himself to
Marianna to remain with her till the close of the
carnival; and as I saw that he was doing violence to
his feelings and hers by this rupture of his word, I
promised to go no further than Florence till he was at
liberty to rejoin me.

For three dreary months, therefore, I remained
alone on the Lung' Arno, weary of myself and the
world, and intent only on my lost Pleiad. Unacquainted with a creature in the place, I pronounced
it to be detestable. On visiting Florence the following
year, it seemed to me that a transformation had taken
place in every object, animate or inanimate.

Towards the close of April Byron rejoined me;
at the beginning of May we stood together in the
Coliseum.

Things fall out strangely in this *imbroglio* of cross
purposes. It had been one of the darling visions of
Byron's life to visit—no! I'll be hanged if I call it
the Eternal City, even in print — to visit ROME.

z

Foscolo, Madame de Staël, Rogers, and a hundred
other talkers to whom the world delights to listen,
had inspired him with an eager interest in the reliques
of the antique world ; and now he was there, he
allowed himself to be ciceroned to all and everything
that classical pilgrims delight to worship. But his
heart and soul were brimful of the wife of a linendraper ; and his chief solicitude, with St. Peter's on
one side and the Pantheon on the other, was to enable
himself to return to Venice within a fortnight.

Yet such is the vivifying power of genius, that the
hurried visit of Byron, rushing from monument to
monument, flying through St. Peter's, glancing at the
Apollo, galloping from the Alban mount to Frascati,
enabled him to add a brighter leaf to the garland of
"the Niobe of nations" than the belaurelling of a
whole century of ordinary travellers.

What provoked me most in the pre-occupation of
his mind and frustration of my plans, was a fact of
which he was himself uncognizant ; that Marianna's
influence was declining, and that his devotion was
a matter of conscience. We are all sad hypocrites
to each other ; even those who pretend to live together
open-hearted as brothers. Byron affected to be as much
in love, and I as much in grief, as ever ; while, in truth,
he was growing sadly *ennuyed* with his living heroine,
and I beginning almost to doubt the existence of my
dead one. I often fancied that I had only indulged in
a dream of Franszetta. But Byron was preserved from
any misdoubtings of that description by the bills of certain Shylocks of the Rialto, for pearls, diamonds, opals,
and rubies, which the lady of his love not only accepted,
but re-sold, as others have since re-sold the more precious intellectual ores of his confiding. He insisted
upon going to see three robbers guillotined while he
was in Rome, and about to return to Marianna. Now
Marianna was a robber !

There was no occasion for me to leave Rome, because
he happened to be hurrying back to Venice, in the

vicinity whereof he intended to hire a villa for the summer months,—La Mira, since so celebrated. I remained there longer than is customary for the English to defy the malaria; then went to Sorrento, and from thence sailed for Messina. Sicily was as much the idol of my dreams as Rome of Byron's; a person for whose taste I have the highest reverence having inspired me with deep interest in its classical remains and modern enchantments, its climate, mild as the sighs of beauty, its gentle landscapes, its meads, its valleys, its Enna, its Hybla.

Now, I have infinite satisfaction in gentle landscapes, meads, and valleys, provided they lie within reach of a city where the eating is good and the opera tolerable. It knew that, in the granary of Italy, corn, wine, and oil were in abundance; and that fruit, which signified more during the dog-days, might be had for picking. Any man can live on figs and water-melons under the clear blue skies of Sicily. It is only when sinking under fog and soot that one cries aloud for the flesh of Southdowns, to enable us to bear up against the climate. A haunch of venison would be as uninviting at Palermo in the month of July as sorbets and *pastecchi* at Edinburgh in that of January.

The island, which seems to form a stepping-stone from Africa to Europe, turning, like some ripe fruit, one sunburnt cheek to the south and one still immature towards the north, did not disappoint my expectations. I spent the winter at Palermo. When I returned to Naples everybody asked me what on earth I had found to detain me there? I told them it was the climate. I shall give the same answer to such of my readers as are bold enough to put the same question. It does not suit me to be more explicit. If any one has any fault to find with my reserve, my card of address lies at my publisher's.

D'Israeli, the Right Honourable, once wrote to me, "Youth is a blunder, manhood a struggle, old age a regret;" a dictum worth reading in a letter worth

preserving. *My* youth, Heaven knows, was a blunder ;
my manhood a struggle ; and now that I am arriving
at old age, the past is beginning to get the better of
the future in my affections.

One of the places I most regret, is Sicily. The spot
is not sanctified, like Cintra or Venice, by a grave ;
but my reminiscences are only the more mournful.
For with Emily and Franszetta abides an atmosphere
of perpetual spring, eternal youth, unchanging beauty.
While in Sicily, time has wrought the same cruel
triumphs as over myself. The face which was beautiful
as an angel's, two-and-twenty years ago, is now that
of a mere mortal.

I pass over my adventures the following season at
Florence. They are recorded in many a diary, still
kept under golden lock and key, and brought out by
their lovely inditers on rainy Sunday afternoons, at
their country seats ; and to give publicity to them in
the teeth of their breathing heroines, were perfidy.
Besides, Doctors' Commons might prove a bitterer
critic than even the "Quarterly Review."

Suffice it, that it was in pursuance of one of these
Florentine episodes I determined to return to England. One of my angels exacted a promise of me to
that effect ; and though I assured her (and the event
justified my prediction) that once established among the
proprieties of English life, she would be the first to forbid
me the house, I felt it a point of conscience to comply.

Another of my prophecies was just as strictly fulfilled. I foresaw that I should abhor London, its
want of graciousness, its want of cordiality, its want of
refinement. I dreaded the supercilious faces of its fine
world, the petty sarcasms which it fancies wit, and its
abject fear of committing itself in the eyes of the
censorship of fashion. All this turned out as I expected.
I look upon the London exclusives, just as the London
exclusives look upon those of New York. Considerable changes and metamorphoses, however, struck me
in the aspect of the great Babylon.

Classical commentators belaud the memory of a certain emperor, on the ground that he found Rome clay, and left it marble.   I had left London brick, and found it STUCCO.   My friend, Sir John Harris, one of the first to greet me on my return (being as stationary in the metropolis as the grasshopper on the Exchange), assured me that England had found in Nash a new Vitruvius, a Palladio the younger ; and though my first glimpse of the glories of Regent Street by no means confirmed the decree, I accepted it with the respect due to the Hephæstion of Carlton House.

I know not whether my ideas had expanded with much travel.   But I remember thinking, one night when we had been playing the pageant of good company, not exactly at Carlton House (which possessed the charm inseparable from all royal establishments, of everything and everybody being in its place), but at the showy residence of a satellite, who affected the form without the spirit of the Carltonian circles.   I remember thinking, I say, that were Primrose Hill to send forth an eruption of cinders and lava, and Herculaneanize or Pompeiify the west-end of London, how greatly A.D. 3001 would wonder at the vulgarity of our taste, and the littleness of our productions. Scarcely a modern mansion one should like to produce to posterity, as our endeavour to vie with the Elizabethan era, or the grander aspirations of Inigo Jones. As to the thousand nameless trinkets invented to amuse the great babies of our enlightened times, our grand nephews will probably decide that there wanted only an enamel rod for lordly fustigation, to complete the play-box of the grown-up nursery.

With respect to the wider field of London society, and what are called by courtesy the gaieties of the season, it was still the reign of mobs on staircases.   An assembly where no carriage was smashed would have been scarce worth speaking of ; while the sacrifice of a fine blood horse, or a coachman or footman carried off on a shutter to St. George's Hospital, conferred dis-

tinction. The greatest happiness of the greatest number
was the professed motto of ball-givers.

I never knew exactly what amended our ways in
this particular. People ascribe the improvement to
the extension of London and its population ; and the
consequent impossibility of giving visiting lists to your
porter, with the sweeping clause of a general invitation.
But such a change would have been progressive ;
whereas mob-assemblies went out with George the
Fourth. An enormous schism arose in society, at the
epoch of the Reform Bill. Parties ran desperately
high ; political, not fashionable parties, which, on the
contrary, fell fifty degrees. The Capulets and the
Montagues of the great world would scarcely meet
in the same room ; though, the moment the great
measure was carried, the effervescence subsided, and
Whigs and Tories, recollecting that, like sea and land,
there must ever exist a junction between them, re-
amalgamated as usual.

But in the interim the revolution was accomplished.
People had discovered the charm of small parties and
moderately crowded rooms. Even the insulting term
" Exclusives," applied to those who were desirous, in
inviting their friends, to secure them from having their
ribs broken and their dresses torn from their backs, did
not frighten the fine world into a renewal of the
exploded system of bear-gardens.

At the period of my arrival London society
flattered itself it was enjoying a peculiar state of bea-
titude. The king had just been crowned, the queen
was just buried,—and the world entertained a notion
that there would be a royal marriage, a female court,
—everything the public eye and mind delights to
dwell on.

But it is not of King George I have undertaken to
write. Kings have their historiographers, who are
paid for praising them ; and it is without a salary I
have undertaken to. commemorate the reign of Cecil
Danby.

Having already hinted that my birth was the first event of public note at Paris after the assembling of the States General, my beloved public will be, of course, ill-natured enough to recollect that, at the coronation of George the Fourth, I must have numbered some two-and-thirty years. Nothing in which people take a more malicious pleasure, than convicting and publishing the ages of their fellow-creatures. Allude in company to the natal date of some absent individual, and you will find everybody endeavouring to prove him older than he acknowledges. Every stranger is better informed on the subject than peerage or parish register, mother, doctor, or nurse.

I am not sure, now I come to think of it, that I did not at the epoch in question affect to be *one*-and-thirty instead of *two*. I knew that to please a lady's eye, thirty is the apex of human perfection ; the moment when the mind begins to mellow, ere the body has begun to decay. Thanks, however, to my mother's obstinate adherence to the age of eight-and-forty, and certain errors of date which she took care should creep into the peerage, I remained thirty longer than most men.

To my great amazement, I found that, as regarded my popularity, age mattered not a jot.

It is needless, I hope, to repeat that the world contained not a roof wide enough for Lord Ormington and myself to dwell under in peace. I therefore established myself in a little snuggery in Cleveland Row, to be within umbrella reach of my clubs, and at a sufficient distance from Hanover Square.

I did not much like the idea of subsiding into "a gentleman in lodgings." When I called to mind the advice lavished upon me by Lady Harriet Vandeleur on my *début*, ten years before, the extreme difficutly she then seemed to anticipate for me of obtaining endurance in society, when backed by Lady Ormington's influence, Lord Ormington's cook and cellar, and my own more than Grecian symmetry of face and form, I could not but perceive the impossibility of making a sensation, now that I stood alone, on means far from princely, with an occasional line of silver perceptible among my glossy curls, and an occasional line of care intersecting my manly brow ; the only " lines on a person of quality," upon which the coteries are apt to be critical.

" Never mind," said I to my Self, when I saw him almost out of spirits on ascertaning a few of these parparticulars from the reflection of an ill-conditioned lodging-house looking-glass, about the size and colour of a cat's eye. " Never mind, old fellow ! There is room for everybody in the world, as well as for every animal in the ark. You have lost the pretension of astounding. Henceforward, you must charm by being agreeable. You were a deuced popular fellow at Naples ; you were much liked at Florence ; and London accepts its favourites on the strength of foreign endorsement. It hissed Pasta, till she had been smothered by the bouquets of La Scala. Be of good cheer. It will not hiss *you.* Take courage, clear your throat, look the public in the face. You will do very well in your way."

Upon this system of philosophy, I prepared myself to fill a secondary place as a stop-gap in dinner parties, and a supernumerary at balls. Judge therefore of my amazement on finding myself super-ascendantly the fashion ; neither a stop-gap nor a supernumerary, but *enormously* the fashion ! I do *not* speak under correction. I say again,—ENORMOUSLY the fashion !

I could scarcely make it out, but so it was. It was not alone that I was invited by all the " leaders of ton;" I was invited in a manner to make acceptance inevitable.

But what could these lovely creatures want of me ? Cecil Danby, my dear fellow, from a man of two-and-thirty the query is unpardonable. Did not the peerage set forth in its record of the Barony of Ormington, Heir Apparent, the Hon. John ; and was it not a matter of

notoriety, that the said Hon. John was in infirm health,
having issue by his marriage only the Hon. Jane? Hadst
thou not therefore every reasonable prospect of succeeding to an ancient title, with a rent-roll of thirty-five
thousand pounds per annum, and as much increase as the
thrifty habits of Lord Ormington might have amassed
in addition? Was not such, in fact, the express origin
of his lordship's still increasing aversion of thy Self?

Yes! such is the foresight of that shrewdest of all
insects, except the ant, a London chaperon, that I was
actually booked among the *partis !* As if it were not
vile enough to speculate upon the Duke of This or
Viscount That, in possession of his dukedom or his
viscountcy, manœuvring mammas look into futurity
with the eye of a seer or an actuary. Were I an earl,
with a marriageable elder son and the consciousness of
impaired health, I should determine the progress of
my decay less by consultations of physicians, than by
examining the nature and quality of the notes addressed to my heir-apparent. If I saw the young
gentleman placed at table by Lady Winstanley next
to one of her daughters, I would go home and order
my coffin.

I *was* placed there. I was invited to her ladyship's
pleasant house in Curzon Street, whenever I liked to
"drop in." I was pressed to join Richmond parties
with them. I was asked to her dinners, both family
and formal.

But it was not alone Lady Winstanley whose
civilities convinced me that Danby was in a critical
condition. Three or four more of the most experienced
chaperons were on the watch to bag me, if I only put
out my nose. I never see a determined elder-son-
catcher going her rounds, like an earth-stopper, or the
parish mole-catcher, or any other setter of springes,
without thinking of the print which adorned the
Aldine edition of one of our nursery classics in
Hanover Square; representing that Mazarin of the
fairy tale book, "Puss in Boots," in a feigned sleep

upon the ground, with his half-open bag baited with parsley lying by his side, to catch the foolish rabbits who might stray into his toils.

My own feelings and views on the question matrimonial are expressed in the following skit, penned one evening after listening to the everlasting chirp of a cricket that haunted my apartment in Cleveland Row.

THE PHYLOSOPHY OF GRYLLO.

CRICKET ! who, these three months long,
Hast beset me with thy song,
Ever restless, never ranging,
In thy notes and haunts unchanging,
Chirping still from noon till night,
Say ! What makes thy heart so light ?
Midst the cursed frost and fog
Rendering man so dull a dog,
Prithee, GRYLLO, whisper me
Thy resource against Ennui ?

GRUMBLER !—quoth the Cricket, thou,
Sauntering home with aching brow,
Sallow cheeks, and yawns amazing
From the halls whose lights are blazing,
Scents exhaling, garlands wreathing,
Music's tones voluptuous breathing,
Jullien, Strauss, and Collinet,
Gunter and the devil to pay,
Beauty drest by Madame Devy,
Say ! what makes thy heart so heavy ?

CRICKET !—In those scenes of sport,
Crockey's,—coterie,—or court,
Hustings, tableaux, or charades,
Steeple-chases, tennis, cards,
Riding twenty miles to cover,
Skulking back to play the lover,
Moonlight, cloisters, and romancing,
Waltzing, reeling, country-dancing,
Dicing, drinking, racing, flirting,
What is it seems so diverting ?

GRUMBLER !—In my chimney-corner,
Free from bore and safe from scorner,
Blest with *ménage* snug and cozy,
All the joys of life *sub rosâ;*

Fair Carlotta twirls in vain,
I've not a pound on Running Rein ;
If stocks look down or bankers smash,
What call have I for ready cash ?
A fig for China ! *Carpe diem !*
Would every man were wise as I am !

CRICKET !—Wert thou one of *us,*
(The Commons and the Omnibus),
Pray, how wouldst thou contrive to shirk
Egypt, Syria, or the Turk ?
Louis Philippe and his trenches,
Cheering from the Treasury benches,
Bonham's boring,—Leader's prating,
All the stuff they call debating ?
Even Charley Buller vows he's
Hipped to death by "both their houses !"

GRUMBLER !—Hadst thou no design
Tully of *The Times* to shine,
Had Ribands red, or green, or blue,
No attraction in thy view,
If Treasury Warrants "please to pay,"
Ne'er tempted thee on Quarter-day,
Nor ays nor noes, nor Lamb nor Peel
Would force the steam up of thy zeal.
'Tis SELF whom thou dost represent
In the High Court of Parliament !

CRICKET !—'Tis *not* because a snobby
I do my duty in the lobby,
Fate doth her blows, as on a cur, vent
Upon your most obedient servant !
Inkson's blackest books I stand in,
Burghart's defaulter I'd a hand in ;
My name is writ with all its vowels,
In ledger seventy-five at Howell's !
By way of assets—Prussic acid,—
A parish coffin,—and—*Hic Jacet!*

GRUMBLER !—I see you think to nick it
By slily making game of Cricket !
No GO !—I'll neither back a bill,
Nor name a spendthrift in my will ;
But take advice, sir,—therewithal
Insects, like men, are prodigal.
☞When house and lands are gone and spent
A prudent match is excellent,
Woman of cents,—I mean the five,
Reclaim the saddest rake alive !

A warm fireside, sir, snug as GRYLLO'S,
A reading-chair, with patent pillows,
A hissing urn and Twining's best,
A Bentley's Mis. to give it zest,
No books but Coutts and Co.'s to bore him,
No debt but Nature's *in terrorem*,
No Almack's, with its varnish'd pumps,
No Travellers', with its "what are trumps?"
With madam, happy as a queen, he
Sings "Jubilate!" like Rubini.

I am not addicted to English misses. I have no
weakness in favour of pretty faces with as much
expression in them as in that of a sunflower. It
was therefore through no seeking of mine that the
whole of that season I had always a Maria or Julia on
my arm or in my pocket ; that I was sung to, prattled
to, danced at, drawn at, rode with, flirted with, by
every muslin frock purposing to promote its muslin
into brocade. Five years' absence from England had
converted me into what the silk mercers call a
" novelty of the season."   Neither mothers nor
daughters were by any means certain what might be
my predilections. I was an open borough. Anybody
might have me, they fancied, who canvassed with
sufficient zeal ; and, as I live by cake, they did not
spare either themselves or me.

I do not much like reverting to Lord Ormington.
The feelings prevailing between us were of too serious
a nature for slight mention. Nay, I look upon our
relative position as the groundwork of a domestic
tragedy of the Christian world, fully as direful as the
wrath of Nemesis, or the persecutions of Neptune or
Jupiter in the pagan. Half the inexplicable antipathies we see in families arise from misgivings or
certainties, such as rendered me hateful in his eyes ;
and if woman in her wanton follies would only please
to remember that, in addition to the shame she is
entailing on herself, she is concentrating hatred and
malice on the head of an innocent being, she might
be restrained in her career of sin. But women

who indulge in wanton flirtations have seldom feeling or sense enough to be touched by such an argument.

I must, however, allude to his lordship so far as to observe that, from the period of poor little Arthur's death, he never held up his head. It had been beyond my strength of mind to attend the obsequies of the poor lost innocent. But Lord Ormington accompanied Danby into Lancashire to see him laid in the family vault, and support the afflicted father. The unbaptized infant was laid at the same time in the grave; and I verily believe that, standing beside those two little coffins, which seemed to complete the extinction of his legitimate branch, Lord Ormington vowed against me a vow of eternal hatred. I am convinced he regarded me in the light of as accomplished an assassin as the cruel uncle of the Babes in the Wood.

He had collected at the time all the newspapers detailing this afflicting calamity; which, as it related to the heir of a noble family, dwelt of course with the utmost pomp and circumstance on the sad event. Morning papers, evening papers, weekly papers, monthly summaries, nay, even the Annual Register, of that disastrous year, were placed apart in his private room; tied up with mourning-strings and bindings, to be perused and reperused whenever he found himself overcoming the force of those grievous recollections. He brooded upon his sorrow, as an old man might be expected to do who knew that *he*, at least, should not survive to witness its obliteration by brighter prospects. For many months, Lady Susan lingered on the brink of the grave; and when the physicians pronounced her out of danger, they acknowledged that it was unlikely she should again become a mother.

Now, had Lord Ormington's affliction been a truly grand-paternal feeling of tenderness for the issue of the loins of the issue of his loins, Danby's little girl,

one of the prettiest and most engaging little creatures
I ever beheld, would have sufficed for his consolation.
But it was not so.   I knew from good authority that
he never evinced the slightest interest in the child.
All his regrets were for the two boys, the heirs of
his titles and estates, the heirs who were to have cir-
cumvented the pretensions of the interloper, Cecil
Danby.   It was me he hated; not poor little Arthur
whom he loved.   Nay, I suspect that in the depths of
his soul, he would not have regretted the death of
Lady Susan, whose illness he affected to take so much
to heart.   He wanted a wife for Danby who was
likely to become the mother of sons.

Meanwhile, the poor old man was shrunken up with
his afflictions, till nothing seemed left of him but his
whiskers.   The wretch, Coulson, his eternal shadow,
was now the shadow of a shade.   We had met once
or twice, when, on my return to England, I went to
pay my respects to my mother, who seldom left the
house; and as nothing had occurred to justify any
overt act of severity towards one who bore his name
and had been introduced into official life under his
patronage, he was forced to meet me on courteous
terms.   He had not even an excuse for referring me,
as he had done ten years before, to his solicitors;
though I accidentally discovered that, after giving up
all hope of an heir from Lady Susan, he had been
engaged day after day in professional consultations
with old Hanmer, concerning the possibility of cutting off the entail of his estates.   The law, however,
stood my friend.   On that point, from the respect
testified toward me by the chaperoning class of the
community, I knew myself to be safe.

But what a cheerless and penitentiary-like aspect
now invested the house in Hanover Square!   It
might be said of its hopes, as of Ophelia's violets, that
"they all withered when my nephew died."   From
that day, the place had never worn a smile.   It
looked doomed, deserted, sorrow-stricken!   An air

of dilapidation may be imparted to a mansion in the best possible state of repair, by trifles imperceptible to its inmates. Lady Ormington, who was now a confirmed invalid (from the effects of a paralytic attack, said by the physicians to be the result of laudanum, whereas her ladyship protested the laudanum to be the result of her illness), never quitted the floor containing her bedroom and dressing room ; and the great saloon, formerly so celebrated through the *fêtes* and fashionabilities of my mother, was deserted.

No one but the housemaid ever entered there. The windows, I suspect, had not been cleaned since I quitted England. But what imparted a still more melancholy aspect than even the thick encrusting of dust and soot streaked off in certain directions by the pelting of April showers, was a row of old flowerpots, the plants in which had been dead for years, but still rustled their dry stalks in the wind ; and the sparrows chose to perch and built round this unsightly rubbish, as though the house contained no living inmate. It was scarcely possible to recognize its dull, dingy, dispiriting façade as the same before which, on leaving college, I found in daily waiting the smartest equipages in town, each with its pair of bloods and snowy-wigged coachman, as proud on his hammer-cloth as a chancellor on the woolsack.

No carriage approached that desolate doorway *now*, save the vehicle of Lady Ormington's daily apothecary, oilskinned and patent-leathered, from the servants' hats to the horses' coats, as if to defy all inclemencies of weather.

I seldom taxed my spirits by entering the house. I was almost as much out of Lady Ormington's good graces, as those of her lord. She was angry with me for being nobody ; reproached me bitterly with having thrown away my prospects in life ; showed me Herries and his two thousand a year, and Sir John Harris and his knighthoods, as examples of what I ought to have achieved ; protesting that had I stuck to the Foreign

Office and persuaded Lady Theresa to stick to *me*, we should now have been Sir Cecil and Lady Theresa Danby, Excellencies at Stutgardt, Munich, Naples, or some other city not demanding a K. B. or K. G. in its ambassadorization.

In vain did I assure her that I was one of the finest gentleman about town ; that I ate the best dinners in the best houses, day after day, from January till July.   She only shrugged her shoulders at my boastings ; muttering something which her paralytic affection prevented from being *very* distinct, about, "Sir Lionel over again ; and like Sir Lionel, he will die in the Bench !"

She was so much impaired in intellect, that it was impossible to resent her attacks.   Nor had I any reason to feel piqued.   Thanks to the manifestations in my favour of Helena Winstanley, and other beauties of the season, I saw that I held four by honours and the odd trick.   I might become pretty nearly what I liked.   Most people might, if they only knew it ; the faculty of knowing it, constituting what the world calls genius.   To be a great writer or a great painter is the mere result of feeling persuaded that you are capable of becoming a great writer or a great painter, and working up to the mark.   A man of genius is, in fact, a narrow-minded man ; a man with a single pretension ; a man who, like Milton or Shakspeare, feels that he is only fit to write poetry ; or who, like Titian, will pass eighty years before an easel.   Whereas a man of great talent is too clever to chain himself down to an oar. *He* understands a little of everything ;. can paint a little, write a little, play a little on every instrument. *He* could not go scraping and polishing away at a block of marble for years, to bring forth at last a Venus de Medicis or Apollo Belvidere ; or confine himself to a single canvas, for the sake of producing a Last Judgment.

Now Cecil Danby was a man of genius, or narrow-minded man.   I was conscious of the power of

becoming dictator to the world of fashion, and I became
so. Even when Brummell was on the throne, ten
years before, I regarded his dazzling supremacy as
Oliver Cromwell in his youth may have contemplated
that of the Stuarts; and in a recent interview with
him at Calais, regarded him much as the Protector
surveys the features of the decapitated king, in Dela-
roche's picture of Charles the First in his coffin.
Already, I was master of his sceptre.

One thing bored me. I entertained a personal
leaning towards George the Fourth, both as the old
friend of my mother, as the patron of my boyhood, and
as a gracious, if not kindly-affectioned man. But I
had wit enough to perceive that, living in a reign
where coxcombry was courtiership, I should be lost by
adhering to the court. At Carlton House, I must of
necessity subside into an imitator, a shadow, an echo,
a nothing. It was only by a schism I had the least
chance of distinguishing myself.

But for my consciousness of power as a coxcomb of
genius, I should probably have attempted some other
means of obtaining renown, for the throne of Dandyism
was already in its Lower Empire. The ornamental
was about to pass away, the graceful to evaporate.
As the decay of religions is perceptible in their recourse
to the accessories of materialism; as Polytheism in its
decline sought aid from the chisel of Phidias, and
Catholicism, when bereft of its influence, strove to
renovate its altars by the pencil of Raphael, so
Dandyism, at its last gasp, called in the aid of
Lawrence.

Ten years later, and I should have been born *too*
late for my vocation.

CHAPTER XVIII.

Jo suis sorti de ma maison, le front haut, le menton relevé, le
regard direct, une main sur la hanche, faisant sonner les talons
de mes bottes comme un auspessade, coudoyant les bourgeois,
et ayant l'air parfaitement vainqueur et triomphal.

> Cosi per entro loro schiera bruna
> S' ammusa l' una con l' altra formica,
> Forse a spiar lor via e lor fortuna !

DANTE.

I HAVE been frequently disgusted in society by the
supercilious air with which people having accounts in
round figures at their bankers, or coronets on their
teaspoons, inquire of some great writer or artist, " what
he has been doing lately ?" as if his only purpose in
life were to paint or scribble. They would be
amazingly surprised if the painter or man of letters
were to retort upon them an inquiry of what they had
been eating or drinking lately ; the only purport of
their existence.

People used to offend me by asking pretty nearly in
the same tone, on my re-appearance in London, what
" Danby was doing with himself?" Of course, I
perfectly understood them to inquire why he had
ceased to speak in the House. From the moment of
his entrance into public life, the world had looked on
him as public property ; and resented his holding his
tongue, when there were so few orators extant in the
most High Court of Parliament. He sat there still,
and still did duty to his constituents and his country,
if not to himself. From the period of that heavy
family affliction, he had not opened his lips. As the
ancients used to cast into the grave of their dead the
most precious objects in their possession, he seemed to
feel that the noblest dedication *he* could make to the

memory of little Arthur, was his reputation as a public man.

I, who had seen him hanging distracted over the dress of the lost child, like Jacob weeping over the bloody garment of his son, could enter into his feelings; and it consequently appeared to me profanation when, in the midst of a crowded ball-room, some trifler suddenly addressed me with questions concerning the seclusion of poor Danby, much as they would have talked of some sulky opera-dancer, or invalid soprano.

"One never hears anything now of Mr. Danby. Does he never mean to favour us again? It is vastly disappointing when a young man makes so promising a throw off, and does nothing afterwards. At one time, it was thought he might end with leading the party. Castlereagh is worn out. Peel will never have pluck to succeed him. Danby has given no pledges, and would be the very man for us, if he could only manage to get up the steam again. To be sure, precocious flowers are the soonest out of bloom. Perhaps his vein was a shallow one. Perhaps he was a squib, not a rocket. I am afraid Emancipation and Abolition were his Pillars of Hercules; and that he will never get beyond them."

The only person who considered him improved as a public man, was Herries. Herries detested oratory. Herries conceived that every man, that is, every member, went down to the House with his mind made up on the questions likely to come before it; and that the only word of any real consequence in his power to utter, was "ay," or "no." Everything else was an interruption to the business of the House. He felt persuaded that the enlightenment of future times would decree that Parliament should be managed like the courts of law; the Houses playing the part of jury, and the Treasury bench and a sort of devil's advocate, the part of plaintiff and defendant. A single speech on either side would serve all purposes of debate. He had no patience with the high-

sounding harangues embroidered by reporters on
the few mumbled words of certain popular members,
as substantial roads are grounded on a foundation of
faggots.

" I'm sure I don't know what they want of Danby,"
was the cry of my brother-in-law.   " He never misses
a division.   What more is wanted."

Herries considered that a strong mind ought to be
inaccessible to argument ; that, even if one rose from
the dead to persuade them, people having a Tory con-
stituency should vote with the Tories ; people having
a Whig, with the Whigs.   An independent member
was a troublesome fool, a stumbling-block in the way
of practical people.

My brother himself, all this while, maintained a
species of dignity, of all dignities to me the most imposing, a self-seclusion wholly distinct from refusals
of dinner-parties, or the surly veto of "not at home."
Danby appeared in society whenever there was occasion for his appearance.   At political dinners, royal
or ministerial, he was a coveted guest ; and those who
met him at such solemnities rarely failed to notice
him as a man of cultivated mind and high intelligence.
He affected neither gloom nor reserve.   He bore his
family afflictions as though they were his own concern,
and not that of society.   His fortitude was as unaffected as it was earnest.

With me, his conduct was angelic.   He saw how
studiously I avoided him ; and as I had not courage
to approach his house, he came straight to *me*.   Except
a slight tremor of the muscles round his mouth as he
cordially shook hands with me, there was nothing to
induce suspicion that he entertained any other feeling
in accosting me, but that of brotherly regard.   I am
convinced that nothing but the dread of inflicting
pain, prevented his throwing himself on my neck and
weeping bitterly.   We had not met since the stone
was rolled to the door of the sepulchre that shut in
all the sunshine of his life.   How could he be other-

wise than deeply moved by the sight of one connected
with such grievous associations ?

He directed the conversation to general topics, as
remote as possible from all that supposed a family
interest between us. He talked of my travels. He
had never crossed the Alps, yet knew more of Italy
than *I*, who had been wandering there for years. He
knew it through the classics, through its modern
writers, through painters, historians, philosophers : I
only by the practical itinerary of post-houses, restau-
rants, Opera-houses. It is true I had stared at the
Coliseum, and wondered at the Vatican. But their
moral influence had entered into the soul of Danby.
He had studied the institutions in which they had
their rise. Dante and Macchiavelli, Petrarca and
Tasso, had imbued his spirit with Italianism : the
utmost *I* could have done to meet him on this ground,
was to spout a little bad Corinne.

But I spared him all mock enthusiasm. There was
something so true in my brother, that to affect spurious
sentiments in conversing with him would have been
like trying to pass a flash note on a child. I admitted
frankly, therefore, that I cared more for San Carlo
and the Scala, than the Duomo or Vesuvius ; and that
the chief captivation I found in Italy, was the blue-
ness of its skies. I said something about green peas
at Christmas, which he was good-natured enough not
to scout ; and finding me as material as ever in my
tastes and feelings, fell upon neutral ground ; talked
of the vegetation of Sicily, the quarry garden of
Prince Butera, the papyrus attesting the Saracenic
occupation of the island, the palm-tree abiding there
like some naturalized foreigner, lingering within reach
of its African home.

" One of my inducements to visit southern countries,
Spain, Portugal, Greece, or Italy, would be the charm
of their evergreens," said Danby. " The laurel is the
only permanent verdure in which we excel ; and I
want to see the ilex, bay, myrtle, cypress, arbutus, in

perfection. I have a passion for evergreens. To me,
they are the nearest approach to the growth of a
celestial sphere. Look at the orange with its flower,
its fruit, its glossy foliage ; at the bay, with its
musky verdure, that seems created to over-shadow
the grave of a poet. Even the agapanthus and
phyllerea of our cottage gardens delight me; even
the yew and holly of our hedge-rows have a
charm. It is only a Frenchman who could upbraid
them as

'Deuil de l'été, parure de l'hiver.'

To me, there is something sublime in their durability.
A very old evergreen, such as the ancient ilexes and
bays I have read of in Spain and Portugal, or the
cedars of Lebanon, or the cypresses of Mexico, conveys to my feelings an impression of awe."

I dare say Danby wondered what there could be in
these remarks, to suffuse my eyes with tears and
cause my lips to tremble. I had never talked to him
of Cintra, never spoken of the grave of Emily, in-
extricably connected in my memory with the espaliers
of orange-trees and myrtle, the rustling of pines,
and, above all, the shapely branches of a glossy
bay-tree.

I tried to change the subject, by expressing my
surprise that he had never been tempted to the
Continent.

"Like most men ambitious of doing too much, I
have done nothing," he replied, slightly shrugging his
shoulders. "I have always laughed at those galloping
tours, whose merit consists in the computation of so
many hundred miles a week ; and so, to borrow from
the epitaph, *per star meglio, sto qui*. I cannot do all
I want, under a year's absence. In early life, I could
not spare so much from my parliamentary duties.
Now, the infirmities of my father and mother forbid
me to quit England. You, to whom the peculiarities
of our family are no secret, must feel that for all our

sakes I ought to be on the spot in the event of the demise of either."

From that first interview, all awkwardness between us disappeared. Yet, on Lady Susan's account, I refrained from the house. Though she extended her hand kindly to me, she could not command the complexion that went and came all the time I addressed her; or the trembling of the lace ruffle of her sleeve, as she extended her thin white hand to mine. Such was the delicacy of her health, that I could not answer to my conscience for exposing her to the struggle of such emotions. I even fancied that an involuntary shudder pervaded her frame when I impressed a kiss upon the forehead of my little niece, now a promising little girl of seven years old.

I inquired of Jane, whether she remembered Uncle Cecil? Instead of replying, she looked so wistfully at her mother, that I saw my name had been an interdicted word in the family.

I resolved, therefore, that the family should be an interdicted source of happiness to me. I could live without them. It is astonishing how much one can dispense with, so long as the illusions of youth surround one with a rainbow atmosphere, reflecting its hues upon the trivialities of social life.

I had brought with me from abroad the facility in receiving and imparting impressions, attained in continental society. The great world found me amusing because I suffered myself to be amused, being itself too fine for any such concession. And if in reality less entertained by the show-off dinners and well-rehearsed wit of the coteries, than by half an hour spent in laughing devilry with Byron on the shores of Como, or an evening passed in some modest apartment of the Faubourg St. Germain, in a circle where every one said his best (adorning with the charms of intelligence, as with a web of costly tapestry, the mean walls and shabby furniture of the place), the delight of being flattered and worshipped supplied all deficiencies.

I should have preferred, I admit, a more matronly order of worshippers. England is called the land of this, and the land of that. It ought to be called the land of MISSES. On the Continent, young ladies are chosen for, in love and matrimony. In England they are forced to strive hard to be chosen. I do not half like the position in which this order of things has placed the poor little dears. They are told to be modest, gentle, undesigning ; then (like the itinerant Savoyards, supplied by their proprietors with a monkey or cage of white mice) sent forth to dance and sing for the captivation of passengers, and threatened with punishment if they return at night unsuccessful. I never blame them when I see them capering and and showing-off their little monkey-tricks, for conquest. The fault is none of theirs. It is part of an erroneous system. However, I should have been an ungrateful brute not to accept with thankfulness the attentions of which I was the object.

It was the spring time of the year, that season when the Gardener's Vade-mecum directs you to *take in* tender plants at night-fall, and when the Chaperon's Guide indicates the same judicious foresight. From April to August, it is equally part of my system to be taken in. There cannot be a more agreeable vocation. Of all occupations for an idle London man, commend me to that of being dupe to the mother of a very pretty daughter, in possesion of a comfortable house and good establishment.

Lady Winstanley was a capital hand at that sort of thing. She had married her two elder daughters to calfish elder sons of country baronets, by the mere charm of an agreeable circle, where these animals found their crib and hay in readiness, and where they were more at home than in their own. The third daughter, being of finer figure than her sisters, was destined by mamma for the peerage. Mamma was right. Helena Winstanley was a tall, graceful, queenly creature; a Duchess D. G., or, at all events, by the letters-patent of Nature.

One night, at a ball at Princess Esterhazy's, I had been struck by the extreme loveliness of a girl of peculiarly English aspect, tall, fair, well-proportioned, natural in her manners, and apparently gracious in her address, for every one seemed pleased whom she accosted. I inadvertently asked her name of Lady Fitzharrington, beside whom I was standing, who immediately turned towards her with, "Miss Winstanley, allow me to present to you Mr. Cecil Danby."

To manifest to one whose bow was so conciliating, my indignation at the liberty taken with my august presence, would have been misplaced. On the contrary, I set about making myself agreeable so diligently, that a dignified, turbaned, chaperonly-looking woman (to whom Lady Fitzharrington whispered a word in explanation of my social position and Danby's state of health) began to look her eyes out in a contrary direction, to conceal her satisfaction at the conquest achieved by her daughter.

Miss Winstanley proved as pleasant as she was handsome. There was nothing very striking in her conversation. But on a young and pretty girl the desire to please confers a charm. When the turbaned lady approached to join in the conversation, I thought it decent to request an introduction, and thus commenced my acquaintance with Lady Winstanley and her family. Having, with becoming assiduity, called her carriage and put on her shawl, I jumped into my cab, and drove straight to White's, to finish the night, thinking no further of the tall ladies, who, I afterwards discovered, went home with the flattering unction laid to their souls of receiving a proposal on the morrow.

I met them again next night, was again civil, and again more than civilly entreated. The following night was Almack's; and as Collinet was in the orchestra, piping the charming valse of "Gentille

Annette," the rage of the season, I turned towards
Miss Winstanley as the handsomest girl nearest to me,
and asked her to dance.   By good luck she was a
charming *valseuse*.   I saw, as well as felt, that we
were acquitting ourselves to admiration, and was
pleased with her for the applause we obtained.   There
was but one way of showing my gratitude.   I took
her into the tea-room, and flirted with her through
two cups of weak bohea, a plate of brown bread and
butter, and biscuits enough to stock an outward-bound
Indiaman for its voyage to Canton.

There is something inexpressibly gratifying in the
envious looks cast at one by members who have not
paired off, as one sits lounging beside one of the handsomest girls in a ball-room.   The significant glance
which looks, "Oh ho !" the determination not to hear
what is going on, displayed in the countenances of the
chaperons seated near one, are vile encouragements
held out to a fellow, to look irresistible and talk as if he
did not know what he was talking about.

I suppose Miss Winstanley understood what Cis
Danby talked of; for at one moment I had serious
apprehensions that she was going to call for a third
cup of tea.   But Lady Winstanley, evidently thinking
the great business of the night accomplished, begged
me to ask for her carriage.   I was forced to stand
half an hour in the old barrack of a waiting-room, till
Townsend got up the family coach, and saw one or two
people smile, as much as to say, "A match!" when they
saw me concealing behind the door, from the air of the
street and the stare of the footmen, the smiling, silent,
cloaked-up girl, so well satisfied to hang on my arm.

Next day I found on my table in Cleveland Row
the card of Sir Gabriel Winstanley.   The next, I left
two at his door, as in politeness bound ; after which
came a formal invitation to dinner.   I had half a mind
not to go ; for one knows beforehand the sort of fussy,
full-dress, grand dinner-party of a country baronet,
with a clumsy old service of plate, and clumsy butler,

and clumsy saddle of fat, home-killed mutton, which looks as if meant for Daniel Lambert to ride on. Having no engagement, however, for the day in question, I refrained from the cruelty of an excuse.

I was agreeably disappointed. Sir Gabriel, a man who spent his life at Boodle's, was a civil, well-behaved person ; who, I conclude, must have been rich in conversational powers, for he certainly never expended any upon his acquaintance. But he looked highly respectable, when carving his own venison (for he had a soul above mutton), and had assembled about him the chief worthies of my ancestral county, wherein he was himself a landed proprietor.

One is always worth five-and-twenty per cent. more among one's county-people than others. It was to Lord Ormington's Lancashire estates I was indebted for Helena's smiles and her father's invitations to dinner. Sir Gabriel had a very accurate notion of our family rent-roll, more so, far, than I had ; and he and Lord and Lady Fitzharrington, Sir John and Lady Styles, and Mr. and Mrs. Whittington Leigh, talked county at me one against the other, till I fairly wished the County Palatine scuttled in the Irish Channel.

I wanted to chat with Helena. It was a very pleasant thing to chat with Helena. Her greenish-grey eyes, fringed with black lashes, her white skin, her expressive lips, united with her joyous, youthful voice, to impart a charm to conversation pretending to nothing beyond rational commonplace. But rational commonplace is, in the long run, that which pleases most. Wit keeps one too much on the alert to watch whether the shafts it launches attain their mark. Humour makes one nervous, lest it should degenerate into coarseness. Refined wisdom oppresses one with a sense of inferiority. Originality is a pretension that renders one critical. But plain, rational, common-sensical conversation, uttered by an agreeable girl, beside whom one is sitting in a comfortable cozy corner, wraps one round with a consciousness of comfort and repose. One has no

fear of being startled, no dread of being quizzed. One
can fancy a long winter evening cheered by such a companion, with the aid of a good fire, good tea, and the
last good novel.

The Winstanleys were now constantly inviting me.
They had a duchess-cousin, of whom they were prouder
than of their whole united family, who often lent them
her box at Covent Garden ; and they had one of their
own, the alternate weeks, at the opera. The boxes
were well situated, the family coach an easy one, and
old Winstanley's wines as good as is usually the case
with that peculiarly inhabitative and well-settled class
of the community, country baronets. I allowed myself, therefore, to be frequently monopolized by Curzon
Street. Helena had a younger sister almost as pretty
and pleasant as herself. The elder daughters were
married, the son was an aide-de-camp in Ireland, the
father a fixture at his club. There was no drawback
upon the agreeable mornings I lounged away in friendly
chat with the mother and daughters.

Now, I just ask my readers whether they discern
any impropriety in my acceptance of Sir Gabriel's invitation ; or see any harm in my allowing Lady Winstanley to carry me to play and opera, Greenwich dinners, and Richmond picnics ? The summer was a fine
one. The Wanstead House sale was going on, to afford
a pretext for rural excursions. Another time, we rattled
down to Kew, to view the Botanical Gardens and eat
our cold chicken uncomfortably on the grass. All
these fits and starts were of the Winstanleys' own
proposing. There was always some engagement in
prospect ; always something that enabled me, in saying "Good bye," to add, "I shall see you to-morrow."

Will anybody be good enough to recall to mind the
epoch when the English world became suddenly shamed
out of its apathy towards the woes of the sister-in-law
kingdom ; that hapless island which, as Delos arose out
of the sea to afford a birthplace to those glorious twins
of nature Apollo and Diana, may be surmised to have

started out of the western main to afford a fatherland to the twins of civilization, Starvation and Riot. Will any one be kind enough, I say, to remember the first Irish ball given under the auspices of George the Fourth? Will any one describe to those who never heard of the same, the brilliancy of the Italian Opera-house, floored into a ball-room, decorated with flags and lustres, garlands and trophies, but, above all, beaming with beauty from box to box?

Lady Winstanley was not the woman to neglect such an occasion for exhibiting her diamonds, her ostrich-feathers, and her daughters. Even Caroline was to be let out of the Misscage for the night.

Of course, I was too fine a gentleman to play fine on such an occasion. Certain of the Winstanley set of dandies, such small things as ensigns in the Guards, and younger brothers of the calfish elder sons married to the elder daughters, expressed considerable uncertainty about "showing in such a mob." "They had taken tickets, but could not make up their minds whether they should go." Whereupon Lady Winstanley looked beseechingly at me, as a hint that I should volunteer to be their escort.

I hate being tied down to time and place on such occasions; when a fit of indigestion, or an amusing paper, or a nap, may render the postponement of dressing indispensable to one's comfort. I therefore expressed as much uncertainty about going, as the poor affected creatures who could be compromised by consulting their inclinations.

But it happened that, by a concatenation of circumstances impossible to record without violating the sanctity of royal privacy (which, from a person admitted to share its hospitalities, I look upon as an act of low treason), I dined the previous day at Carlton House, where I found myself required to give my arm to one of the most beautiful women of the time.

One never objects to shine in public as the satellite of a fair planet, unless one happens to be in love else-

where, which I was not ; and it was agreeable enough
to secure one of the best places of the night, and the
entrée of the private staircase, by the small concession
of attending on one upon whom every eye was turned
on her entrance.

It was not, however, till towards the close of that
brilliant *fête* that, in traversing the ball-room, whispering somewhat closely to the lovely woman on my
arm, we came suddenly upon Lady Winstanley's party.
I saw the cheeks of Helena flush crimson, then turn
to an ashy paleness. Five minutes afterwards, as I
caught a glimpse of them again, Lady Winstanley was
anxiously despatching my cousin, Lord Wolverton
(whom the reader may remember, when paying his
court to Lady Harriet Vandeleur, as "little Squeamy"),
in search of the carriage. I would have given much
to offer my assistance ; but the heaviest set of darbies
is scarcely a greater obstruction to a man's liberty than
a beautiful woman hanging on his arm.

This little incident spoiled the satisfaction of my
evening. All the rest of the night I was haunted by
Helena's pale face. I flatter myself that, in my worst
of times, I was never much of a monster to these
tender creatures.

> Quando leoni
> Fortior eripuit vitam leo ?

I was never more cruel to them than could be
nelped. Why, why has Providence created them with
such feeble temperaments, or the coarser sex with such
powerful attractions ?

By one of those inexplicable chains of association which, more than all the preachments of the
churches of Asia or Europe, establish the immortality
of the soul, my eyes were irresistibly upraised
towards that fatal box, that hateful box of the
d'Acunhas, usually undistinguishable among its fellows, but now rendered remarkable by a chandelier
placed before it and a waving banner appended to its

façade. My eye seemed fascinated to the spot. I fancied I could see the well-remembered curls of chestnut hair still drooping behind its curtains.

Nec tamen hic oculos falli concedimus hilum,

* * * * *

Proinde animi vitium hoc oculis adfingere noli.

The result of my compunctious visitings was highly favourable to Helena. I recalled to mind the disastrous result of delay on a former occasion ; and next day, not later than two o'clock, was at her door.

Lady Winstanley was never visible at that hour. But *I* was privileged. The servants admitted me, saying they would "let my lady know." Down came "my lady" in her dressing-gown, looking as agitated as an aspen in a sou'-wester. Poor woman. I am convinced she thought I was come to propose for Helena ; for she instantly mentioned that her daughter was indisposed with a headache from the extreme heat. Yet by the nervous anxiety with which she watched the door every time the slightest sound was audible, I saw that she was expecting her down.

She came at last, and lovely indeed she looked ; that is, lovely to *me*, who did not fail to attribute a certain redness of the eyelids singularly at variance with the smiles of joy that dimpled her mouth, to a sleepless night, occasioned by the supposed infidelities of a certain Cecil Danby.

From that day my attentions became more pronounced. All I said was spoken in whispers, and my looks said more than words. I took to dancing again, dancing being the only privileged occasion for *pressing* declarations which are no declarations at all ; and not a supper-room in London whose door might not have told tales of the earnestness of the handsomest man in town, when leaning against it with his eyes fixed in unclouded sunshine on those of one of its prettiest girls.

Lady Winstanley looked triumphant. She was in

a perpetual course of smiles. Though I could see, when approached with congratulations by rival chaperons who longed to tear her eyes out, that she vehemently begged no one "would suppose there was anything *in it*" (what English these women talk !), "the lady did protest too much ;" so much, indeed, as to leave a conviction on their minds that the marriage settlements were in process of engrossment. Helena protested nothing. She only listened, only smiled. And though the three distinct words which would have been more to the purpose than all the sighs and looks I was lavishing, were never even hinted at, she had reason to expect that any moment might startle formal proposals out of my lips.

Mammas get nervous when the month of June expires without the undecided man coming to the point. When July sets in, the landed proprietors grow harvest-bitten, and want to have a look at the crops. Sir Gabriel, I suspect, bored them amazingly with his peas and beans. For I could see that Lady Winstanley grew horribly agitated every time he opened his mouth, lest he should fix the day of their departure from town. Helena still smiled on, in happy serenity. She saw me every morning in our riding parties, every night at our balls. She was content. She took no thought for the morrow. No more did I.

The king was to visit Scotland at the close of the session, and I had received a gracious invitation to be of the party I had long been desirous to see the capital of the ancient kingdom, with whose beauties it is a disgrace to an Englishman not to be acquainted. Whenever the expedition was alluded to, I could perceive a smile twinkle in the eyes of Lady Winstanley. *Why,* I can't pretend to say.

One morning, towards the end of July, as I was coming out of Watier's to go home to bed, by that peculiar, greenish, aqua-marine light, through which one never sees anything moving in London but dandies and watchmen going their rounds, and squares, I was hailed by Sir John Harris. He was driving home from Carlton House, and sat swelling in his many-buttoned coat, as if it contained something to be proud of.

Though he wanted only to acquaint me with the exact day of our start in the royal yachts, which were to be steamed to Edinburgh, he saw fit to add, " But perhaps, after a match with a country baronet's daughter, you will not like to show among us ? "

"*Who* says I am about to marry anybody's daughter?" said I gravely.

" All the world."

I expressed myself with suitable emphasis concerning the folly and impertinence of all the world.

" I am glad to hear you plead not guilty, Cis," replied Sir John. " I have said what I can to exonerate you in certain quarters. I have gone so far as to contradict the report, at White's, on my own authority ; but no one believes me."

" I believe you," said I, drily.

" They all protest," continued Harris, not perceiving my sneer, " that you are perpetually with these people, and seen dancing with the girl, night after night."

" What would you have ? The Winstanleys invite me to their house. I can't help their having a daughter. But it does not follow that I am to marry her."

" It does, I can tell you, in the eyes of—"

I made a coarse rejoinder by way of interruption ; whereon, Sir John touched his fine horse on the flank, and away went the cab and its two brutes, at the rate of fifteen miles an hour.

But the blow had struck home. I made a very late, and very short, visit to Curzon Street that day. Instead of riding, I sauntered to the tennis-court.

On my return home, there was a little flummering three-cornered note from Lady Winstanley, reminding me that I was to meet them at Vauxhall, as she had a supper-party afterwards. To which I wrote a civil

2 B

answer, "how could I possibly forget, &c., &c." But
I never went.

The following day I was at Hampton races,—a party
from Oatlands. We made two pleasant days of it;
and on my return to town, I was so busy arming for
Scotland, that I found not a moment to call in Curzon Street.

At the end of the week came another note from
Lady Winstanley. "What was become of me? They
were anxious lest I should be indisposed." Not having courage to show my face in reply to these kind
inquiries, I stayed away: played more tennis, more
écarté; saw Nicholls about my stocks, Elvey about
refitting my dressing-case, and divers other persons,
concerning whom there is no need to trouble the
public. I went through all the duties, in short, of a
coxcomb on the eve of leaving town.

August was come—tawny, copper-coloured, heart-
achiferous August—the terminator of so many projects,
the blight of so many hopes. Lady Winstanley's last
little note informed me that they were about to leave
town; and as, though I had no thoughts of marrying
Helena Winstanley or Helena anybody else (how was
I to marry, a gentleman in lodgings, with an embarrassed income of five hundred a year?)—though I had
no thoughts, I say, of making her Mrs. Cis, I had just
as little desire to make her unhappy. So I resolved to
go and take leave of her in the handsomest manner,
attributing my previous neglect to indisposition, and
expressing a hope that we should meet in Lancashire
in the autumn.

I had lived on terms of sufficient confidence with
my brother-vagabonds at Watier's to know how very
few words whispered in a proper tone, to a girl who is
leaving town, by the fellow who has been flirting with
her throughout the season, suffice to send her into the
family coach, happy and contented, with renovated
hopes for another spring.

It was a deuced hot day; the sort of day when one

begins to think about shooting-shoes and percussion caps, and a destructive propensity connects itself with the name of the Moors. I sauntered into Gunter's on my way to Curzon Street, for a white currant ice, the only species of nutriment in the dog-days.

When cooled, composed, and comfortable, I drew down my light brown beaver hat, drew up my straw-coloured gloves, and nodding to the girl at the counter, as much as to say, "put it down to my account," lounged out of the shop, and through Lansdowne Passage ; that emblem of a younger brother's fortunes, mean, dispiriting, and without prospect, with over-flowing wealth and enjoyment bounding his views on either side.

I noticed, as I proceeded along Bolton Row, that grass was growing between the stones. But the Winstanleys' door discovered a still more positive proof of the emptiness of town. Straw was scattered there ; *not* the thick trusses announcing the advent of sons and heirs ; but scattered straws, as when magpies are building their nests, or family waggons departing to the family seat, with all the lumber not included in the family coach.

GONE ! No need to knock and inquire. The windows were closed. A maid of all-work was in charge of the house.

" Another vanished," sighed Cis, as he turned from the door—

(Perchè, dubbiosa ancor del suo ritorno,
Non s' assicura attonita la mente.)

" Well ! I am not sorry to be spared the leave-taking ! Helena is a sweet creature. I could scarcely have borne to witness her emotion."

Relieved from all fear of meeting them, I ventured that night to one of those charming little close-of-the-season parties (where one says and does all one forgot to do and say in June), at Lady Devereux's who, under Lady Harriet Vandeleur's pernicious instructions, had progressed into all that was "pleasant but wrong."

It was a charming little circle, a circlet of stars ; people who were of the expedition to Scotland, or above even that. I observed that Lady Harriet (who, like many women after losing their last vestige of good looks, had lost her last vestige of good-nature) seemed rejoiced to see me enter. I was consequently prepared to find her ready with a handful of sarcasms to fling in my face.

" You are quite right to go to Scotland, " was her reply to my announcement of my plans. " The further you get out of hearing of the outcry raised against you by those people the better."

" What outcry ?   What people ? "

" The country-baronet people, whose daughter you have used so ill. They are going to take her to Clifton. She is in a deep decline."

" The only daughter of a country baronet with whom I am much acquainted," said I, coolly, " is Miss Win-stanley, who is in blooming health at her father's place in Lancashire."

" I don't know what you call blooming health," retorted Lady Harriet.   " But rely upon it that her mother has been intrusting in strictest confidence to one (hundred) or two of her intimates, that Mr. Danby has behaved infamously to her daughter, paying her the most serious *attentions*, without serious *intentions* ; and —"

" I swear they ought to publish a Hand-book, or Flirting Manual, for the youth of both sexes, " interrupted I, " to prevent these misunderstandings.   I went constantly to Lady Winstanley's, because she constantly invited me.   How was I to know she intended me to marry her daughter ? "

" She invited you because she thought *you* intended it.   Everybody thought so."

" I can't see why everybody should trouble itself about the matter."

" Public flirtations are public property."

" Did people expect me to be uncivil to a pretty girl who did me the favour to gratify my passion for waltzing. I never saw more in Miss Winstanley than a partner. The ' everybody' you quote as sitting in judgment upon my proceedings is aware that I am a younger son, without a guinea at my disposal."

" A younger son, whose elder brother is in declining health, without issue male. *That* fact is pretty well known. Lady Cork asked me to present you to her, to be the lion of one of her dinner-parties, as the man who had got rid of a nephew standing between him and his inheritance ; the blackest of uncles since him of the Babes in the Wood. Fact, 'pon honour ! Don't look so indignant. You know how fond we English are of a sensation. One of the things which made you so much the fashion this season, was—"

" My reputation as an assassin ? Thank you, both for myself and the honour of London society. Miss Winstanley is quite justified in going into a decline, to get rid of such a monster. Meanwhile, pending my next murder, what say you to some *macédoine ?* "

But however indignantly I might scout Lady Harriet's assertion concerning Helena and her disappointment, I felt a little uneasy. Her touching look on seeing me whisper to my fair companion at the Irish ball recurred to my recollection. I would have given worlds that the family had been still in town, that I might pour balm into the wounds of that loving heart.

It may be a weakness. But I cannot bear the thoughts of a woman dying for love of a wretched thing like me.

> Imperet bellante prior, jacentem
> Lenis in hostem !

I swore that she should *not* die ; and proceeded to mutter Portia's charming panegyric upon the twofold virtue of mercy.

CHAPTER XIX.

I wonder how the deuce anybody could make such a world ;
for what purpose, for instance, dandies were ordained, and
kings, and fellows of colleges, and women of a certain age, and
many men of any age, and myself most of all.

                                        BYRON'S JOURNAL.

Ταυτοματον ἡμων καλλιω βουλευεται.

                                            MENANDER.

WE love to have a laugh against the ancients for
any little absurdity we dig out of Herculaneum, or
unroll out of the mummies of Egypt—that is, not a
laugh, but a prose ; the English would sooner get a
prose out of anything except ten per cent.

We love, I say, to inflict long exhortations upon
young gentlemen whose ideas are shooting in the preserves of classic lore, touching the vices of Epicurus,
the follies of Alcibiades, the enervation of the Syba-
rites, and so forth ; and if ever I am Lord Rector of
the University of Glasgow, to which, being a long-
sighted and long-eared fellow, I have pretensions, I
keep some uncommon fine writing in my desk, with
which I mean to pepper my address to the schools.
Now I only ask any reasonable being (and consequently do not address the inquiry to professors, ushers,
or schoolmasters), whether any weakness recorded of
the enervation of Rome or Greece ever exceeded the
make-believe sailorship of Royal yachting ?

Of all times and places where luxuriousness is *out* of
place, commend me to the wooden " castle on the
brine " of the British sailor. Whether we regard a ship
clergymanically, as a spot where a plank divides one
from eternity, or fine-gentlemanically, as a spot where
the human heart heaves with emotions anything but
tender, we must admit that manly plainness is the

style appropriate to the deep, deep sea. French varnish, satin bolsters, gilded lamps, and arabesque mouldings, are fit only for the vulgarity of a Yankee steam-packet. One of the wags of Watier's was pleased to say that, " in the fitting up of his yacht the King showed a great deal of taste, and bad enough it was."

Not being responsible for this error of judgment, I contented myself to enjoy our voyage in all the luxury of a progress, as brilliant by sea as Queen Elizabeth's by land ; and must own that even *my* apathy was deeply moved by the aspect of Edina, mad· as Ophelia with joy to welcome the King and his yacht's company.

My heart warms to the tartan. All that is left of poetry or hardihood in the British islands is concentrated in the land which *deserved* to have Sir Walter Scott among her sons. The Muse, steam-engined out of England, starved out of Ireland, has taken refuge, I suspect, in some Highland bothy, " o'er the muir among the heather ; " to commune with the storms of heaven and consecrate the earnest virtues of that peculiar race, who adhere to the virtues of their ancestors, though robbed of the pomp and circumstance of regality which endears the throne to the cockney perceptions of Cheapside.

People talk of the coolness, caution and reserve of the Scotch. I wish those who regard them as cold had seen them fling up their bonnets for King Geordie. Edinburgh not only honoured and obeyed us, but fed and cherished us, as though "bonnie Prince Charlie" were come again. It was generally noticed, indeed, in the papers of the day, that a distinguished individual in the royal suite bore a remarkable resemblance to the portraits of that unfortunate prince (produced, perhaps, by dressing after them), but whether the " individual " were myself, or Sir William Curtis, history must determine. But not a son of the mist threw his Highland flings more strenuously, or more ardently enjoyed the "sparkie" which inspired the effort.

I love a reel ; *"furor brevis"* perhaps, but one of the pleasantest little bits of madness in the world. Among the hills, and with a sonsie lass for a partner, I could keep it up from July to eternity. When Pope wrote about " wafting the soul upon a jig to heaven," he was clearly thinking of a Highland reel.

The only thing that kept down my spirits at Holyrood was the idea which, in spite of my efforts, *would* intrude, of what might be going on at Winstanley Manor. I had no means of obtaining information. Lady Harriet's intelligence might be accurate. With the fatal experiences of my past life, and the memory of Cintra and Venice vivid in my thoughts, I had some reason to be anxious. So long as I lived with Byron, the romance of life was smoked out of my head, like Tobit's fiend, by the extreme practicality of his habits. But after being some time absent from him, the finer impulses of the soul budded again, like an esculent cut down for the vulgar uses of the table, and sprouting anew at the return of spring.

I don't know how it may be with the young fellows of the present day. People eat better than they used ; and I have observed, that where the cooks are good the morals are indifferent. Perhaps, therefore, the lads I hear boasting of their conquests and flirtations may be less accessible than we used to be in *my* time to emotions of pity and terror, when we heard of some gentle creature sorely tempted by the fish-pond in her papa's pleasure-grounds, or the phial labelled "laudanum" in her mamma's medicine-chest. Poor Helena ! It was just the time that prussic acid began to be talked of as an accessory in heroic life. And the reader will be pleased to bear in mind that, as yet, stomach-pumps were not. After all, we London men have much to answer for. There is a worse place waiting for us than the limbo of vanity.

It was a relief to obtain, through Sir John Harris,

(by whose means all things were obtainable, from a mitre to a Guelphhood), his Majesty's sanction to my quitting the royal *cortège* at Edinburgh, and cutting across the country to Ormington Hall. I had made up my mind never to enter the domain again. But I found that his lordship was with Danby, in the south, and seized upon the pretext for visiting Lancashire, as a means of hearing something of Sir Gabriel Winstanley's daughter.

It is a hazardous thing to storm a country-house during the absence of the family. Though it was the month of August, Ormington looked as dreary and smelt as mouldy as the family vault. The country servants ran about as if I had headed an incursion of the Picts and Scots. The steward talked about killing a sheep (I would have knocked him down had he proposed a calf !) and everybody laboured hard to make me aware that my arrival was as much out of season as a hare in March.

The only person from whom I had hopes of learning what I wanted was the Reverend Dr. Droneby, who was lucky enough to have succeeded to the family-living which my Oxford follies placed within his reach ; a dry, solemn old chap, supposed to have considerable influence with Lord Ormington. His parsonage lay half-way between Ormington and the Manor ; so that he was likely to be well-informed touching the movements of the family. But it was scarcely possible to get a word out of him. He was, of course, a magistrate ; and looked at me precisely as if he had a warrant of the peace against me in his pocket. I was glad to bow myself out of his presence, with the information that the Winstanleys were not at home.

In reply to my inquiry as to what had taken them back so suddenly to the south, he replied, with a grim smile, that he believed the journey was undertaken on Miss Winstanley's account ; and looked so maliciously pleased when he said it, that I felt sure something afflicting was in progress. Recalling to mind the

horrible consequences of my delay in Lisbon, that very
night I got into the London mail.

An hour or two after my arrival in town, I breakfasted at my club.   The morning papers, fresh ironed,
were on the table ; and, while my dry toast was
crisping, I took up the *Morning Post.*   A disagreeable
presentiment assailed me as I unfolded the sheet.   On
my way from Cleveland Row up St. James's Street, I
had been instinctively repeating to myself those touching lines of Byron :—

> When we two parted
>   In silence and tears,
> Half broken-hearted,
>   To sever for years ;
> Pale grew thy cheek and cold,
>   Colder thy kiss !
> Surely that hour foretold
>   Sorrow to this !
> They name thee before me,
>   A knell to my ear ;
> A shudder comes o'er me,—
>   Why wert thou so dear ?

and I swear a knell *did* seem to sound in my ear,
and a shudder to gooseflesh me, as I cast my eyes
upon the tittle-tattle of that confounded *Morning
Post.*

Already the name of Winstanley had caught my eye.
Helena,—*my* Helena !

" We understand that Thursday next is appointed
for the solemnization of the hymeneals between the
young EARL OF WOLVERTON, and HELENA, third
daughter of SIR GABRIEL WINSTANLEY, BART., of
Winstanley Manor, in the county of Lancashire, and
Moy Park, in the county of Fermanagh."

Little Squeamy, by all that was preposterous. Little
Squeamy, and my Helena !

    *   *   *   *

I leave to the imagination of my readers, though
not the strong point of the British idiosyncrasy, the
fussy self-consequence of Lady Winstanley under such

circumstances. Just as the calfish elder sons united with her elder daughters had been thrown into the shade by the younger son of an earl, was the younger son swamped by the Right Hon. Earl of Wolverton, a man with a park, with a villa, with a house in town, with family diamonds, with everything a man who respects himself ought to possess, to propitiate the right-feeling mother of a right-thinking daughter. He was a donkey; but what then? Did not William Shakspeare allegorize, in Titania and Nick Bottom, the disproportionate passion of the fairest of fairies for a fellow with an ass's head?

I do not ask my readers to share my indignation on discovering from Wolverton, whom I met one day coming out of Gray's shop with a ring-case worth £900 in his hand, that he had been accepted on the very night of the Irish ball : that the red eyelids of Helena, and tremours of mamma, were tributes to *his* merits, not to mine.

Let me sum up in the fewest possible words the sequel of the adventure. Trusting to my *à-plomb* to prevent my chagrin from being apparent, I got through a visit of congratulation, and was invited to the wedding. There was not a soul in town to be the wiser for it. But I thought it would look well in the papers, for both our sakes, if I patronized the performance.

Let the public conceive the Mercury of John de Bologna, dressed by Stultz, curled by Smith, and booted by O'Shaughnessy, in order to picture to itself Cis Danby, while standing, as near as decency and the bishop would allow, to the altar of St. George's Church ; in contrast with the puny earl of Wolverton, a little black aphis, who wanted only a needle run through him to fasten him into a glass case, to form an interesting addition to any cabinet of natural history. I trust the contrast was dramatic. I flatter myself that Hyperion and a satyr occurred to others besides myself.

The insect hopped and skipped about merrily, however, at its wedding breakfast ; though poor Helena
was too blinded by tears to notice its saltations.   For
my part, I had courage to remain at the window with
the rest of the party, to see Sir Gabriel place her in
her bridal chariot and four, while the populace stood
by applauding.   Our eyes had not met since the
announcement of her marriage.   I am glad she did
not see me *then*, for I suspect I cut a sorry figure.
Sir Moulton Drewe, turning towards the breakfast-
table, invited me to take a glass of sherry with him,
in a tone that plainly inferred "You had better, or
you will never get through it."

This roused my courage.   On quitting the house, I
persuaded him to send away his cab (for, at that de-
populated season, any equipage but an errand-cart
depositing hares and partridges attracts attention),
and saunter to White's for a game at billiards.   It
was indispensable that he should do justice to the
steadiness of my hand ; which he *did*, to the tune of
a pony or two, before we parted.   At that moment,
I loathed him.   He was the friend and confidant of
Wolverton, and must have guessed, pretty nearly to a
pang, all I was suffering.

On reaching my lodgings, I despatched a letter to
Byron, telling him to expect me shortly in Italy.   But,
somehow or other, peevish and irresolute, I loitered in
England through the winter ; undergoing a severe
course of country-houses.   We are proud of our country-
house life ; and as regards good eating, drinking, sleeping, hunting, and shooting, nothing can exceed the
attraction of some dozen or so of our "residences of the
nobility and gentry," who are obliging enough to keep
open house for our diversion and their own ruin.

But, generally speaking, I have found the thing a
bore.   Sixteen hours of twenty-four is too much to
devote to one's fellow-creatures.   In a country-house,
one can never be alone.   When sinking under the
labour of having been agreeable and chatty through

the evening, fellows *will* come and talk scandal in one's room at night. The women get up piques among themselves, to relieve the monotony of the mornings when their male moieties are hunting or shooting ; or worse still, private theatricals or charades, to *prevent* the hunting or shooting. And then the groom of the chambers prohibits smoking in the bedrooms ; and, just as one gets inured to the detestabilities of the house, just as one has found out the deaf side of the host, the easiest armchair and coziest corner, it is time to go away, and begin one's experiences in

Fresh fields and pastures new.

As to the gaiety of a country-house in the Christmas holidays, it is as forced as its pineapples, as much "got up" as its theatricals. Either the party is as dull as a dormouse, a sort of vapid compromise between public and domestic life ; or enlivened by a monkey-man or two, invited for the purpose, and pestiferous to gentlemen who are disposed to take things in an easier manner. I could almost as soon amuse myself among a showman's puppets, as with those who must be moved by a master-hand, to endow their wooden nature with vitality.

All this time, the Wolvertons were at their place in Ireland ; and the papers gave an eloquent account of the roasting of oxen and firing of cannon to welcome the young countess, which must have caused the heart of Lady Winstanley to sing for joy.

Our first meeting after her marriage was at a concert given at Almack's by Rossini, the following spring ; where poor Maria Garcia made a *début* little in accordance with the after fame of Maria Malibran. While pressing as near as I could to the piano, to catch a glimpse of Rossini's masterly accompaniment to his wife's miserable singing, my attention was attracted by a tremendous blaze of diamonds. I seemed to recollect the face to which that gorgeous tiara and those splendid girandoles imparted lustre. I looked

again.   The cheeks were hollow, the eyes far less
brilliant than the diamonds. Beauty was there, but
beauty on the wane.   Even when convinced by the
observations of those around me that it was no other
than Lady Wolverton, I could scarcely bring myself to
believe that the bony arms and shoulders before me
ever belonged to the fair, round, symmetrical figure of
my Helena. She looked worn, woebegone, harassed.
Was the gratification derived from the sparkling
diamond tiara sufficient compensation for all this ?

A day or two afterwards, I met Wolverton at
White's. Bustling up to me, he made a sort of
ostentatious show of inviting me to his house ;
talked about the taste displayed by Gillow in fitting
it up, as if to decoy me into a visit ; and hinted at the
merits of his cook, as if *that* were a sufficient induce-
ment.   I would rather have " chopped " at the " Blue
Posts," as I once did, fifteen years before, with
Sir John Harris, before our faces were as well known
on the *pavé* as the effigy of Britannia on a penny-
piece.

In process of time, the countess of Wolverton was
presented at court ; the countess of Wolverton was
most graciously welcomed by the king ; the countess
of Wolverton figured in the lists of Almack's and at
the *fêtes* of D—— House.   I hope she was satisfied ;
that is, I hope Lady Winstanley was satisfied. But
she did not look so. A son and heir was in expectation.   It might be that such an accession was indispensable for the completion of Helena's worldly peace.
It was clear that *something* was wanting.

I left cards at her door, sent an excuse to Wolverton's formal invitation to dinner ; and, to spare *her*
feelings or my own, was careful to avoid her amid the
mobs of fashionable life.   One night, at a Saturday
supper party at Lady L.'s, after the opera, I met her
on the stairs ; and, seeing that her situation rendered
it difficult to her to ascend, could not avoid offering
her my arm. I did not speak, however, more than

the mutter indispensable to the occasion; and she accepted my aid in the same silence. We walked up slowly together, without exchanging a syllable, then separated. It was the only time I approached her after her marriage; the trembling of her arm and mine mutually betraying to each the agitation of two persons but a year before all in all to each other; and now, far less than nothing.

The most offensive part of the business was the self-importance of that wretched little item of humanity, Squeamy, I beg his pardon, the earl of Wolverton. Who will presume to undervalue the importance of birth and fortune, when we find them invest a pigmy with the attributes of a giant; and make a man of a mouse? Thanks to this twofold endowment, had not the most insignificant atom in human nature pinned to his sleeve the handsomest girl in London?

Thousands and thousands of times have I wished I had been at Jericho, Genoa, Coblentz, or anywhere else, sooner than have come in contact with Helena, that night at the supper party. Just as she was dropping my arm in the lobby, the light of the lustre over our head fell upon her half-averted face, betraying certain glitterings, *not* proceeding from her diamond coronet, since she wore round her head only a garland of blush roses. Years afterwards, her tearful eyes haunted me. *Those* diamonds were as thoroughly *my* gift to Helena as the tiara of the Right Hon. Earl of Wolverton. All I had done in return for her young affection was to wither up her beauty, and tinge her bridal honours with misery and remorse.

Even altered as she was, however, the world was amazingly struck by her loveliness, her simple dignity of air, her gentleness of manner. The fine ladies were astonished to see anything so distinguished emerge from the park of a Lancashire baronet. The fine gentlemen whispered, " By Jove, Cis ! you are a more prudent fellow than *I* should have been in your place."

Lady Winstanley, meanwhile, went fussing every day to her daughter's fine house in Berkeley Square, seeming to have lost all recollection of her elder daughters and their calves. It was a bitter mortification that, in Helena's delicate state of health, Lord Wolverton would not hear of giving a ball ; not only because to a vulgar woman a ball appears a mighty triumph, indispensable to confer the honours of canonization in London society, but because she thought that Helena owed to the younger sister the chances of promotion insured by such an advertisement. But the little earl was inflexible. When he had made up his little mind, it was as firm as the minds of bigger men.

All the time, I was secretly patting him on the back ; encouraging his resistance, and begging him, above all things, to beware of giving way to the influence of Lady Winstanley. I described a mother-in-law to him in such terms, that I flatter myself he made himself sufficiently disagreeable to avenge my wrongs and those of Helena.

Meanwhile, balls delighting me no longer nor ball-givers either, I profited by the weather of a delicious June, to betake myself to Cowes. I had nothing to do in London—that is, London had nothing for me to do ; and at a certain period of the year, provided the summer do not set in *too* severe, I am usually affected with the marine epidemy peculiar to the English constitution. I suppose it is because Britannia rules the waves that Britannia's sons and daughters, cetaceous monsters ! cannot rest contented without once a year rushing *into* them.

I am almost ashamed, at this time of day, to indulge in a rhapsody about yachting ; now, as vulgarized as coaching, or steeple-chasing, or any other pastime of the Paradise of Fools. But when I and George IV first indulged in the delicious recreation, regattas were in their infancy, and the high seas a highway for gentlemen. I used to delight in it, when one had the Isle of Wight almost to one Self; that is, almost to the little knot of elect which ought to be esteemed as one man.

Merepark, who was the fortunate proprietor of the *Morning Star*, as well as of the charming Lady Theresa, proposed to me to accompany him that year, in a cruise to the Mediterranean. Lady Merepark was to be of our crew. I had rather she had stayed at Cowes; but *that* regarded the will of her ladyship's and the *Morning Star's* lord and master. I did not, however, so much regret her being with us, when, on fine moonlight nights, the harmonious couple were good-natured enough to amuse me and the dolphins by singing duets; and if most " silver-sweet sound lovers' tongues by night," I can assure my readers that the Notturni of Lord and Lady Merepark as we sat together on deck, enjoying the fragrant breeze from shore off the coast of Sicily, were as mellifluous as the song of the Sirens.

I liked Merepark's singing as much better than his talking, as I had once been disposed to prefer his conversation to his vocal efforts. Since his secession from diplomatic life, he was growing domestic as George III.; resided three-fourths of the year at Chippenham Park, and was, of course, as crotchety and dogmatical as all people who choose to exempt themselves from the modifying influences of society.

From the days of Plato, I scarcely know an individual qualified to think for himself, in opposition to his times and country. It requires about a million of men to form an opinion with a degree of force intitling it to be stereotyped. I hold (I fear it may be a Danbyical dogma), that there are about a dozen capital Thinkers in Europe, patented to have notions of their own; viz., London, Paris, Petersburg, Vienna, Rome, Berlin, Madrid, Munich, and so forth. These have a right to argue among themselves, on all topics affecting the enlightenment or melioration of mankind. But little rap-on-the-knuckles disputations between the egotism of John Thompson and the egotism of Tom Johnson, or between Cis Danby and Lord Merepark, are just as much to the purpose as the spitting of tabby cats, or the snarling of terriers.

Whenever Merepark began to dogmatize, accordingly, I said to him, as nature did to Béranger,

Chante, chante, pauvre petit !

which he did, divinely ; and left the balance of power and of the budget to those M.P.'d into the privilege of prosing. Lady Merepark did not look at all obliged to me. She knew, probably, that the whims and fancies which *I* did not choose to accept as infallible, would be inflicted on *her*, like a papal bull, *per* tyranny matrimonial, at Chippenham Park.

Poor thing ! She was the pattern of a wife. How little I surmised, when in my puppy-days at Maybush Lodge, I pronounced her to be a nonentity, how charming a compound part of the monotonous domestic happiness of an English earl, such a nonentity might become. She was the very thing for a nine months-in-the-country sort of life ; a loving mother to little Lord Chippenham, and a loving wife to his father. All her ambitions were bounded by the park paling.

If I should ever live to accomplish a park paling, I trust Providence will send me precisely such a wife. And why not ? It is impossible to guess how one may end. The jocose old screw of a lawyer, whom I had found rubbing his hands in a barn in Southampton Buildings, in 1810, was now, in 1823, a wealthy baronet, residing in a handsome house in Chandos Street, Cavendish Square ;—Pepper-and-salt being replaced by a butler, square and solemn as the Principal of a college, but better dressed.

Such progresses are of daily occurrence in England. A wealthy landowner's man of business is as sure to fatten in means, as his stalled oxen in flesh ; and a baronetcy is cheap requital for such services as killing off a young lady likely to inveigle one of the junior branches into matrimony ; more particularly when there is a borough in the family, and only one younger son to provide for.

It is true Sir Joseph Hanmer had achieved the comforts of life after losing the five senses that might have enabled him to enjoy them ; and now, he lay, like a superannuated wolf in his lair, feeble and edentated, yet shunned and dreaded through his former ill-repute. The creature had even sat in parliament for half a session. Think of such a man as old Hanmer being called, by such a man as Danby, "my friend, the Honourable Member for Sneakington!"

I know not why I recall, at this portion of my memoirs, the name of one who occupies small space in my regard ; unless because the reminiscences therewith connected were painfully revived by a visit I paid to Cintra, while touching at Lisbon in our cruise.

The Mereparks were, of course, occupied with the city, the opera, the embassy, Mafra, the Necessidades, the Ajudas, and the various lions of the place. We were to be at anchor only a couple of days. The first of these I devoted to a pilgrimage of grace to San José.

The quinta was all but in ruins. Old Barnet's property had been converted into a chancery suit by Messrs. Hanmer and Snatch ; and was, perhaps, the remote origin of the comfortable house in Chandos Street, Cavendish Square. The roof was falling in, and there were stems of oats which had sprung up and withered between the flooring of the drawing-room, where poor Yilko formerly sidled on his stand.

The garden was a wilderness. The orange-orchard had run almost as wild as the chestnuts and cork-trees springing from the rifted rocks of the Peninha. The espaliers of myrtle, untrimmed for years, were sheeted with snow-white blossoms ; closing up, by their intermingling branches, the road to the postern door. For

years, no one had passed that way. It was useless to
think of reaching the cemetery in that direction.

It was easy enough to make the circuit by the
public entrance. To accomplish this, I had to penetrate through the grove of pine-trees; of all the objects
that presented themselves, the one which had experienced least alteration in the lapse of those thirteen
busy years. Sir Joseph's chancery job had effected no
change in the mystic characters upon the venerable
bark of those majestic trees. The same mossy fibrous
ground was under my feet ; the same dim, chastened,
cathedral-like light was diffused around me.

From this mysterious twilight, I emerged into the
little burying-ground. Death had not been inactive.
Of the many despatched by the caprice of northern
physicians to end their consumptive days in Lisbon, a
few repose at Cintra. Since my last visit to the spot,
tombs had arisen, marble columns, crosses of granite
within trellised enclosures, gloomy with cypresses or
bright with flowers.

I passed them by unheeded. I made my way straight
towards the spot overhung by the outstretching branches
of the bay-tree. I could have reached the spot blind-
fold. And it was well for me that my memory was so
retentive, for not a trace remained of the stone tablet.
Within the railing I had caused to be erected around
it before I quitted Lisbon, the honeysuckle planted by
my hand had sprung up in wanton luxuriance ; and no
friend of the family being at hand to direct or remu-
nerate the gardener of the cemetery to whom was consigned the care of the other tombs and funereal gardens, it formed an entangled mass of blossoms over the
grave, concealing all record of her who slept beneath.

The sun was crimsoning the west when I reached
the spot ; and the overpowering fragrance which evening dew extracts from the pale tassels of the woodbine
pervaded the air.

And it was thus the memory of Emily deserved to
be embalmed. Nature remained faithful to a grave to

which none survived to offer the tribute of their tears. I looked towards the craggy summits visible above the dark cypress trees, on which the evening sun was shedding its effulgence, and prayed that from the regions of the blessed the anguish of my soul might bring down forgiveness of my fault.

Next day we sailed for England. But the influence of these renovated associations saddened me for the remainder of the voyage. I could enjoy nothing ; neither the sweet music of the Mereparks nor the calmness ot those halcyon summer nights so far more enjoyable than the fervour of garish day.

The Mereparks having engagements with visitors at Chippenham Park, altered their plan of touching at Cowes, and made straight for Southampton. It was a delicious evening on which we sailed up the river. After the languid atmosphere of the sweet south there was something refreshing in the stirring air of home ; more especially intermingled as it was with the breath of gardens and emanation of the oak-woods from the shores of the Southampton river.

As we sat together on deck I persuaded Merepark to indulge me for the last time with a favourite ballad, the words of which originated, I suspect, in the sunny climes we had been traversing.

She look'd so fair when, fresher than the morn,
   Her happy laugh rang through the greenwood boughs ;
She look'd so fair when, from the golden corn,
   Tearing the wild flowers to adorn her brows ;
She look'd so fair when, calm, at dewy even
   Watching the streamlet's waves go listless by ;
She look'd so fair beneath the moonlit heaven,
   Her earnest face uplifted to the sky !

How fair, when o'er her thrilling lute she hung
   Till from its chords unearthly music stole !
How fair, when, whisperingly, her faltering tongue
   Reveal'd her modest eloquence of soul !
How fair, when, in the old cathedral aisle,
   Upon her knees absorb'd in silent pray'r ;
The poor still crowding round to court her smile,
   As though a saint from heaven were kneeling there

How fair, how passing fair, when in the dance
　Her buoyant footsteps wild outflew the rest ;
How fair, how passing fair, when at her glance
　The proud grew humble, and the humble blest.
How fair !—And yet, too young to LOVE !—The spell
　Was yet unspoken !—But the time may come !
Ah, hush !—ah, hush ! Hear ye the funeral knell ?—
　Yon nodding bearse hath borne her to her home !

But it was no moment for a strain so doleful.　The Mereparks were in high spirits because about to be re-united to their children and park palings ; I, from the force of sympathy.　The tide took us in at dusk.　The cheerful lights of the city were gleaming in all directions ; and the familiar cries of an English crowd greeted us as a friendly salutation.

On arriving at the hotel we were eager for dinner ; hailing as delicacies those much contemned simplicities of cod and oyster sauce, partridges and panada, with other items of English fare that would make Paris die of indigestion.　Merepark and I resolved to make a carouse of it.　I never felt in higher glee.　I had a charming autumn before me : first, a week at the Royal Cottage ; next, a capital party for pheasant shooting at —— Abbey ; and after roughing it for a few weeks, the smooth sumptuosities of a lordly establishment are not to be despised.

As we were to start early, Lady Merepark wished me good night when she retired from the dinner-table ; and Merepark and I ordered a fresh bottle of claret, drew our chairs closer to the fire, and began to give way to the social feeling which the first fire of the season is sure to inspire.　England is the only country in the world where men shut out the chaste creation and prose over their wine ; which I conclude is what renders our morals so superior to the residue of civilized Europe.

On that occasion we indulged.　We talked over adventures of our old Downing Street days, and laughed over events of more recent occurrence at Palermo, till we neither of us saw any fault in our claret, a proof that we did not see very clearly. Nay, having persuaded Merepark, who, though now on dry land, was half-seas-over, to indulge me with a drinking song he had learnt at

Fair Cadiz, rising o'er the dark blue sea,

from a rollicking Spanish muleteer, the room began to be filled with shapes resembling those that clustered round the loneliness of St. Anthony. I have little doubt that Byron, when galloping, half-mad, half-intoxicated, through the pine-woods, after solemnizing those terrible obsequies of Shelley, felt much as I felt that night.

I know not what else prompted me to blaspheme as I did all that was good and fair. If in Satan's memo-randum-book be enregistered the abominable falsehoods interchanged between man and man on such occasions, the account will contain many a crime unwhipped of justice ; and Merepark's maudlin wonder and applause encouraged me to exaggeration, till I began to describe all sorts of imaginary adventures with the graver of Callot and the periods of Matt. Lewis.

At last it was time to retire. The fire was burnt out. The wine was drunk out. The candles were about to follow their example, and disappear also. We went laughing and pushing each other upstairs like two silly schoolboys. Everybody was in bed in the house, but the drowsy waiter who had sat up to give us our bed-candles. When we reached No. 4, Merepark, after several ineffectual attempts to turn the handle of the door, blundered in, wishing me good night, while I proceeded towards the end of the corridor, to the room where, before dinner, I could just remember having washed my hands.

I suppose the wine I had drunk did not tend to in-crease the clearness of my perceptions ; for, having reached the one I conceived to be mine, I threw it open with violence, bursting in, to take possession of my territories.

An exclamation of "Hush!" was the first sound
that saluted me.   Unnecessary, however, for the
startling spectacle before me sufficed to paralyze my
faculties.   It was the chamber of death.   A gorgeous
coffin,—*two* gorgeous coffins, with lights burning at the
head, and domestics in deep mourning, keeping watch
over the dead.

Sobered by the spectacle, and deeply ashamed of my
intrusion, I was retreating in haste.   Already the
waiter was at my heels, with apologies, explanations,
and offers to conduct me to my own room.

"They had said nothing about *the body*, thinking it
might be disagreeable to the lady to sleep under the
same roof with a corpse.   But they could assure me
that it was only there for the night.   The funeral had
arrived late in the evening, and was to be embarked
early in the morning for Ireland.   The bodies were on
their way to my lord's family vault in the county of
Limerick."

I had reached the threshold of my own door when
the fellow made this communication.   Staggering to a
chair, I had just strength to demand the *name* of the
family seat in the county of Limerick.   I had not
courage to pronounce that of the dead.

"I think the butler said Craig's Castle, sir; but
Lord Wolverton has another seat in——"

 * * * * * *

I heard no more.   Helena, my Helena!—While I
was defiling her innocent name, by words that ought
to have festered my lying lips, she lay dead—dead—
dead—within my reach.

The uproar of my senseless merriment must have
shaken the heavy folds of her pall.

CHAPTER XX.

As the warm heart expands, the eye grows clear,
And sees beyond the slave's and bigot's grasp.
                                        PROCTOR.

One who saw,
Observed nor shunn'd the busy scenes of life,
But mingled not ; and 'mid the din, the stir,
Lived as a separate spirit.   ROGERS.

PEOPLE are apt to assert that nothing consoles us more for the loss of those dear to us, than to find their death a cause of general lamentation.

This may be the case with statesmen and heroes, whose fame is the breath of nations. But as regards a young and delicate woman, the regrets showered upon her grave serve only to increase the bitterness of grief. I could not take up a newspaper just then, but it was filled with paragraphs relative to "the bereaved Earl of Wolverton," or "the late lovely and lamented Countess of Wolverton." There was a detailed account of the funeral and the " affecting embarkation of the bodies of the mother and child. All that the worst taste could perpetrate in the way of fine writing, was twopence-a-lined by the *Limerick Chronicle*, announcing in letters half a yard long, the arrival of THE CORPSE (how I hate that word!) of the son and heir of the ancient house of Wolverton ; as if the little atom of clay, deposited on a spot wherein it had never exercised even its puny powers of vitality, were worthy of mention in the same page with the wreck of all that was gentle, all that was beautiful ; martyrized by the splendours of life, as though her diamond tiara had been a crown of thorns.

How often do the old fix their cold, callous, lustre-

less gaze upon the young, either living or dead, as if
they were *too* young to have suffered.   Blockheads.!
It is *only* the young who are capable of real sorrow or
real enjoyment.   In after life, the selfishness of human
nature supplies a styptic for every wound !   and Utili-
tarianism has her pockets filled with Family Cerate, to
salve it over.   We recall to mind that it is not worth
while to harass our few remaining years with regrets,
that all will soon be over.   We call this philosophy.
It is simply decadence of mind under the growing
ascendancy of material nature.

In the sunshine of girl and boyhood, on the contrary,
the expanding blossoms of the soul are readily
withered by sudden frost.   To the very young heart,
the stab of the moral assassin conveys a death-blow.
At thirty, one calls in a surgeon ; at ——ty, the flesh
has become mere cartilage, and defies the rapier's
edge.   Though snatched from earth with the down of
childhood still soft upon their cheeks, the heartbreak
contained beneath the pall of Juliet, or the velvet
coffin of the Countess of Wolverton, were sufficient to
have tinged a long after-life with despair.

I knew it.   *I* understood it.   The gossips of society
observed, that autumn, over their pineapples and
peaches, their claret and Burgundy, or clustering
round their blazing fires after dinner, with due regard to
their satin dresses and Mecklin lace, " What a shocking
thing it was that poor Lady Wolverton dying in child-
bed so soon after her marriage.   Such a beautiful
creature, with such a charming house in town, and
such a fine place in Hampshire.   Really everything
to make life desirable.   I wonder whether Lord Wolverton will marry again ?"   No one but Cecil Danby
knew what a glorious escape she had had from the
charming house in town, and fine place in Hampshire ;
that she had been tormented into avenging herself
upon an ingrate by a brilliant match, then broken
her heart, offering to Heaven the atonement of her

tears, and the sacrifice of penitence and prayer. But she was at peace ; yea ! at peace. Nothing could touch her further.

I hope and believe that I *felt* on the occasion. Not indeed with a sorrow as in my brighter days at Cintra. But when I struggled back into society the following spring, scarcely a fellow at White's but saluted me with " Hallo, Cis, my boy ! What on earth have you been doing with yourself ? You look as if you came out of the tombs."

Why admit to such men that I had been undergoing martyrdom ? Had I displayed to them the wounds of my agony, instead of being convinced, like the incredulous Apostle, they would have persisted in their derision. I did well to hold my peace.

Will the world believe, I mean the real world, that these scorners attributed my anguish to *another* death, which had occurred in the interval, that of Lady Susan Danby ? They thought me anxious lest Danby should marry again, and disappoint my expectations by a son and heir.

They were, perhaps, justified in the surmise ; for if *my* despondency had another origin, the exultation of Lord Ormington was disgracefully genuine. It was frightful to see with what glee he wore his broad hems and black coat. I doubt whether any family event, since Danby's wedding, had inspired him with such ardent imaginings as poor Lady Susan's funeral. He saw apparitions of crowned children rising out of her grave, like those in the vision vouchsafed by the weird sisters to Macbeth.

He was not, however, the only person who speculated upon the event. Lady Harriet Vandeleur, now approaching her fiftieth year, who had adopted habits more becoming her years than flirting or flippancy, began to fire off batteries of tracts and serious books at the widower. She was grown evangelical, much in the same spirit of wrongheadedness she had once fan-

cied herself an infidel; and it was with a view of
enlarging her sphere of benevolence, that perhaps she
thought the rent-roll of the future Lord Ormington
might be advantageously added to her jointure.

Danby was a person who took all things so quietly,
that I verily believe she thought herself making an
impression, by her strenuousness in advising him about
the bringing up of his daughter, and her officious
counsels on topics too sacred to be introduced irre-
verently into pages like these; when, in fact, he
listened without hearing, regarding the former
bosom-friend of his mother as a sort of troublesome
aunt.

Lord Ormington, with his usual charity, chose to
infer that I promoted her Ladyship's views, in order
to secure myself from the new Arthur who might
arise from a more propitious alliance. He was mistaken. If I did not vehemently oppose the foolish
woman's advances, it was because I knew my brother
need not be placed upon his guard against giving such
a successor to Lady Susan. I was, in fact, too deeply
overpowered by a new and most unexpected affliction,
to trouble myself with her proceedings. An event
occurred which wrung from my lips the same exclamation as from those of Trelawney, "The world has
lost its greatest man; I, my best friend!"

BYRON, who, to borrow the elegant quotation of
Moore, was fated to gather in Greece a crown of palm
or ,cypress, "*o cipresso, o palma acquistar.*" Byron
sank under the influence of bad diet and a bad climate,
at Missolonghi; or, to speak more truly, was bored to
death by the practicalities of war-making, and the
impracticability of the Philhellenic Committee.

The world raised its usual foolish clamour over the
grave. The dull preached. The bitter sneered. *The
wise* WEPT! And lo! his name is excluded from the
pomps of Westminster Abbey, where only the right
divine entitles the sinners of this world to be inurned

and inscribed for evermore in the land's language, and the memory of all who venerate the glories of genius, even when tarnished with human frailty; like the improvidence of Scott, or the greater sin of the greater Bacon.

As Pindar sings, "let the ravens croak and clamour, the eagle pursues his flight towards the sun :"

$$\Delta\iota\grave{o}\varsigma \ \pi\rho\grave{o}\varsigma \ \check{o}\rho\nu\iota\chi\alpha \ \vartheta\epsilon\tilde{\iota}o\nu.$$

Deeply depressed, I confined myself that season to the society of my own family. I was fond of dining quietly with Danby, in Connaught Place. My little niece was now ten years old; the most graceful and engaging creature I ever beheld. All the leisure my brother could spare from the duties of public life, he devoted to the education of Jane. But the indulgence and adoration with which he surrounded her, prevented her from imbibing the pedantic formality usually affecting the mind of a girl modelled by instruction unfitted for her sex. She was gentle and childish in manners, as became her years; and her singular intelligence rendered her a charming accession to our family circle.

Of Julia, too, I was the frequent guest. But the society of Herries I could have dispensed with. My brother-in-law already wrote himself Right Hon., and occupied a lucrative post in the administration. But he was so completely be-officed, so overwhelmed with business, that the parish dustman is more his own master. In conversation, it was easy to see that he never afforded more than the attention of the eye. In argument, he fought with a reed. He disdained conquest. He cared not for victory, unless in the House or before the Privy Council. He had no longer a part in the ordinary enjoyments of life; no longer leisure to be glad or sorry; his very thoughts and feelings were technical.

The same harassing anxieties that worried poor Lon-

donderry out of his wits and Canning out of his life,
deprived Herries of all pretence to domestic comfort.
When a man rises in public life by abilities and industry, his highborn colleagues take care that plenty
of occupation shall tax his abilities and industry.
Like the mules expiring in the sunshine, while toiling
with heavy loads of the precious metals of the Cor-
dilleras, Herries was overwhelmed with the greatness
of his charge. But for the sympathy of his wife, he
would have sunk under his task. But the weariness
of which he was conscious, he of course inflicted upon
others.

There was another member of the family from
whose company I humbly request the reader to spare
all exclamations of surprise at finding me derive satisfaction : Lady Ormington.

I never pretend to virtues beyond my calibre; and
shall not waste my ink in affecting that it was filial
piety, or gratitude for the partiality lavished on my
cockadehood, which induced me to spend my evenings
in her ladyship's drowsy boudoir, whenever I could
induce Miss Richardson to solicit a holiday. Prematurely aged, she would sit for hours coaxing a little
King Charles's spaniel, almost without uttering a
syllable ;—like a tree motionless beside some rolling
stream.

There we sat together ; musing, if not amusing; in
the self-same chamber where my first survey in the
glass of my own beauties made a coxcomb of me for
life; and where I had seen her ladyship rehearse her
worldly scenes of serious comedy. The gay Axminster
carpet had given way to one of more sombre hue ; and
the great toilet-glass was replaced by a highly varnished *armoire*, containing within its polished ma-
hogany, as a marble sarcophagus conceals unsightly
bones, patent medicines of every dye. The old furniture,—the chairs and tables, were the same as of old ;
grown dingy and quizzical by contrast with modern

inventions. I fear the human lumber of the spot shared the fate of its chairs and tables.

But it was on this very account I felt so comfortable with my mother. We had progressed over hill and dale together. Our selfishnesses were enlisted under the same banner. Our interests were in common. If we did not love each other so passionately as some mothers and their offspring, each loved the other as much as it loved any other created being besides its Self.

A warm room, excellent tea, and an amusing periodical, always awaited me in Hanover Square; and I suppose it needs no other proof that I was in the wane of my rouéism, than that some of my pleasantest evenings in the summer of 1824 were spent by Lady Ormington's fireside. So long as we can interest ourselves in a book, we are not much to be pitied. Whoever reads with a warm, cordial, and expansive spirit, becomes king, knight, pope, philosopher, as he listeth :

> Ad summam, sapiens uno minor est Jove, dives,
> Liber, honoratus, pulcher, rex denique regum.

For Jupiter, read of course, King George; the Jove of *my* Olympus.

The proposition has been made a text for prize essays, whether the king who dreams every night that he is a beggar, or the beggar who dreams every night that he is a king, be the happier man. On this point I have not made up my mind. I seldom *do* make up my mind. All questions are to *me* open questions. But I am satisfied that among the faculties most to be dreaded for the young, and most to be desired for the old, is a busy fancy. Reverie is the bane of twenty, the antidote of fourscore.

I was somewhat betwixt the two, when I found solace in dreaming away my evenings in Lady Ormington's boudoir. I fancied myself hand to hand, heart

to heart, with Byron on the sands of the Lido, or
among the green pastures of Vévay; exchanging
speculations on those solemn topics on which men
have speculated for four thousand years, without
having so much as determined whether the tree of
knowledge were a nonpareil or a crab. I fancied
myself watching once more the lightning-like corus-
cations of his genius, as developed in word and
glance.

I was living, in short, in the past. One is apt to
retire from the scene of life, like a Lord Chamberlain
from the presence of Majesty, *à reculons*. At thirty-
five, one's pleasantest days lie in the rear. One can't
help looking back. I do not mean that some men at
five-and-thirty are not, like oaks and yews at a
century, still in their infancy. But a Cis Danby
becomes at forty " a very foolish, fond old man,"—more
foolish and more fond than Lear at double the age.
After undergoing two or three desperate heartquakes,
the structure of one's nature loses its equilibrium.
Cracks are perceptible on all sides, and one's mind
exhibits as perplexing a study for the curious in
mathematics, as the leaning Tower of Pisa.

The first public indication I gave of moral decrepitude was by accepting a place at Court. I refer my
readers to the Red Book of 1825, for the specification
of my office. My motives for re-entering public life, I
rise to explain.

As regards human nature in general, we have Milton's
authority for the servility of mankind. " Half the
world," saith he, " prefers living under masters." As
regards human nature in my own person, I found the
vindictive hints of Lord Ormington that my inactivity
arose from views upon the inheritance of my brother,
every day more insupportable; and I was consequently
grateful to the friendship with which his Majesty, on
his return from his tour, once more tendered me an
appointment in his Household. I was literally forced

into the assumption of ambition, by having incurred an odium inevitable among the evils of an origin obliquitous as mine.

Moreover, I felt capable of doing the state, or rather the country, some service. I have dwelt modestly on my personal merits; conceiving them to be sufficiently manifested in my deeds as the prowess of the lion is attested by the whitening bones of his victims, heaped round his den. But it becomes my duty to declare that my inborn graces were now refined by much travel, and much converse with all that is best and brightest in civilized Europe.

To extinguish such acquirements in the obscurity of private life, was not altogether fair. The true patriot sacrifices himself to the interests of his fatherland. If the sale of the Houghton collection of pictures to a foreign power were an act of profanation, I felt that I should " stand accountant for as great a sin," in withholding from public example those merits of mind and manners which so amply fulfilled the promise of my cockadehood.

The public hailed my appointment with satisfaction. The Court was regarded just then as the head-quarters of taste. The Court gave the law to the town, the town to the country. There was no appeal.

A considerable lull was perceptible in public affairs. With the exception of Spain (a country, which having an unlucky knack of matching its right hand against its left, was, as usual, at fisticuffs with itself), there was very little fighting going on, except among the patronesses of Almack's. The Holy Alliance still consolidated the kingdoms of the earth. The three-cornered hats of the Jesuits had the best of it in France; the cocked-hats of the standard footmen of the exclusives, in London. Fashion here, and fanaticism there, was the ascendant influence. The becalming, in short, produced the same results as that described by Coleridge, in the Ancient Mariner.

2 D

A satisfactory state of things to me. My notion of enjoyment is to take the busiest life in the quietest way ; to sit in a patent reclining chair, and behold affairs of state delineated by a camera-obscura. I detest a hermitage, whose mossy couch is full of earwigs, and whose maple dish full of raw carrots. My vegetables must be dressed *à la maître d'hôtel;* and my mattresses, not my shirt, be of horsehair. In other words, the Royal Cottage comprised my *summum bonum* of human felicity.

The time is gone by for kings to retire from the world into a cloister. The example of that wrong-headed emperor, Charles V., has convinced his royal successors, that since, in all communities, intrigues and factions must arise, it is less worrying to arbitrate the squabbles of lords and ladies, than the animosities of frowsy monks.

It was about three months after accepting my appointment, that one night, at a charming party—— But alas ! dear reader, it is denied me to gratify your curiosity with the narration.

Just as I find myself at ease in your company,— just as I have attained unbounded confidence in your discretion,—just as I was about to intrust to you some of the choicest adventures of my life,—comes the fatal fiat of the publisher. The pages allotted me to fill, are expended. No reprieve, no renewal of my lease, no sixth act to the melodrama ! The brimstone and blue lights are blazing. The green curtain waits only the signal of the prompter's whistle, to conceal me for ever from your view.

But must it be indeed my last appearance ? Is there no hope of being called for, like other favourite performers, when the piece is at an end ?

Dear Public,—dear *unindulgent* Public,—

I do, as is my duty,
Honour the shadow of your shoe-tie,—

For once, be generous as well as just. Shake me
kindly by the hand at parting, and admit that it will
give you pleasure to meet me again. At all events,
confess that seldom have you been beguiled into idling
away an hour or two of your precious life by a more
gentlemanly fellow, or more agreeable companion,
than,

Your most obedient humble servant,

CECIL THE COXCOMB.

THE END

COX AND WYMAN, PRINTERS, GREAT QUEEN STREET, LONDON.

BY CAPTAIN MARRYAT.

In fcap. 8vo, price Eighteenpence each, boards.

PETER SIMPLE.	NEWTON FORSTER.
MIDSHIPMAN EASY (Mr.).	DOO FIEND (The).
KING'S OWN (The).	VALERIE. (Edited.)
RATTLIN THE REEFER. (Edited.)	POACHER (The).
JACOB FAITHFUL.	PHANTOM SHIP (The).
JAPHET IN SEARCH OF A FATHER.	PERCIVAL KEENE.
PACHA OF MANY TALES (The).	NAVAL OFFICER.

" Marryat's works abound in humour—real, unaffected, buoyant, overflowing humour. Many bits of his writings strongly remind us of Dickens. He is an incorrigible joker, and frequently relates such strange anecdotes and adventures, that the gloomiest hypochondriac could not read them without involuntarily indulging in the unwonted luxury of a hearty cachinnation."—*Dublin University Magazine.*

BY THE RIGHT HON. B. DISRAELI.

Price 1s. 6d. each, boards.

THE YOUNG DUKE.	CONINGSBY.
TANCRED.	SYBIL.
VENETIA.	ALROY.
CONTARINI FLEMING.	IXION.

Price 2s. each, boards; or, in cloth, 2s. 6d.

HENRIETTA TEMPLE.	VIVIAN GREY.

BY J. F. COOPER.

In fcap. 8vo, price Eighteenpence each, boards; or, in cloth, 2s.

LAST OF THE MOHICANS (The).	DEERSLAYER (The).
SPY (The).	OAK OPENINGS (The).
LIONEL LINCOLN.	PATHFINDER (The).
PILOT (The).	HEADSMAN (The).
PIONEERS (The).	WATER WITCH (The).
SEA LIONS (The).	TWO ADMIRALS (The).
BORDERERS, or Heathcotes (The).	MILES WALLINGFORD.
BRAVO (The).	PRAIRIE (The).
HOMEWARD BOUND.	RED ROVER (The).
AFLOAT AND ASHORE.	EVE EFFINGHAM.
SATANSTOE.	HEIDENMAUER (The).
WYANDOTTE.	PRECAUTION.
MARK'S REEF.	JACK TIER.

" Cooper constructs enthralling stories, which hold us in breathless suspense, and make our brows alternately pallid with awe and terror, or flushed with powerful emotion : when once taken up, they are so fascinating, that we must perforce read on from beginning to end, panting to arrive at the thrilling *dénouement.*"—*Dublin University Magazine.*

THE USEFUL LIBRARY.

In fcap. 8vo, price One Shilling each, cloth limp, unless expressed.

1. A NEW LETTER WRITER.
2. HOME BOOK OF HOUSEHOLD ECONOMY.
3. LANDMARKS OF HISTORY OF ENGLAND. 1s. 6d.
4. LANDMARKS OF HISTORY OF GREECE. 1s. 6d.
5. COMMON THINGS OF EVERY-DAY LIFE.
6. THINGS WORTH KNOWING.
7. LAW OF LANDLORD AND TENANT.
8. LIVES OF GOOD SERVANTS.
9. HISTORY OF FRANCE.
10. LAW OF WILLS, EXECUTORS, AND ADMINISTRATORS.

London: ROUTLEDGE, WARNES, & ROUTLEDGE, Farringdon Street.

ROUTLEDGE'S
CHEAP SERIES.

In boards, 1s. per Volume, unless specified.
Ditto   1s. 6d.   ,,   marked (*).

www.ingramcontent.com/pod-product-compliance
Lightning Source LLC
Chambersburg PA
CBHW030824110726
47900CB00006B/1729